ENEMY CONTACT

Weaving from side to side, the LOH worked its way southward with Barnes's gunship in pursuit. The C&C aircraft was going to attempt a pickup, and the clatter from their door guns almost drowned out the voices of the gunpilots laying down protective fire. "C'mon, c'mon," muttered Barnes, "pick 'em up, get 'em outta there." Straining to hear more about the downed crew, Barnes allowed the gunship to drift to the right. A static-filled transmission flooded his earphones. He couldn't understand.

Then he heard what sounded like popcorn popping, and the windshield began to disintegrate. . . .

FEW DIE WELL

David R. Olson

J

JOVE BOOKS, NEW YORK

Grateful acknowledgment is made for permission to reprint the following:

Four lines from ''An Irish Airman Foresees His Death'' by W.B. Yeats. Reprinted with permission of Macmillan Publishing Company from *The Poems of W.B. Yeats: A New Edition*, edited by Richard J. Finneran. Copyright 1919 by Macmillan Publishing Company, renewed 1947 by Bertha Georgie Yeats.

''WE GOTTA GET OUT OF THIS PLACE'' by Barry Mann and Cynthia Weil. Copyright © 1965 SCREEN GEMS–EMI MUSIC INC. All Rights Reserved. International Copyright Secured. Used by permission.

FEW DIE WELL

A Jove Book / published by arrangement with
the author

PRINTING HISTORY
Jove edition / April 1991

ISBN: 0-515-10544-9

Jove Books are published by The Berkley Publishing Group,
200 Madison Avenue, New York, New York 10016.
The name ''JOVE'' and the ''J'' logo
are trademarks belonging to Jove Publications, Inc.

PRINTED IN THE UNITED STATES OF AMERICA

10 9 8 7 6 5 4 3 2 1

ACKNOWLEDGMENTS

It would not be fair to allow this book to be published without publicly thanking those individuals who contributed greatly to its realization.

Thanks to: Ted Stanton of the University of Houston, whose enthusiasm for writing is contagious; Michael Doran of Southern Literary Agency, who provided invaluable editorial advice; Cheryl and James Olson, who provided crucial early feedback; R. K. Nelson, whose comments at the outset helped me maintain focus and perspective; and Terri Jendry, who painstakingly plowed through the text in search of mistakes.

A special thanks to Harold, Lorna, Eric, Mary Beth, Kysa, Laura, Karl and Charlie Olson for their unflagging interest and support.

And finally, my deepest thanks to my wife, Catherine Lamboley, who sacrificed much so that I could write full-time. Her confidence in my ability was the antidote for my doubts.

This book is dedicated to:

WO1 Thomas J. Moore
KIA 02/19/68

CW2 Ronald K. Nelson (Ret.)

CW2 Leonard L. Robbins (Ret.)

CW2 David W. Timm
KIA 04/05/68

INTRODUCTION

Although this story is fictitious, the names of real Vietnamese cities and villages are used. In addition, most of the military installations mentioned actually existed during the war.

There were several air cavalry troops operating in the central highlands of Vietnam during the time period covered by this novel, but there was no E Troop, 5th Squadron, 14th Cavalry. To the best of the author's knowledge, the E Troop call signs (other than Red, White and Blue, which were standard call signs used by many units) were not used by any actual air cavalry units in the highlands from October 1967 to June 1968.

There were a limited number of ways in which helicopter operations could be conducted in Vietnam, thus it would not be surprising if some of the incidents concocted by the author resemble—in part or *in toto*—actual events. If such parallels occur, they should be taken for what they are: coincidental conjunctions of fact and fancy.

The men and women depicted in this book are fictional characters. They are born of the author's imagination, and any resemblance to actual persons is purely coincidental.

Readers not familiar with military helicopters and military terminology are urged to peruse the appendices and the glossary.

I am afeard there are few die well that die in a battle.

—SHAKESPEARE, *Henry V*

PROLOGUE

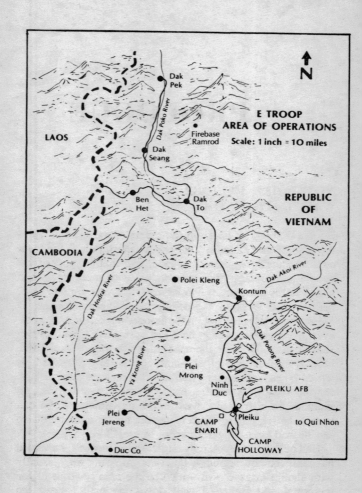

NOVEMBER 13, 1982
WASHINGTON, D.C.

He stood about halfway up the grassy slope that ran from the base of the Vietnam Veterans Memorial up to the level of Constitution Gardens. His face, like that of most of the people surrounding him, was etched with more lines than a man in his late thirties should have. It was a somber face, befitting the occasion: the dedication of the monument.

His thoughts were not on the impending ceremony, however; they were on a man he'd last seen more than fourteen years before. Both of them had thought they would come back from Vietnam alive—and maybe they both had. It would be easy enough to find out. There were several park service volunteers nearby, each of whom was carrying an index of the names inscribed on the monument; all he had to do was ask one of them about the man's name. Yet, so far, he had been unable to bring himself to do so.

Had he not been so deeply engrossed in thought, he would have noticed how strangely quiet the gathering was. Usually with such a large crowd—it filled the area in front of the memorial and stretched well down the mall toward the Washington Monument—there was a constant undercurrent of noise, like the steady hum from a hive full of bees. But this crowd was silent.

The only sounds to be heard were erratic snappings of flags and banners waving briskly in the gusting wind, and the muted strains of "Chariots of Fire" that wafted forth from two large speakers placed about 150 feet apart on the grass just behind the top edge of the memorial.

Set vertically against the flat side of a semicircle-shaped depression in the mall, the shiny black monument looked like it was made of two tall, narrow triangles that had been laid on their sides and joined at their bases. The bottom edge of the monument at its lowest point was about ten feet below the level of the mall.

From his vantage point on the slope, the man thought it looked like a cubist's drawing of a giant raven with its wings spread. There was no head or torso, just two long wings, each tapering to a sharp point. He likened the horizontal rows of tightly spaced, grayish lines to the veins of a bird's feathers.

But unlike real veins, which were conduits of life, the striations on the wall were hollow lines of death. Each was formed by letters etched in the granite, letters spelling the names of nearly fifty-eight thousand American soldiers.

He hugged himself against the cold, his arms folded across his chest and his hands tucked into his armpits. Obscured behind his right wrist was a circular patch sewn to the pocket of his faded field jacket. It depicted the head of a snarling, pug-faced dog, which was sandwiched between the word BULLDOGS, and the words E TROOP GUN PLATOON.

During the previous three days, he had searched for other jackets sporting the patch, but his search had been in vain. He was not surprised. There were thousands of veterans there, and the odds of encountering someone he knew were small. There was another reason why the odds were small:

many of his old friends had their names etched in the black granite.

He squinted at the wall, his eyes tearing—partly from the bitter, icy wind blowing across the Potomac River, and partly from the emotions welling up from within him.

All during the five-day "Salute to Vietnam Veterans," he had fought to suppress his feelings, but he had lost the battle the day before. After seeing the names of friends from long ago inscribed on the wall, years of pent-up emotion finally poured out. Sitting on the wet grass near the center of the memorial, bent forward with his face in his hands, he had wept—something he had not allowed himself to do since returning from Vietnam.

It had been a tremendous release, and he knew that if the tears came again today, he would gladly let them flow. There would be no embarrassment; he was surrounded by people who shared the same loss.

Immediately after the Welcome Home parade, he'd gathered at the memorial with the other marchers, even though the start of the dedication was more than two hours away. The march down Constitution Avenue had been uplifting, a joyful and boisterous occasion in which many veterans had felt pride in their Vietnam service for the first time since they'd returned from the war. Now the excitement had waned and each person seemed lost in reflection.

Standing in the silent crowd, he felt as if the ghosts of Vietnam that had dogged him for so long were being carried away by the blustery wind. Not all of them perhaps—there was still the one major piece of unfinished business—but almost all of them. He felt strangely tranquil and was in no hurry for the dedication ceremonies to begin.

Then abruptly, his feeling of contentment came to an end. Somewhere in the throng of people filling the mall area to his right, a chant began. He could not see the group of people making the noise, but he could see a Vietnam Veterans Against the War banner bobbing up and down above the crowd, keeping time with the chant. At first he could not understand what was being said, but the voices gradually grew louder: "We won't be used again! We won't be used again! We won't be used again! . . ."

There were angry murmurs from several men standing near him, but no one responded directly to the chanters. He listened as the protesters' voices grew louder, and he shook his head slowly. *This isn't the time, man, this just isn't the time.* Trying to recapture his feeling of peaceful solitude, he focused on the wall. It was a time for quiet reflection, not a time for protest.

"Hey!"

The booming voice came from behind him. He turned and saw a man in a faded flight jacket standing in the crotch of a small tree at the top of the slope. The tree jiggled as the man shook his fist at the protesters.

"Shut up, ya fuckin' sissies," he bellowed. "I volunteered and I loved it!"

The man on the slope turned slowly back around and thought again of the friend whose fate he didn't know. His friend hadn't loved it, but he'd fought as best he could.

PART ONE
SAVOR OF
BREAD

It is the savor of bread broken with comrades
that makes us accept the values of war.
    —SAINT-EXUPÉRY, *Wind, Sand and Stars*

CHAPTER 1

**NOVEMBER 14, 1967
KONTUM PROVINCE, NEAR POLEI KLENG**

The meager light penetrating the thick, dank cloud layer cast the world below in a monochrome of pallid grays. Peering through the morning mist, Warrant Officer Michael R. Danly watched the group of D-models churn northward toward Dak To. Like a flock of wary, migrating birds, the eight slicks stayed closely bunched in a tight, V formation.

Whenever they passed through the infrequent pockets of light turbulence, the slicks would bob slowly up and down, one after another, like horses on a slow-moving merry-go-round. From Danly's vantage point—a gunship flying slightly above and to the left and rear of the formation— the periodic bouts with unsettled air made it appear as if a lazy ripple of energy was passing from the point of the V out along its legs.

As the rotor blades sliced through the sodden air, tiny beads of moisture were slung free from the blade tips by centrifugal force. The droplets formed a faint gray ring around each set of spinning blades. Danly smiled at the irony of halos framing a scruffy set of decidedly unangelic war machines.

At times, whenever a low-lying cloud bank obscured the jungle below, the formation showed no sense of forward movement. The slicks seemed to hang suspended in a corridor of clouds. Danly thought it was during those moments that the formation possessed a somber, ghostly beauty.

Below and perhaps a quarter mile in front of the slicks was a group of four LOHs. The formation of scout helicopters was arranged roughly in the shape of a diamond, which would change dimensions as the formation zigzagged around patches of thick scud.

Occasionally as Danly watched the other aircraft, he would reach up and rub the bridge of his nose with the back of his left hand. It was a recently developed habit. Not really a nervous mannerism, it was more of a random, detached gesture that seemed to have a life of its own. But it had been born of tension.

He yawned. Sleep had become a precious commodity, and he had not been getting nearly enough. He envied those pilots who could catch a quick nap during flight; he had never been able to sleep in a helicopter. It wasn't because of the helicopter's constant vibrations or the erratic movements caused by low-level thermals. He found the rhythm of flight relaxing. It was like the calming clickety-clack of a passenger train: the C-model's broad, heavy blades provided a steady bounce, which was as soothing as the regular bump of train wheels rolling over joints in the tracks. He truly was relaxed by the varying sensations, but he could not sleep in an upright position.

He yawned again. The radios were uncharacteristically silent, attesting to the weariness of all the flight crews. The only sounds penetrating the thick, rubber earphones in his helmet were the heavy whine of the turbine and the occasional whopping noise when the rotor blades slapped through pockets of turbulence.

Totally relaxed, Danly relished the serenity of the moment. Suspended between the silent layers of drifting clouds, and wrapped in the morning's soft, gray mist, the flotilla of helicopters seemed immune to the danger far below them. He easily pushed the day's menace from his mind; it would come soon enough. Too soon, in fact.

DAK POKO VALLEY

Danly lit a cigarette, leaned forward in the armored seat and searched the skies ahead of the gunship for some patches of blue. His search was in vain and he sat back, scowling. He had hoped the cloud layer would be broken north of Dak To, but it remained solid. The overcast stretched the entire length of the valley and engulfed the top half of the mountains south of Dak Pek.

"Well, Book," he said to the man flying the aircraft, "it looks like we go through the pass."

"Sure does," replied Bookman, his eyes darting nervously back and forth from the instruments to the gloomy panorama outside. He was very tense and he hoped his voice did not betray that fact. Having recently graduated from flight school, he felt very much out of place sharing the cockpit with the calm, experienced man who sat in the copilot's seat.

He was pleased that Danly let him occupy the pilot's seat, but it also increased his nervousness. He wasn't sure if Danly expected him to perform like a veteran, or if he just let him sit in the right seat in order to bolster his confidence. If it was the latter, he could certainly understand. His confidence needed all the bolstering it could get.

During the morning briefing he had listened intently as the operations officer, Captain Holman, had described the situation in the area surrounding Dak Pek. It had not sounded good.

The Special Forces camp at Dak Pek had received mortar and rocket fire sporadically throughout the night, and its defenders had repulsed two ground assaults. Two miles to the west, a combined force of Fourth Division infantrymen and South Vietnamese Rangers had fought off several NVA attacks, which enabled them to maintain a shaky hold on their ridge-top position. Shortly after dawn, a medevac helicopter from Dak To was fired upon while flying through the Krong Bak Pass south of Dak Pek.

Although he had just arrived in Vietnam the previous week, Bookman had already been to Dak Pek once. The surrounding area scared him. Covered with thick jungle, the rugged, mountainous terrain had a sinister, forbidding aura. He tried to take some comfort from the fact that today he was flying with Danly, a man reputed to be one of the best pilots in the unit.

"Maybe the gooks that shot at the dustoff have left," he said as casually as possible, trying not to show his fear. He hoped fervently it was true.

"Fat fucking chance," blurted Gunther, the crew chief.

Bookman realized at once he'd been too obvious. He looked over his left shoulder at the slender man sitting in the open doorway. Gunther's loose-fitting fatigues flapped in the slipstream, and he grinned as he waved the muzzle of his M-60 at the jungle below.

"They're falling all over each other now. Where the hell could they go? Ain't no more room."

Danly glanced across the cockpit and suppressed a smile. Bookman was sitting stiffly, his cheeks turning red below the dark Plexiglas visor that covered the upper half of his face.

"You never can tell, Gunther. Mister Bookman could be right," said Danly, trying to ease Bookman's embarrassment. The younger man obviously was frightened and Danly was sympathetic. "They might have *di-di*ed the area."

Gunther grunted. "Bullshit, sir."

Danly allowed himself a short laugh, but quickly shifted his attention back outside the helicopter. Inhaling deeply from his cigarette, he leaned forward and stared at the cut in the mountains that was rapidly coming into view. With the cloud base so low it obscured the tops of the ridges on either side of the pass, the helicopters would have to go through the V-shaped opening that was approximately three hundred meters across at its widest point. Much of the triple-canopy jungle that covered the slopes within the pass had been destroyed by bomb strikes and the fires that they ignited, thereby reducing the number of places the NVA could hide. But Danly knew the NVA still had one thing in their favor: there was not much room in the narrow pass for the helicopters to maneuver.

At least he didn't have to worry about the slicks; they had landed at Dak To. The ground troops were to be held in reserve. The LOHs were still out in front, however, and Danly kept a close watch on the lead LOH, which was skimming the trees along the edge of the winding ribbon of water. The other three LOHs were spread out behind the leader, sweeping over the jungle on both sides of the river. Danly knew the other three gunships maintained a crude semblance of a staggered trail formation behind him.

The usual early-morning banter among the pilots was still absent as the aircraft flew up the valley, and Danly pondered the silence. All of the aircraft commanders were experienced—several had already been decorated for heroism—and they did not usually approach trouble with worried silence. Irreverence and profane bravado were more the norm. He hoped their silence was indeed due to fatigue and not to concern about their current destination.

Dak Pek seemed to have developed a mystique. Gradually changing from just another place to get your ass shot, it was getting the reputation of being a malignant gouge in the mountains, an evil "black hole" where no amount of skill or luck would keep you from being sucked from the sky into the suffocating jungle.

Danly had little use for such thinking. The fighting near the border with Laos and Cambodia had intensified, but there were no "evil" forces involved. The North Vietnamese were simply pushing more and more men and supplies into South Vietnam, and Special Forces camps like Dak Pek were hampering their operations. Danly was sure Dak Pek had to be a royal pain in the ass for the local NVA commander—it sat astride a major supply line. It almost begged to be overrun.

As the lead LOH approached the entrance to the pass, Danly decided to take over the flying chores. Placing his feet against the pedals, he took hold of the controls and squeezed the transmit button on the cyclic halfway, activating the intercom.

"Okay, Book, I've got the aircraft."

Nodding, Bookman let go of the controls and tried to relax. Danly maneuvered the gunship so its line of flight stayed to the left of that of the scout helicopters. The voice of the scout pilot in the first LOH crackled in Danly's earphones.

"White Two-six, Red One-two. I'm in the pass."

"Two-six, roger, right behind you," replied Danly.

He didn't expect to get fired upon on their way through to Dak Pek. The NVA weren't usually stupid; they knew gunships heading north were likely to be fully armed. He figured if the aircraft were going to get shot at, it would probably be when they were headed back south, low on ammunition.

But he hadn't stayed alive as long as he had by relying solely on assumptions, so he carefully scanned the jungle as the LOHs, hugging the treetops, entered the gap. Skirting the steep slopes on the west side of the pass, Danly kept his gunship above and behind the small aircraft. When the lead LOH suddenly banked sharply to the left, Danly's muscles tightened as if he'd received a small jolt of electricity.

"He's taking fire!" Bookman exclaimed.

Danly forced his muscles to relax. "I don't think so, Book," he said calmly.

"Two-six, this is One-four." It was the high-pitched

voice of Egan, one of the newer scout pilots. "We spotted some fresh bunkers down here."

"Roger," answered Danly. "You take fire?"

"One-four, negative. But my observer's pretty sure he saw some dinks in the holes."

"Two-six, roger, we got the spot. Just keep on going . . . break . . . white team keep to the left going through."

As the other aircraft acknowledged his instructions, he motioned for Bookman to take control of the gunship. Pulling a map from where it was wedged between his seat and the radio console, Danly unfolded it and spread it across his lap. Locating the spot where Egan had seen the bunkers, he noted the coordinates and wrote them on the plastic map cover with a grease pencil.

He frowned. The bunker discovery was about the last thing he needed. The morning's mission was to support the beleaguered troops on the ground west of Dak Pek, not to get into a pissing contest with a few NVA hiding in the pass. That could wait.

He had the feeling, though, that the troop commander was not going to agree. And if so, it wasn't going to set any precedent—he and Major Patterson had had serious disagreements before. Anticipating yet another clash, he took a deep breath and exhaled slowly. Here goes nothing, he thought.

"Striker Six, White Two-six."

"Two-six, this is Six. Go ahead."

Danly reached to turn down the volume of the UHF radio as Patterson's booming voice rang in his earphones.

"Six, we've got a small bunker complex at coordinates Yankee Bravo, nine five one, five nine eight. Negative contact, but One-four confirms Charlies in the holes."

"Roger, Two-six, what's your present location?"

"We're two klicks north," replied Danly, "en route Delta Papa."

"Negative!" yelled Patterson. "Hold your position!"

Danly tilted his head back and closed his eyes. *Here we go. He's going to fuck something up!*

Bookman tapped him on the arm. "What now?"

Danly made a sweeping motion with his right arm indicating that Bookman should enter a right-hand orbit over their current location. As the other helicopters settled into the orbit, forming a large circle, Danly stared at the thick carpet of jungle revolving slowly beneath him. A crooked line of dark green foliage, marking the edges of the river, wound its way northward amid the lighter green treetops that blanketed the undulating valley floor. He thought it ironic that such beautiful scenery also served such a deadly purpose: it concealed the enemy. With a touch of melancholy, Danly realized he preferred looking at the ugly, defoliated, bomb-pocked areas—they held fewer surprises.

He glanced at Bookman, who was fidgeting in his seat. Bookman had yet to be fired upon, and Danly wondered how Bookman was going to react when it finally happened. He was certain it would not be long before they both found out.

"Two-six, this is Striker Six!" Once again Patterson's voice blared in Danly's earphones.

Danly looked at Bookman. "I wonder if the bastard can talk in a normal tone of voice."

Bookman grinned uneasily. He felt uncomfortable with derogatory comments about superior officers, particularly in the presence of enlisted men. He looked over his shoulder and saw that both Gunther and the door gunner were wearing wide grins. "Um . . . I don't know," he mumbled.

Danly squeezed the transmit button past the intercom detent. "Go ahead, Six," he said.

"Two-six, I'm about one-five minutes from your position. Take the White team, proceed to the AO and contact Blue Hat Six. Tell the scouts to hold; I'll want One-four to mark the bunker location."

"Two-six, roger. One-four, you copy?"

"One-four, affirmative."

Scowling, Danly reached for the map that he had tucked back between his seat and the console.

"I gave Patterson the damn coordinates, Book. He shouldn't need Egan's help to find the spot. Can't the son of a bitch read a map?"

Bookman suddenly found the jungle to be quite interesting. He stared out the window and pretended he didn't hear.

Danly shot him a disapproving glance and returned his attention to the map. It only took him a moment to locate the coordinates.

"Six, this is Two-six."

"This is Striker Six."

"I'll say again the location of the bunkers, over."

"Negative," snapped Patterson. "One-four will mark it."

Shaking his head in disgust, Danly removed a small code book from his pocket. The book, which had the letters soi stamped on the front page, contained the call signs and radio frequencies for all the American and Vietnamese units in the area. Locating the entry for Blue Hat, he tuned the FM radio to the frequency indicated.

"Blue Hat, Bulldog Two-six, over."

Danly listened intently for a response, but the radio was silent. "Blue Hat, Blue Hat, this is Bulldog Two-six, over."

There was a sudden rush of static punctuated by the sound of small explosions and the syncopated chatter of automatic weapons. A high-pitched voice was barely audible above the noise.

"Bulldog, this is Blue Hat Three, over."

"Blue Hat, I've got gun support for you. What's your situation?"

"We've been picking up fire all morning. It just got a little heavier, over."

"Roger. Say your location."

"Stand by. . . . Don't know the exact coordinates. Just fly due—" The sound of an explosion drowned out the voice and the radio clicked off.

"Oh, Jesus," said Bookman. "He—"

Danly held up his hand like a policeman stopping traffic and cocked his head to the left, as if the act of straining to hear would bring the radio back to life.

Bookman grimaced. "He must have—"

Abruptly the cacophony from the ground resumed. "Bulldog, fly due west from Dak Pek," said the shaky voice on the ground, "and we'll pop a smoke."

"Two-six, roger. We're on the way." Taking over the controls, Danly pushed the cyclic forward and pulled the collective up about two inches, using all of the aircraft's remaining power. The nose of the gunship dipped and the whole fuselage vibrated strongly, protesting the added strain.

Strung out in a ragged line and struggling to gain a few extra knots, the gunships neared Dak Pek. The Special Forces camp was located on a plateau that jutted from the base of the mountains in the southwest corner of a picturesque valley. Framed on two sides by steeply rising terrain, the square table of land was split by a north-south runway, which lay about fifty meters to the east of the octagon-shaped camp. On the northern edge of the plateau, a sheer cliff dropped from the end of the runway about two hundred feet to a narrow river that curved across the valley floor. The eastern edge of the plateau gave way to a shallow slope, its washboardlike surface undulating its way down to a large rice paddy bordering the river.

The asphalt runway, which was approximately one thousand feet long, was bordered near its north end by two large knolls. Danly looked down as he passed over the black strip and saw the wreckage of a Chinook strewn near the base of the largest knoll. Almost directly across from the skeleton of the cargo helicopter, on the other side of the runway, lay the charred remains of a twin-engine Army Caribou. Reminders—as if Danly needed any—of the camp's tenuous location.

About three miles to the west, looming in front of the

gunships, was a huge, sinister-looking mountain, its upper third disappearing into the dirty-gray overcast. Between it and the camp, like the rows of spiny projections on a lizard's back, lay a series of parallel, jagged ridgelines. Passing over the first of them, Danly and his crew scanned the terrain ahead for some sign of the besieged infantry unit.

The door gunner was the first to spot something. "I see some smoke about two o'clock, sir, on the third ridgeline."

Looking in the direction that Bolger had indicated, Danly saw several faint columns of gray smoke emanating from the heavy jungle. As he turned toward the ridge, he saw a bright flash followed by more smoke.

"Blue Hat, Two-six. I think I got you in sight."

"Roger," cried the high-pitched voice. "I see you to the southeast of us. I'll pop a smoke."

After a few seconds, yellow smoke began billowing up through the trees adjacent to where Danly had seen the explosion.

"Okay, Blue Hat, confirm yellow smoke."

"Roger, that's us. Put your fire about fifty meters to the south of the smoke on both sides of the ridge."

"Are all the friendlies north of the smoke?"

"That's affirmative, Two-six."

Danly turned north to parallel the ridgeline.

"Okay, White team, we'll be going in northeast to southwest. You all copy Blue Hat on the friendlies' location?"

"Two-three, roger."

"Two-seven, roger."

"Two-eight, got it."

During a sweeping left turn that would bring the gunships in line with the target azimuth, Danly reached to the console with his left hand. Flicking up a bright red safety cover, he moved the armament switch to the ARMED position. As he pushed the gunship's nose down to begin his attack, his concentration was interrupted by the frantic voice of Patterson.

"Two-six, Two-six, return to my location ASAP! One-four is down in the pass!"

Bookman stared across the cockpit at Danly. "What do we do now?"

Danly momentarily rolled his eyes toward the slate gray clouds. "Jesus H. Christ!" he said in disgust. "Okay, Two-seven, you and Two-eight make one run here and then haul it back to the pass . . . break . . . Blue Hat, we're hot."

He steadied the rocket sight on the trees just beyond the last wisps of yellow smoke and pressed the red button on the left side of the cyclic grip. In seconds, a pair of rockets tore through the treetops and disintegrated in two angry bursts of red-orange light.

"That's right on 'em," yelled Blue Hat.

Danly pressed the button again and then banked hard to the right as two streams of tracers arched toward him from a gully on the left side of the ridge. A sharp cracking sound made him flinch and he looked down between his feet. There was a hole in the chin bubble.

"Two-six, this is Six."

"Dammit! Stand by, Six!" Danly snapped. More tracers flashed by on his left. He pulled the gunship into a steeper bank and watched his wingman ripple-fire three pair of rockets at the spot where the tracers were coming from. Clouds of smoke billowed from the trees, and the tracers stopped.

"Looking great," Blue Hat shouted happily.

Danly swung around behind the remaining two gunships as they began their one-pass attack on the ridge. Placing covering fire beneath Two-eight as he broke off to the east behind Two-seven, Danly cursed silently as the UHF radio came to life again.

"Two-six." Patterson's voice was thick with anger. "You got those birds on the way?"

"Roger," Danly replied tersely.

"Two-six, when you return to home plate, report to me ASAP."

"Two-six copies. Out."

CHAPTER 2

NOVEMBER 14, 1967
PLEIKU AIR FORCE BASE

In the sweltering heat of midday, Barnes trudged across the large concrete parking ramp toward the small building that served as the airport terminal. A small sign—he had barely been able to read it when he'd first walked down the ramp of the C-123—was nailed to the side of the building facing the runway. On the sign, in hand-painted block letters, was written the message:

> WELCOME TO
> PLEIKU

As he drew closer, he saw there was a brief commentary appended to the message. Immediately to the right of the *u*, someone had scrawled a comma followed by the word *sucker*. Barnes's first reaction was one of irritation at being labeled a patsy for doing his duty, but the mild surge of anger faded quickly.

He trudged around the corner of the building, lifted the heavy overseas bag off his shoulder and let it flop to the pavement. On one side of the bag, his name, rank and serial

number were stenciled in black. The serial number was
partially obscured by a large grease mark, but the rest was
clear: WO1 RAYMOND J. BARNES.

He leaned back against the building, seeking the meager
shade afforded by the small overhang from the roof. Christ
it's hot, he thought as he reached into his pants pocket and
took out a large, olive-drab handkerchief. He removed his
cap, wiped his forehead, and then ran the handkerchief over
his close-cropped, light brown hair. Although he was almost
six feet tall and twenty-three years old, his youthful face
somehow made him appear smaller and much younger. He
looked more like a high school sophomore than an Army
pilot.

"Hey, buddy, your name Barnes?"

Turning to his left, he saw a disheveled man sporting a
thick, brown moustache hop out of a jeep and walk toward
him.

"Yes, it is," answered Barnes.

"Name's Spradling, Wendell Spradling. If you're the
Barnes who's going to the Fourteeth Cav, I got a ride for
ya."

"That's where I'm headed all right, but how—"

"Good!" interrupted Spradling. He reached down,
grabbed Barnes's bag and then began walking rapidly to the
jeep. Barnes paused for a moment, then shrugged and fell
in behind him. He was unsure what to make of Spradling.
There was no clue as to his rank; the only insignia visible
was a patch over his left breast pocket that showed the
snarling head of a bulldog. Spradling's fatigues were wrinkled and smudged with grease, and his boots were scuffed
and dirty. Barnes was certain of one thing: Spradling could
not be an officer.

As he approached the jeep, Barnes was feeling uncomfortable. The man's slovenly appearance and lack of military
courtesy could not be ignored. He did not enjoy confron-
tations with enlisted men, but clearly some corrective action
was necessary.

Spradling had already tossed the overseas bag on the backseat and started the engine by the time Barnes got to the vehicle.

"Hop in! We've got to take a little detour on the way to Camp Enari," Spradling said with a grin. "Got a little business to take care of. A deal with the Air Force."

Barnes steeled himself. "Where's your rank, soldier?" he asked sharply.

Spradling's cheeks bulged and then he emitted a sound like a Bronx cheer as the air rushed out between his lips. "So . . . so . . . soldier?" Spradling sputtered as his eyes grew wide and he began to laugh. "Soldier? Oh man," he said, laughing even harder, "you got a couple of things to learn. Come on, get in."

Disarmed by Spradling's laughter, Barnes's ire evaporated and he climbed meekly into the passenger seat.

"This may come as a shock," said Spradling as he accelerated quickly out of the parking area, "but I'm a warrant officer, just like you. I'm assigned to the weapons platoon, but I'm also the fucking motor pool officer; that's why I've got this jeep. Ya just can't beat having your own vehicle over here," he said with a wide grin. "Hang on!"

Instead of continuing on the road that curved to the right toward a large cluster of wood and cement-block buildings, Spradling made a sharp left turn onto a bumpy dirt road that led past the end of the runway toward some Quonset huts on the other side of the field. He ignored the large sign next to the road that warned:

STOP!
UNAUTHORIZED
VEHICLES
PROHIBITED!

"The thing about the Air Force is that they've got a lot of things that we need," Spradling said. "And even though we don't have anything that they really need, we've still

got a lot of stuff they want. You know, NVA stuff, like
uniforms, flags, knives, guns—all that kind of shit. Since
most of the Air Force guys who aren't pilots never get near
the fighting, they need a source for war souvenirs. And I'm
their man.''

Barnes hung on tightly as the jeep bounced and lurched
across the uneven road. It seemed to him that the swaying
vehicle might flip over at any moment, but Spradling sped
on, seemingly oblivious to the violent movements.

''As you're gonna see, right around here people are living
pretty good. They've got permanent buildings with tile
floors, real toilets, and hot and cold running water. That's
the Air Force—first class all the way. Now over at Enari,
which is the Fourth Division's base camp, it's typical Army.
There's a lot of permanent buildings all right, but they're
not as nice. No flush toilets or running water. The showers
are gravity feed and the latrines are regular outhouses. Under
each shit hole there's a half an oil drum. Every couple of
days one of the gooks that works on the base opens a wooden
flap in the back of the latrine, drags out the drums, pours
some diesel oil on all the crap, and lights the whole mess
on fire. Barnes, you ain't lived till you get a good whiff of
them burning honeypots.

''But hell, it could be worse. There's some units you
could get assigned to where you'd be lucky to even get a
shower once a week.

''Now, the Cav tries its damnedest to live like shit, but
don't worry. Despite living in tents, we've got us a few
comforts. We've got a couple of refrigerators, including the
generators to run 'em, and we've got a shower that'll produce steam in about ten seconds. And we got 'em all from
the Air Force.

''Now we'll see if I can arrange for some tile for the
hootch floors,'' he said as the jeep bounced off the dirt road
and onto an asphalt apron that ran alongside the Quonset
huts.

"I thought you said you were living in tents," said Barnes.

"We are, but they're gonna build some wood barracks with cement floors sometime in the near future. I want to be prepared."

Spradling wheeled the jeep into a parking space marked RESERVED 149TH TAS. He nodded toward a heavyset sergeant who was talking to two Vietnamese workers near the corner of the building.

"I'll see what the fat fuck wants in trade for some tile."

Spradling hopped out of the jeep, and the sergeant waved him toward the doorway of the Quonset hut. After they went inside, Barnes turned his attention to the two Vietnamese who were now squatting next to the building waiting for the sergeant to return. Barnes did not want to make eye contact with them because he did not want them to approach him. It seemed like every Vietnamese he'd encountered so far tried to beg something from him.

When he had gone outside the Army compound at Qui Nhon the day before his flight to Pleiku, he had been particularly unnerved by the horde of children that descended upon him. They had pleaded for cigarettes, candy and money, all the while trying to force their hands into his pockets.

When he had refused to give them anything and had tried gently to brush their groping hands away, several had pinched his arms as hard as they could before darting quickly out of reach. The adult Vietnamese standing nearby had watched impassively, making no attempt to control the children. Retreating into the compound, he had felt disappointed and confused; it had not been the sort of reception he had anticipated. In fact, contrary to his expectations, there had been no indication thus far that any of the Vietnamese were pleased to see him. All they seemed to care about was what he had in his pockets.

Barnes noticed that the two workers were staring at him, and in spite of his intention to ignore them, he felt compelled to at least nod. They nodded in return, one of them offering a thin, crooked smile. They remained by the building, however, and Barnes was relieved when it was apparent they were going to stay where they were. Different from the Vietnamese he had seen so far, the men had darker skin and their features were broader. He decided they had to be Montagnards, the fiercely independent tribal people who inhabited the highlands. His thoughts were interrupted by the return of Spradling.

"Business concluded," he said as he climbed into the driver's seat, "and we're on the go." He backed the jeep away from the hut and aimed it back toward the dirt road. Oh no, thought Barnes, not again.

They bounced back across the field toward the terminal and then turned left onto the blacktop road that led out of the Air Force base toward Pleiku City. As they approached the main gate, Spradling reached behind his seat and produced two flak vests.

"Here," he said, handing one of them to Barnes. "Put this on. We're supposed to wear these when we're out of the compounds. Also, there's a steel pot behind your seat and an M-16 under your overseas bag. Grab 'em. You're now the door gunner."

After leaving the base, they followed a convoy of trucks into the city. Spradling kept up a running commentary about Pleiku and the surrounding area while Barnes, not listening very closely, became engrossed with the passing scenery. He was struck by how dirty everything seemed. A thin layer of rusty-red-colored dust appeared to have settled upon everything, and refuse of all sorts was scattered about. As they neared the center of the city, the streets became very crowded; most of the inhabitants appeared to be in a hurry as they scurried about through the teeming congestion. The notable exceptions were the small groups of young men who were perched on motor scooters, staring sullenly at the bustling activity around them. As if it were some sort of requirement, all the young men wore mirrored aviator sunglasses. Several made obscene gestures at any military vehicles that drove by them. Spradling indicated that the young men were often thought to be Viet Cong, and while that was undoubtedly true in some cases, he figured they were mostly either draft dodgers or street punks trying to be the Vietnamese version of the Hell's Angels.

Also ignoring the bustle of their countrymen were the prostitutes. Leaning against the doorjambs of sleazy bars and run-down houses, their hips cocked in the languid fashion peculiar to prostitutes everywhere, they watched the passing traffic with heavy-lidded eyes. Most wore dresses slit almost to the hip, revealing smooth thighs and taut calves flexed above a pair of stiletto high heels. Some of the women would call to the soldiers in passing vehicles, while others employed a more graphic approach. They would form a circle with the thumb and forefinger of one hand and push the forefinger of the other hand back and forth through the opening.

"If you ever start thinking of messing with that stuff, think again," said Spradling. "They got diseases you ain't even heard of. The exceptions are the whores over in boys-town near Camp Enari; they get checked by Army docs. But that ginch is for the enlisted men only. Officers are supposed to stay the hell away from there."

"So, what are the officers supposed to do?"

"Find a Red Cross girl, or if they get real lucky, an Army nurse. Otherwise it's standard issue."

"Standard issue?" asked Barnes.

"Yeah," replied Spradling, starting to laugh. "At birth, all officers are supplied with at least one hand."

Barnes laughed, but to his surprise felt somewhat embarrassed. He decided to change the subject.

"How come you're not wearing your rank?"

"Because," replied Spradling, accelerating around a slow-moving deuce-and-a-half, "only enlisted men are allowed to drive motor vehicles, and a driver can be a pain in the ass. This way, I just look like your average PFC and nobody looks at me twice when I'm over at Pleiku setting up a deal.''

"Oh yeah," said Barnes, "I forgot to ask. Are you going to get the tile?"

"Sure, if I can get the fat man what he wants."

"Which is?"

"A jeep."

"Too bad," said Barnes, shaking his head. "That's got to be a problem."

Spradling grinned. "Easy," he said.

The trucks in front of the jeep stopped, a pair of oxen blocking their path. The large beasts had halted in the middle of the road and despite the frantic pleas of their owner, refused to move. As soon as the jeep rolled to a stop, a small mob of children crowded around it begging for cigarettes and candy. Barnes became very uneasy and tried to ignore the numerous little hands that plucked at his clothes. Spradling's demeanor, on the other hand, appeared to remain unchanged. His characteristic good humor seemed to extend to the throng of children. He tossed sticks of gum to them and made faces that made them laugh. When he spoke, however, his voice was flat and businesslike.

"Watch these little bastards closely, Barnes. They'll steal anything they can grab, and some of 'em will cheerfully drop a grenade in your lap if they get the chance."

Barnes watched the group of small beggars warily, and was thankful when the oxen finally moved and the jeep began to edge forward. As the children backed away, a small boy who had been pleading with Barnes for cigarettes spat on his leg.

"Fuck you, G.I.," the child said, his dark eyes cold and glistening like little black marbles.

Barnes felt a momentary urge to reach out and smack the boy in the face, but it quickly passed and he began to feel ashamed of his reaction. He sat quietly as the jeep increased its speed.

At the outskirts of Pleiku, Spradling continued west while

the trucks turned south. He explained that the convoy was going to a small Army base nearby named Camp Holloway, which housed an assault helicopter company and a Chinook unit.

"If you need to refuel on a night flight, that's the place to go," he said. "Enari's refuel point usually isn't lighted and the pumps are slower. At Holloway you can get in and out fast and easy."

"How much night flying do you do?"

"Not a hell of a lot. We fly mostly up around Dak To, and night flying's not too healthy up there. Ain't about but one nav aid up there, and there's mountains all over the fucking place. Near here, though, it's pretty flat; you'd have to be flying real low to hit anything. About all there is is Dragon Mountain over by Enari."

"Dragon Mountain?"

"Yeah," said Spradling. "It's just a big hill actually; easy as hell to avoid. But somebody was flying with his head up his ass, because there's a wrecked H-model near the top."

Barnes frowned. He was sure he'd never be that careless.

Once clear of the city, they sped west on the asphalt road that sliced across the patchwork of fields blanketing the highlands plateau. In the distance toward Enari, Barnes could see a long, narrow, rust red cloud hanging just above the trees. Not being close enough to determine its origin, he shifted his attention to the passing fields. Scattered groups of peasants, their conical straw hats bobbing up and down, worked their way slowly along the rows of plants. To the north—Barnes guessed the distance to be about eight miles—the flatlands gave way to rolling foothills, which quickly butted against the steep slopes of a dark, blue-green line of mountains. Framing the peaks was an azure blue sky, dotted with small popcorn-shaped clouds. The scene reminded Barnes of a travel poster he'd once seen extolling the virtues of the Orient.

Drawing closer to Enari, the source of the dust cloud

became obvious. A long line of armored personnel carriers was moving westward, parallel to the road, on a wide, dirt path fifty yards south of the blacktop. Clanking forward on what was clearly a well-traveled route, the boxlike vehicles churned up clouds of fine red particles of dirt with their heavy treads. Group of soldiers sat huddled atop the APCs. Their faces and uniforms, like the vehicles beneath them, had taken on the reddish hue of the swirling dust. To Barnes, the scene had a surrealistic aura. It seemed to him as if he were viewing through red-tinted glasses some netherworld army. His concentration was broken by Spradling's voice.

"That ought to make you glad you're not a grunt."

"Yeah," said Barnes, thankful not only that he was not in the infantry, but also that the light breeze was blowing the dust south, away from the jeep. "But tell me something: why are they riding on top? Why don't they ride inside, out of the dust?"

"You ever been inside one of those things on a day like this? Those poor bastards have only got a choice of being cooked inside or suckin' dust on top."

"Oh," said Barnes, feeling a bit foolish, knowing that he should have been able to figure it out for himself.

Spradling, however, didn't seem to think his question out of the ordinary and was now pointing to a large mound not more than a mile away. It seemed to rise out of the table-flat plateau like the hump of a camel. "That's Dragon Mountain, the highlight of the Enari resort community."

As they drew closer, Barnes could see five long zigzag rows of barbed wire that formed the northern perimeter of the base. Just behind the wire, at intervals of approximately fifty yards, there were sandbagged guard towers rising fifteen feet in the air. Outside the wire, the ground had been plowed bare for a distance of almost one hundred yards.

"Looks secure," said Spradling, "but you'd be surprised how them skinny gooks can sneak through that wire, and it's no problem for 'em to lob a few mortar rounds in either."

He grinned at Barnes. "But what the hell, it's home sweet home."

━━━━━━━━━━

Barnes lay on his cot with his eyes closed, listening to the music blaring from a radio in an adjacent tent. He had hoped to settle into his new environment with as little difficulty as possible, and it seemed to be working fine. After Spradling had dropped him off at the small, wooden building that served as troop headquarters, the company clerk told him he was the first of three new pilots due to arrive that afternoon. Captain Thomas, the executive officer, welcomed him and told him that because he was the first replacement to arrive, he should think about whether he wanted to fly slicks or guns—it would be his choice. Barnes could scarcely believe his good fortune. Ever since the gunnery training portion of flight school, he had wanted to be a gunship pilot. Slicks or guns? There was nothing to think about.

After completing some paperwork, he had been met by a pilot named Steven Gray, a quiet, slender man with blond hair, who gave him a tour of the troop area. Laid out like a small town, it was in the northeast corner of the sprawling base camp, adjacent to an artillery battery.

"When they fire at night you may have some trouble sleeping at first," Gray had told him, "but you'll get used to it. There's also an advantage. You'll learn real fast how to tell the difference between incoming and outgoing shells."

Approximately forty tents, along with a few wooden, tin-roofed buildings, were arranged in small squares, much like city blocks. Most of the tents were GP-mediums—rectangular tents about twenty-five feet long that housed eight men each. Surrounded by chest-high walls of sandbags, each tent was set on a frame made of two-by-fours. Wooden planks nailed to the base of each frame provided a raised floor about three feet above the ground. The sides of the tents were two layers thick. The outer layer was canvas; the inner layer consisted of mosquito netting. The canvas sides could be rolled up and secured to the top of the frame, thus allowing better air circulation while still providing protection from mosquitoes. Barnes decided that on the whole the living conditions weren't bad at all.

Gray had shown him to his new home, which was the end tent in the row nearest the latrine and the shower. "You'll be sharing the tent with myself, Mike Danly, Jug Hill, Jack Winters and Walt Bookman. Bookman's pretty much a new guy like yourself, but everyone else is an old-timer. Danly's the best; won a Silver Star his second week in country."

"How'd he do that?"

"He was flying with a crazy bastard named Holcomb. They were part of a heavy gun team covering a medevac when it had an engine failure shortly after coming out of the LZ. It crash-landed in a clearing, and even though Danly and Holcomb were flying a gunship, they decided to go in after it. As soon as they landed they started taking fire. While Holcomb and the door gunner fired into the surrounding treelines, Danly and the crew chief unassed the aircraft, ran to the wreckage and started pulling guys out.

"The crew chief got his kneecap shot up and Danly had to drag him and the three survivors of the crash over to the gunship one by one. He was wounded twice in the process. After they got everybody aboard, they dumped all the excess weight they could, including the rocket pods, and still almost didn't clear the trees."

"Damn!" Barnes exclaimed. "I look forward to meeting them."

"You're too late to meet Holcomb. As a matter of fact, that's his bunk you're getting."

"He's gone home already, huh?"

"He's . . ." Gray paused. "Yeah, he's gone home."

Noting Gray's hesitation, Barnes started to ask about

Holcomb, but was interrupted by two men entering the tent. One was a thin, red-haired pilot who appeared to be barely eighteen years old. He introduced himself as Winters. The other man was tall and muscular. He greeted Barnes with a condescending smile and said his name was Hill. Both men had told him how lucky he was to be assigned to the weapons platoon.

"Slicks are for kids," Hill had scoffed. "And scouts are for dumb shits."

The clatter of approaching helicopters roused him from his thoughts. He had hoped to get some sleep between dinner and the evening briefing, but too many thoughts kept tumbling through his head. He decided to go outside and watch the aircraft pass overhead.

Sitting nearby on a wall of sandbags, Winters and Hill glanced up briefly at the approaching formation.

"Must be Danly and the group," said Hill.

"Think you're right, Jug," agreed Winters, who then, as if he had just remembered something startling, quickly looked skyward again. "Shit! There's a loach missing."

Hill arched his thick, black eyebrows and turned his head toward Barnes. "See, I told you you're in the right platoon."

FOURTEENTH CAV FLIGHT LINE, CAMP ENARI

Danly hovered the gunship forward slowly toward the narrow gap between the chest-high walls. The revetments, constructed to protect parked helicopters from shrapnel during mortar and rocket attacks, were proving to be as much of a threat to the aircraft as enemy shells. Each revetment consisted of two four-foot-high parallel walls, each fifteen feet long and two feet thick. They were made of wooden frames filled with sand, and occasionally, concrete.

As he eased the gunship into the revetment, he silently cursed the builders. The walls had been constructed too close together, leaving less than two feet of clearance on each side for the helicopters with gun mounts. Several helicopters had been damaged—two seriously—because their pilots had been unsteady while hovering between the walls, and the gun mounts had begun bumping against them. Danly regarded the revetment construction as just another sorry example of stupid planning.

He lowered the gunship gently to the ground and quickly went through the shutdown procedure. Pulling the logbook from its holder on the side of the console, he handed it to Bookman.

"Book, sign us off, will ya? I want to check the back."

Stiffly, he climbed out of the cockpit and flexed his legs several times. His buttocks were sore and his left leg ached. The familiar tingling sensation that signaled his leg had once again fallen asleep spread throughout his left thigh. Twelve hours of flight time in one day was too damn much, he thought as he massaged his thigh. The guys who designed the revetments must have designed the armored seats, too; both were a pain in the ass.

Instinctively ducking as the rotor blades gradually slowed above him, he limped toward the rear of the gunship, barely squeezing between the gun mount and the revetment wall. Gunther and the door gunner were standing near the tailboom, beneath the tail rotor, looking at several holes about the size of a penny.

"We took six hits, sir," said Gunther. "Four here and two up forward underneath."

Nodding, Danly stepped closer to inspect the punctures in the tailboom's thin metal skin.

"Doesn't look like much, Gunther."

The crew chief wore a pained expression. "Maybe not to you, sir, but I'm the one that has to patch the damn holes."

Danly suppressed a smile; to Gunther, bullet holes were like badges of honor. "How many does that make so far for this crate?"

Gunther paused. "I think it's seventeen."

"Well, at that rate you'll have no problem getting a hundred before the year's up."

"Thanks a fuckin' lot, sir. That's all I need to hear."

Danly grinned and continued his slow stroll around the gunship, inspecting it for any further damage. Finding none, he walked toward Bookman, who had gathered up their flight helmets, maps and other gear and was waiting in front of the revetment for the truck that would take them back to the troop area.

Danly eyed the younger man, who was staring blankly at the eastern perimeter, and was sure he knew how Bookman felt. After his first battle, he'd felt a great feeling of relief because he hadn't panicked, and he'd been almost euphoric from the thrill of fighting—and from the fact that he was still alive. But it sure wasn't like that anymore; now all he felt was kind of a dull pleasure at having made it through another day.

Bookman heard him approaching and turned around. "Well, Mike, things went pretty good out there today!"

Danly stared at him expressionless, then cocked an eyebrow. "Not for Egan they didn't."

"Oh yeah," responded Bookman sheepishly, "I . . . I meant after that."

"Yes," said Danly. "After that things went okay." He felt a twinge of regret for shattering Bookman's euphoric mood. "You did a good job, Book," he added.

"Thanks," said Bookman, turning to look at the parked gunship. He closed his eyes and pictured the rockets slicing through the air, tracers flitting across the sky, and smoke swirling above the shredded jungle. He could hardly wait until the next morning when he would be in the air again.

Danly rubbed the bridge of his nose and yawned. He looked north toward the troop area, hoping to see the truck.

Barnes sat on his cot holding the thick, dog-eared, loose-leaf binders that Gray had given him.

"Dull as they are," Gray said, "those two binders contain most of the information you'll need about troop rules, regulations and basic operating procedures. It takes a good while to read all that crap, though, so there's a couple of things I'll tell you about now. While you're waiting around to get your in-country checkout, if someone comes up to you and asks if you want to ride along as an observer, tell him to forget it. In this unit the term *observer* means someone who rides in the copilot's seat in a loach. Usually it's an enlisted guy who knows how to fly just enough to land it if necessary, but some gunpilots and slick drivers like to get loach time on their days off. I think that's stupid. We get shot at enough without begging for more.

"Another thing you ought to know right away is our call-sign setup—it's probably different than anything you've heard of before. Instead of one call sign for the whole troop, we've got several. The CO, XO and operations officer use 'Striker' at all times. Each platoon, however, has a different call sign depending upon whether we're talking to our own aircraft or to someone in a different unit. If we're talking among ourselves, it's simple: the scouts are 'Red,' the gun platoon is 'White,' and the lift platoon is 'Blue.' If we're talking to other units, then the scouts use 'Hunter,' the slicks are 'Jitney,' and we're 'Bulldogs.' Confused?"

"A little," replied Barnes, leaning over and setting the binders on his footlocker. "But I'll get used to it. Two questions, though."

"Shoot."

"Why all the different names?"

"Either bureaucratic excess or a plot to confound the Vietnamese," said Gray. "Take your pick."

"It's probably both," said Barnes, smiling. "My second

question's probably dumb. What's a jitney?''

"A British cab. The gunpilots think it's a real appropriate name. If there was a wrong side of the road in the air, the slick drivers would certainly be driving on . . .'' Gray stopped talking and cocked his head as the heavy whine of a deuce-and-a-half engine rapidly grew louder. "I think that's the guys that were at Dak Pek.''

The truck came to a halt outside the tent, and Barnes could hear the repeated thud of boots slapping the clay as men jumped from the back of the vehicle onto the road. The sound of footsteps grew louder and he looked up to see two men enter the tent. The first man, who appeared to be in his late twenties, was about six feet tall and sported a thick, black moustache that drooped well beyond the corners of his mouth. He was followed by a shorter, heavier man who, like Barnes, looked rather young.

"Mike, what happened?'' asked Gray. "I hear a loach bought it.''

"Egan got shot down in the pass south of Dak Pek,'' answered the man with the moustache.

"Did they get him out?''

"A medevac pulled him and the observer out about an hour after they went down. They were alive, but that's all I know.'' Danly tossed his flight gear on top of his sleeping bag and sat down wearily on the footlocker near the end of his cot.

"By the way, Mike,'' said Gray, "this is a new gunpilot, Raymond Barnes.''

Barnes stepped forward and extended his hand. "Nice to meet you.'' Danly's grip was strong despite his obvious fatigue, and Barnes winced slightly as they shook hands. Although Danly greeted him cordially enough, Barnes felt uneasy, as if he were being measured.

"So, how'd it happen?'' asked Hill, who was sitting on his cot near the opposite door.

"Simple. Egan got hit because Patterson's a fucking idiot, and because Egan didn't use his head either,'' replied Danly.

"What did Major Shithead do this time?"

"We were on our way to Dak Pek for a support mission and Egan spotted some bunkers in the pass. I gave the coordinates to Patterson, but he decided to make Egan hang around until he could get there. In the meantime he had me contact some grunts west of Dak Pek to see if they needed help, which they damn sure did.

"When Patterson arrived at the pass, he told Egan to fly back over the area and check the location of the bunkers. Egan told him the coordinates I gave were right, but Patterson told him to go mark the spot with a smoke grenade. Egan should've told him to get bent, but he didn't and ended up getting his ass shot. Then Patterson calls me and says to bring all the guns back to cover the downed loach. Problem was, the grunts were in deep shit. So I had Reinke and Mackin make one pass and then hook it back to help Egan. Coombs and I ran the NVA off, but if they'd had a bigger force, we'd've been in big trouble with only two gunships."

Hill snorted angrily. "Patterson ought to be strung up by the balls!"

"You keep mouthing off," said a low, raspy voice, "and that's what's going happen to you."

Barnes turned and saw the tall, rangy form of the platoon leader, Captain Hawkins, standing in the doorway.

"I've heard a few too many negative comments about Major Patterson from you people," Hawkins continued, "and that shit's going to stop. He's your commanding officer and will be respected as such." He turned toward Danly. "Mike, the major's waiting to see you."

Danly stopped unlacing his boots and worked his jaw back and forth in a simmering anger. "Oh yeah. I forgot."

"Hey, Hawk," said Hill, smirking, "how 'bout if I just *think* bad things about the major?"

Hawkins motioned impatiently to Danly. "He wants to see you right now, Mike. Let's go."

As he turned to leave, Hawkins paused and glared at Hill,

whose smirk quickly disappeared. Hawkins' voice was cold. "Don't push it, Jug," he said slowly, dragging the words out for emphasis.

"Sorry, Hawk," said Hill, looking at the floor. Barnes found himself enjoying Hill's discomfort. The man's cocky, condescending manner had irritated him since their first meeting.

Hawkins turned and strode from the tent, followed closely by Danly.

"What's going on?" Barnes asked.

"Major Patterson's pissed at Danly because he swore at him and didn't send the gunships back to the pass right away," Bookman replied.

"That's no big deal," Gray said. "He'll chew on 'em for a while, but nothing serious is going to happen. Patterson may not like him, but he knows Danly is one of the best pilots he's got."

"But the major could do something, couldn't he?" asked Barnes. "I mean, Danly did disobey a direct order."

"Jesus!" exclaimed Hill, his usual demeanor restored. "Save us from the new guys. Barnes, this is the real world for Christsakes, not warrant officer candidate school. If some RLO gives you a dumbfuck order, you ignore it."

Barnes was puzzled. "RLO?"

Groaning, Hill fell back upon his bunk.

"Real live officer," said Gray. "And it's not quite that simple. If you disobey an order, make sure it's over something worth risking your ass. You also better be damn sure you're right."

———

The melody kept popping up in his head. Staring through the darkness at the tent roof, Barnes wondered why he couldn't ignore it and go to sleep.

He had recognized the melody as "Camptown Races," but the words had been different. With the new lyrics it was called the "Body Bag Song." He had also understood its singing to be a ritual—it was always sung to new pilots when they first arrived—but he felt the ritual should have been postponed, considering the circumstances.

Shortly after the evening briefing, when most of the pilots were gathered in the tent that served as the officers' club, the news had arrived. A scout pilot had come into the tent and said that Egan died in the Seventy-first Evac hospital. The pilot, a small, tough-looking man named Snead, delivered the news in a matter-of-fact manner, but Barnes sensed that Snead was deeply affected. For a minute everyone was silent, then Snead said, very quietly, "He should have been smarter."

Barnes had thought the gathering would end then, but it did not. The drinking resumed and soon he found himself standing in a corner with the other new pilots, facing the rest of the men.

With a grand sweep of his arm toward the veteran pilots, Winters had said, "Gentlemen, may I present the Corpse Container Chorus."

Led by Spradling, the singing had begun:

You're going home in a body bag, doo dah, doo dah;
you're going home in a body bag, oh, doo dah day.
Shot between the eyes, shot between the thighs;
they'll ship you home in a body bag,
                    oh, doo dah day.

Even after Barnes had finally left and returned to his tent, he could hear the voices grow more raucous as additional verses were sung. They should have waited, he thought. Didn't Egan deserve more respect?

He tried to relax, to make his mind let go of the present. He closed his eyes and finally the melody faded away . . .
ship you home in a body bag, oh, doo . . . dah . . . day.

CHAPTER 3

NOVEMBER 17, 1967
CAMP ENARI

The E Troop pilots sat in a large semicircle facing Captain Holman, the operations officer. Immediately behind him on the wall was a large map of the area surrounding Dak To. On the sheet of clear plastic covering the map, someone had drawn seven large rectangles, each enclosing an area of about one hundred square kilometers. Holman had marked each rectangle with a different letter and was explaining that E Troop would be responsible for the reconnaissance of rectangles A through D, while C Troop was going to handle areas E, F and G.

Within each area there were a few blue dots, each of which indicated the presence of American or South Vietnamese troops. The crews were cautioned that the friendly locations were based on reports from Fourth Division operations received the previous night and should be considered approximations only.

In grave tones, Holman talked about the mission, which was simply to locate enemy troop concentrations. All indications were that the North Vietnamese had been steadily moving men and materials across the Cambodian border

west of Dak To and were preparing for an assault on yet-
to-be-determined targets in the northwestern area of the
central highlands. Dak To and Kontum were considered
strong candidates.

Sitting near the front of the room, just to the right of the
map, Gray watched the other pilots while Holman droned
on about the tactical situation. The newer men were paying
close attention to Holman's monologue, but the more experienced pilots were showing signs of boredom. Hill and
Reinke were both leaning against the hootch wall with their
eyes closed; Danly appeared to be reading a letter; Mackin
was engrossed in trying to repair the chin strap on his helmet;
and several others were more concerned with consuming
what was left of their C ration breakfasts than listening to
Holman.

They had remained attentive when the mission require-
ments, frequencies, codes and locations of friendly troops
were given, but they had ignored the general-situation portion of the briefing. Gray shared their disdain. What the
hell? he thought. It's the same damn thing every day: NVA
were sneaking across the border in significant numbers and
were going to attack something. No shit. What else is new?

Once during Holman's daily attempt to sound like Edward
R. Murrow, Hill had leapt to his feet and with exaggerated
gravity exclaimed, "Jesus! Does Westmoreland know about
this? We'd better tell him ASAP; this could change the
course—" Hawkins had cut him off in midsentence, but
by that time Holman was so flustered he had lost his place
and had to start over from the beginning. Spradling had
later suggested to Holman that he could save a lot of effort
if he would just record his Monday briefing and then play
it back at each briefing during the remainder of the week.
Holman had not been amused.

Gray returned his attention to the meeting as Holman
concluded his spiel and asked if there were any questions.

Reinke, his eyes closed, was still leaning against the wall.
"Who're we supposed to get the call sign and frequency of

the 173rd grunts in sector B from?'' he asked.

"Contact the Fourth Division TOC when you get to Dak To.''

"Last time I asked 'em for a frequency they gave me the wrong one.''

"Well, that's who you contact anyway,'' snapped Holman. "Are there any more questions?''

"Yeah,'' responded Mackin, tugging on the end of his moustache. "You suppose you could get the squadron C&C to stay out of the way when we're working an AO? Yesterday Colonel Bensen came flying through on the deck while we were doing a recon. Almost had a goddamn midair collision with him!''

Holman assumed his best indignant air. "It's your responsibility to keep a sharp eye out whenever and wherever you're flying. The command and control aircraft will periodically be flying low-level whenever the squadron commander needs to get a firsthand look at—''

"Phil,'' interrupted Hawkins, "we know the colonel can go any place he damn well pleases, but it's going to really screw something up if he keeps cruising in unannounced. See if you can get the S3 to pass the word when he's going to be in the AO.''

"Well, I don't know. The way we've always done—''

"Just give it a try, Phil,'' said Hawkins.

"All right,'' said Holman, obviously unhappy at the prospect of requesting a change in established procedure. "Anything else?''

Spradling belched.

"All right, at ease,'' Holman said sourly. "You're released to your platoon leaders.'' He turned and stalked from the room.

The gunpilots stayed where they were while the scouts followed Captain Miller out of the hootch, and the lift pilots gathered around Captain Resnick who had moved to the far end of the room. Hawkins removed his pipe from his shirt pocket and pointed the stem at a broad-shouldered, fair-skinned lieutenant who was holding a clipboard.

"Lieutenant Horvath will give the crew and aircraft assignments. As usual, keep your heads on a swivel out there . . . *and,* tighten up the radio procedures. Some of you people are bullshitting too much." He nodded at Horvath. "Albert."

"Okay, listen up. Captain Hawkins and Mister Coombs are in seven three one, they'll be Bulldog Six; flying wing will be Reinke and Webb in zero zero six, they'll be Two-four. Next team is myself and Gray in seven three five, Bulldog Two-one; and Spradling and Winters in seven three two . . ."

As Horvath continued with the crew assignments, Gray looked across the room at Reinke and Hill. Reinke shook his head slowly, and then made the sign of the cross. Hill smirked and began to mouth the words to the "Body Bag Song." Gray held up his fist and flashed his middle finger at them. He dreaded the coming day. Being assigned to fly with Horvath—according to the current joke—qualified you for double hazardous-duty pay. Horvath was a nervous, fidgety person, who most of the pilots felt should never have been allowed to graduate from flight school. While as yet he hadn't done anything catastrophic, most of the men considered it just a matter of time.

Gray was fairly certain he could take over the controls in most situations if Horvath was doing something dangerous, but just having to put up with his nervousness and rough handling of the controls was trial enough.

One of the first things Gray had learned about flying in Vietnam was that a fully loaded gunship was not anxious to leave the ground. Not only was it a problem to execute a takeoff, it was also a major task just to get the heavy aircraft to hover. Spradling had once said that a loaded gunship had the same aerodynamic characteristics as a hippopotamus with wings. Gray agreed.

But he had learned how to coax the sluggish aircraft into

the air. Being smooth on the controls was absolutely crucial—sudden, erratic movements of the controls dissipated
lift. He remembered a demonstration from flight school
when his instructor had held the aircraft at a three-foot-high
hover, and then had started moving the cyclic in a small
circle, as if he were mixing pancake batter. The helicopter
had quickly settled back to the ground. Horvath's "control
touch" was much worse than the instructor's had been during the demonstration.

It was going to be a long day.

━━━━━━

Barnes stood with his arms folded across his chest sur-
veying the flight equipment laid neatly on his bunk. There
was a flak vest; a flashlight; a large, clear-plastic map case;
a shoulder holster containing a .45-caliber pistol; a sturdy
cloth vest—called a "chicken-plate"—that had a large
pouch in both the front and back, each of which contained
a thick piece of armor shaped like a square shield; an olive-
drab flight helmet; flight gloves; and a blue, plastic case
containing sunglasses. With the exception of the gloves and
sunglasses, all of the equipment had been used before.
Barnes felt a little disappointed; he had counted on receiving
new equipment.

The flight helmet was scratched and nicked, and the name
Dingo was printed on the back in black Magic Marker.
Whoever Dingo was, he apparently didn't take good care
of his equipment; the flak vest had also belonged to him,
and it was torn near the left shoulder.

Well, Barnes thought, at least I won't be using this. He
picked up the flak vest and dropped it into the bottom of
his footlocker. Danly had said the flak vests were unbearably
hot, and in addition, were far too cumbersome to wear along
with a chicken-plate.

Extracting the .45 from its holster, Barnes chuckled to
himself. The pistol was going to provide protection in a

way he had never thought of. Gray had told him about how
a lieutenant named Wilbanks had been shot on the inside
of his upper thigh. Another inch to the left and Wilbanks
would have been hit in the testicles—or worse. Wilbanks's
experience had led to the other pilots' wearing their shoulder
holsters around their waists during flight, with the holster
being positioned directly in front between their legs, like
an athlete's protective cup.

Barnes had scoffed at the idea at first, but upon reflection
decided he'd do the same thing. He wanted to have all his
parts in working order next time he saw his girl. He frowned
at the thought. Seeing her wasn't something he really wanted
to mull over too much—a year was going to be a long time.
And around here, he thought, a long time can quickly become forever.

He placed the pistol and holster back on the bed and sat
down on his footlocker. Am I really going to make it through
the year? he wondered. He'd never doubted it before—good
luck had always followed him around like a devoted little
brother—but now he wasn't quite so sure. Luck might not
be enough. Egan, according to Spradling, had thought of
himself as a lucky man, and he was dead. Dead because
of his own mistakes.

Barnes thought of Danly's comment to him the night of
Egan's death. "One thing you need to do over here, Barnes,
is always keep in control. Keep in control of the situation
and—most importantly—keep in control of yourself."

As he surveyed the equipment arrayed on the blanket,
equipment designed to help keep him in one piece, Barnes
was struck by the reality that he himself was the most important piece of protective gear he would ever have. The
idea chilled him.

═══════════

Since arriving in Vietnam, Gray had already seen two
gunship accidents, one minor and one major, as a result of

poor flying technique during takeoff attempts. Now, as Horvath attempted to move the helicopter from the refueling area to the runway, he began to wonder if he had a ringside seat for a third accident. His earlier confidence about intervening in time to prevent a crash began to wane.

With the load of ammunition and fuel necessary for the mission, the gunship would barely hover, so Horvath was trying to move it to the runway by using a series of short hops. He would briskly pull pitch, which would bring the gunship to a hover but at the same time would cause the RPM to drop to a dangerously low level. During the few seconds the gunship remained airborne, Horvath would hover it a few yards closer to the runway before it sunk back to the ground. Gray wished he were more religious—maybe praying would help.

His gum chewing rapidly increased in tempo as Horvath finally bounced the helicopter into position for takeoff. Gray sighed as he reflected on how simple it could be if Horvath would just relax. Getting a gunship into the air was just a matter of making smooth, almost minuscule control movements. Like the old saying went: it knows how to fly better than you do. The trick was to coax it off the ground, not to force it. The procedure was to get just enough pitch in the blades to get the helicopter sliding forward on its skids, but not so much as to cause the engine and rotor RPM to drop. Once the helicopter was steadily accelerating, it would gain extra lift from the more rapid passage of air through the rotor system, and it would begin to fly.

Spradling, taking off behind them, had obviously executed the procedure correctly, for he flew past on the left while Horvath was still bouncing the gunship down the runway. He grinned at Gray on the way by. The end of the asphalt strip was rapidly approaching and Gray was about to grab the controls, when the gunship grudgingly began to fly. The engine RPM was dangerously low and Gray put his hand firmly on the collective to prevent Horvath from attempting to pull more pitch. He was more sure than ever that it would only be luck that could keep Horvath from wrecking an aircraft someday.

Spradling made a wide circle to fall in behind Horvath as the gunships joined the two LOHs, which had flitted away from the refuel point as nimbly as hummingbirds. With his index finger, Gray began to trace their flight path along his map. Turning north, the helicopters flew a course paralleling and about five miles east of Highway 14, which ran from Pleiku to Kontum. Abreast of Kontum, the helicopters angled slightly to the northeast, and in less than ten minutes arrived at the funnel-shaped valley they were assigned to search. Two parallel ridges, running north to south, were situated in the narrower part of the valley. Except for a few widely spaced clearings, the ridges were covered with the usual tangle of jungle.

Nearing the crest of the easternmost finger of land, the pilot of the lead LOH called to explain how he wanted to work the area. "This is One-five. We'll start on the first ridge here and work our way south, then hop over to the next one."

Horvath acknowledged and banked the gunship to enter a circular orbit above the LOHs. Gray thought Horvath was acting even more strained than usual. The left side of his mouth had developed a twitch, and he had removed his right hand from the collective and was nervously rubbing his chin. He looked at Gray.

"Are we in the right location?"

"Yeah," said Gray, focusing on the corner of Horvath's mouth, which now looked as if it were being jolted by a pulsing electric current.

"I don't think so," said Horvath, looking down at the ridge. "This just doesn't look like it should. Are you sure?"

"I'm sure," Gray sighed. "You want to look at the map?"

"No, no. That's okay; I believe you."

Horvath began muttering to himself as he stared down at

the LOHs, which were hovering slowly just above the treetops.

Ignoring the fact that it was very difficult to see through
the thick foliage even when right on top of it like the LOH
pilots, Horvath occasionally would jerk the gunship into a
steeper bank as he strained to peer beneath the leaves from
the higher altitude. With each abrupt movement of the controls, Gray would tense and then slowly grind his teeth in
anger. It doesn't matter if Ho Chi Minh himself is down
there, he said silently, fighting the urge to grab the controls.
You don't have to jerk the goddamn aircraft all over the
sky.

"You want me to fly for a while?" he asked, trying to
sound casual.

Horvath turned his head quickly, as if startled. "What?"

"Do you want me to fly for a while?" Gray repeated.

"No. I've got it."

Yeah, I guess you do, thought Gray, and it would probably take a good hour to pry your fingers loose from that
death grip on the controls.

Gray slumped in his seat and watched the LOHs proceed
slowly along the ridge. The scout pilots worked cautiously
as they strained to see signs of the enemy through the thick,
green canopy of leaves. Occasionally, when their pilots
suspected immediate danger, the small aircraft would dart
back and forth, resembling a pair of hummingbirds uncertain
of their destination. After a while, though, the darting
ceased, and Gray's attention began to wander. This was not
normally a healthy thing to do, but experienced pilots—the
good ones, anyway—developed a sixth sense about danger.
They could feel its presence.

Gray believed he possessed the sense. He knew Danly
did—Danly probably had it more than anyone. Hawkins
had it, so did Hill, so did Mackin. Many pilots who didn't
develop it didn't make it home.

Danly had once said there was nothing mysterious about

it, just a combination of good observation and the knowledge gained from experience.

Snead, who was one of the best scout pilots, had echoed the sentiment about experience being the best teacher. He had shown Gray the bullet-hole scars on his right leg that served as a constant reminder of his narrow escape near a tiny creek in a serene-looking valley. Snead had said that from then on, whenever he flew in a new area, he would be especially careful near any body of water, no matter how small.

Gray had argued that if it was just observation and experience, then you would always be conscious of what to look for and know how to interpret what you saw.

Not necessarily, Danly had replied. Often the process was a matter of the subconscious interpreting things you had seen but had not been conscious of noticing. Perhaps it was the behavior of birds—nothing dramatic like a sudden, startled flight, but something simpler and subtler, like their casual avoidance of a certain area. Maybe it was a faint bit of dust in the air kicked up by the movement of unseen men—enough to register in the back of your mind, but not enough to be consciously aware of. Maybe it was the shape of the terrain, or a fraction-of-a-second glimpse of something through the dense jungle that would, like a subliminal advertisement, only be noted by the subconscious.

Gray had not known exactly what to believe about how it worked, but he was sure the sense existed. And he was just as sure, as he sat looking down through the hazy sunlight at the two snooping LOHs, that there were no NVA on the twin fingers of land below.

A few Americans, yes, but no NVA. On the situation map at the morning briefing, there had been a small blue dot representing an American unit on the western tip of the second ridge. It was a small patrol that would slowly be working its way east. Gray figured it would be about two hours before the LOHs would encounter the patrol, and then

the mission would be over. In the meantime, there was
nothing to do but ride herd on the LOHs. Gray thought it
was a colossal waste of time for all concerned. Too bad the
somebody at headquarters saw it differently.

When the LOHs first moved over to the second ridge,
Gray had had momentary hopes of a change of mission.
Snead had radioed Holman, who had just arrived overhead
in the C&C aircraft, and suggested that the mission be
scrapped. He had been emphatic, telling Holman there had
been "no gooks on these ridges since Jesus was an altar
boy." But Gray's hopes for a change of mission evaporated
when Holman curtly replied that they were to proceed as
planned.

However, that course of action did suit Horvath, who
was still muttering about how suspicious the area looked.
He insisted upon doing all the flying, and as the afternoon
sun baked the cockpit, Gray grew bored and had to fight
the urge to doze. Suddenly his head was snapped to the side
as Horvath jerked the gunship into a steep right-hand bank.

"There's the gooks! Open fire!" yelled Horvath.

It was several seconds before Gray could focus on the
area Horvath was pointing to. There was a small clearing
a few meters down from the peak of the ridge, and several
men were moving slowly along its edge. Gray felt a moment
of panic when he saw the familiar camouflaged helmet cov-
erings.

"Fire into that clearing!" Horvath yelled as he swung
the rocket sight into position and pushed the cyclic forward
to start a dive.

"NO, NO!" screamed Gray. He grabbed the armament
toggle switch, which Horvath had just moved to the ARMED
position, and flipped it off. He waved his right arm frantically at the crew chief and door gunner. "Don't fire,
they're friendlies!"

The door gunner had not been able to see the clearing,
but the crew chief had and had immediately recognized the
troops as being American. He stared angrily at Horvath, the

muzzle of his M-60 pointed at the back of Horvath's head.

Gray grabbed the controls. "I've got the aircraft," he snapped.

His hands shaking, Horvath relinquished the controls and fumbled for his cigarettes. "Damn," he said with a tremor in his voice. "They looked just like NVA at first. You know, sometimes it's hard to tell right off." He looked at Gray as if entreating him for a word of agreement.

"Hey, what's the problem, Two-one?" It was Spradling, puzzled by the sudden, erratic movements of Horvath's aircraft.

"No problem," answered Gray, his pulse still racing. "But be advised we found the friendlies. They're a lot farther down the ridgeline than they're supposed to be."

He did not know what to say to Horvath. He was sure now that Horvath's fidgeting was due to more than just a nervous disposition. Horvath was beginning to unravel. Something would have to be done.

"Steve, that was too close for comfort," Horvath said with a nervous laugh.

"Yeah."

"You know, just as you yelled, I got a better look at them and saw they were our guys," Horvath said, sounding more in control of himself. "Still good that you yelled, though, that was good teamwork."

Gray stared straight ahead and did not respond. He thought Horvath's efforts to gloss over the incident were even more pathetic than his original actions.

CHAPTER 4

NOVEMBER 21, 1967
KONTUM PROVINCE,
WEST OF PLEI MRONG

Dotting the landscape of the highlands plateau, there were
many circular, thatched huts topped with conical roofs. From
the air, they looked like huge mushrooms sprouting randomly
across the landscape. Most were located in the patchwork
fields of the flatlands, but an occasional hut could be seen nes-
tled in a hillside clearing. Although some functioned as permanent dwellings, most were used for storage or served as
temporary lodging for peasants working the nearby fields.

Barnes was not sure which purpose was served by the
hut on the hill below him. It sat in the middle of a cultivated
clearing about the size of a football field. A well-worn path
led south from the hut, cutting across the clearing and disappearing into the dense grove of trees surrounding it. Next
to the hut were several small, neat stacks of cut bamboo.
Though it was obvious the hut had been used recently,
neither Hill, who was flying the aircraft, nor Barnes could
detect any movement in the clearing.

On Barnes's map there was a thick, black line drawn

around the area designated as a free-fire zone. As he attempted to match the features of the small hill with one of the hills depicted on the map, he wondered if it was within the zone. It was hard to determine at first—there were many hills that looked like the one below—but using a nearby river as a reference point, he counted the number of small hills between it and the hut. He decided the hill in question was outside the black line.

Barnes was puzzled by Hill's interest in the hut; it was no different from any of the other huts they had flown over. Maybe it's boredom, he thought. They had spent the entire morning searching an area near Kontum and had found no signs of the enemy. Hill's restlessness had been quite evident. Now, with an hour to wait until they were due at Dak To for a briefing on a new mission, Barnes guessed Hill was just seeking a diversion.

Having circled the hut three times, Hill lowered the gunship's nose to descend for a low pass. Swooping over the clearing, he narrowed his eyes and compressed his lips into a tight smile as the gunship passed barely fifty feet above the small straw building. He turned to Barnes with a lopsided grin as he pulled back on the cyclic and the gunship began to climb.

"Looks like a goddamn VC motel. I think we ought to lob a couple of rounds in there, see what comes out."

"I don't know," said Barnes, feeling uneasy. He was fairly sure the hut was outside the free-fire zone, but he hesitated to question Hill's decision.

"Yeah," said Hill, still grinning, "we'll put a couple of chunkers in there. Hey, Two-nine, how 'bout a little recon by fire?"

"Number one!" was the cheerful response from Mackin in the second gunship.

"Okay, Two-nine, we'll be making our runs east to west."

Despite his inexperience and his wariness of Hill, Barnes decided he had to say something.

"Ah . . . look, Jug, I'm pretty certain we're outside the free-fire area."

"Naa," responded Hill, still staring at the hut. "I've been practically living in this goddamn area for the last six months; there's no problem."

As Hill flew further east to set up the gun run, Barnes hurriedly examined the map again. He was sure; the hut was outside the black line.

"You want to check the map quick?" he asked, extending it toward Hill.

"Fuck it!" snapped Hill, pushing the map away. "I know where we are." He turned the aircraft back toward the west and reached across the console to flip the grenade-launcher power switch to the HOT position. "All right," he said, glancing over his shoulder at the crew chief and door gunner. "If anybody comes out of that hut, blast their ass."

"Roger that, sir," responded the crew chief, nodding his head and pointing the muzzle of his M-60 toward the clearing.

As he lined the gunship up with the target, Hill motioned to the grenade-launcher sight hanging just above Barnes's head.

"You're the new guy; you get the honors."

Barnes began to reach for the sight, but stopped. Suppose some innocent peasants were in the hut avoiding the heat of the midday sun? Chewing on his lip, he looked across the cockpit. Hill seemed to know what he was doing; why worry? Barnes started to reach for the sight, but again stopped. He could not decide what to do.

"I . . . I just don't know, Jug," he said slowly.

Hill looked at him coldly for a few seconds, then shrugged. "I'll fire it; I can always use the practice." He increased the gun elevation setting with his left hand and pushed the cyclic forward to start a dive.

Thump . . . thump . . . thump . . . thump . . . The rhythmic recoil of the snub-barreled gun jarred the aircraft. Barnes watched the small grenades arc from the front of the gunship toward the hut. The stubby canisters with the domelike heads seemed to curve toward the ground in slow motion. The first two landed short, kicking up small geysers of dirt, but the third grenade hit the front of the hut, and the fourth crashed into the roof. Hill banked the helicopter sharply to the right, and the tilting horizon seem to slide across the windshield as the nose of the aircraft swung back to the east. Mackin's gunship was already diving toward the target, and Barnes could see a steady stream of black ammunition links trailing beneath it like stringy wisps of dark smoke. Tracers poured into the hut from the miniguns and the door gunners' M-60s.

"See anybody, Two-nine?"

"Negative," Mackin answered, his voice barely audible above the din.

"Okay then," said Hill, "we'll just make one more pass."

The hut roof had begun burning, set ablaze by the volley of tracers. As they dove toward the target a second time, Barnes winced at the sight of the fire spreading rapidly throughout the hut. He could not push the idea from his mind that a farmer, maybe even with members of his family, might have been resting in the hut after lunch to escape the broiling sun. Barnes had a sudden image of several terror-stricken Vietnamese huddled on the floor as bullets and shrapnel tore through the structure.

"Whoooooooeeeee! Look at that sucker burn," Hill exclaimed. He grinned and began to whistle happily as he turned the helicopter toward Dak To.

CAMP ENARI

Foam spurted from the can and the white flecks that landed on Danly's jungle fatigues quickly dissolved, leaving an irregular pattern of dark green wet spots. He placed the can opener on his footlocker and took a long drink from the dark gold can. The beer was warm, but he savored it none-theless. He lay back on top of his sleeping bag and propped the can of beer on his stomach. This is all I want, he thought, just a couple of beers and some peace and quiet. That shouldn't be too much to ask.

But he knew it was, of course. Privacy was almost non-existent. It was a rare day when he would be the only person in the tent not scheduled to fly.

Being extremely tired after flying fourteen days in a row, he had still gotten up early that morning. He wanted to take the opportunity to write several long-overdue letters, without the usual distractions. He had not written to anyone in more than a month, and the most recent correspondence from his mother had urged him with both sarcasm and genuine concern to "please write and let us know you're still alive." Feeling suitably guilty, he had scratched out letters to his parents, both his sisters, his brother, and several friends. It had taken him most of the day and had drained what little energy he had had to start with.

Avoiding the mess hall—solitude took precedence over hot food—he had squatted listlessly on the steps of his tent and slowly consumed a box of C rations. His plan had been to finish eating, drink the three cans of beer stashed in his footlocker, and then fall asleep before his tentmates returned.

Now, as he took the first long swallow from the third can, he realized he had taken too long to savor the beers. The sound of a deuce-and-a-half was growing louder, and Danly was sure it must have come from the flight line. Shit, he thought, I should've gotten some sleep earlier. He quickly guzzled the remainder of the warm fluid and slid the empty can underneath his cot. Feigning sleep, he lay quiet, hoping to be ignored.

"Well, well," drawled Hill as he stepped into the tent, "musta been a tough day for the garrison troopers; here's one fucking laid out already." He nudged the edge of Danly's cot as he walked by. " 'Course I don't know, maybe he's actually dead."

Danly's only movement was to flick up the middle finger of his left hand.

"Naw," laughed Winters, following Hill into the tent. "It's just another candy-assed Yankee run outta gas."

Gray said nothing as he walked slowly to his bunk.

After dropping their flight gear on their cots, Hill and Winters continued to taunt Danly good-naturedly before finally leaving for the mess hall. Gray sat slumped on his footlocker, wearily rubbing the back of his neck.

"Hey, Mike," he said softly, "I need to talk to you."

"Later," replied Danly, remaining motionless.

"It's important."

"Later," repeated Danly.

"C'mon Mike, I'm not kidding."

"Neither am I."

"Goddammit! This is serious," Gray said angrily. He stood up and began to pace. "Horvath fucked up bad out there today."

Danly, mildly surprised by Gray's sudden outburst, had opened one eye. "So what's new?" he asked, watching Gray stroll back and forth along the row of bunks.

"What's new is he started to come unraveled and damn near shot at a platoon of Fourth Division grunts. They were walking across a clearing and any idiot could've seen they weren't NVA."

Danly opened his other eye and propped himself up on his elbows. "That bad, huh?"

"Yeah. Something has got to be done with that guy."

"You talk to Hawkins?"

"I told him what happened, but he didn't seem to listen very closely. When I tried to emphasize the problem, he just nodded distractedly and said something about giving Horvath a couple of days off. Hell, Horvath's problem isn't a matter of being tired," Gray said emphatically. "His problem is he's cracking up. He shouldn't be flying anymore."

Danly nodded in agreement. "Won't argue that. Shouldn't have been flying to begin with."

Gray stopped pacing and turned to face Danly. "Mike, you gotta talk to Hawkins; we've got to get Horvath grounded."

"I'm not sure my talking would do any good. I think Hawk might chalk up complaints about Horvath to the bad feelings between some of the warrants and the commissioned officers.''

"Hawk respects you, Mike; he'll listen.''

Danly closed his eyes and rubbed the bridge of his nose with the back of his hand.

"Mike?''

"All right," he said, rolling on his side, his back to Gray. "I'll talk to him. Now let me get some damn sleep.''

Danly sensed the presence of someone standing nearby and debated with himself whether to open his eyes. He had been drifting toward his longed-for sleep, but was not quite there. How long has it been since Gray left? he wondered. Couldn't have been more than a few minutes.

"Mike, you awake?''

Danly opened his eyes. "I am now.''

Barnes fidgeted, wondering if it was a bad idea to bother Danly. "Uh . . . you're the guy that's been around here the longest and there are a couple of questions that've been bothering me.''

"Which are?''

"Well, first, what happens if you fire outside of a free-fire zone?''

"You mean without having been fired upon?''

"Yes.''

Danly sat up and yawned. "It depends entirely upon the circumstances." He stared at Barnes. "I've got the feeling this question's not just academic. Something happen?''

Barnes was suddenly sorry he'd started the whole thing. He'd overlooked the possibility that Danly and Hill might be good friends. "Aw, it's nothing.''

"Nothing my ass. You just woke me up; now what's this about?''

"Forget—''

"*What happened*, Barnes?''

Barnes began to wilt under Danly's hard gaze. "I was flying with Hill and he did a recon by fire outside the zone.

Destroyed a hootch and it kind of bothers me.''

At the mention of Hill's name, Danly's lips had parted into a thin, mirthless smile. ''Look, Barnes, you might as well get used to that sort of thing; it happens now and then, and Hill's not the only one who does it.''

''Do you?''

''No.''

''But doesn't it bother you when . . .'' Barnes grimaced. He hadn't meant to question Danly's conduct. ''I'm sorry; I've got no business—''

''Barnes, just relax and shut up for a minute. Does it bother me when other people ignore the rules? It depends. If it's because of negligence or stupidity, yeah; if it's for a good reason, no. Look, Hill's no dummy; he knows the area. Do you think the guys that set up the free-fire zones are omniscient, that they always know everything that goes on in the AO?''

''No, I guess not.''

Danly lay back down and put his hands behind his head. ''If Hill would've hurt a civilian, then you'd have to report it. But if you went to Patterson with this business about Hill shooting up a hut, he'd laugh in your face.

''Look, I'm not telling you that what Hill did was right. What I am telling you is that rules don't always fit the circumstances. Things aren't all black and white over here— there's a lot of gray. You haven't been around too long, so it's kind of tough for you to judge.''

''I guess it gets easier, then?''

Danly closed his eyes. ''Not necessarily. Look, what's important is that you do what you think is right; it doesn't matter what Patterson says or what I say or what anybody says. You're the one that has to live with your conscience. You're going to have to make some tough decisions about when to pull the trigger, so start thinking about it.''

''Yeah, uh . . . thanks.'' Barnes walked away, not sure if the conversation had made him feel better or worse.

CHAPTER 5

**NOVEMBER 22, 1967
KONTUM PROVINCE,
SOUTH OF POLEI KLENG**

The chicken-plate covering Barnes's chest was bothering him. Although he much preferred the protection it offered to that provided by a flak vest, it was proving to be more uncomfortable. He had removed the plate from the rear pouch of the armored vest—the aircraft seat provided ample protection for his back—in order to feel a bit cooler and to make it much less awkward to lean back against his seat. But the ensuing weight imbalance had presented another problem. No matter how he adjusted the straps that secured the vest, the weight imbalance caused the front of the vest to sag until the plate in the front pouch pressed against his thighs. Invariably, one of his legs would then go to sleep.

Digging into his pants pocket for his lighter, he felt the familiar tingling sensation spreading through his left leg and he cursed. The discomfort caused by the vest was not his only problem; the incident involving Hill and the destruction of the hut was still weighing on his mind. Conditioned by training and temperament to ''play by the rules,'' he was still disturbed by Hill's disregard of the free-fire zone boundaries. Sure the hut had almost certainly been empty, but suppose, just suppose, it hadn't been. Then somebody was dead. Was it soldiers or civilians? And if it was the latter, could Barnes have prevented it?

His frown deepened. He had anticipated the physical discomfort of the war, but not the emotional. He did not want to be troubled by the kind of uncertainties that Hill's actions presented. Shifting his weight onto his right buttock, he lifted the edge of the chicken-plate with his right hand and massaged his thigh with his left. The gunship bounced as it flew through a pocket of mild turbulence, and the chicken-plate slipped from his fingers, landing sharply on his aching thigh. Barnes swore.

"Problem?" asked Winters, smiling across the cockpit.

Barnes just grunted, unsure whether Winters was trying to cheer him up or merely laughing at him.

"You want to fly for a while?" asked Winters, still smiling.

"Yeah," replied Barnes, eager to do something besides sit and brood.

"This is what, your third flight in-country?"

"Yeah. Had an orientation flight and then flew with Hill yesterday."

"Well, just be sure to keep the loaches in sight at all times and vary your flight path so you don't keep flying over the same spots. Some of the loaches move around pretty quick, so you gotta be alert to stay on top of 'em. No pun intended."

Barnes nodded and began to relax. It was easy for him to keep the little helicopters in sight. There was one trouble, though: it was also boring. He had expected something different. He had thought that for gunship pilots boredom would be confined to the time spent on the ground waiting to "scramble" for combat assault missions. He was learning that reconnaissance, the air cavalry's primary mission, was often slow, tedious, and dull work. All his flight time thus far, excepting the five-minute attack on the hut, had consisted of flying in circles while the LOHs flitted back and forth just above the treetops.

Around and around in a wide circle he steered the gunship, while the sun beat relentlessly on its dark green top. Even with the breeze that circulated freely through the open windows and cargo doors, Barnes felt uncomfortably hot. Small rivulets of sweat crept from inside his helmet and trickled down his cheeks and along the sides of his nose. He could not imagine how anyone on the ground could tolerate the heat while trudging through the stifling jungle. Thank God I'm not in the infantry, he thought.

"How do you like the heat, man?" asked Winters, as if reading his mind.

"I'll get used to it—I hope."

Winters nodded. "How'd you like to be one of them NVA troopers, humpin' it all the way down from Hanoi, carrying a couple of mortar rounds like some damn pack mule?"

"No thanks," said Barnes emphatically.

"Fuckers must be crazy. But then," said Winters with a rueful grin, "ain't we all?"

Barnes nodded and watched closely as the LOHs began to fly in a circle. They had been following a well-used path that cut through a wide valley. The narrow trail was seldom visible from the gunships' altitude, but Barnes had occasionally caught glimpses of it while passing over those areas where the vegetation was thinner. Suddenly the second LOH banked sharply to the right near a huge tree protruding above the surrounding vegetation.

"Two-seven, this is Red One-one. You see where I just turned?"

Winters looked at Barnes. "You see where he's talking about?"

Barnes nodded.

"Affirmative," answered Winters. "What have ya got?"

"There's four dinks huddled down near the base of that

big tree. At least two of 'em have got A.K.'s.''

"Okay, One-one, we'll put it on 'em." He glanced at Barnes. "No sweat; it's just like gunnery training at Fort Rucker. Get the reticle on the target and squeeze. After you fire a couple of pair, break off and come round again."

Barnes wished he could match Winters' calmness, but his stomach muscles were already drumhead tight, and his breathing was shallow and rapid. His hands began to tremble, and he squeezed the controls in an attempt to steady himself. Relax, he said silently, concentrate. He reached above his head and swung the rocket sight into position in front of his face. After aligning the aircraft on the target axis, he lowered the nose of the gunship until the iridescent red circle in the middle of the sight overlaid the large tree. The aircraft's speed increased rapidly and the ensuing vibrations caused the circle to bounce erratically. Grimly fighting the controls, Barnes attempted to keep the sight centered on the target. His breathing became more rapid and he clenched his jaw. Keep it centered, keep it centered, he repeated to himself.

For a brief moment the circle held rock-steady, framing the lower half of the tree. Barnes squeezed the red button on the side of the cyclic. He heard a loud *whoosh* as on each side of the aircraft a thin rocket escaped from its tube and rushed toward the target. The two white contrails looked to Barnes like a pair of powdery railroad tracks angling toward convergence on a dark green horizon. The illusion quickly faded as the rockets ripped through the foliage of nearby trees and exploded on the ground near the base of the huge tree.

Barnes's pulse raced, as now accompanied by the whirring blat of miniguns and the staccato bursts of the door guns, he squeezed off another pair of rockets. He was transfixed by the sight of the sleek, white cylinders streaking toward the target followed closely by a tight spray of red tracers. His entire consciousness had narrowed to the small section of ground near the giant tree, a plot of earth turned deadly by the barrage of flying metal.

He jerked as if doused with ice water when Winters nudged him and made a sweeping motion to the right with his hand. Barnes cursed under his breath; he'd flown too close to the target. Banking hard, he felt the pressure of the turn press him firmly to the seat. A slow, hopping vibration from the main rotor system made him realize the blades were partially stalled, and he eased the back pressure of the cyclic. He suddenly realized he could "feel" the aircraft like he never had before; all his senses were sharp and clear. He was exhilarated.

The target fixation he had experienced did not reoccur during the second gun run, and he knew it wouldn't happen again. It seemed to him he could see and hear and smell everything with amazing clarity. His rockets were on target, his flying was smooth and controlled, and his voice was calm as he responded to Winters' command to break off the attack.

"Let's make one more run. Be sure we got 'em."

"Naa," said Winters, looking down at the smoke curling up from burning elephant grass near the big tree. "There's nobody gonna be moving around after that."

"Hey, One-one, this is Two-seven."

"Go ahead, Two-seven."

"Why don't you check and see if any of those guys are still in one piece?"

Barnes circled overhead as the LOHs made two fast passes over the target. He knew his fire had been accurate, because the small aircraft slowed quickly, and one of them came to a hover directly above the big tree.

"Looks like you gunnies lucked out again; I count four K.I.A.'s down here."

"Roger, One-one, we'll relay that to Striker Three." Smiling, Winters gave the thumbs-up sign to Barnes. "Nice going. Take a break; I'll fly for a while."

Barnes grinned and sat back. Now he knew what Bookman had been talking about the other night. Bookman's situation had been somewhat different—Bookman had been under fire and Barnes had not—but it didn't make that much difference. The threat had still existed, and Barnes's adrenaline had flowed wildly. Barnes had enjoyed it immensely.

Yup, he thought, pleased with himself, this is more like it.

CAMP ENARI

The brilliant orange in the western sky was gradually giving way to the somber gray of dusk. Lengthening shadows crept slowly along the ground, the dark outlines making distorted shapes, like reflections in a fun-house mirror. The point of the shadow cast by the tent roof across the road nudged the toe of Danly's boot. He sat motionless on the ground, leaning against the wall of sandbags that surrounded the platoon leaders' tent. Watching the changing color in the sky reminded him of those lazy summer evenings on his father's farm in Iowa. He had liked nothing better than sitting on the wide porch as the sun slowly settled behind the dense forest of cornstalks in the sprawling "west forty." On most summer evenings, the entire family was usually there: his mother and sisters chatted happily, while he and his brother played checkers under the watchful eye of their father. It had been a regular routine, one that he'd grown to enjoy immensely.

Sometimes though, as the sun went down, he would wander off by himself and sit in the long grass at the edge of the cornfield. He enjoyed looking back at the house as its gleaming whiteness changed to a shimmering orange, and then finally, as it was enveloped by the night, to a soft gray.

Occasionally, usually in the later part of the summer when the early harvest would increase the amount of dust in the air, there would be such a stunning display of oranges, reds and purples at sunset that everyone on the porch would be rendered mute. Even his mother's lilting voice, which seemed to dance lightly along the porch railing before diffusing into the crisp evening air, would suddenly become silent as the vibrant hues spread across the western sky.

There were other good things about those summer nights. As the days dissolved into darkness, little flickers of light would suddenly appear all around the vast lawn. He and his brother, and later when he was in high school, his girlfriend Kay, would roam about the lawn catching the lightning bugs and putting them in jars, which they would then set on the porch railing. Later they would sit on the porch swing and listen to the frogs and the crickets, and watch the lights blink on and off in the jars.

Some nights there would be a different kind of light show, and he and Kay would sit on the swing and gaze in awe at the huge, crackling pitchforks of lightning that accompanied a late-evening thunderstorm. They would sit close, his arm draped protectively about her shoulders, and silently marvel at the dazzling display.

But all that was from another time. Often it seemed to Danly like a goddamn lifetime ago. Instead of dozing to the lazy rhythm of a creaking porch swing and breathing air filled with the sweet odor of new-mown hay, he now spent nights surrounded by the pungent odor of dried sweat, his sleep often interrupted by the wail of a warning siren or the grating snores of his tentmates.

Instead of puzzling over Kay's erratic behavior, he was now burdened with Horvath's peculiar actions. Instead of being filled with youthful hope and enthusiasm, he was becoming more infused with the cynicism and indifference of a middle-aged man growing tired of his life.

Danly was tired all right; he knew better than to try to kid himself about that. But he was determined not to give in to the weariness. The only thing to do in Vietnam, he had decided, was to take the days and the troubles one at a time. Otherwise they could overwhelm you.

Danly remembered the first real trouble that had affected his life—the disintegration of Kay's mental health. He had been ill-equipped to handle her increasingly erratic behavior. Her bizarre stunts and emotional outbursts had left him confused and scared. If only he had had the maturity he had gained in the past few months, it might have ended differently. He cursed softly through clenched teeth and forced her memory from his mind.

His problem now was Horvath. The lieutenant's frightened antics could easily result in disaster for anyone unlucky enough to be near him at the wrong time, and there was no sense in giving the NVA any help. They were knocking off enough people on their own. There were plenty of things to be concerned about, but Horvath was now at the top of the list.

The sun was almost down. Danly sat quietly, watching the last faint streaks of orange fade from the sky. *Just take one problem at a time.*

Danly heard Miller's thin laugh ricochet off the sandbag walls as the three captains emerged from Patterson's hootch. Well, he thought, the old man must've been in good humor this evening. The shithead. Four more enemy K.I.A.'s today for E Troop—Patterson must figure he's looking pretty good. That makes about thirty for the week that "his boys" have dispatched. Yes sir, under his leadership the gooks were dropping like flies. That would impress the hell out of 'em up at squadron.

"Hey look at this," laughed Miller as he, Resnick and Hawkins got close enough to the tent to see Danly. "We got our own personal sentry."

"Somebody's got to look out for your ass; lord knows *you're* not capable," said Resnick. "Hey, Mike, how ya doing?"

Danly looked up and feigned surprise. "For a minute

there I thought the three stooges had been drafted. Evening, sirs.''

"That's all right, don't get up," Miller said. "We're only captains—you know, your superior officers?"

Danly yawned.

"In all ways, I might add," Miller said, smiling. "You here to try and recoup your poker losses from the other night, Mister Danly?"

"That was blind luck, Miller," answered Danly pleasantly. "Just like your flying."

"Hawk, some of your people got no respect."

"Some of them have no brains either, although that doesn't apply to Mister Danly here; he's just short on manners."

"*Au contraire*, sir. I always enjoy chatting with your lovely companions."

Danly rolled quickly to his right as Miller pushed a sandbag from the top row, just above Danly's head. It landed with a loud plop, right where he had been sitting. Shaking his head slowly in mock sorrow, he stood up and looked at Miller with a pained expression. "There's just no hospitality anymore."

Miller and Resnick laughed and entered the tent.

"What do you want?" asked Hawkins.

"Need to talk to you for a few minutes. Privately."

The two men walked across the troop area and stopped next to the wall of sandbags surrounding the supply tent.

"Hawk, I think Horvath ought to be taken off flight status."

"You do, huh?" asked Hawkins dryly.

"He's nervous as hell and I think he's dangerous up there. The guy's about to crack up."

"You become a flight surgeon in your spare time?"

Danly ignored the sarcasm. "Did Gray tell you about the incident with the friendlies?"

"Yes, so what? Horvath's not the first pilot that ever confused friendlies with gooks. I talked to him and he said he realized his mistake just as Gray yelled a warning, so he wouldn't have fired even if Gray hadn't intervened.''

"It wasn't just the mistake itself; it's why he made it: he panicked. Look, Hawk, that wasn't the first fuckup for Horvath. You must've heard about that deal two weeks ago when he hit the top of a tree during a gun run. He froze. If Webb hadn't grabbed the controls, it would've been a lot worse than just getting a few branches caught in the rocket pods. Other guys have had problems with Horvath also. Hell, I had to grab the controls one time when he was about to fly us into a ridgeline.''

"He's the only guy you've had to take the controls from?''

"Of course not. But it's usually brand-new guys.''

"Yeah, and that includes warrant officers, too, doesn't it?''

"Hawk, this isn't a warrant-versus-commissioned thing.''

"Oh no? You think I'm not aware of what the warrants think of Horvath? Just because he came into this unit expecting the proper military courtesy—you know, like yes sir, no sir, and a few salutes, things you and your cronies are a little short of—you guys have had it in for him.''

"Sure we think he's an asshole, but that's not it.''

"Bullshit!'' Hawkins exclaimed angrily. He pointed his forefinger at faced Danly. "I think that's *exactly* it. Maybe not so much with you, but I think it is with the rest of 'em. You guys seem to think you're in some goddamn fraternity, just a little bit better than everybody else. You all better think again. This is the Army; you don't blackball anybody around here.

"What the hell do you people know about the pressures on Horvath, or any other commissioned officer? You warrants get done flying and it's whoopee time, head for the beer. You don't have command responsibility, and damn few of you have any extra duties. But Horvath does, and he works damn hard at them. Did it ever dawn on you

people that he might just be one hell of a lot tired than any
of you?''

Even in the deepening shadows, Danly could see how
much thinner Hawkins' dark face had become in the past
few months. The strain seemed to be showing on everyone.
Danly was silent for a few moments, then said quietly,
''With all due respect, Hawk, that ain't it.''

The outburst had drained Hawkins' energy and he relaxed
as he reached into his pocket for a cigarette. ''I don't think
you and I are going to agree on this one, Mike. Look, I'm
going to give Horvath a few days off; I think he'll be all
right.''

''I hope so, because a few guys are talking about refusing
to fly with him.''

''Oh?'' asked Hawkins, his anger returning.

''Yeah. As a matter of fact, they're thinking of going
right to Patterson about it.''

''That,'' Hawkins said with a thin smile, ''would be a
big mistake.''

''Well, Hawk,'' said Danly, ''at least we agree on something.''

_____

Gray sat staring at the blank piece of paper. With the pen
that he held loosely in his right hand, he drummed an irregular beat upon the makeshift desk. Great things you can
do with ammo crates, he mused. You can use them to store
things, you can use them as braces, and best of all, you can
use them to make furniture. You can even use them as
coffins for thin midgets.

Wincing at his black humor, he dropped the pen on top
of the paper and looked at the picture sitting on the corner
of the desk. He could not seem to conjure up much in the
way of humor anymore, and when he did, it was always of
the grim variety. Laughing used to come easy, especially
when he was with Karen.

He stared at the small photograph and the faces of a little girl and a dark-haired woman smiled up at him, the smaller face a miniature version of the woman's. Fran had always been cheery; Gray was sure she had inherited her mother's laughter genes. He stared at the images of the two people that gave meaning to his life and he felt the familiar ache of loneliness.

At first he had thought that was the source of his increasing depression, but he had gradually realized it was something else. His separation from Karen and Fran may have been the catalyst, but it was not the main thing that was troubling him. Stumbling to his bunk one evening, his weariness and ill-humor fed by an excess of alcohol, he had accidently knocked the picture off the desk and had stepped on it. "That's how we get them dinks around here," he had mumbled drunkenly to himself. "Knock 'em down and step on their asses." Tottering backward, he had removed his jungle boot from atop the picture. Two faces had beamed at him from the dusty tent floor, their smiles partially obscured by a tread mark from his dirty boot.

It was then that the fear hit him. Suppose they were to die? Suppose something snuffed out their lives as suddenly as it happened to other people every day in Vietnam? He shuddered. Bending over to pick up the picture, he had lost his balance and tumbled onto his cot. The tent had seemed to spin and he surrendered to the alcohol and fatigue, tightly clutching the bent photograph as he passed out.

Ever since that night—there was no getting around it— he had been bothered by the fact he was killing people. Initially he supposed it was just the shock of finally seeing men fall as the bullets from his miniguns riddled their bodies. For several months and maybe a hundred missions, he had fired upon and killed numerous men, but had not actually seen what he had done. The rockets and tracers would pour into the jungle and it wasn't until later that he would find out exactly what had happened. The infantry would count bodies and the "score" would be posted in operations. It was decidedly impersonal.

It was impossible to tell exactly how many NVA he had actually killed—when there were several gunships firing, it could only be considered a group total. Dividing the casualties among the pilots would give a rough approximation, but he had not bothered to do that; it hadn't mattered.

But ever since the "turkey shoot," as Hill had called it, Gray found himself wondering just how many people were no longer living because of him. It had only been two weeks ago, although it seemed much longer than that, when they had caught the twenty NVA troops in the open. It was a gunpilot's dream. Laden with supplies, the men were struggling through waist-high elephant grass in a large clearing. The ensuing scene had reminded Gray of one of those nature documentary film clips shot from an airplane in Africa. As the plane swoops down on some herd of antelope or gazelles, they start fleeing in a mad frenzy, bumping into one another and zigzagging wildly across the plain. It had been just like that with the NVA. When they heard the helicopters, they had frantically attempted to flee. Running crazily through the grass, they had desperately sought the cover of the jungle at the edge of the clearing. They never had a chance.

The gunships simply mowed them down.

Gray did not really feel sorry for them—hell, they were carrying enough ammunition to kill a couple hundred Americans. It was just that he did not like the fact *he* had been shooting them. He had never felt that way before, and his growing concern with the matter confused him. He was not against the war; he believed in what he understood the purpose to be: fighting communism. But still he was finding himself increasingly hesitant about pulling the trigger.

Reluctantly, he began to believe he was just one of those people who was just not cut out to kill. It was a hell of a trait for a gunpilot in Vietnam.

CHAPTER 6

**DECEMBER 5, 1967
CAMP ENARI**

At the sound of the jeep's horn, Barnes tossed the paperback he'd been reading onto his cot and hurried out of the tent. Spradling sat at the wheel of the vehicle, and behind him in the backseat were two enlisted men. They both had the same rumpled appearance as Spradling. One of the men sat immobile, hiding behind a pair of black-framed wraparound sunglasses that contrasted sharply with the whiteness of his shaved head. The other man, who was in desperate need of a haircut, nodded at Barnes and smiled.

"How ya doin', sir?"

"Fine," Barnes grunted. He had a strong premonition of trouble. The man's smile was like that of a pool shark trying to lure a sucker into a game.

As Barnes raised his leg to climb into the front seat, Spradling held out his arm like a school crossing guard, stopping him halfway.

"Go get your flak vest and your steel pot."

"What the hell for? I thought we were going to the PX."

"We are. Then we're going over to Pleiku Air Force Base."

"Why?"

"Because some USO girls are giving free blowjobs on the runway. What do you care? Just get your shit and let's go."

"Shouldn't I notify Horvath or somebody that I'm leaving the base?"

"We'll put in a call to Westmoreland later. C'mon, hurry up."

Despite his misgivings, Barnes decided to get his gear. Being around Spradling was seldom dull.

The scenery within Camp Enari wasn't much to look at, Barnes had to admit. The setting was merely a huge swath of the highlands plain that had been skinned bare by the behemoth bulldozers of the Corps of Engineers. The top layer of loose soil was scooped up by even the gentlest of breezes. Later it would float down like microscopic red snowflakes, giving a rust-colored tint to everything in sight. Had the roads remained bare, it would have been much worse. But several tanker trucks periodically patrolled the miles of roads crisscrossing the camp, recoating them with a gooey, black film of liquid tar called "Pentaprime."

As he had done on his ride in from Pleiku that first day, Barnes settled into a state where he divided his attention between Spradling's travelogues and the passing sights. He gazed with mild envy as they drove past the rows of long, low wooden barracks. He figured there must have been hundreds of them spread across the camp. There were a few pockets of tents, such as those used by E Troop, but most of the soldiers lived in the more permanent structures. He hoped Spradling had been correct about E Troop building wooden barracks; he was tired already of living in a tent.

The thoughts of new quarters faded from his mind, however, when he realized that Spradling had become uncharacteristically quiet. They had just entered the PX parking lot, but instead of turning into the nearest space, Spradling began to cruise slowly between two long rows of parked vehicles. Barnes glanced behind him and saw each of the men in back peering intently at each parked jeep as they cruised past.

Oh, shit! thought Barnes. I'm about to get in trouble.

"Wendell, what in—"

Spradling shook his head irritably and motioned for him to keep silent. The man behind Barnes suddenly tapped Spradling on the shoulder, and Spradling brought the jeep to an abrupt halt. After quickly scanning the immediate area and determining no one was nearby, he nodded. The two men in back scrambled out and walked rapidly to the jeep, which was parked abreast of Barnes. The driver had forgotten to chain the steering wheel.

"Dammit, Wendell! Why didn't you tell—"

Spradling waved him silent again and accelerated smoothly, aiming the jeep for the far entrance to the parking lot. Once out of the lot, he increased speed rapidly, turning onto the road that led toward the main gate. Barnes looked over his shoulder and saw another jeep following close behind. The private wearing the beatnik sunglasses sat behind the wheel grinning broadly.

Barnes turned around and leaned forward, covering his face with his hands. "Why me?" he moaned.

"Aw, relax," said Spradling. "This isn't the first time we've done this, you know."

"I don't want to know about any other times; I don't even want to know about this time. If we get caught, so help me God, Wendell . . ."

"Raymond, my man, better get a hold of yourself. You being the only officer here," Spradling smiled and pointed to his bare shirt collars, "you're in charge of this little convoy. If there's any question about the trip ticket for our spare vehicle, the lunkhead MPs at the gate are going to come to you for answers."

"Hey, I'm not going to be a part of this. Pull over and let me out."

"Too late," laughed Spradling, pointing ahead at the gate

that was clearly in view, "they'll see you and get suspicious. Calm down, Ray; I was just shitting you about the paper-work. My men know what they're doing."

Barnes tried to appear relaxed, but felt as if he were oozing guilt from every pore. He was certain the MPs would notice his nervousness and know something was wrong. But to his surprise, nothing happened. The MPs made a bored, cursory inspection of the trip tickets and waved them through.

Spradling began to hum cheerfully as they sped down the road toward Pleiku. Barnes sat glumly, wondering what would prove to be more dangerous: flying or hanging around with Spradling.

———————————

PLEIKU AIR FORCE BASE

The transaction at the Air Force base was handled quickly and efficiently. The fat sergeant that Barnes had seen when Spradling had picked him up the first day was sitting in his own jeep waiting for them. It then became a convoy of three vehicles speeding rapidly toward a large hangar used for servicing transport planes.

Barnes had to marvel at the coordination of activities; the sergeant's cohorts had wasted no time in getting the stolen jeep aboard the waiting C-123. In fact, the big plane had had its engines running—Barnes figured someone in the sergeant's office must have phoned the flight line when they first drove up—and its ramp down. The loadmaster had waved the stolen jeep aboard, and within four minutes after Spradling's men had hopped from the transport's doorway, it was lumbering down the runway headed for Phan Rang.

Spradling then decided a small celebration was in order and drove to the snack bar next to the terminal.

Barnes idly twirled a long french fry in a small mound

of catsup and glared at Spradling. He was still angry at not being told ahead of time about the theft.

"Wendell, why in the hell didn't you tell me what you had planned?"

"Because you wouldn't have come."

"You're damn right I wouldn't have come. I came over here to fly, not to get strung up by the balls for stealing some colonel's jeep."

"I kinda like to think of it as an interservice equipment transfer."

"It's not funny, Wendell; it's serious."

Spradling's grin disappeared and he sighed. "That's where you're wrong. It's not serious. Stealing stuff and sending it home is serious. Selling military property on the black market is very fucking serious. But *rearranging* the location of property among military installations isn't serious. Everybody does it.

"Come on, Barnes, do you think the normal supply system provides everything everyone needs? Christ, there's enough trouble trying to get basic supplies, to say nothing of getting a few extras to make life more bearable. So everybody helps themselves. It's just a big game, Raymond, that's all."

"I'll bet it's not a game to the poor bastard who forgot to chain the steering wheel."

"Aaaah, now we're supposed to worry about someone payin' for his own foolishness. Forget it. Anybody, I mean *anybody*, with a brain in his head will come up with another jeep within a couple of hours, if not sooner. Motor pools have been known to have a few extra items laying around, and I don't just mean sheet-metal screws and brake pads."

"Aw . . . I don't know," Barnes said, his anger beginning to fade.

"Ray, you gotta learn not to take anything that happens over here too seriously. Otherwise you'll end up like Horvath, acting like you got a hole in the brainpan and a bad case of palsy.''

''Yeah, maybe you're right.''

''No maybe about it. Look, you just got your first taste of action a few days ago; what did you get, four gooks?''

Barnes nodded.

''How did you feel about it?''

''What do you mean?''

''Did you enjoy it?'' Spradling's grin returned.

''Um . . . no. I don't get a kick out of killing people.''

''Nobody does unless they're sick, but that's not what I meant. I mean, did you enjoy the thrill of the action?''

''Yeah, I guess so.''

''Well, it's gonna get better. Everything will. The flying, the excitement, the women—when you're lucky enough to find one—the risks, everything, man.''

Barnes appeared dubious, and Spradling leaned across the table and looked at him earnestly. ''You remember Dickens from high school, right? 'The best of times and the worst of times.' Well that's what you've got comin' up. Vietnam sucks real bad, but it's also the most fun you're ever gonna have.''

CAMP ENARI

For Barnes, writing letters was a difficult job. As far as he was concerned, he was not very good at it under the best of circumstances, and the current circumstances were hardly the best. He was not sure of what he could safely write about without upsetting his family. He was afraid that any detailed stories about the war would cause them unnecessary worry.

There was also another problem: he was superstitious. He thought the most heartrending type of story to come out of any war was one where some poor guy would express his gut feelings in a letter, only to die shortly thereafter. The letter would invariably be eloquent, despite the author's limited writing abilities, and the net effect was usually enough to move even a cynic to tears.

Thus each time Barnes considered expressing his true feelings in a letter, he was restrained by the nagging fear that he might produce some noble sentiments that would somehow precipitate his death.

He knew it was foolish, but the superstition was hard to overcome. He would have fantasies about his family after they'd received the news. Grief-stricken, they would tearfully pass around his last letter. It would be doubly painful for them because the letter would be as eloquent as any he had ever written. It would end on a positive note, which would only increase the melancholy of the family. Each member would shake his or her head ruefully at the sad irony: Raymond had been so positive, so brave, and now . . . now it was over for him. It was a sad scene to be sure, and Barnes could hardly think about it without coming close to tears himself.

But nevertheless, he still had to write home, and he had to include at least some account of what was going on. If his letters were too vague, his loved ones would naturally think he was trying to conceal some horrible truths from them. Yet, if he was too candid, the dreaded superstition lurked. It seemed to him to be a no-win situation.

Electing to write his girlfriend first, he forged ahead, describing in as much detail as possible the attack on the four men hiding under the tree. He exaggerated a few things, but rationalized his "creative writing" as being necessary to convey properly the aura of the situation.

Immediately after rereading what he had written, he felt satisfied with his efforts. But when he had folded the letter and was putting it into an envelope, he felt a twinge of doubt. Maybe his embellishments were too good. Maybe he'd trigger the dreaded jinx after all.

"What's the matter, Barnes? You forget to sign it 'love

and kisses'?'' Hill sniggered sarcastically from his bunk in the corner.

Feeling sheepish, Barnes shook his head no and put the letter in the envelope.

"Letter to your girl, huh?" asked Danly, who was lying on his side reading a book.

"His girl?" exclaimed Hill, feigning astonishment. "Who'd be waiting for him 'cept his old mama?"

"Yes," Barnes said to Danly.

"Where does she live?"

"Washington, D.C."

"You're wasting your time," said Hill. "There's probably some candy-assed civilian getting in her pants right now."

Barnes's jaw tightened, but he did not respond.

Winters winked at Hill. "Jug's probably right," he said gravely. "Your girl's gotta be pretty horny already."

Hill snorted. "Who's talking about his girl? I was talking about his mama."

Barnes stared at the floor as Winters and Hill burst into laughter. Although he was not bothered that much by the talk about his mother, he was irritated by Hill's obvious attempt to make him angry. He guessed it was a test of his manhood, but he couldn't decide how to react.

"What's her name?" asked Bookman.

"Joan," answered Barnes quietly, hoping the subject would soon be dropped.

"Ah, Joanie sweet Joanie." Hill was once again wearing his malevolent grin. "Girls just love all that power in Washington. I'll tell ya, Ray old buddy, she'll be suckin' some senator's dick before the month is out."

Barnes stiffened. Spradling's warning about taking things too seriously popped into his mind, but he pushed it aside. Hill was asking—no, begging—for trouble. Hill was bigger, but if the insults continued, Barnes knew he would have to stand up to him.

"Of course if your mother was in Washington, it'd be

different," Hill continued. "Then she and sweet Joanie could get it on without any senator."

Barnes lurched forward, but was stopped by Danly who leapt from his bunk and snagged Barnes's arm. "Ignore him, Raymond."

Hill's grin had disappeared and he glared at Barnes. "Why don't you just let the boy go, Mike?"

Danly spun Barnes around and pushed him toward Bookman, who grabbed him and pinned his arms behind his back. Danly's voice was soft, but menacing. "Take a fucking hike, Jug."

"What are you now, king of the tent?"

Danly did not answer, but began walking slowly toward Hill, his right hand curled into a fist.

Hill suddenly stood up and began moving toward the door. "Aw, shit," he said, smiling. "I ain't gonna fight you, Mike. You get hurt and I just gotta fly more." He motioned to Winters. "C'mon, let's go get a beer."

Barnes winced as Bookman released him. The soft-spoken man had deceptive strength. Barnes felt as if his arms had been clamped in a large vise.

Turning around and staring at Barnes, Danly shook his head from side to side. "You really better learn something: nothing is sacred around here. You let shit like that bother you and it's going to be a long year."

Barnes nodded soberly and wiggled his arms, trying to get the circulation back to normal.

Danly flopped back upon his cot and put his hands behind his head. "Besides, Raymond," he said with a thin smile, "Joanie probably really will be sucking some senator's dick before too long."

PART TWO
A PALE HORSE

And I looked, and behold a pale horse: and his
name that sat on him was death . . .
—*Revelation 6:8*

CHAPTER 7

JANUARY 24, 1968
CAMP ENARI

As the helicopter cleared the barbed wire at the east end of the runway and started a climbing turn to the north, Gray watched the stream of vehicles and people below him moving slowly to the southeast. The exodus to Qui Nhon was in full swing. Apparently many of the Pleiku residents had gotten the same idea as Gracie.

Two days before, Gray had been sitting on the steps of the tent watching Spradling and Webb engage in a tobacco-juice-spitting contest, when she suddenly appeared. She was called Nhu, but he did not know her full name. Spradling had tagged her with the nickname of Gracie the day she began work as a hootchmaid. She was small, even by Vietnamese standards and her skin was mottled and leathery. When she smiled, which was seldom, she displayed a set of worn, dark brown teeth, badly stained from years of chewing betel nut. Gray had no idea how old she was, but he suspected she was much younger than she looked. He figured a person could age pretty fast when her life consisted mostly of drudgery and fear.

"Hello, Nhu," he said, smiling. She nodded, but did not reply.

When Spradling heard her name mentioned, he whirled around and spread his arms wide.

"Gracie! You're just in time; I need your help."

Nhu smiled shyly. Spradling was the only person who could make her smile, even though most of the time she had no idea what he was talking about.

"I'm losing to this dud, Gracie; you got to help me out." He held out a rumpled package of Beechnut chewing tobacco. "Grab a chaw, Gracie, and we'll kick ass."

She backed away, smiling and shaking her head from side to side.

"C'mon, Gracie, you can spit with the best of them."

Putting her hands over her mouth like an embarrassed schoolgirl, she peered up at Spradling, still shaking her head no.

"Oh, how stupid of me," said Spradling. "You don't want to ruin your teeth."

Webb doubled over laughing, and Nhu, not understanding, smiled nervously behind her hands.

"Nhu, what do you want?" asked Gray.

"Me go. For many days," she answered softly.

"Where?"

"Go Qui Nhon."

"Ah!" exclaimed Spradling with a grin. "You and your old man gonna get it on on the beach."

Again Webb laughed, and Gray could not help but join him. Nhu looked quizzically at Spradling.

"Why," he asked. "Why you go Qui Nhon?"

"Many VC come."

"VC?" snorted Spradling. "For Christ sake, Gracie, most of 'em are dead. You could get all the VC left alive in the central highlands in one goddamn tent. Ain't nothing around here but the fucking North Vietnamese Army."

She watched Spradling, her eyes wide, understanding

almost nothing that he said. But when she heard the words *North Vietnamese*, she nodded her head vigorously.

"Yes, yes. Many North Vietnamese come."

Spradling arched another tan glob of saliva toward the line marking the farthest launch so far. "Out-fucking-standing," he laughed. "I'd like to see the bastards come marching along in one big group."

Nhu was startled as Spradling spun around, bent over and hugged her. "Gracie," he said, looking at her fondly, "you're just like an American—as soon as you hear your relatives are coming, you skip town."

Now Gray wondered, as he passed over the stream of people leaving Pleiku, whether he would ever see the woman again. He wished she would have been able to speak English, or he Vietnamese, because he had grown very curious about her. In contrast to the other hootch-maids, who would chatter constantly among themselves in the rapid, singsong cadence that was total gibberish to him, she had always remained quiet and solemn. He had learned from an English-speaking hootchmaid that Nhu's two children had been killed, one by an unknown disease and the other by a stray bullet during an attack on Nhu's original home, the village of Dak Seang. The hootchmaid had also told him about Nhu's husband. A lieutenant in the South Vietnamese Army, he had been killed in action the previous June near Dak To. Spradling had not known of her husband's fate when he made his joke, and Gray had been thankful for once that she did not understand much English. Her world had been collapsing over the previous months, and now what little security she had in Pleiku was also being lost.

Gray was not certain why he worried about her—there was nothing he could do to improve her lot in life. But he cared just the same.

A mental exercise he often indulged in was to imagine what it would be like for people if they were in vastly different situations. With Nhu, he tried to imagine what it would be like for her now if she had been transplanted to America at a young age. He figured she would be a secretary, or maybe an administrative assistant. Quiet, serious, industrious—she'd be a valuable employee. Hell, she would probably be pretty good-looking, too. Without the crushing stress of war, and with the benefit of hygiene, she would probably have white teeth, silky black hair and a smooth, wrinkle-free complexion.

He could even imagine her being hooked up with Spradling. Since she obviously liked him now when she seldom knew what the hell he was talking about, she would really go for him if she could understand him. The combination of his good humor and her industriousness would make them quite a pair.

"Hey, Steve, take this thing, will ya? I gotta adjust this goddamn chicken-plate."

Startled from his thoughts, it took Gray a moment to respond. Nodding at Spradling, he grasped the controls. The helicopter was passing over Pleiku and he could see people carrying possessions from their houses, preparing to join the long line of other residents fleeing the city.

Aw, the hell with it, he thought, trying to be stoic. No point in worrying about any of those people, especially Nhu. She was never going to smell of fine perfume or be decked out in the latest fashions. She was just going to join that tide of humanity scuffing along on the road beneath him, wearing her soiled, threadbare, pajamalike clothes and leaving in her wake the pungent odor of someone badly in need of a bath.

Pleiku slid by underneath him and the jungle-covered hills were rapidly approaching. He scanned the instruments. Time to start paying attention and forget the maudlin stuff. Xin loi, *Gracie. Like a lot of other people, you're just going to disappear into the misery of this lousy war.*

DAK TO

The C-130 rumbled down the runway and noisily powered its bulk into the hot, humid air. Leaning against the tailboom of Danly's gunship, Hawkins wiped the perspiration from his brow and waited for the noise to subside. His expression was grim as he addressed the semicircle of gunpilots.

"Well, it looks like the shit's really starting. Some NVA types overran a firebase about twenty klicks southeast of Dak Pek last night. Name of the place is Firebase Ramrod. Two companies of the 173rd Airborne are going to be inserted just west of there, and the Fourth Division's going to put in three companies to the east. That's supposed to put the gooks in a box. We're going to team up with the 170th guns to support the 173rd insertion. I'll be the C&C, call sign Striker Three.

"The LZ's gotta be hot, so don't save anything. I want two teams up at all times until the situation on the ground stabilizes. If we need 'em, we've got two extra ships on standby here. Danly's team and Mackin's will be up first; they'll crank at ten-thirty. You can get the call signs and frequencies from Mister Mackin. Any questions?"

No one spoke.

"Okay, the LZs are marked on the map." He tossed the map to Mackin and motioned to Danly, who was sitting on the skid, near the cockpit door. "Mike, I need to see you a minute."

Danly rose slowly and followed Hawkins to the gunship parked nearest the runway. Hawkins opened the cockpit door on the right side and reaching inside, removed the canteen from the web belt hanging on the seat. He poured some water on a handkerchief and drew it slowly across his forehead.

"You don't look too good, Hawk."

Hawkins grunted and sat down wearily in the rear of the

aircraft. "Mike, you probably wonder why I got you and Horvath flying together today."

"The thought crossed my mind, yeah."

"Well it isn't because you convinced me that he's a basket case. It's because I'm not feeling too hot and if I can't last the day, Horvath's in charge. You've got a lot more experience and I want you up with him to help out if he needs it."

Danly said nothing.

Hawkins squeezed his eyes shut and rubbed his forehead. "I think everyone's going to step in some shit today and we've got to stay on top of it." He grimaced at the unintended pun.

"Agreed," said Danly. "That it, Hawk?"

Hawkins nodded and lay back on the helicopter floor. Danly started back toward the other pilots when he heard Hawkins call his name. Returning to Hawkins' aircraft, he noticed how bad the platoon leader looked. His face was flush; his eyes were rheumy and he seemed thinner than ever.

"I don't want anybody hurt by mistakes, Mike. If Horvath starts losing it, don't hesitate to take over."

"I won't," said Danly.

═══════════════

WEST OF FIREBASE RAMROD

Checking his watch, Danly noted that it was five minutes until the first slicks were due to touch down. The area chosen for the landing zone was a small clearing downslope from the overrun firebase. Only three slicks at a time could land in the clearing, and it would be a tight fit. The ground sloped steeply from the center of the clearing toward the side of the ridge, thus preventing the helicopters from making their approaches all the way to the ground—the troops would have to jump out while the aircraft were at a low hover.

Although several LOHs had made rapid passes over the surrounding area and had not received fire, Danly was sure the NVA were there. They were patient; they knew troops were coming.

He held the gunship in a shallow bank at 4,100 feet, carving a wide circle in the haze just north of the approach path. Glancing over his left shoulder, he looked for his wingman. All he could see was empty sky. He shrugged, and with his left hand dug in his pocket for a cigarette. Wherever Spradling and Gray were at the moment did not concern him; they would be right where they were supposed to be when the firing began.

No getting around it, he thought as he inhaled the harsh smoke from a stale Camel, there are two kinds of people over here: those you can rely upon, and those you can't. That was about as basic as you could get. A guy could be the biggest asshole in the world, but if he was reliable, that's the person you wanted flying with you or near you. He coughed as the stale smoke irritated his lungs and noticed Horvath jerk at the sound. He sighed, stubbed out the cigarette and searched the sky to the southwest. Three black dots moving slowly to the north stood out in contrast to the pale haze blanketing the horizon. Behind them were more dots, strung out in groups of three.

"Here come the grunts, Lieutenant."

"What?" asked Horvath, as if he had just been awakened from a long sleep.

Danly tilted his head toward the dots, which were now assuming the profiles of helicopters. "Slicks will be here in about zero five."

Horvath nodded, then looked back out the cargo door opening, straining to see Gray's gunship.

"I don't see Gray back there," he said.

Danly raised his eyebrows in mock concern, but did not reply.

"I better give him a call," said Horvath, reaching to turn the radio selector switch from intercom to UHF. "Two-nine, this is Two-four, are you still with us?''

The radio was silent.

"Two-nine, Two-nine, this is Two-four," Horvath said urgently.

There was still no reply and Danly smiled. He could picture Gray and Spradling relishing Horvath's discomfort.

"Two-nine, Two-nine, say your position, over."

"Your position, over."

At the sound of Spradling's voice, Horvath's jaw tightened and his face began to turn red.

"Two-nine," Horvath began angrily, "this is—"

"You got the slicks in sight, Two-nine?" Danly quickly interrupted.

"Roger," answered Spradling crisply.

"All right, we'll pick 'em up about even with that bare knob two klicks west of the Lima Zulu."

"Two-niner, gotcha."

Two teams of 170th gunships began to pour rocket and minigun fire into the jungle surrounding the clearing as Danly began his descending turn to be in position to escort the lead trio of D-models. He noticed Horvath gripping the map tightly as the chatter of the 170th gunpilots filled his earphones.

"Buc One is inbound; . . . Same-same for Buc Seven; . . . One's breaking left, got some fire from the top of the ridge; . . . Buc Three, rog; . . . Seven, I got flashes from that ravine; . . . Three, they're on your left! They're on your left! . . . Eight, we see 'em; . . . You hit, Three? . . . Negative; . . . Watch your break, Eight, more Charlies in the treeline. . . .''

Dotted lines of red tracers snaked through the air and puffs of white smoke from exploding rockets mushroomed from the foliage. As the Buccaneer gunships continued their relentless assault, Danly once again found himself thinking how happy he was not to be an infantryman, especially on the other side.

"Buc One, this is Striker Three." Hawkins' voice was thin and tired.

"This is One, go."

"The slicks are inbound, what's it look like?"

"We were getting small arms and some automatic weapons from the ravine, but I think we shut 'em up."

"Striker Three, roger. Confirm you're not presently taking fire."

"Buc One, that's affirmative, not at the moment."

"Striker Three, roger . . . break . . . Chariot Two, Striker Three."

"Striker, this is Chariot Two, we copied Buc One, but understand LZ could still be hot. We're on long final."

Danly swung abreast of the lead D-model. "Buc One, Bulldog Two-four is inbound with Chariot Lead."

"Okay, Bulldog, we shot our wad. Bucs are breaking off."

Danly looked at Horvath as the Buccaneer gunships fired the last of their ordnance and broke away toward Dak To. Horvath's hand was wrapped tightly around the minigun sight, and he stared intently at the landing zone. Sweat dripped from his chin and his jaw was tightly clenched.

"Sir," said Danly, "you might like to get your visor down."

His hand trembling, Horvath reached up for the little knob that held the protective eye covering in the stowed position. After giving the knob a twist, he pulled it downward, forcing the clear visor into place. "Thanks," he said nervously. "Wouldn't want to get hit in the baby blues."

Feeling a bit sorry for him, Danly forced a grin and nodded. Christ, he thought, the guy is absolutely scared shitless.

"Two-four, Striker Three." Hawkins' voice sounded very weak.

"This is Two-four," responded Horvath, "go ahead."

"You've got the show, Two-four . . . break . . . All aircraft be advised Striker Three is departing the AO, contact Bulldog Two-four."

Well, Hawk, you could pick a better time to get sick,

thought Danly. "Okay, Lieutenant, looks like we're now running the show." Horvath did not answer, but continued to stare down at the clearing, which looked deceptively peaceful.

Lowering the nose to begin the firing run, Danly glanced to his right. On the other side of the lead D-model, Mackin had begun his dive toward the ridge on the right side of the landing zone. The gunship began to vibrate more as its speed increased, and Danly moved the controls with a smooth precision that was born of the hundreds of previous firing passes. Jiggling in time with the shaking airframe, the rocket sight became aligned with the treeline bordering the north edge of the clearing. Danly squeezed the trigger, and a familiar *whoosh* filled the cockpit as a pair of rockets fled their tubes. Almost at the same moment, Horvath and the door gunners began firing. Danly was oblivious to the din as he fired another pair of rockets and scanned the jungle for muzzle flashes or movement. Nothing was visible but the explosive puffs from the rockets and the red blur of tracers disappearing into the leaves.

He banked sharply, feeling the familiar G-force pressing him into his seat. As the aircraft swung through the turn, rolled almost on its side, he craned his neck to see through the window directly above his head. Gray had begun firing, and the D-models were beginning their deceleration as they closed with the landing zone. Danly leveled the aircraft and flew away from the target toward the line of inbound slicks, then swung quickly around for another pass.

Troops were now jumping from the D-models, even though the helicopters were still several feet above the ground. Laden with equipment, the men sprinted awkwardly toward the trees on the east side of the clearing as the three D-models rose quickly.

"Chariot Lead's on the go."

"Chariot Two-three on short final." The second group of helicopters was about two hundred feet behind the first. Danly concentrated on firing as the second batch of slicks deposited their troops and rapidly exited the area.

"So far, so good," said Horvath. He still sat rigidly, as if wearing a body cast, but his voice was calmer.

"Yeah," said Danly noncommittally. It was still early, and when he had last glimpsed the third group of inbound aircraft, its flight path had not looked right.

As he swung the aircraft around and headed outbound, his first impression was confirmed. The approach of the third group of slicks looked awful. They were too slow and too high, making themselves perfect targets.

Danly cursed as they flew by him in the opposite direction. Spradling was in position to provide cover, but if the gunships hadn't yet driven off the NVA, there was serious trouble ahead.

"Damn. Two-four, what are they doing?"

"Don't know, Wendell. Stay on their ass. I'll get turned inbound soon as I can."

Looking back over his shoulder, Danly could see the first D-model slow even more. Two hundred feet short of the clearing, the aircraft on its left suddenly broke formation and began to accelerate, turning to the north.

"There's a guy wants to grow older, Mike."

"Roger that, Two-nine. Break. Chariot on final, this is Two-four; go around."

As Danly started his turn inbound, he could see tracers from Spradling's miniguns spraying the trees short of the LZ. "I say again, Chariot, *go around*!"

The two slicks continued their slow descent.

"Goddammit!" Danly cursed through clenched teeth. He jerked the gunship through the turn and pushed it into a dive. Out of the corner of his eye he noticed Horvath clutching the edge of his seat. "Don't go south on me now, Lieutenant," he said under his breath.

Suddenly the first slick rocked violently from side to side and then dove sharply to the left.

"He's hit!" shouted Horvath.

The stricken aircraft banged into the ground, tipped over

and began to break apart as it tumbled down the slope toward the trees. Several infantrymen, thrown from the aircraft when it slammed into the slope, were crushed as it rolled over them.

As Danly began firing, he saw two figures emerge from the blazing wreckage. Their clothes were on fire, and one of them collapsed almost immediately. The other stumbled up the slope, his arms flailing wildly at the flames.

"My God!" Horvath exclaimed softly.

The other D-model had turned right, and its pilot was yelling, "Mayday, Mayday! Chariot Three-four is taking fire!"

"Where from, Chariot?"

There was no response as the stricken helicopter continued its right turn and descended into the trees. Danly then heard the ground commander saying his troops were being fired upon from the east and south, and that the heavy fire toward the helicopters was coming from the ravine. As he turned outbound, he saw the next group of slicks abandon their approach and turn toward the west.

"Bulldog Two-four, Tiger Six. They're coming at us; we need some more help down here!"

Danly looked at Horvath. The lieutenant's jaw was sliding back and forth, grinding his teeth in frustration and fear. Danly could imagine the turmoil taking place in Horvath's mind. If he ordered the slicks to continue the insertion, more aircraft could be lost. On the other hand, if he did not get reinforcements for the men on the ground, they might be overrun. Either way, more men would probably die.

What was needed was some napalm and bomb support from the Air Force, but there was no way Horvath could be certain of when it would arrive. Could the gunships provide enough support for the men on the ground until the help arrived?

Horvath chewed on his lower lip as his hands squeezed the sides of his seat tightly.

"Two-four, you copy Tiger Six?" The voice of the ground commander was pitched higher than before and it could barely be heard above the clatter of the weapons firing in the background.

"Roger, Six," said Danly. "Can you mark your forward positions?"

"Tiger Six, affirmative; smoke's out. We *need* that help, over!"

"Stand by, Six." Danly saw two columns of green smoke snaking upward from the trees and he looked quickly across the cockpit. Horvath's body was still frozen in its rigid position while his jaw moved slowly back and forth.

"Lieutenant, what are you going to do?" As he asked the question, Danly remembered a scene played over and over on the parade ground in flight school. Training officers would gang up on a student, yelling contradictory instructions at him, and then smile sadistically while the befuddled man tried to figure out what to do. Finally, one of the officers would step close, putting his mouth within an inch of the student's ear, and scream: "DO SOMETHING, EVEN IF IT IS WRONG!"

The lesson had been simple: inaction is the worst alternative under fire.

Danly could wait no longer. "Do *something*, Lieutenant!"

Horvath still did not move. Christ! thought Danly, the son of a bitch is frozen solid. He looked to his right and saw Mackin's team pouring fire into the ravine. He couldn't wait any longer.

"Chariot Three-seven," said Danly, "Bulldog Two-four."

"This is Three-seven, go."

"Three-seven—" Danly stopped as Horvath waved his hand.

Like someone awakening from a deep slumber, Horvath blinked and shook his head. "Chariot, I want your flight to stay real low and come in single ship from the northwest until we're sure we've got those automatic weapons silenced.''

"Three-seven, okay. We'll give it a try."

Well I'll be dipped in shit, thought Danly. A command decision.

Horvath's face was ashen.

CAMP ENARI

Barnes lay on his bunk, dressed only in shorts. It was midafternoon and the heat was stifling. The sides of the tent had been rolled up to allow the rare, transient breeze to blow through, but the air was dead still. He had tried to sleep, but his discomfort from the heat made that impossible.

His thoughts returned to the fighting. There was no doubt that a major NVA offensive had begun, and that was fine with him; he was eager for his chance to fight. He had not been involved in any action since the day he and Webb had killed the four NVA. Although suitably frightened at the prospect of being shot at, he still wanted it to happen soon. He was sure he could handle the fear, and it was a way to earn the respect of the other pilots.

Hands behind his head, he lay staring blankly at the roof of the tent. Imagining combat situations, he indulged in wild fantasies. One of them, his favorite, kept reoccurring: Although seriously wounded, with his crew incapacitated, he would swoop down through a barrage of enemy fire to rescue the crew of a downed gunship. Dragging its occupants one by one back to his own ship, he would be wounded twice more and then just barely escape, coaxing his overloaded helicopter from the tight LZ just ahead of an onrushing hoard of enemy soldiers.

When the fantasy was over, he always felt a bit foolish, but he was sure he could do just what he had imagined if it became necessary. Pretty sure, anyway.

It was the waiting around that he could not handle very well. Webb had come from operations just before lunch and told him all hell had broken loose south of Dak Pek during an insertion, and that as soon as an aircraft became available from maintenance, he and Barnes were to depart for the area. Barnes had hurriedly begun to dress.

"What are you doing?" Webb had asked with a bemused smile.

Barnes had been puzzled by the question. "Getting ready to go to the flight line."

"Barnes, I'm just alerting you so you don't go marching off to the PX or something; they'll call us when an aircraft is ready."

"But shouldn't we get down there so we can take off as soon as a ship is fixed?"

Webb had looked at him as if he couldn't believe his ears. "*You* can go down and squat in the sun for a couple of hours and work up a good case of hemorrhoids, but me, I'm going to stay up here and try to get some fucking sleep. They'll call us when an aircraft's ready." He had started to leave, then stopped and looked back. "The war ain't going to end this afternoon, Barnes; you'll get your chance."

And so, while assorted bugs probed lazily for gaps in the tent's mosquito netting, Barnes lay sweating, trying without success to relax. Waiting was hard to get used to.

DAK TO

Danly climbed from the cockpit onto the metal planking that covered the parking area on the south side of the runway. He removed his flight helmet, the rubber earpads sliding easily along his sweat-slickened hair. The odor from the helmet was strong, reminding him of the stale smell that always clung to old athletic equipment. He looked inside and saw strands of hair adhering to the brown padding. Spradling had once said they'd all have heads like cue balls before the year was over, and Danly was beginning to believe it. He tossed the helmet onto the pilot's seat, then pulled on the Velcro strips that secured his chicken-plate. The peculiar tearing sound of the Velcro separating was a welcome relief from the cacophony of gunship noises he had endured for the past several hours. The whine of the turbine, the noise and static from all three radios, and the intermittent din of the guns were torture without earplugs. He vowed he would never forget them again.

Slowly, he shrugged his shoulders, gingerly moving them up and down several times. Then, much like a gymnast warming up, he swung his arms in circles trying to drive the stiffness from his shoulders. They ached and he felt a dull throb at the base of his skull. Jesus, he thought wearily, this must be how it feels to be eighty; I need some goddamn time off. Maybe Horvath had the right idea: start going nuts and you get a three-day vacation.

That had been Patterson's solution, anyway. He had sent Horvath to Vung Tau for a short R&R. He had even stopped Danly next to the mess hall one day and said that Horvath had earned the R&R, and that if Danly and his friends ever hoped to get a similar break, they had better emulate Horvath's work habits.

Danly had stood mute, staring at Patterson with as much interest as he would show while gazing at a rock.

Patterson had had to fight to control his anger.

"You seem to have some difficulty paying attention, Mister Danly. You've got an insolent attitude and if I chose, I could make you change it. But I'm not going to bother with you at the moment. You see, one of these days you're going to make a serious mistake, and I'm going to be right there when you do." Patterson's lips separated into a mirthless grin. "You will end up being *very* unhappy."

Massaging the back of his neck, Danly smiled at the

recollection. Patterson was a real piece of work—the king of melodrama.

The sound of the copilot's door closing returned his attention to Horvath. The lieutenant was walking slowly away from the helicopter toward the shade of a revetment. Very pale, he moved as if he were exhausted. His sweat-drenched fatigues stuck to his body, outlining his bony frame.

Danly paused and mentally reviewed Horvath's actions during the mission. After Horvath's initial hesitance when the two D-models were shot down, he had responded well to the situation. It had taken an enormous amount of energy and self-control, but he had controlled the entire operation for almost two hours, until Patterson had arrived to take over. During that time Horvath had coordinated the remainder of the insertion, which had included two companies of Vietnamese Rangers that had been on standby at Polei Kleng. He had coordinated the movements of helicopters from three different units, in addition to the medevacs, and had made good use of Air Force firepower when several Phantoms finally arrived to help.

The remainder of the troops had been put on the ground without further helicopter losses. Several aircraft had been damaged by enemy fire, but none seriously. Fire support had been accurate and the ground troops had sustained as few casualties as could have been expected. The American and South Vietnamese units had moved out of the landing area and were pushing the bulk of the enemy forces toward the other American units that had been inserted to the east.

Danly had made some suggestions during the operation, but for the most part, Horvath had run the entire show. Danly admitted to himself that he would not have done things much differently. Other than the shaky beginning, the whole operation had been a textbook air assault, and Danly was sure that any of the other officers would have been pleased with the results had one of them been in charge.

But Danly could see that Horvath was incapable of reflecting on the positive aspects of his performance. Controlling his own fear and anxiety, in addition to controlling the operation, had drained all of Horvath's energy. Watching him shuffle away, Danly doubted if Horvath would ever recover. He resembled a vacant-eyed old man whose spark of life was close to flickering out. Maintaining his composure during the battle had required a superhuman effort, and the lieutenant had no more to give.

Danly lit a cigarette and wondered what the difference was between them. He felt confident that he would never react like Horvath, but how could he be absolutely sure? Why was one man beaten down in the face of pressure while another man was not? It bothered him that he did not have a ready answer.

―――――――

FIREBASE RAMROD

Pieces of the wrecked helicopter were strewn about the clearing, and Barnes could see the twisted fuselage resting against the trees. Further up the ridge, men could be seen piling sandbags and laying concertina wire around the firebase. He searched without result for traces of the second D-model, which had crashed into the jungle below the landing zone.

By the time a gunship had come out of maintenance for him and Webb, details of the assault had begun to filter back to operations. They had fueled his imagination and he had been increasingly anxious to get to the area before the fighting had ceased.

But after arriving at the landing zone, they had continued circling for more than an hour, awaiting a call from the ground troops. But some of the NVA had somehow melted into the jungle, avoiding the trap, and the American and South Vietnamese troops were digging in for the night. Barnes guided the gunship over the landing zone once more, maintaining the monotonous orbit, and wondered when he would finally get involved in some serious fighting.

Webb had grown quiet and Barnes looked across the cockpit. Webb sat with his eyes closed, a cigarette dangling precariously from the corner of his mouth.

"Hey, Webb," he said softly, hoping he would not startle him and cause him to drop the cigarette into his lap.

"Umph," grunted Webb.

"There's something I don't understand. Why don't they just let us hose down the jungle where there's not any friendlies? Might just pick off a few stragglers."

Webb reached up and pinched his cigarette, slowly removing it from his mouth. "Because," he yawned, "wasting bullets costs money and Lyndon might get pissed."

"Come on, I'm serious. Why not?"

Webb inhaled deeply and blew a stream of smoke toward the Plexiglas windshield. "Barnes, it's gonna be a long war. We don't have enough time, energy or ammunition to run around shooting up the goddamn countryside just because some gooks *might* be there."

"But there's no *might* about it. We know they're down there somewhere."

"I'm with Mister Barnes," said the door gunner. "Let's try an' kill something."

Webb laughed. "Bolger, this morning you were moaning like hell because you were getting called away from a skin book to go fly on your day off. Now you want to be Audie Murphy."

"Who?"

"You tell him, Barnes; you're the gung ho motherfucker around here."

"Bulldogs, this is Six." Patterson's resonant bass filled Barnes's earphones. "That's it for today, let's go home."

"Aw, too bad," drawled Webb, looking from Bolger to Barnes. "I know it's hard on you trained killers, but we got to go to the house."

Barnes looked back at the clearing as he swung the aircraft around toward Camp Enari. He saw a large section of a main rotor blade laying in the landing zone. The blunt end of the blade lay upslope, and the jagged end—where it had broken off near the mast—was aimed like the tip of a giant arrow at the wrecked helicopter resting against the lower treeline. Barnes thought there was something very noble about the broken blade. It lay like a fallen sentinel, pointing at the grim evidence of the terrible cost of battle.

He was very sorry he had missed the action.

CHAPTER 8

JANUARY 28, 1968
CAMP ENARI

Barnes cupped the five cards carefully in his hands, and with his left thumb slowly spread them apart just far enough to see the markings. They were all hearts.

"C'mon, Ray," Winters said irritably. "You going to call or not?"

Pushing the cards back together, Barnes let his hand hover over the small stack of chips in front of him and glanced quickly around the table. Winters was staring at him anxiously; Danly and Gray had both thrown in their cards; Spradling was tapping his fingers restlessly on the table; and Hill was leaning back in his chair smiling benignly. Barnes looked at his hand again.

"This ain't bridge," Spradling said wearily. "Therefore, you don't have to stare at your fucking cards till everybody falls asleep. Either you hit your straight or you didn't."

"Don't harass the boy," Hill said. "He's trying to learn. This is quite a switch from playing Michigan rummy with his mommy and daddy."

"All right," said Barnes, glowering at Hill. "Call. *And* . . . raise five bucks."

Hill continued to smile.

Tossing his cards facedown on the table, Winters glared at Hill. "You just had to piss him off, didn't you, Jug?"

"If the game's too rough—"

"I'll call," interrupted Spradling.

Hill pushed a small stack of chips into the center of the table. "So will I. He doesn't have a straight—do you, Barnes?"

"Nope," said Barnes, spreading his hand on the table with a triumphant smile. "Better."

Hill shook his head from side to side. "Rookies," he sighed. "They always overestimate their hand." He turned his cards over to show two jacks and three sevens.

Barnes stared at the full house, then cursed softly.

"Kiss my ass," moaned Spradling, flipping his cards in the air. "I didn't have to come all the way to Vietnam to throw away money; I coulda done this at home."

"How did you end up over here, Wendell?" Winters asked as he gathered up the cards. "I know you didn't flunk out of college—you weren't smart enough to get in in the first place."

"Bite it, Winters."

"Yeah, Wendell," said Hill. "What happened? You couldn't find your way to Canada?"

"I'm here for the same reasons you are. I was a fuckoff, dropped out of college and was about to get drafted. I enlisted for flight school, figuring I'd be rubbing elbows with a higher class of people. Christ, was I wrong."

Winters laughed. "I had kinda figured the same thing. But I'll bet it ain't the same for Danly and Gray. They look like straight-A students."

Danly just grunted and reached for the cards that Winters had dealt him.

"Yeah," said Spradling. "You're halfway bright, Steve. How'd you get caught?"

"I didn't. I'm here because I want to be."

"*Want to be?* Jesus, Gray! Nobody wants to be here. Not

even Mister 'I Love to Kill Dinks,' here,'' Spradling said, nodding toward Hill.

Gray had to smile. "You're right, Wendell. Let me put that in the past tense: *wanted* to be. Now that I'm here, I'd rather be anyplace but."

"Yeah, but why'd you join the Army in the first place?"

"I wanted to fly. Couldn't afford to finish college, so that ruled out the Navy and the Air Force. The Army·was it."

"This is fucking it, all right. You musta wanted to fly *real* bad."

Gray laughed.

"How about you, Mike?" asked Barnes.

Danly looked at his cards and tossed them on the table. There was no point in trying to explain the emptiness that enveloped him after Kay's suicide, or how he had to get as far away from home as he could.

"I wanted to see a Bob Hope show for free."

Spradling slapped the table and laughed. "I knew it, goddammit! I knew it. Danly, you've got the soul of a comedian. You hide it well, but underneath you're a fucking barrel of laughs. You—"

"Wendell," growled Hill. "Shut the fuck up and play cards. Are you going to open or not?"

"You in a hurry? You got to go kill somebody?" Spradling leaned back and began a leisurely examination of his cards.

Barnes looked at the hand Winters had dealt him, but his thoughts had wandered back to when the seeds of his Army career had been sown. He remembered, how at the age of ten, he had wandered into his uncle's study and idly picked from a shelf the first of the war books that would shock and fascinate him. Bound in dark red leather, the six volumes comprised a pictorial history of World War II. He had been particularly captivated by the photographs of aerial combat. His imagination fueled by the heroics of fighter and bomber pilots, he had spent hours pretending he was among them—

testing his courage in countless imaginary battles.

But there were also pictures that shocked him and made him squirm with revulsion: the photographs taken of the concentration camps. He had had to look away, afraid the gruesome images were going to make him throw up. Later, he had asked his uncle how such terrible things could happen. His uncle had said they resulted from a twisted, evil part of the human spirit, a part that could never flourish in a free society.

He had vowed then that if America was in a war when he was old enough to fight, he would volunteer to serve. And there had been no question in his ten-year-old mind that he would be a pilot. He could not think of a better thing to be.

"Barnes!"

Startled, Barnes jerked his head up. "Huh?"

"Jesus!" Hill snorted. "I just love playing with zombies. Call or fold?"

"Bet he was thinking of his girl again," Spradling said.

"No," Barnes answered, absentmindedly tossing a chip on the small pile in the center of the table. "I was thinking about why I'm here."

"Not that anybody cares," said Winters, "but go ahead and tell us."

Suddenly feeling embarrassed, Barnes shook his head. "Doesn't matter."

"Come on, Barnes, tell us," said Hill with his usual condescending grin.

Barnes's embarrassment gave way to anger at Hill's mocking smile. "I'm here because I'm patriotic and I hate communism."

Hill arched his eyebrows and his grin disappeared. "Well I'll be damned," he said. "Barnes, you and I *do* have something in common."

Winters stared at the three aces in his hand and sighed. "Now that the war bond rally is over, can we fucking play cards?"

The dull thump of mortars beat an irregular tattoo above the wailing of the siren. Gray could hear men fumbling about as they searched in the dark for their flak vests and steel pots. How long had it been since the card game broke up? He didn't know, but was sure he hadn't been asleep very long. Keeping his eyes closed, he pulled the blanket up over his head. He was too tired and too depressed to care about the warning; he sleepily decided that maybe a mortar round landing on his head would be a blessed relief. The bunker was safer, but his body insisted upon sleep.

He felt someone bump his cot, and then a hand grabbed his left ankle and tugged on his leg.

"C'mon, Steve," said Barnes urgently. "We've got incoming."

"Get lost," mumbled Gray into his blanket.

Barnes shook him again. "Wake up, man. We're under attack."

As Gray groggily pulled the blanket tighter around his head, he heard Danly's voice.

"Barnes, he heard you and he doesn't give a fuck. Some of us would rather sleep. Good-bye."

"But they said when the siren blows everyone has got—"

"Barnes, don't you fucking listen? We're staying here!"

"Okay, okay," said Barnes. He turned and hurried from the tent.

Gray heard Danly roll over, and the sound of snoring from the far corner indicated that Hill had not been disturbed at all by the commotion. When Gray had first arrived in-country, the sound of the siren would cause adrenaline to surge through his body and he would be wide awake in seconds. He would be so keyed up that he seldom could get back to sleep for at least an hour. Several consecutive nights of sirens had turned him into a zombie, and it had been clear he would never last the year if he could not get sufficient sleep. He had tried to train his body to relax so he could go to sleep at will, but was unsuccessful. He had then decided he must somehow conquer his fear. Hill and Danly, the two men who seemed to be the least afraid of anything, were also the ones who were least bothered by the sirens. He had asked Danly about it.

"I'm as afraid of getting bopped by a mortar round as anybody," Danly had said. "But I'm not going to waste time worrying about it. Look, they're not trying to hit us anyway; they're after the ammo dump or the flight line or maybe the goddamn general's trailer, and we're not close to any of that shit. If a mortar round hits the tent some night, then it'll just be an unfortunate, random event. I'm not going to spend time worrying about it; I need my sleep."

It took more force of will and more practice, but eventually Gray got the hang of it. When the low wail began, he would just push his fear from his mind, roll over and ease back to sleep. It had been working fine.

However, when Patterson took over command of the troop, Gray's problems started all over again. Patterson issued an order instructing everyone to go to the nearest bunker as soon as the siren started. For a while Gray complied like most of the men, but the routine of getting up, running to the bunker, sitting crammed together in the stifling structure and then trudging wearily back to the tent was severely interrupting his sleep once again. Then he noticed that a few people, like Danly and Hill, never bothered to get up. They continued to stay in their bunks, while the rest of the men in the platoon would jam into the bunker and wait uncomfortably in the fetid air until the all-clear signal.

Since the platoon leaders did not seem to care about compliance with Patterson's order, Gray had decided to stay in bed like Danly and Hill. But he was beginning to get nervous about it.

Patterson had recently begun checking, inspecting the tents and going from bunker to bunker demanding that his platoon leaders account for all their men. Displeased with the lack of compliance with his order during the last night-time shelling, he had assembled the platoon leaders, and with an impressive tirade, convinced them that henceforth all personnel would move to the bunkers when the siren sounded. Gray had heard Hawkins stress the importance of complying with the order, but still Gray had gotten the feeling that Hawkins really didn't care that much.

Gray closed his ears to the metronomic regularity of Hill's snoring and the singsong wail of the siren. His body began to relax again, and he waited for sleep to take over.

＝＝＝＝＝＝

As he trotted toward the bunker, Barnes wondered what would happen if Patterson decided to check and see who was there. Surely there would be several asses in a sling, including the platoon leaders'. Looking to his right, Barnes paused for a moment. Tracer rounds arched from the east perimeter toward a small gully. Several parachute flares were swaying gently toward the ground about a thousand meters to the northeast, faintly illuminating the shadowy figures of men still scurrying to the bunkers. He could hear the dull thump of explosions off to the south. It sounded as if the incoming mortar rounds were landing near the fuel storage point, but he couldn't be sure. As he resumed his progress toward the bunker, a man hurried past him in the opposite direction. It looked like Hawkins.

＝＝＝＝＝＝

Gray floated in that warm space between sleep and con-sciousness. Random thoughts wafted through his mind as he slowly drifted toward slumber. Then suddenly, a sharp pain in his knee caused him to jerk upright, struggling groggily to regain full consciousness. As he heard Hawkins' voice, he realized he had been either punched or kicked in the leg.

"All right, gentlemen, get your goddamn asses down to the bunker. NOW!"

"Aw, c'mon, Hawk. We need our sleep," protested Hill wearily.

Hawkins strode quickly to the corner of the tent, jerked the end of Hill's cot up level with his chest, and then let it crash to the floor.

"Jesus Christ!" Hill exclaimed in surprise. He tumbled to the floor and began scrambling for his clothes.

"Tonight marks the end of your 'we set our own rules' bullshit," Hawkins said angrily. "You people are going to start toeing the goddamn mark. Now MOVE!" he yelled, throwing open the tent flap and vanishing into the darkness.

"What in the hell got into him?" asked Gray, now wide awake.

"Patterson," answered Danly as he pulled his pants on. "What else?"

As the three men emerged from the tent, two parachute flares suddenly popped open two hundred meters beyond the east perimeter. Bathing the ground in a sickly, yellow light, the swaying flares caused the men's shadows to oscillate as they moved down the row of tents toward the bunker.

"Hey, wait a minute," said Hill. "We're about to get a show."

They stopped, crouching against a row of sandbags encircling the nearest tent. From the pitch-black sky above the flares came the drone of airplane engines, followed by a flash that instantly turned into an iridescent stream of red. The bright column then began to separate as it plunged toward the ground, breaking into countless strands of red dashes. As the rain of tracers hit the ground, the ricochets gave the impression of large sparks dancing along a dull yellow grid. Almost immediately there was a second stream of tracers, followed quickly by a third as the C-130 gunship unleashed the power of its arsenal of miniguns.

Hill whistled. "Whoooooeeeee. This is better than the Fourth of July."

"How'd you like to be a Charlie out there right now?" asked Gray.

"Them poor motherfuckers," said Hill, but his voice gave no hint of sympathy. Gray peered at him in the dim light. The reflection from the tracers glinted red in Hill's eyes and, coupled with his hard, malevolent smile, gave his face the appearance of a sinister mask.

Gray's pleasure at the vivid display of color in the sky vanished and he stood up. "We'd better get to the bunker before Hawk comes back out," he said and moved away quickly.

In a serene trance, Hill stared at the tracers for a few moments more, then turned and moved away in the darkness.

Neither the look on Hill's face nor Gray's startled reaction to it had escaped Danly. Their expressions represented the opposite ends of the emotional response to war: love and hate.

Danly wondered what his true feeling about war was, and finally decided he didn't have one. He saw himself existing in a self-protecting emotional vacuum, insulated from the overpowering feelings that were distorting his comrades' perceptions of the violence they were involved in.

He glanced once more at the waterfall of tracers cascading earthward from the ink black highlands sky, then shrugged and walked toward the bunker.

The heat inside the bunker was oppressive, and the stale air was rife with a mixture of body odors and cigarette smoke. Except for the occasional flash of a match and the small glowing dots at the ends of several cigarettes, it was completely dark. Most of the men sat with their backs against the sandbags; a few lay stretched on the ground trying to sleep. As Hill and Danly entered, a flashlight flicked on and a beam of light passed across their faces. From the darkness behind the beam, they heard Hawkins' voice.

"Nice of you to join us."

Hill started to respond, but was cut short by Hawkins' sharp command. "Sit down and shut up!"

There was a long pause before Hawkins continued. "I'm not sure why, but a number of you warrant officers feel that the rules and regulations of the military don't apply to you unless they happen to be convenient. You seem to think that you can just kind of pick and choose, and your section leaders and platoon leaders will put up with it. Big-time pilots. The Army needs you, so what the fuck? What are they going to do? Send you to Vietnam?

"Well, I'll tell you what we're going to do: we're going to start making your lives miserable if you don't knock off the crap. You might think they can't get more miserable than they are right now, but I assure you they can. There aren't going to be any more warnings; from here on out, you either shape up or pay the goddamn price.

"Gentlemen, I'm unhappy. I'm not a goddamn baby-sitter, yet not long ago I was out running around trying to shepherd your asses down here. Now why in the hell is that? Major Patterson has made it clear that everyone in the troop without alert-crew responsibilities will go to the nearest bunker when the siren sounds. That's pretty easy to understand, as far as I can see. So why am I and the other platoon leaders out policing you goddamn people up?

"Well, we know the answer to that, don't we? This is one of those 'we know better' deals. Camp Enari is a big camp and when the gooks lob a few mortar rounds in, they're always going for the POL point or the ammo dump. They're not going to bother with a few tents off in the corner. Naa, no point in getting excited, just roll over and get some sleep—why worry about it?

"BECAUSE IT'S AN ORDER, THAT'S WHY. You've been told to go to a bunker and from now on you are goddamn well going to go. Now, does anybody have any *problem* with that?"

The men remained silent. Jesus, thought Danly, what a stupid bastard Patterson is. He tells people to do stupid things in the AO, which puts them at greater risk, but then makes a big deal about safety during a pathetic mortar attack. Christ, there was a better chance of getting run over by a deuce-and-a-half on the flight line than there was from getting hit by a mortar round.

Danly felt sorry for Hawkins. Hawkins knew as well as anybody that the whole thing was bullshit, but he did not have any choice but to read the riot act like he just had. Patterson would have his ass if his men weren't complying with orders. He leaned his head against the sandbags and tried to get comfortable. *Fucking Army, nothing changes.*

He had almost dozed off when he heard footsteps outside the bunker. A figure, breathing heavily, entered and crouched in the doorway. Hawkins' flashlight flicked on briefly, illuminating Patterson's face, and then clicked off.

"Platoon leaders, is everyone accounted for?"

"All my people are here, sir," said Miller.

There was a pause before Resnick spoke. "No, sir. Mister Wallace is not here."

"Where is he?"

"I don't know, sir."

"Well, when you locate him, and that *will* be tonight, tell him to report to me at oh-six-hundred."

"He's scheduled to be on the flight line at that time, sir."

"Not anymore. Captain Hawkins, are all your people here?"

"Yes, sir."

"How about Mister Danly, did he see fit to join us?"

"Yes, SIR," said Danly, before Hawkins could respond. Patterson turned and left.

• • •

When the all-clear signal finally sounded, Danly remained seated, content to wait until almost everyone had gone. Several flashlights had been turned on, and grotesque shadows danced against the sandbag walls as the remainder of the men moved toward the door.

"Mike, hang around a minute, will you?" asked Hawkins.

Danly sat down next to the door and waited until he and Hawkins were alone. "What is it?"

"I didn't get a chance to talk to you yesterday, but I understand that Horvath did okay."

"Yeah, he did. Hawk, you still look bad. What was the matter?"

"I don't know, a lot of puking and diarrhea. Must've ate something bad. Look, back to Horvath. No problems? He had control of everything?"

"He did fine, but he was a wreck when it was over. Hawk, I'll bet my paltry paycheck he's going to crack. I don't think he can handle much more."

Hawkins stared at the ground. "I don't know," he sighed. "Maybe you're right. It's got me puzzled, though; he doesn't seem to be a coward. I don't remember him ever trying to get out of a mission." He scratched the stubble on his chin thoughtfully. "I've never heard any complaints about him backing off during a firefight, either. Have you?"

"No, not like that guy . . . aw, what was his name? You know, that loudmouthed CW3."

"Dirkerman."

"Yeah, him. He was my wingman the day of that big firefight at Hill 875. When I made my break, I found out that not only was the son of a bitch not covering me, I couldn't even see him. He was up there floating around in a circle at four thousand feet. Claimed he felt a vibration when he started his gun run. If he'd been solo, I'd've shot his ass down.

"Anyway, no, Horvath's not like that. It seems like he gets a kind of tunnel vision of the mind. He gets all wound up, focuses on only one thing and lets everything else go right to hell. When I first flew with him, I thought he was just afraid of screwing up, but I don't think so anymore. I think maybe he's just scared of dying like the rest of us, only there isn't much room between the start of his fear and his breaking point. And they're getting closer all the time.''

"I gotta admit," said Hawkins, "I thought for a while that it was some more of that warrant-versus-commissioned shit, but I've been mulling it over and I think maybe you're right. Problem is, neither Patterson nor the flight surgeon are likely to agree." Placing his fingertips on either side of his forehead, he massaged his temples. "I needn't tell you that all this has gotta stay between us."

Danly nodded.

"From now on, I'm going to make sure Horvath's always paired with an experienced pilot. That means," he continued with a thin smile, "that you, for one, are going to see a lot more of him."

"Swell," said Danly, rolling his eyes.

"Well, would your rather see me send him out with new guys like Barnes?"

"I can tell you where I'd *like* to see you send him."

Laughing, Hawkins got to his feet and walked to the door. "Better see the chaplain, Mister Danly. Sounds like a personal problem to me."

CHAPTER 9

FEBRUARY 1, 1968
CAMP ENARI

Still groggy, Barnes raised himself to a sitting position. It can't be morning yet, he thought. What the hell is going on? His eyes were red and puffy, and the single light bulb hanging from the tent roof seemed like a spotlight. He groped for his watch and, finding it, squinted at the dial.

"Jesus," he groaned. "Three-fifty!"

"Come on, Barnes, quit bitching and get dressed." Winters' voice was annoyingly cheerful.

Barnes rolled his eyes and groaned again.

Bookman laughed. "Remember, Ray: ours is not to reason why; ours is just to fly and die."

"Yeah," Barnes responded wearily. He swung his legs over the side of the cot and rubbed his eyes.

"Well, Ray, you've been wanting some action. Looks like you're about to get your wish."

"What are ya talking about?"

"I've been duty officer since midnight and reports of attacks have been coming in like crazy. It ain't any Cong shit either; it's NVA regulars attacking in force."

Barnes tried to snap out of his groggy state. "Where?"

"All over the place," replied Bookman. "Everywhere in the highlands, probably the whole country."

Barnes's pulse began to quicken and his head began to clear. "About time," he said.

As the pilots gathered around the radios in operations, the reports of fighting continued to flow in. They were not favorable—American setbacks were mounting: Dak Seang defenders were suffering heavy casualties; the perimeter at Kontum had been breached; Plei Jereng was under attack; Plei Mrong was partially overrun; Duc Co was being overrun; Polei Kleng was under siege; and Ninh Duc was overrun. The pilots waited anxiously, eager to get into the air, while the radios continued to crackle with the litany of disasters and near disasters. It was no longer a case of plugging holes in the dike; the whole dike was collapsing.

Barnes was unable to sit still. He paced back and forth, keeping one ear tuned to the steady stream of radio traffic, the other to the discussion taking place among the other pilots. As bad as the situation sounded, they were still eager to get into the air. They had long yearned for a main-force battle. The hide-and-seek frustrations of the guerilla war were being swapped for a high-risk showdown, and Barnes was glad to be a part of it.

Holman finally entered the briefing room. His remarks were brief. E Troop was assigned to help repulse the attack on Kontum. Crank at 0500.

Barnes poked Gray in the ribs and smiled. "We're finally going to get to kick ass."

Gray gave him a funny look and turned away. Momentarily puzzled, Barnes shrugged and then walked to the flight activity board to check crew assignments. He was happy when he saw he was assigned to fly with Spradling. Spradling had an infectious eagerness for just about everything, and Barnes couldn't think of a better partner for his first foray into serious fighting.

• • •

After departing Camp Enari, the flight of gunships flew north toward Kontum, passing over the western outskirts of Pleiku. Numerous clouds of smoke towered over the buildings. Barnes could see two Air Force Spads making gun runs in the northwest corner of the city. American and ARVN tanks were moving along the west edge of the most heavily populated area, firing point blank into various buildings. Further to the southeast, a group of helicopter gunships were attacking targets near Camp Holloway.

"Damn!" exclaimed Spradling as he watched the turmoil in and about the city. "We're gonna melt the goddamn gun barrels today."

Barnes grinned and continued to watch the fighting until it passed from view behind him. This was more like it; this was what he had anticipated long ago—direct, sustained fighting, not the fly-around-in-circles-looking-for-them crap that he had already grown weary of. Finally it looked like a real war.

But despite his eagerness, he could feel the tentacles of fear trying to strangle his fledgling resolution of bravery. Well, at least the cat-and-mouse games are over for a while, he thought, steeling himself for whatever lay ahead.

KONTUM

As he circled over the south edge of the city, Barnes could not believe his eyes. There, directly below him in a large outdoor market, people were going about their business as if nothing out of the ordinary was happening nearby. Only three hundred feet above them, eight helicopters were clattering about; there were explosions mushrooming along the east side of the city—no more than one mile away; acrid smoke from several fires just to the north was casting a shadow over the market; and to the west and north .50-caliber tracers were making glowing, dashed arcs across the horizon. Still, incredibly, the people in the market haggled about their daily provisions, ignoring the turmoil surrounding them.

"Look at 'em," exclaimed Barnes in awe. "They're acting like nothing's happening around here. They gotta be crazy."

"Naa," said Spradling. "There's just a strong chamber of commerce in this city."

Barnes grinned and continued to watch the activity below him in disbelief. There was traffic flowing in and out of the market in all directions, but most people seemed to be coming from the area immediately to the west. One street, much wider than the rest, ran due north from the edge of the market all the way to the perimeter of the city. A large church, its steeple protruding high above the surrounding buildings, was situated on a corner of the street, about two miles north of the circling gunships. There was no one visible near the church.

"Wonder how many NVA are in the city?" mused Barnes.

"A shitload, I would imagine," said Spradling. "They overran those ARVN compounds to the northwest and they're probably all over the goddamn place by now. Shit, some of 'em are probably below us doing some shopping."

Looking down at the teeming crowd, Barnes was glad that he wasn't on the ground with the job of trying to sort out the bad guys from the good guys. He was happy to let someone else figure it out, and then just tell him whom to shoot at. He was also anxious to get started.

━━━━━━━━

Gray didn't like the looks of it at all. This was the sort of situation he had been dreading ever since he had arrived in Vietnam. Up until this moment, it had been easy—when you saw people out in the mountain areas, there was seldom any doubt about which side they were on. It was easy to

tell the NVA from American or ARVN troops, so the only
question concerned the Montagnards. But a simple plan for
dealing with them had been developed also. If they were
carrying weapons that were not American-made, they were
to be shot. If they were unarmed, they were left alone. It
was a pretty straightforward system, and Gray never lost
any sleep worrying about whether he had shot civilians.

Here, however, separating the good guys from the bad
guys looked like a real problem, and he derived no comfort
from knowing that he would not be the one who made the
decision about whom to fire at. The fact remained that it
was entirely possible that he could find himself killing civilians. He hoped the E Troop gunships would be used to
go after the NVA surrounding the airfield. There would be
little confusion there as to who was who.

As a matter of fact, he could not figure out what the hell
the people in charge were waiting for. Explosions and tracer
rounds were visible all around the edges of the city, and
here were eight gunships floating around in a circle above
an outdoor market like a bunch of Cessnas at a country
picnic fly-in.

"White team, this is Six." It was Hawkins' voice.

About time, thought Gray.

"Two-three, Two-seven, and Two-eight will come with
me, the rest will stay with Two-six. Acknowledge."

Gray grimaced as he watched the four gunships led by
Hawkins turn in the direction of the airfield. He was sure
now he was going to be placed in the situation he was
dreading. Listening to the litany of "rogers" as the pilots
responded to Hawkins, he saw a short stream of tracers fly
over the roofs of some houses near the church. He could
not be sure being as far away as he was, but they appeared
to come from its steeple.

"Two-six," said Hawkins, "you're to contact Boar
Six."

"Two-six, roger," answered Danly.

Gray began to search his SOI for the proper frequency,

but Danly was on the radio almost immediately.

"Okay, Bulldogs, go up from Larkin, four point six."
Danly was using the quick method of giving a frequency
without using the shackle code. Larkin was an older warrant
officer, who was easily fifty years old, but who still insisted
he was only forty-one. The gun platoon commonly used his
claimed age as a base for giving a frequency that would
otherwise have to be given in code. Gray switched the FM
radio to 45.6.

"Boar Six, Bulldog Two-six."

"Boar Six here, go ahead."

"Roger, Six, I've got some gunships for you."

"Outstanding. We've got some NVA holed up in that
big church north of the market, approximate coordinates,
Zulu Alpha, two six zero, eight nine six."

"Roger, we got it. Where are the friendlies?"

"They'll all be at least fifty meters to the north, or on
the other side of the street west of the church."

"Roger, on the way."

Surrounded by a small courtyard, the church sat on a
corner lot in the middle of several blocks of houses. A public
square fronted the church and in its midst were the remains
of a once colorful pagoda, which now lay in shambles. Even
while passing well to the east, Gray could see the church
was a sturdy structure. He guessed the walls were fairly
thick, and if Boar Six had no tanks at his disposal it was
obvious why the gunships were wanted. Gray doubted, however, that even the rockets would do much good, unless
someone got lucky and put a couple through the doors or
the small church windows. He thought it was far more likely
that an errant rocket or two would damage one of the surrounding houses.

"Boar Six, what about those houses near the church?"
asked Danly, as if echoing Gray's concern.

"Our ARVN guy says they're empty."

Gray looked across at Coombs. "Bullshit! I'll bet nobody
knows."

"Maybe," said Coombs, shrugging, "but it don't make any difference."

Gray cursed. If there were civilians in any nearby houses, they stood a good chance of getting hurt.

"I don't like this," he said bitterly.

Coombs did not reply.

━━━━━━━━━

Sweeping low, just above the rooftops, the gunships flew in an easterly arc until they were about two thousand meters northeast of the church. Then, they began to climb and turn back south. Barnes saw several columns of colored smoke curve upward as the ground troops marked their forward positions.

He listened while Danly, speaking in a relaxed but businesslike manner, began the attack.

"Bulldogs, keep it on the church and break left. Two-six is inbound."

Webb's ship was second in line as Danly began his dive, and Barnes clutched the minigun sight tightly while Spradling swung in behind Webb. Danly's first pair of rockets landed short of the church in the square, but the second pair crashed into the front of the building, kicking up small, thin clouds of powdered granite. Bullets from the miniguns and door gunners' M-60s raked the church's facade, spawning a mass of tiny puffs of dust.

"Two-six breaking left."

"Two-three's inbound."

Barnes felt his legs twitching with excitement as Spradling lined up behind Webb's diving gunship. "Let's go, let's go," he whispered to himself. Four more rockets flew toward the steeple. Three of them hit the church, but one corkscrewed to the right and slammed into the roof of a nearby house.

"Receiving fire!"

Webb's voice rang in Barnes's earphones and he watched

the attacking gunship bank hard to the left. Barnes's heart pounded. Muzzle flashes were visible from the steeple and the house closest to the west side of the church.

"Roger, we see 'em," said Spradling.

Barnes had never felt anything remotely like this in his life. Diving at the church, the steeple growing larger in his minigun sight as the lines of tracers swept across it, his fear vanished, replaced by euphoria. Even the continuous sparkle of muzzle flashes from the house and the church did not bother him. He was finally getting what he'd been waiting for.

Smoke and dust erupted from near the church doorway as one of Spradling's rockets scored a hit. A few moments later, three men scurried from the entrance and ran around the edge of the church toward the houses behind it.

"Got some gooks moving to that house back there," called Spradling as he pulled the gunship into a hard left turn.

"Roger that," answered Coombs.

Barnes looked back over his shoulder to watch Gray and Coombs dive toward the church. As they began firing, Barnes saw two figures bolt from the side of the house behind the church onto the boulevard. They seemed to run right into the minigun fire sweeping the area and tumbled to the street before they had gone ten yards. One of the two people was very small—Barnes was sure it was a child.

DAK TO

As the main rotor blades turned slower and slower, winding to a halt, it was easy to see the holes. There were four of them in one blade and three in the other. Barnes and Spradling strode to where Coombs was standing with the crew chief looking up at the blades.

"Coombs, that's the third time this week," said Spradling. "You better take a vacation."

Coombs turned around and stepped toward him, and Spradling jumped back in mock horror.

"Don't get near me, magnet ass! Bad luck rubs off."

"It can't be all bad," said Coombs, grinning. "I'm still here, ain't I?"

"Physically maybe," answered Spradling taking another step backward. "Hey, what's with your partner? He afraid to look?"

Coombs glanced back into the cockpit where Gray sat staring vacantly at the instrument panel. "No," he answered quietly. "He's still thinking about the kid that was shot."

"Damn!" exclaimed Barnes. "Those people ran out of that building right into his fire. Wasn't his fault."

"I know that," said Coombs, "but *he* thinks it was."

"Shit," said Spradling. "The grunts were firing too; *they* might've got 'em. Hey, Gray, quit hiding! We know you fucked up this helicopter."

Gray heard Spradling, but ignored him. All he could think about was the dead people. He could not get the picture out of his mind of the two of them tumbling to the street, particularly the image of the child as it spun to the ground, its arms flailing helplessly. He didn't mean to shoot them—they just ran out of the house, right into the goddamn bullets. It wasn't his fault—or was it? At first he'd only seen the movement out of the corner of his eye. Had he given a little twist of his wrist, causing the guns to spray further to the left? Had he, for a split second, thought he'd seen some NVA and reacted accordingly? He had been sweeping the area near the church with minigun fire, sure, but had he consciously given it a little extra turn to the left?

He bent forward in the seat and put his head in his hands. If only he could be sure. Closing his eyes, he played the scene over and over in his mind, trying to visualize exactly what had taken place. He strained to picture the event once again. But it was no use. His mind's-eye version was like an old, fuzzy newsreel—jerky and slightly out of focus. He squeezed his eyes shut even tighter. Did they run into the spray of bullets or did he turn it on them? His fingers clamped tighter on his forehead and he gradually became aware that his entire body was rigid.

He forced himself to relax. Sitting up straight, he took a deep breath and opened his eyes. Fifteen yards in front of him, squatting on the hard, red clay that surrounded the runway, was Danly's gunship. Oil stains spotted the underside of the tailboom, the paint was blackened and blistered just aft of the exhaust, and its faded green body was covered with a film of red dirt.

It did not have the sleek aloofness of the Air Force jets or the placid strength of the fat transports. Rather, it possessed a dogged, plodding grace resembling the defiant posture of a weary but undaunted foot soldier. Squatting on the bumpy ground, tough and grimy, it embodied the heart and soul of the war—it was the infantry of the air.

Gray had always liked the workhorse ugliness of a C-model. But he didn't like it very much now and he wondered if he ever would again.

He closed his eyes and the small body went spinning to the ground once more. He groaned, realizing he would never know for sure if it had actually been his fault.

CHAPTER 10

FEBRUARY 10, 1968
DAK TO

The asphalt seemed to undulate in the early-evening haze as it released the heat absorbed from its day-long baking under the relentless sun. Danly stood next to his helicopter, staring across the ramp toward the gaggle of worn huts and swaybacked tents south of the runway. They all had the faint reddish tinge resulting from the ever-present red-clay dust. The scene reminded him of the many desultory collections of sharecropper shacks he'd seen in rural Alabama —clusters of decaying shanties dusted by the dry, red-orange soil. Slowly yielding to the elements, the weather-beaten shacks would sag like tired derelicts wearily forestalling their inevitable collapse.

Dak To had a similar quality of slow decay. It had an aura of resignation, an acceptance of the fact that the war just wasn't going anywhere, that there was no resolution in sight, no end.

Even at that, Danly thought, there was still something about Dak To that could not be stifled by the glumness which overlaid it. There was an underlying current of dogged defiance, an unshakable resolve never to give in.

During his first few months in Vietnam, he thought he could see real progress in the war, but the longer he was there, the more he was convinced it was a stalemate. Dak To was a microcosm of the whole war, a prime example of the futility of the "enclave strategy." The North Vietnamese would never overrun Dak To, and the Americans and the ARVNs would never kill enough of them to make them stop trying. Enemy body counts would steadily increase, but so would the stacks of American corpses in the refrigerated conexes setting next to the runway.

Wrapped in body bags and stacked like cordwood, the bodies would remain at Dak To until the conexes were full. Then they would be hauled off in a C-130 to some other stockpiling destination before they were finally shipped home.

Due to some strange coincidence of timing, almost every time he passed by the body-storage area, the doors on the large, white containers would be left ajar. He had gotten in the habit of looking closely, because the space within provided a measure of the intensity of fighting in the area. By observing how rapidly the empty space in the conexes was filled, he could get a good idea of whether things were going well or poorly.

But even during the worst of times, Danly was still comfortable flying in the mountains surrounding Dak To. He knew the terrain well and could predict trouble with a high degree of accuracy. There was much to be said for a lack of surprises. From the center of Dak To, no matter which direction you looked, you could be pretty sure that underneath the jungle canopy there was a sizable group of NVA soldiers. They were all over the damn place.

Fighting was always hard on the nerves, but the waiting, the idle time spent between engagements that allowed a person to muse upon the dangers, that was worse. At least when he flew in the vicinity of Dak To, he usually did not have to wait too long for something to happen. But it wasn't just the predictable action during the day: Danly also felt comfortable with the often subtler tension of night. After being energized by sporadic jolts of adrenaline throughout the day, it was easier for him to adjust to the viselike menace of the Dak To darkness than to adjust to the placid security of Camp Enari. Enari was too much of a change from the rigors of combat. There was television, cold beer, hot meals, stereos, and for many troops, real beds with sheets and pillows. The lights of Pleiku City shone in the distance and the evening breezes blew gently across the plateau, helping to cool the mass of tents and barracks.

Camp Enari could be pleasant, like a Boy Scout camp during the summer, and the back-and-forth transition from Dak To to Enari was hard on the nerves. What should have been a welcome haven was not. It was like getting comfortable with a mirage—before too long it would vanish and you'd be right back in the middle of the desert. Enari was reasonably secure and comfortable at night, but before the sun was fully risen, you'd be on your way back to the menacing isolation of the highlands' mountains, on your way back to Dak To.

It was like being continuously shuttled from a mansion to a shanty, Danly thought. The difference was unsettling; it ate at the nerves. Danly decided he'd just as soon stay at Dak To if he could.

When night enveloped the sagging tents and scraggly barbed wire, there were no lights in the distance. The profiles of the surrounding hills and mountains merged with the blackness of the sky. If an overcast blocked out the light from the moon and stars, it was like being in a giant inkwell. Rather than sleep in the aircraft, Danly usually spent the night in an old hex tent near the runway. There was a dirt floor, a single light bulb, and four cots covered with dusty blankets. If the light bulb was burnt out, which was usually the case, there was nothing to do but lie in the dark and think. Wrap yourself in the dark void and think about your life . . . or of home . . . or better yet, of nothing at all.

Yeah, it was easier to keep in sync with the war at Dak To.

But Danly knew that tonight they were going to return to Enari, and for once he was glad. The crews were tired—mentally and physically exhausted. For almost two weeks, most of them had logged more than ten combat flight hours every day. They'd been up before dawn and seldom to bed before midnight. The heavy fighting was wearing their nerves thin. The constant tension, lack of sleep and oppressive heat had made them logy. Mistakes were becoming more frequent and had already caused the loss of two aircraft. The crews badly needed some rest.

Danly found himself contemplating the luxury of a hot meal, an even hotter shower, and the comfort of his own cot. The only thing to worry about now was a last-minute mission. He tried to push the thought from his mind.

"Mister Danly, Six is on the radio!"

He walked across the asphalt ramp toward the crew chief, who had yelled at him from his position beside the ammunition bunker. Gothard was sitting next to Span, the door gunner, on a bank of red clay piled against a wall of sandbags. A PRC-10 radio was propped on top of the bunker wall, its bent aerial angling toward the hills to the north.

"What've you been doing," asked Danly, eyeing the mangled aerial, "tying knots with this thing?"

"No, sir," Gothard responded lazily. "It just sits on the floor of the aircraft and gets banged around cuz of the way you fly."

Feigning anger, Danly narrowed his eyes and jerked the microphone from its slot on the side of the radio.

"Six, this is Two-six."

"Roger, Two-six, all units are to return to home plate, except"—as soon as he heard the "except," Danly knew he wasn't going directly back to Enari—"I want you to take your team to Kontum and contact Cannonball Six."

"Two-six, roger. Out." Disgusted, he tossed the microphone in the air. It made a loud clunk as it landed on the radio's metal casing.

"Shit! Why is it always us, sir?" asked Gothard.

Danly pushed the radio off the wall and it tumbled down the clay bank between Gothard and Span. "Because you gentlemen haven't taken the time to break this goddamn thing." He turned toward the parked helicopters, raised his right arm and swung it in a circle like he was twirling a lariat. "Wind 'em up!" he yelled. "We're going to the house!

"Most of you, anyway," he added to himself.

As the line of gunships and slicks continued south to Camp Enari, Danly broke away from the formation and, followed by Mackin, headed toward Kontum. A thin layer of fog was beginning to form near the ground as the dusk gave way to darkness. The lights of Kontum slowly came into view, giving off a fuzzy, yellow glow beneath the developing mist. After making contact with Cannonball Six and being asked to stand by, Danly began orbiting over a wide, flat area southwest of the city.

He looked down and frowned. Whatever the mission was, he hoped they would get on with it as soon as possible. The white layer congealing near the ground was not the kind of fog that would remain patchy. There was much dust and smoke in the air—the haze from that alone would make night flight difficult—and that coupled with the abnormally cool temperatures meant a thick, solid layer of fog was imminent.

Danly was not sure what the mission was going to be, but he suspected it had something to do with the reports he had heard earlier about a convoy being ambushed south of the city. If he was correct, and the mission required flying among the hills and mountains in that area, then it was going to be a tension-filled night.

He looked at the fuel gauge and swore softly. This is

starting off real poorly, he thought. We're low on JP4; I'm hungry; my ass is numb; I smell like a damn goat and I can barely keep my eyes open. And here we are, driving around in the gathering mist waiting for some jerk-off on the ground to decide what he wants to do.

"Hey, Webb. I'd better find out what in the hell's going on down there before we get too low on fuel."

Webb, who had been slouched down in his seat and leaning his head against the door, slowly straightened up. He reached under his visor and rubbed his eyes.

"You woke me up just to tell me that?"

Danly laughed. "Standard crew briefing."

"My ass," said Webb, lighting a cigarette.

"Cannonball Six, this is Bulldog Two-six."

"Two-six, this is Cannonball Three, over," responded a young-sounding voice.

"Jesus," scoffed Webb. "What're they doing now, drafting grade-school kids?"

Danly chuckled. "Three, tell your Six if you don't get moving soon, we aren't going to be of any help. We're low on fuel."

"Cannonball Three, roger, please stand by."

"Don't know if you should've done that, Mike. They seem to have enough trouble without something else to think about. You shoulda waited a few more minutes and then told them we're *di-di*ing the area."

Fifteen minutes passed and there was still no response from the ground. "Let's go home. Looks like they forgot about us," grunted Webb.

"I fucking wish," Danly replied.

The radio came to life once more. "Bulldog Two-six, Cannonball Three."

"Yeah, go ahead, Three."

"Roger, sir, Six wants you to refuel and return ASAP, over."

"Figures," muttered Danly. "Okay, Three, I copy. Out."

CAMP ENARI

Barnes sat on his footlocker, a warm can of beer in his left hand, and reflected on the events of the previous few days. Hectic as they were, they had given him the opportunity to test himself. He was satisfied with the way he had handled the pressure. Any lingering doubts he'd had about his ability to cope had been dispelled.

Not that he hadn't been scared. He'd been as frightened as he'd ever been in his life. The fear had soured his stomach and made his mouth so dry he'd barely been able to talk. But still, he'd kept his composure. That made him happy.

But best of all, he'd finally crossed over the invisible line that separated the newer pilots from the veterans. He now had some respect. Being a new guy, an outsider, had been very difficult to handle. He thought it was kind of like when he was an eighth grader and was allowed to tag along with his older brother. His brother's friends would treat him well enough, but there'd never been any doubt that he was not really a part of the group; he was just being tolerated.

It had been the same situation when he'd joined the weapons platoon. But the reason had nothing to do with age, of course; it had to do with the all-important consideration of whether he possessed the qualities that would allow the high-time pilots to trust him with their lives.

Barnes was sure he'd gotten that trust two days earlier, and it was Danly who'd made it possible.

It was funny about Danly. Barnes had thought Danly exhibited an aloofness that indicated he basically cared for no one but himself. True, he had done Barnes a couple of favors, not the least of which was keeping Barnes from getting into the fight with Hill, but Danly's attitude had seemed to Barnes more like that of a commander keeping order than that of a friend helping a friend.

But the events of two days ago made Barnes think differently.

A placid-looking, narrow valley northwest of Dak To had transformed itself with disconcerting speed into a dangerous, ugly gash. One minute three gunships were flying in a lazy circle above a Ranger unit that was casually waiting for a medevac to pick up a heat casualty, and the next minute they were diving and feinting, locked in a violent exchange of fire with NVA troops.

A few seconds before the frenzy began, Barnes had caught a glimpse through the patchy jungle of the black-clad figures moving down the ridge toward the Rangers. His heart pounding, he had stomped on the floor intercom switch.

"Mike! On the—"

But Danly had already begun to bank the gunship toward the ridge. "Bulldogs, Two-six. Got some Charlies, ten o'clock." He quickly glanced over his shoulder at the crew chief and door gunner. "Gunther, Doss, put your fire just below the ridge."

As if to punctuate Danly's directions, Barnes directed a stream of minigun tracers on the spot Danly indicated.

The firefight didn't last terribly long, but long enough for a round to come through Barnes's door, zip by his knee and lodge in the radio compartment. When the fight was over, more than a dozen NVA bodies littered the ridge.

It was later, at Dak To, while Barnes sat on the ground with the other crews while they broke open their C rations, that Danly helped him over the hump.

"Good thing you spotted the gooks when you did, Mike," Hill had said. "That dustoff would've passed right over them fuckers about a minute later."

Danly shook his head. "Barnes is the one who saw them, Jug."

Spradling dropped his jaw in mock astonishment. "Not Barnes—how could he, flying with his eyes closed?"

"And that's not all," Danly continued as he used a plastic spoon to scrape off the layer of grease on top of his cold meatballs and beans. "He lost his cherry. A round about took off his kneecap, but he never missed a beat."

Hill had leaned over and punched Barnes in the arm—a bit harder than necessary, Barnes had thought—but Hill's praise had seemed genuine. "All right, Ray! Way to fucking go."

Barnes drank the remainder of the warm beer and contemplated the favor that Danly had done him. Sure he had seen the NVA, but Danly had spotted them a second or two sooner. Sure he had kept his composure when the round just missed him—that's because he hadn't known it at the time. Danly pointed out the bullet holes after they'd landed. He owed Danly, that was for certain.

Respect. That's what he'd longed for. Settling back on his cot, he felt the slight stiffness in his body dissolve. He could relax a bit now; he'd finally been accepted.

Sleep came quickly, but not before visions of tracers and muzzle flashes danced across the backs of his closed eyelids. At first, he dozed fitfully, dreaming of the flying and fighting. But eventually his body relaxed, and a small, satisfied smile creased his face.

CAMP HOLLOWAY, PLEIKU

As the two helicopters climbed back into the darkness from the dimly lit runway, Danly was pleased to see that the fog was not forming over Pleiku. It looked as if it would not spread that far south, but stay confined to the valleys and plains to the north. So, if it got too bad around Kontum, he knew they could get out of the soup by flying to Pleiku. A little further to the southwest, the skies around Camp Enari also looked as if they would remain clear and bright.

While refueling, Danly had tried to get the mission canceled, citing the buildup of fog. Operations had been adamant, however: E Troop was firmly committed to supply

gun support for the Kontum mission. A deuce-and-a-half
had been disabled south of the city during an ambush of a
convoy, and the truck, loaded with 105-mm mortar rounds,
was still sitting by the side of the road. A small work party
was going to try to retrieve the vehicle so the ammunition
wouldn't be carried off during the night by the NVA. Danly
had explained to Holman that visibility was already lousy
enough to cast doubt on their ability to provide close support, and it was undoubtedly going to get worse. But Holman said the retrieval party had already left Kontum in
search of the truck, and the brigade commander, Cannonball
Six, was not about to call it back. The mission was still on,
and Danly was to contact the convoy commander, Sweeper
Six, when he returned to the area.

The gunships churned northward through the ever-
thickening haze, a few dim lights in the distance providing
the only reference to the ground. The horizon had vanished,
merging with the murky shadows of the surrounding mountains. Webb glanced back out the cargo door and saw that
Mackin, obviously concerned with losing sight of them, had
drawn much closer in order to maintain visual contact. Webb
frowned. He hated formation flying—that was for slick
drivers. Gunpilots needed room. Although Mackin hadn't
moved in close enough to form a tight formation, he was
much too close as far as Webb was concerned.

"If those fartheads in the command bunkers had to be
up here," he said disgustedly, "you can bet this mission
would be called off already."

Danly did not respond. His face, bathed in the soft, red
glow of the instrument lights, was impassive. His jaw
worked slowly on a wad of gum as his eyes flicked back
and forth between the instruments and the hazy gloom in
front of the aircraft. Webb probed angrily in his pocket for
his cigarettes. *Goddamn Danly; he'll stay out here all night
if they ask him. He just doesn't know when to quit.*

After several attempts, interspersed with Webb's grousing
about ground-bound assholes, Danly was able to contact

Cannonball Six and obtain the frequency and call sign of the search party. Moving slowly and cautiously, the three-vehicle convoy was now about three miles south of the city, waiting for the gunship protection to arrive. Flanking the road on both sides were two companies of ARVN troops, but Danly had the feeling the convoy commander was not putting his faith in the ARVNs' ability to protect him in the event of a determined assault. Many American commanders seemed to trust only the ARVN Rangers and considered other ARVN units to be unreliable.

"Sweeper Six, Bulldog Two-Six. I think we're somewhere near you, but I can't see anything on the road."

"Roger, Two-Six, we're blacked out," answered a surprisingly cheerful voice from the darkness below. "Stand by, we'll give you a light."

"What the hell's he so happy about?" Webb asked sourly.

Danly peered downward, but nothing shone through the blanket of darkness. "Anybody see anything? Gothard? Span?"

"No, sir."

"Me neither, sir."

"How about you, Art?"

"Nope."

"Sweeper, still haven't got you."

"Okay, Two-six, no problem. You know that small bridge about five klicks south of the ARVN compound?"

"Affirmative."

"Well, we're just a little bit south of that. You guys sound like you're almost right above us."

"Roger," replied Danly. "Problem is we can't see much of anything through the fog. I'll bring it down closer. Wait about zero five and then give me a couple more flashes."

"Will do. Sweeper, out."

Danly pushed down gently on the collective and the gunship began to sink slowly. He knew the road was about two thousand feet above sea level at that point and that several nearby hills were almost five hundred feet higher than the road. "Art, keep an eye on the altimeter. Can't get lower than twenty-six hundred feet."

"Roger on that," said Webb, becoming more anxious by the minute. Dividing his attention between the altimeter and his map, he saw there was not much room for error. Within a half mile of the road there were two hills with elevations of 2,502 and 2,494 feet, respectively. About another two miles to the south were two larger hills flanking either side of the road. Their tops exceeded three thousand feet.

Webb stuffed the map down beside his seat and stared at the small, iridescent needle on the face of the altimeter. His frown deepened as the needle swept through three thousand feet.

Passing through 2,650 feet, intermittent patches of thick, soupy fog would momentarily envelop the gunships, causing a bright glow right outside the cockpit as the navigation lights were reflected by the mist.

"Getting close," said Webb nervously.

Danly began to pull up on the collective, when suddenly he saw a flickering red light.

"Sweeper, Two-six, I got ya now," he said quickly. "But be advised this stuff is getting worse. Don't know how long we'll be able to see enough to help you."

"I understand, Two-six. Just do what you can for us."

"Two-six, roger . . . break . . . Two-eight, why don't you climb up clear of this crap. No sense bumping into each other."

"Amen to that, Two-six; we're going up."

Not wanting to advertise the convoy's exact position, Danly turned off the aircraft's exterior lights and began a tight orbit off to the southwest. He could track the convoy's movement by observing the periodic signal from the flashlight as the convoy continued to move away from the protection of the last ARVN outpost. Circling above a convoy was the sort of boring, tiresome flying that Danly had learned to accustom himself to. It was the kind of flying that tended to dull the senses, inducing a state of lethargy that could result in serious mistakes. By force of will, he had trained himself to remain alert while still relaxing to the monotonous rhythm of flight. But, occasionally—always the result of weariness—his resolve would flag.

As he settled into the monotony of the orbit, he knew it was going to be difficult to stay properly alert. The cumulative strains of the recent chaotic days had worn him down. He doubted he was capable of falling asleep at the controls, but if it was possible, it would be in a situation like this. Suspecting the crew chief and door gunner of already being asleep, he looked over his shoulder. Both were slumped against their respective sides of the gunship, their heads resting against the closed cargo doors. He shifted his gaze to Webb. The smaller man sat motionless, but his eyes were moving back and forth from the instruments to the darkness outside.

When the gunship was in the part of the orbit where it faced Kontum, the lights on the ground, which were slowly fading beneath the thickening fog, formed a horizon. But as the aircraft turned away, there was only darkness. After flying in a left-hand orbit for a half hour, Danly felt a spate of vertigo as he rolled the aircraft level and then into a right turn. Shrugging off the momentary dizziness, he increased the volume on the radio as Sweeper Six reported his progress to Cannonball Six.

Progress was slow. Fearing another ambush, the convoy was moving without lights and had to pick its way slowly around the vehicles disabled from the ambush that were partially blocking the road. As the convoy inched its way along, the red-lensed flashlight would periodically flicker to keep Danly aware of the convoy's location.

Danly hoped the men on the road were realistic about his ability to help them in case of attack. About the best he would be able to do is provide covering fire while they tried to retreat to the nearest ARVN position by the bridge. If they got caught in a serious firefight, it might be all over for them. It was a high-risk, stupid mission for all concerned.

Suddenly the dim lights of Kontum totally vanished as a thick patch of fog surrounded the aircraft. Webb shifted nervously in his seat. They had to be getting close to the three-thousand-foot hills.

"Mike, why don't we just pull the plug on this goddamn fiasco. Just call the TOC and tell 'em we can't see shit and have to get the hell out of here."

As the helicopter broke free of the fog, Danly rubbed his nose wearily and pondered Webb's suggestion. It made sense. But he hadn't backed out of a mission yet and did not want to start now.

"No, as long as we can see anything at all," he said slowly, "we'll stay with 'em. I don't think Cannonball will pull them back just because we leave, and they damn well might need us."

Webb stared hard at Danly and shook his head in exasperation. He began to argue, but stopped as a conversation began between Sweeper Six and the TOC. The ARVN troops guarding the bridge had decided to retreat to their compound in Kontum and had done so without asking permission or notifying anyone. When he learned of it, the American advisor at ARVN headquarters was furious, but unable to get the ARVN commander to order the troops back out. The bridge was now unprotected, and if the NVA snuck in behind the convoy and took the bridge, Sweeper was trapped.

"Just fucking great," sighed Danly. He looked at the fuel gauge. "Sweeper, this is Two-six. We copied that your ARVN buddies have flown the coop. Be advised we can only stay up here another four zero."

"Roger, understand," said the voice from the road, and the flashlight flickered again.

Forty minutes of flight time would be pushing the limit; Danly hoped they'd find the truck soon.

"Cannonball Six, Sweeper Six, over."

"Go ahead, Sweeper."

"I think we ought to scratch this and pull it back in."

"Negative! You will continue, out."

So, there's more of them like Patterson, thought Danly. The convoy commander was in a tight spot. He was probably a low-ranking officer, who, left to his own judgment, would have called a halt to the proceedings long ago. But he wasn't that lucky. Cannonball Six was unquestionably a bird colonel, and Sweeper didn't have much choice but to do what he was told—up to a point, anyway. Eventually he'd have to make the big decision himself.

Suddenly several clicks were heard on the FM radio. Someone had keyed a microphone three times in rapid succession. The clicks were then repeated, and after a pause, repeated again.

"Span, Gothard, wake up!" said Danly urgently as he watched for a signal from the red flashlight. Finally it flickered, followed immediately by Sweeper's whisper.

"Still got us, Two-six?"

"Roger," Danly replied softly. There was no doubt that the convoy had encountered something. Danly tightened his orbit so as not to lose the convoy's position. Occasionally he could get a glimpse of large dark shapes on the road, but most of the time the vehicles were not visible. It seemed to him like it had been an hour since Sweeper had clicked out the initial warning, but when he looked at his watch, he saw that only fifteen minutes had passed.

Keeping his eyes on the murk below, with only occasional glances at the dimly lit instruments, it suddenly dawned on him that it had been too long since he'd been able to see the lights of Kontum. At first he thought he might be looking in the wrong direction, but as the compass swung through 005 degrees, where there should have been lights, there was nothing but ever-thickening haze.

Shit, thought Danly. We've got to get out of here.

"Two-six, this is Sweeper." The voice was louder now.

"Go ahead."

"I'm all for God, country and apple pie, but this shit's ridiculous. We've got some bad-ass company out in front of us, so we're heading back in. Can you hang with us to the bridge?"

Danly hesitated, then the gunship popped clear of the fog bank once more and he saw three pairs of lights moving back toward Kontum, zigzagging around the damaged vehicles partially blocking the road.

"I think so. Good try."

"Thanks. Appreciate your help, buddy."

The lights of Kontum reappeared and then immediately disappeared in the swirling fog. As Danly rolled the aircraft level, he once again fought a twinge of vertigo. He realized he was sweating heavily and was suddenly aware of a dull ache that ran all the way from his right shoulder to his hand. He relaxed his grip on the cyclic and glanced across the cockpit. A small, glowing red dot vibrated in the darkness as Webb's trembling hand removed the cigarette from his mouth.

"Sweeper Six, Cannonball Six, over."

Danly could barely see the lights on the road below, but they seemed to pick up speed.

"Sweeper Six! Sweeper Six! Cannonball Six, over!"

There was no response to the TOC as the half-moons of light continued moving rapidly down the road.

Webb sagged in his seat and exhaled slowly. He wondered just how long Danly would stay alive.

CHAPTER 11

MARCH 5, 1968
CAMP ENARI

The lights in the tent flicked on, illuminating the smirk on the face of a boyish-looking private. Obviously relishing the morning's duty, he moved the light switch back and forth rapidly, producing a strobe effect.

"C'mon," he bellowed at the now half-awake men huddled beneath their blankets. "Time to get your asses up, sirs!"

Bookman, who had the day off, lifted his head and squinted at the figure in the doorway. "Turn off that goddamn light," he threatened in a groggy voice.

Not intimidated, the private flipped the switch a few more times and then sauntered out the door leaving the lights on.

"Little bastard," muttered Bookman, shutting his eyes and pulling the blanket over his head to shield himself from the light.

Danly felt as if he had only been asleep for a matter of minutes. Slowly he crawled from his bunk and began to get dressed. His watch indicated four-thirty, and he knew he had not gotten to sleep until after one. As he slowly pulled his pants on, he wondered how long he could stay reasonably

alert while adhering to such an absurd schedule. Yesterday
it was almost fifteen hours of flight time; no telling what it
would be today.

While lacing his boots, he made a halfhearted attempt to
compute how many hours he had flown in the previous
month, but suddenly realized he really didn't care. He also
didn't care—and didn't know—what day of the week it was,
whether he had written his parents lately, or how many days
in a row he had flown. Such bits of information had ceased to
be important anymore. His entire focus was upon flying. The
hell with the other mundane details of life. Lives depended
upon his ability to think straight and shoot accurately, and
anything that detracted from that was to be avoided.

When he had first arrived in Vietnam, his main concern
was doing his part to help win the war. He had still harbored
a degree of idealism and had been eager to help the South
Vietnamese fight for their freedom. His idealism had faded
rather quickly. It had become his impression that many of
the Vietnamese did not give a real big damn who won the
war. All they wanted was for the bombs and the bullets to
stop. They seemed to feel that they weren't going to fare
particularly well no matter which side came out on top.

He had questioned his changing attitude, thinking that
perhaps he had read too much into the situation, that it was
really just his own doubts and feelings that he was projecting
onto the Vietnamese. But after seeing too many times the
vacant and sullen stares of war-weary peasants, he was hard-
pressed to abandon his newly found conviction that all they
wanted was to be left alone.

He knew it wasn't that simple, of course. There were
also many Vietnamese who hated communism with a pas-
sion and were very frightened of falling under domination
from the north. He was still willing to fight, but his idealism
had become tainted, and his initial eagerness had been
blunted by the realization that the war was not being fought
in a manner that would bring military victory. His months
of fighting had consisted primarily of stopgap, scattershot

responses to NVA threats. Camped in almost total safety within Laos and Cambodia, the North Vietnamese could move large numbers of men up and down the border, pushing into South Vietnam whenever and wherever they deemed it advantageous.

Danly had begun to feel like a man battling a forest fire while being constrained by an arbitrary boundary. Forced to scramble to and fro, extinguishing flare-ups born of wind-blown sparks, he was restrained from attacking the real source of trouble—a forest-gutting fire that blazed with an ever-increasing ferocity.

His initial optimism about winning the war had waned in the face of reality. It had been replaced by a dogged determination to avoid defeat. He still believed a South Vietnamese democracy was worth fighting for; he was just no longer sure that the majority of Vietnamese were willing to sacrifice for that end. He hoped he was wrong.

His changing view had presented him with a new quandary. Why take any chances? Why not be extremely cautious, put in your time and get the hell out in one piece? Initially, having accepted his disillusionment, he found the questions difficult to answer. Why indeed, given the circumstances, should he "hang his ass out"?

After wrestling with the question for a while, he realized the answer was there all the time. It was simple, really, and it had been exemplified by the actions of a medevac pilot during a mission west of Dak Pek in late December. Danly had flown gun support for the medevac's attempts to pick up the wounded. An infantry unit had run into a deadly ambush and was under heavy attack. In tears, the ground commander had pleaded for evacuation of the seriously wounded. In spite of the torrent of enemy fire, the medevac pilot had not hesitated. Using the support of E Troop's gunships—inadequate as it was in the face of such concentrated enemy fire—the medevac pilot had made two extractions of wounded men before being shot down going in for a third load. There had been no indecision on the pilot's part; there were people who needed his help desperately, and he damn well was going to do everything he could to provide it.

And there it was; it couldn't be any more basic than that. The life of another soldier was always worth the risk of your own. If you weren't willing to take that risk, then you were a disgrace to the uniform.

Danly knew what he had to do.

"Hey, Mike, you gonna get some breakfast?"

Barnes's voice interrupted his thoughts, and he realized that he had been sitting, motionless, staring at his boots. *Come on, old man, wake the fuck up. Another day, another piaster. Hi ho, hi ho, it's off to war we go.*

"Mike?"

"Yeah, I'm coming." It took more effort than it should have to stand up.

Danly and Barnes took their trays to a long table where a large group of pilots was already eating. Spradling was talking with a great deal of animation, capturing the attention of everyone at the table.

"You guys hear about what happened with Wendell and the squadron commander?" asked Webb, as they sat down next to him at the end of the table.

"Not me," answered Barnes. Danly shook his head no.

"Hey, Wendell," Webb yelled, pointing at the new arrivals, "start over. They didn't hear the beginning."

"Then they ought to get the fuck up like the rest of us," said Hill.

"Hill, the only reason you're up right now is you had diarrhea this morning from someplace other than your mouth," said Spradling. "I saw you running like hell for the latrine earlier. Ain't going to help you though; you could shit for a week and your eyes would still be brown."

"Up yours," scowled Hill.

"Me and Reinke," said Spradling, turning toward Danly and Barnes, "were sitting at Kontum yesterday while you

guys were at Dak To, and we get a call from Dragon Six
to go help out some ARVNs just west of the city. They got
some NVA trapped just north of the Ya Krong. Well the
ARVNs were fucking around instead of just moving in and
nailing 'em, and the advisor's getting tired of all the bullshit,
so he calls us in.

"But, before he calls us, this was one of those deals
where he had to go back through the ARVN honchos, and
then they call the 173rd, and then the 173rd calls the Fourth
Division and, you know, they're talking to every-fucking-
body but Westmoreland himself. Of course squadron's in
the loop, and Bensen decides he's got to come out and take
a look. But as usual, the dickhead—" Spradling stopped
suddenly and grimaced, ducking his head like an animal
sensing danger. He looked cautiously around the mess tent,
and seeing no one from squadron, relaxed.

"As usual," he continued, regaining his enthusiasm,
"Colonel Dickhead doesn't bother to tell us he's around.
Now, by the time we finally get the word to go start shooting
at the bastards, probably every goddamn NVA commander
between here and Hanoi knows what's going on. The gooks
that were trapped certainly got the idea,'cause they decide
to make a break for it. At the same time, the gooks on our
side are down there farting around, trying to figure out when
to break for lunch or something.

"So, all hell breaks loose. Some of the NVA suddenly
charge the ARVNs, while the rest of 'em make a break for
the river. Dragon Six starts popping smoke and yelling for
help, and all we're concentrating on is the mess on the
ground, trying to sort out who's who."

"Incidentally," said Reinke, interrupting Spradling's
monologue, "you should know that Bensen's C&C wasn't
on any of the same frequencies that we were."

"Right," said Spradling emphatically. "The guy's flying
around out there and he doesn't know one goddamn thing
that's going on. So, when Dragon popped the smoke, Bensen's nearby and decides to fly over and take a look. Mean-

while, we're getting lined up to fire. So, I start the gun run, and I can see a group of the bastards moving toward the river, and that's all I'm focusing on. I punch off a pair of rockets, and—'' Spradling shook his head slowly, as if he still couldn't believe it ''—out of the corner of my eye, flying right into view in the middle of the rocket sight is a helicopter. It's fucking Bensen!''

"Please," said Webb with an eager smile, "tell me you shot his ass down."

"For an instant, I figure, 'Jesus! I'm in the Long Binh jail for the rest of my life.' Then I see the rockets might miss. One of them goes right underneath him; the other is one of those corkscrew numbers that's wavering around all over the place, and finally it goes by him right between the tailboom and the main rotor. I can't believe it; I'm saying 'Thank you, Lord, thank you, Lord' over and over, but then I get worried again. I figured I must've at least scared him half to death and I'm still gonna go to the Long Binh jail for life."

Laughter filled the mess tent as Hill slapped the table in mock anger. "You missed?" he asked incredulously. "You had him in your sights and you missed?"

"There went your best chance for a DFC," said Winters.

The laughter continued and Barnes was surprised when he noticed that Danly had not joined in. Danly had shown a small, fleeting smile, but that was all. Barnes was puzzled, but shifted his attention back to Spradling, who had resumed his story.

"A little later, we're back at Kontum to refuel and we see Bensen's ship parked in a nearby revetment. I notice he's not aboard—I figured he was off somewhere drawing up the court-martial papers—but Lieutenant Pauley gets out and comes walking over toward us. He's white as a fucking sheet. He tells us he'd been sitting in the left seat—Bensen was doing the flying—and he'd seen us just as we fired. Nothing he could do; the rockets were on top of him immediately. He just thought he'd had it.

"But the good part," said Spradling with a grin, "was that the colonel never saw the goddamn rockets. Didn't even know what happened, and Pauley's too scared to even talk. Hell, Pauley's always been been scared to fly with that dud, anyway, but after this I think he's goin' AWOL."

There was more laughter as the men began to get up and leave for the flight line. Soon only Barnes and Danly were left.

"How about the ARVNs sitting around doing nothing? I didn't know they were that bad," said Barnes.

"They're not. Aw, they got some units that aren't too sharp, but others, like the Rangers, are pretty good. You've also got to consider that they've been fighting over here for about three decades, and they don't have our sense of urgency. Why be in a hurry when nothing much has changed in thirty years?"

"Yeah, I guess so," replied Barnes, though he really couldn't understand not being eager to fight. He also was puzzled by Danly's earlier reactions.

"Mike, you didn't seem very amused by Spradling's story. I thought it was pretty funny."

Danly nodded. "It was funny." He drank the last of his coffee and stood up. "The problem is I started thinking about Patterson. It should have been him rather than Pauley eyeballing those rockets. Having one just miss his ass might have scared some sense into him.

"He's a hell of a lot more dangerous than Bensen and Horvath put together," Danly said gravely.

As a rule Danly did not care for uneventful days while flying. They tended to lull people into a false sense of security and to dull their reactions. But for once he had welcomed the boring day that had just passed. The easy flying had allowed the crews to give their overworked nervous systems some rest. Danly had greatly enjoyed the respite from the usual activities. He had spent most of the quiet afternoon thinking about the cold beer that now sat in front of him, and had had no intention of pondering any weighty issues while he consumed it. But Horvath's difficulties were once again commanding his attention.

When Danly had first entered the officers' club, he hadn't noticed Horvath. This struck Danly as being rather funny when he finally did see him, because there were only three other people there. I gotta start getting more sleep, Danly thought; Horvath's not *that* inconspicuous. But as he watched the lieutenant, who sat hunched over a table intently studying some kind of chart, he reconsidered. In spite of the fact Horvath was of average size, he often seemed much smaller. He had developed a reclusive, insular quality that somehow made him blend in with his surroundings.

Leaning against the bar and nursing his beer, Danly began debating with himself about whether to go over to Horvath and try to initiate a conversation. Maybe Horvath's biggest problem was that he had no one to talk to. The warrant officers didn't want anything to do with him, and recently the commissioned officers, with the exception of Patterson, had exhibited only a polite tolerance toward him. He was, as near as Danly could determine, a man devoid of friends.

Danly didn't know if that was always the case—he hadn't even bothered to notice before—but ever since the onset of Horvath's nervous troubles, he was seldom seen with anyone else. He ate alone, drank alone, went to the PX alone—did everything alone. Horvath's situation reminded Danly of a wildlife documentary he'd seen once that showed the pathetic plight of an injured antelope being stalked by lions. Hobbling pitifully, the crippled animal would try to blend in with the rest of the herd. But the other antelopes would shy away from the cripple as if its disability were contagious. There was strength in numbers, but only if each member of the group was reasonably healthy. A vulnerable animal was a magnet for danger, and the herd would keep moving away from it. If the injured one became lunch for the lions, too bad. The others weren't going risk their necks by associating with it.

Danly knew all too well that the same thing was true of humans. When Kay had begun acting strangely, her friends had quickly drifted away—some out of fear, some out of disgust, and some because they just didn't want to be bothered. Emotional instability could be frightening, so he could understand their fear; it was the last reason—the not wanting to be bothered—that he couldn't stomach. He had hated her so-called friends who had abandoned her because she had become an inconvenience, or because they were afraid their popularity would suffer if they hung around with a "loony." He had sworn he would see her through it, that he would stand by her and love her and force her to get well, that he would persevere despite the fact she resisted all help.

But he had failed.

Finally her manic highs and lows had worn him down like they had everyone else. He had tried to help as best he could, but one day, for his own sanity, he had given up. He couldn't bear to see her anymore.

Now he found his feelings affected by Horvath's situation, which was similar to Kay's. His contemporaries' self-preservation instincts made them keep away from him. It did not matter whether he was sick or just weak; his instability could be fatal and that was reason enough to avoid him. Nervousness and fear could be contagious.

Danly took another swig of beer and wondered why the hell he should care about Horvath. People had to learn to be tenacious, to fight and overcome their maladies and weaknesses. Why couldn't they just take care of themselves? He thought again of Kay and what she once was. He could still picture her: laughing green eyes, a broad smile, and soft, red hair framing her gentle face. *Why did she quit, dammit? Why did she quit?*

He looked over at Horvath, who was still making notations on his chart, and an old guilt feeling began to prod him. He sighed. *Okay, what the hell? Maybe it's worth a shot.*

Horvath's head jerked up as Danly pulled a chair away from the table and sat down.

"Hey, Lieutenant," Danly said with a smile, "how are ya doing?"

Horvath tensed. "What do you mean?"

Oh boy, this is going to be tougher than I thought. "I mean," said Danly, "what's going on? How're they hanging? What's happening?"

"I'm doing some work. What do you want?"

"Nothing," shrugged Danly. "This is just an attempt at sociability. Look, Lieutenant, things have gotten kind of tense around here lately. People have been overextended and nerves are getting stretched a little taut. I think it's time maybe we all tried to relax. No sense in aggravating one another or being at each other's throat."

Nervously scratching his chin, Horvath eyed Danly warily. "I doubt cordiality will change things much."

"Okay, have it your way, sir," Danly said as he began to get up. "I'll let you get back to work."

"No . . . ah . . . wait a minute. Sit down, Mike. Why did you really come over here?"

"Like I said, it's about time people started being more than just barely civil to one another."

"So, you want to be friends in other words."

Danly nodded, noticing the small twitch that had jerked to life at the corner of Horvath's mouth. "Couldn't hurt."

"Look, Mike, I've never disliked you; unlike your contemporaries, you usually act in a professional manner. I've always felt we got along all right. But I'm not stupid—you and I both know we're never going to be friends. What do you really want?"

Danly paused. "Okay, the truth. You seem to have been having a rough time of it lately and—"

"And now I'm the object of pity, in addition to ridicule? I . . . I know what Hill and Gray and the others think of me. So you think I'm a chickenshit also?"

"No, I don't," Danly replied honestly. "I just think you ought to talk to a—"

"You're out of line, Mister Danly!" snapped Horvath.

His mouth was now twitching rapidly and he had begun to wring his hands. "I'm a professional soldier and I don't give a shit about your immature friends' puerile jokes, and I don't need any words of wisdom from you!"

Danly sighed. It was not going as he'd planned. "Look, Lieutenant—"

"Look nothing! That'll be all, Mister Danly."

Slowly, Danly stood up and walked back to the bar. "A waste of fucking time," he mumbled to himself. A fleeting image of Kay flashed through his mind once again, and he shrugged. *Didn't work last time either.*

CHAPTER 12

MARCH 11, 1968
DAK TO

An early morning storm had passed, leaving just a few small clouds in its wake. Gray watched the scattered puffs of white float lazily toward the south and tried to forget the gruesome photographs. The scenes they showed were horrible. Wrapped in bloodstained clothes, shapeless forms—many of which were not recognizable as having once been human beings—were scattered across a large field. Some of the photographs, taken at close range, showed bowels and internal organs lying in sticky blobs, the center of attention for clouds of shimmering, blue-black flies.

The bodies in the photographs were those of North Vietnamese soldiers. They had been killed two weeks earlier while attacking a company of Fourth Division troops south of Polei Kleng. Most of them had been hit by rocket fire, and Gray had been among the gunpilots firing the rockets.

The pictures of the carnage had been the source of great interest to the flight crews that gathered around Gray's aircraft. Hill, with whom he was flying, had produced the pictures with undisguised glee. Part of Hill's happiness was derived from the look of revulsion that shone on the faces of some of the men, and part was derived from the fact that he had been involved in the action that caused the enemy deaths. If anything in the photographs bothered Hill, he gave no indication of it. On the contrary, he seemed to revel in the macabre scenes.

"See this guy here?" said Hill, holding up a picture for one of the crew chiefs and pointing to the most badly mangled body. "I got 'im."

"How in the fuck could you know?" Reinke scoffed with a mixture of weariness and disgust. He turned away and walked toward his own aircraft.

"Because," Hill shouted at the retreating figure, "he's next to that big tree by the footbridge, and I put a couple pair right on the roots." The crew chief laughed and Hill grinned crookedly.

After the photographs had been passed around, and the men had returned to their aircraft to await the next mission, Gray sat quietly in the cockpit. How anyone could enjoy viewing such sights was beyond him. Curiosity, even of the morbid variety, he could understand, but the pleasure exhibited by Hill and some of the others was unfathomable to him. How could anyone gloat over the remains of other human beings?

While he sat ruminating about the photographs, his right hand, moving as if controlled by an unconscious urge, slid forward and grasped the cyclic. He looked down as his thumb began absentmindedly caressing the little red button on the side of the grip. Startled, he jerked his hand back as if jolted by an electric current.

For many months he had operated the weapons, and for many months he had been far removed from the results of his actions. From the air it was all so clean and neat. Push the shiny red button and two sleek, white cylinders flew to the ground to cause a bright orange flash and a crisp puff of smoke. Come around in a circle and do it again. Repeat as necessary.

Hill, who had been talking with the crew chief, circled

the aircraft and leaned on Gray's open cockpit door.

"Hey, Steve-o, you want another look at these before I put them away?" he asked with an innocent grin, waving the stack of photographs.

Gray turned his head slowly and glared at Hill. "You really enjoyed that, didn't you?"

"What?" asked Hill, still wearing the innocent grin. "Showing the pictures or killing the gooks?"

Gray pursed his lips and looked away.

"Yeah," said Hill leaning toward Gray, his grin vanishing. "The answer to both questions is: yeah, I enjoyed it. Would you rather we'd have let the sons of bitches get away? Would you rather look at pictures of civilians that the bastards kill?" His eyes narrowed. "I'm proud of what I do; I ain't afraid to look at my handiwork. The grunts gotta look 'em in the eyes when they kill 'em. You too good for that, Stevie?"

Gray said nothing.

═══════════

EAST OF DAK TO

Whistling between puffs on a small, black cigar, Hill maneuvered the gunship to keep a close watch on the LOHs. He seemed to have forgotten the unpleasantness over the pictures and attempted several times to engage Gray in conversation. Gray kept his responses to a minimum and tried, without much success, to pay attention to the mission. He stared at the sky while thinking about Hill's earlier comments. Maybe Hill had a point.

Until recently, Gray knew that he, too, had been proud of being a gunpilot. He hadn't really minded shooting people. Hell, most of the time, if he saw any NVA at all, they didn't even seem like people, just little stick figures scurrying through the elephant grass. It had been pretty abstract really, just like shooting targets in an arcade.

The worst part about it, he thought, was that he had not even tried to think about them as human beings—just some ephemeral, armed phantoms called "the enemy." Blow the fuckers away. A few less dinks and everyone is better off. But the grotesque, bloody bodies in the pictures weren't better off. And there was certainly nothing abstract about them, either.

Gray was jolted from his thoughts by the abrupt movement of the gunship as Hill banked it sharply to the left. Gray realized Hill was peering intently at a knoll about a quarter of a mile to the west, half of which was completely covered by a large field of elephant grass. The entire expanse of grass undulated in the gentle breeze, ripples and waves pulsing through the sea of long blades like small swells on the surface of a lake. As the grass swung back and forth, portions of a well-worn path were exposed.

"Goddamn," Hill said slowly. "I saw something moving over there."

"On that path?"

Hill nodded. "Hey, Two-nine, Two-seven. I think I got something on this hill over here. I'm going to take a look."

"Two-nine, roger." Mackin sounded bored.

More of the path, which ran from north to south across the field, was visible as they flew nearer, and Gray saw the two men on the path at the same moment as Hill. They were dressed in dark-colored clothes, walking briskly toward the trees at the edge of the field.

"Well, well. Looks like a couple of dinks trying to get away, eh Lewis?" asked Hill, looking over his shoulder at the crew chief.

"Damn straight, sir; let's get 'em," responded Lewis, who was already leaning out over the skids pointing his M-60 at the hill.

Gray watched the figures moving along the trail. They appeared to have increased their pace, but he wondered if it wasn't just due to the nervousness some peasants felt whenever helicopters approached. He couldn't tell if they were armed.

"Two-nine, Two-seven, got some Charlies in the open."

"Two-nine, roger; we're on the way."

"Jug," Gray said hurriedly, "let's just see if we can get them to stop, and then have the scouts pick them up."

"No, they're going to haul ass any second. If they make the treeline, we'll lose 'em."

Hill moved the armament switch to the ARMED position and began a shallow dive. Gray's mind raced. They were not in a free-fire zone, but this area was pretty desolate. If these guys aren't NVA, he reassured himself, then neither is Ho Chi Minh. But still, goddammit, they aren't running away. At least let's give them a chance to stop and surrender.

Clenching his jaw, Gray unhooked the minigun sight and swung it into place. The aircraft began its familiar shaking as it gained speed in the dive, and the vibration gave the illusion that the two men, who were now looking up over their shoulders at the onrushing gunship, were bouncing up and down in the gunsight reticle.

"Oooookay," drawled Hill and he squeezed the rocket firing switch. As a pair of rockets whooshed out of the tubes, Gray bit his lip and fired the miniguns. The men, who had just begun to run, quickly collapsed under the onslaught of bullets and shrapnel. Gray saw no reason to continue firing and released the trigger. The hail of metal continued, however, as the door gunners tried to direct their string of tracers into the bodies, and more rockets kicked up plumes of dust and smoke.

Then it was over.

Dark stains dampened the clothing covering the crumpled bodies, as the LOHs moved across the hilltop. The small helicopters buzzed the surrounding area several times, and detecting no further activity, began to fly slower. Cautiously they swept over the clearing, the turbulence fanning downward from their rotor blades flattening the long-bladed grass. Satisfied there were no more people in the area, one LOH landed near the bodies, and the observer hurried from the aircraft. Tugging at and occasionally kicking at the limp forms, he searched them, rolling them over and removing items from their pockets. Finally he tore loose a pouch that had been fastened tightly to one of the dead men's belts and trotted back to the LOH.

Gray, trying to maintain a detached air, watched him work and wished he could wash his hands of the whole business. He could see that Hill, on the other hand, was visibly excited. Like a jackal picking over a carcass, thought Gray.

"Two-seven, this is Red One-two."

"Go ahead, One-two."

"Looks like these guys were NVA couriers. We got a bunch of documents and a couple of pistols."

"Outstanding, One-two, we'll call it in." Hill looked across at Gray. "Way to shoot, Steve," he said with genuine appreciation. "We got two less dinks to worry about and some intelligence to boot."

Gray nodded, still wishing he had not been a part of it.

===

DAK TO

Sickness and maintenance difficulties aren't always bad, thought Barnes. Depends upon the circumstances. He whistled happily to himself as the heavy gunship grudgingly labored against gravity and slowly gained altitude. Today he was an aircraft commander and it mattered not at all that it cost him his day off.

In midmorning, he had been engrossed in a novel, when Gunther entered the tent and said a pilot was needed for the standby crew. Hager, the aircraft commander, had become ill. Only three pilots had been in the troop area, and two of them were new arrivals. So despite the fact that Barnes was woefully short of experience, he became an aircraft commander by default.

The call for the standby aircraft had come at noon. Spradling and Winters were stuck at Kontum with a hydraulics leak, and a replacement aircraft was needed immediately. Barnes fully expected some crew changes to be made once he arrived there—it was troop policy always to have an experienced pilot in command. But as he neared Kontum, operations radioed him to proceed directly to Dak To to refuel, and then to join up with the other aircraft near Ben Het.

Struggling to conceal his excitement at being in command of an aircraft, Barnes forced himself to move in a measured—almost lazy—fashion, so as not to reveal his true state of mind. He casually reached for the map tucked alongside the radio console.

Ben Het was just a tiny dot near the juncture of South Vietnam, Laos and Cambodia, and it took Barnes a few moments to find it on the crinkled surface of the map. It was easy to see why the small firebase was often under pressure from NVA units coming across the border. Carved into the bald knob of a small hill, it sat in the middle of a flat-bottomed valley that started in Cambodia and spread east into Vietnam. The terrain formed a perfect infiltration route.

Operations said that the perimeter had been probed several times the previous night and E Troop's mission was to scour the surrounding jungle in hopes of finding the main part of the enemy force. Barnes didn't know as much about the area as the veteran pilots, but he knew enough to make him nervous. Hill had once said "the whole goddamn area is *always* crawling with dinks," and although Barnes treated most of Hill's pronouncements skeptically, that one he believed.

As the gunship continued climbing to the west from Dak To, Barnes set the map in his lap and scanned the terrain in front of him. He could see the mouth of the Dak Hodrai River valley in the distance, slightly to the left of his course. The valley wound its way to the south, just east of the Cambodian border. In front of Barnes to the right, crossing under the remnants of Highway 16, was the Dak Poko River, which originated just the other side of Dak Pek, twenty-five miles to the north. There were flat areas of intermittent vegetation near the rivers, but the flatlands quickly gave way to the more heavily wooded hills, which in turn merged with the surrounding mountains. The thick, lush foliage carpeted all the higher ground and imparted a deceptively tranquil appearance to the entire area.

But Barnes knew that underneath the serene, picture-postcard foliage, North Vietnamese soldiers swarmed like colonies of ants, preparing for continued assaults on all the American firebases nearby. And the nearest one, Ben Het, was smack dab in the middle of a key infiltration route—a big American thorn in the paw of Ho Chi Minh's tiger.

Barnes wondered what it would be like to live on a forlorn firebase like Ben Het. Isolated, constantly under the threat of being overrun, it had to be a nerve-racking place to be. It would have to be particularly ominous after sunset on those days when bad weather precluded any air support. He imagined the menace of darkness tightening around the small outpost, squeezing out the confidence of its inhabitants, making them feel like they were slowly strangling. It made the freedom of the air all the more appealing.

After flying due west for about ten minutes, he saw several aircraft circling high above the bald knob of the hill upon which the firebase was built. His copilot, a thin, studious-looking man named Mullen, was chewing rapidly on a wad of gum. It was Mullen's first combat flight. Wanting to set a good example, Barnes continued his efforts to adopt the studied casualness that was the demeanor of so many experienced pilots. The "I am fairly hot shit and don't have to work too hard at this" attitude had always appealed to Barnes, and now that he was in charge, he thought it important to project that image to the new guy.

Barnes had been briefed on the radio while refueling. After linking up with Two-four and Red One-eight, they were to scout an area just to the southwest of the firebase in an attempt to find the NVA that had been probing the perimeter. As he neared the circling aircraft, Reinke told him to move in behind One-eight. Other groups of gunships and scouts were breaking out of the orbit toward the north and west for similar missions.

"All right, Mullen," said Barnes, attempting to imitate the laconic delivery of Danly, "we've got to keep One-eight in sight at all times and be in a position to put fire underneath him. As soon as he calls receiving fire, start hosing down the area. There's no friendlies out here to worry about."

"Okay," gulped Mullen.

"You guys all set back there?" asked Barnes, looking over his shoulder.

The door gunner nodded, and Gunther pulled an unlit cigar from his mouth. "Always am, sir," he said.

"Okay, One-eight, we're with you."

The LOH started a left turn, descending rapidly toward the treetops. Barnes lost sight of it and felt a moment of panic before he saw the little aircraft roll level just above the jungle. Dropping down to treetop level and keeping to the left of the LOH's course, Barnes tried to maintain a good covering position. The LOH flew rapidly up the right side of a long, shallow draw, and Barnes struggled to keep up. Glancing to his left, he saw Mullen hunched forward, peering intently through the minigun sight. Barnes smiled to himself. Jesus, was I like that on my first mission? he wondered. Looking forward again, he saw that the LOH had already made a sharp turn out of the draw. Barnes swore at himself. *Dammit man, concentrate!* Executing an abrupt turn, he popped out of the draw and again swung in behind the small aircraft.

Weaving from side to side, the LOH worked its way

southward with Barnes's gunship in pursuit. Radio calls
from the helicopters working to the north indicated contact
had already been made with the enemy. An LOH was down,
but apparently the crew had scrambled out and were fleeing
toward a small clearing. Barnes turned up the volume on
all three radios and tensed involuntarily at the increased
urgency of the voices. The C&C aircraft was going to attempt a pickup, and the clatter from their door guns almost
drowned out the voices of the gunpilots laying down protective fire. "C'mon, c'mon," muttered Barnes. "Pick 'em
up; get 'em outta there."

The treetops moved by rapidly just under the chin bubble
as Barnes turned right again, following the LOH back into
the draw. Straining to hear more about the downed crew,
he allowed the gunship to drift to the right, thus duplicating
the LOH's flight path. He cocked his head as a static-filled
transmission from the C&C aircraft flooded his earphones.
He couldn't understand. Then the voice from the C&C came
through louder—the men had been picked up. All-god-
damn-right! thought Barnes. Number one!

Then he heard what sounded like popcorn popping, and
the windshield began to disintegrate.

━━━━━━━━━

"This is really fucking stupid," exclaimed Spradling between puffs on a cigarette. Danly was flying, keeping the
LOH covered as it skimmed the rolling terrain in the small
valley due west of Ben Het.

"They send us out here," Spradling continued, "to find
out where the gooks are at. Where they're at? What a fucking
joke. They're all over the place."

"Yeah," chimed in the crew chief. "They ought to just
bomb the shit out of the whole valley."

Spradling nodded vigorously in agreement. Earlier at Dak
To, just after receiving the details of the mission, Spradling
had begun grousing loudly about the assignment.

"Go *find* them?" he had asked. "*Go find them?* Somebody's got to be kidding. You could stand right in the center of that miserable firebase, close your eyes, turn around a few times, then just point in the direction you're facing and that's where they'd fucking be. They are all over the damn place. Don't the meatheads in command understand that?"

"I think I've heard all this before," yawned Danly. "Only last time it was about Dak Pek . . . or was it Dak To? You gotta get a new routine, Wendell."

"Routine my ass," Spradling said vehemently. "It's fucking true!"

"Hey, cheer up, Wendell." Webb grinned, delighted he was going to use Spradling's own favorite saying to bait him. "It may not be much, but it's the only war we got."

"Blow it out your ass, Webb."

Danly had worn a solemn expression as he watched Spradling stalk off. "Things must be getting really bad; Wendell's losing his sense of humor."

Now, after sweating through the radio reports of the LOH crew rescue, Spradling was angry again. "Mike, you gonna tell me this shit's a good idea?"

"Doesn't much matter; we're here."

"What the hell kind of reasoning is that?"

"*Mine*," said Danly. "Now shut the fuck up for a while." He did not like the distraction of Spradling's continuous grumbling. He needed to concentrate. Always think ahead and concentrate. It was when your attention wandered that you got hurt.

━━━━━━━━━

An instant before he heard the popping noises of the AK-47s, Barnes knew he had made a mistake. Instead of maintaining a flight path to the left or right of the LOH he was following, he had allowed the gunship to drift laterally and was passing over the same ground the LOH had flown over a few seconds earlier.

It was a stupid and very serious error.

Winters had once told Barnes that if you were close enough to them when they fired, AK-47s sounded just like a batch of popcorn cooking. Now, as his adrenaline surged and his pulse quickened, he remembered Winters' comment. Damn, he's right, thought Barnes as yells from his crew filled his earphones.

It all happened very fast and seemingly at once. Mullen yelled that he had been shot in the foot, and the door gunner was screaming. Barnes felt blood dripping from his nose. Something had torn by, or into, the little finger on his left hand and the entire hand was numb. He was afraid to look and see if his finger was still there. The Plexiglas windshield, dotted with holes, had begun to crumble—much of it looked like a sheet of crushed ice—and the sharp odor of an electrical fire pierced his nostrils. He looked down and saw wisps of smoke emanating from the radio console. When he tried to make the standard radio call about receiving fire, there was no feedback in his headphones—the radios were dead. He could no longer hear anyone. Gunther's M-60 was firing, but other than the whine of the engine, there was silence.

He scanned the instrument panel, focusing first on the engine gauges. His relief at their indications was short-lived. The smell of the electrical fire was stronger, and as he looked between the seats at the console, he felt another moment of panic. Many of the emergency warning lights were lit, including both the engine and transmission oil pressure lights, and both fuel boost warning lights. His heart felt as if it were pounding against his ribs. Afraid to make any sharp control movements, he gingerly turned the gunship to the south, aiming it toward a flat, open area southeast of the firebase. He prayed for the engine to keep running.

Feeling began returning to his hand and reluctantly he peered at it. His flight glove had been ripped open along the outside edge of his palm and little finger, but other than a modest streak of blood, there was no damage. He marveled at the effect the force of the passing bullet had had upon his hand, and then shuddered at what could have happened if the shell had taken a different path.

The aircraft was now pointed toward the clearing, and Barnes turned his attention to Mullen and the crew.

Mullen was bent over, holding his ankle, but he mouthed a silent "I'm okay." Barnes nodded, and fearing the worst, yelled over his shoulder. "Are you all right back there?"

There was no response, but he was afraid to look away from the gauges to see what had happened to Gunther and the door gunner. He had the eerie feeling that the small, gently vibrating needles in the engine gauges were somehow dependent upon his attention to keep them from dropping lifelessly to zero. Keep running, just keep running, he pleaded silently.

His upper body jerked involuntarily as he felt something on his shoulder, and he felt foolish when he realized it was a hand. Gunther was on one knee, leaning forward between the pilots' seats.

"Kraft's all right," he yelled, his voice weaker than usual. "I dropped a smoke, but I didn't see it come up."

"Okay," yelled Barnes, doubly relieved that Gunther didn't appear to be hurt either. "Strap in."

He lowered the collective and started the approach to the clearing. The smell of the electrical fire continued, but the smoke curling up from the console had diminished. The needles in the engine gauges stoically held their positions, and Barnes sighed in relief. The gunship was going too fast as it touched down, and it bounced roughly, but Barnes was too relieved to care about the lousy landing. He battled the controls briefly before the aircraft slid to a halt, churning up a large cloud of dust. He froze when he looked at the engine gauges—the needles had just fluttered to zero.

"C'mon, sir," yelled Gunther, who was helping Mullen from his seat. "Get out of here."

Nodding dumbly, Barnes scrambled from his seat. What was wrong with Gunther? He looked ghostly pale. He started around to Mullen's side of the aircraft, but stopped as an LOH banked steeply above the treeline on the north edge of the clearing, leveled itself and then quickly dipped to the ground. It landed about thirty meters from the gunship. Motioning frantically at Barnes, the observer hopped out and ran toward him.

"Nobody's sure where the fire came from; we didn't see any smoke. They need somebody to mark the spot," the man yelled at him breathlessly.

"I'll do it," said Barnes, and he ran to the LOH. As he buckled himself in, he saw Gunther fall to the ground. The crew chief's pants and the part of his shirt covering his stomach were now wet with blood. As the LOH climbed from the clearing, Barnes watched the figures on the ground helplessly. Mullen, limping badly, and the observer were dragging Gunther toward the nearest trees, while Kraft wandered aimlessly in the opposite direction.

CAMP ENARI

"This isn't very cold," Gray apologized as he handed Barnes a can of beer, "but I don't imagine you care too much tonight."

"No, no I don't," Barnes said quietly. He took the beer and sat down heavily on one of the wood stools that lined an L-shaped structure made of used ammunition crates. Webb, Mackin and Gray stood behind the makeshift bar and looked at Barnes with a mixture of amusement and respect.

"Hear you had a close one today," said Mackin.

"Yeah, a lot closer than I'd like."

"So, in your own words, with no false modesty, tell us what the fuck happened," Webb said. He raised his eyebrows and assumed an awestruck look. "But first," he added, leaning over and putting his hand tentatively on

Barnes's shoulder, "let me just touch the man who spit in death's face."

Mackin and Gray laughed, and Barnes, sheepishly, joined in. He stared at the top of his beer can. *If only they knew, they wouldn't be patting me on the back and joking; they'd be avoiding me. Fuckups aren't too welcome in the flying fraternity.*

He took a long drink of beer. *What should he tell them? That he violated one of the simplest rules of combat flying and got some people hurt? That he not only got them hurt, but almost got them killed?* He looked up slowly.

"Not much to tell really," he said quietly. "We were reconning this draw about a klick from the firebase when they got us. Shot out our commo, part of the windshield and tore up the electrical system, starting a fire. I was afraid the ship was going to quit running, so I set it down in a field back off the southeast side." He paused and took a long drink. "I'll tell you something, if there's any hero, it's Gunther. He was damn good. He was hit in the groin and never said a word. He got a smoke out immediately, although it must have fallen in the river or something because it didn't come up, and he was firing back right away. They got him medevacked pretty quick. I hope he's gonna be okay."

"Shit, he's a tough kid," said Webb. "No problem."

Barnes scowled, remembering the door gunner's actions. "The door gunner was something else, though. He screamed he was shot and then froze. Didn't fire, didn't drop a smoke, didn't help Gunther, didn't do shit. Thing was, he wasn't even shot. Just had a nick in his cheek from flying Plexiglas."

"He's done flying," said Mackin, emphatically, "that's for fucking sure."

"What about Mullen?" asked Webb.

"He'll be all right. He thought he was hurt worse than he was. From what I understand, the round had slowed down enough coming through the floor that it just barely made it through the bottom of his boot. It cut a little notch around the side of his foot, but he ought to be back here in a few days.''

"He's only *been* here a few days," said Gray.

"Well, if that's how his tour is going to go," said Webb, "we need to get him back here for a few choruses of the 'Body Bag Song' . . . before it's too late.''

Barnes laughed again with the others, then grimaced. His nose still hurt from whatever it was that had nicked him when the first rounds went through the cockpit. He quickly finished his beer and motioned to Gray for another.

Stumbling as he neared his tent, Barnes barely managed to keep from falling face first on the hard-packed clay. Tottering, he brought his beer can up to his lips, then grinned crookedly as he realized it was just as empty as when he had tried to drink from it two minutes ago. Well, well, he thought, no more beer for the fucking cavalry. He flipped it over his shoulder, and it bounced off the row of sandbags with a muffled clunk. Unsteadily, he pushed aside the door flap and stepped into the darkened tent. As his hand groped for the light switch, he lost his balance and took three halting steps toward the middle of the tent. Barely balancing on the balls of his feet, he wavered precariously, like a sailor negotiating a pitching deck.

"Shit," he mumbled, "I'm gonna break my fucking neck just trying to get to bed.'' Abandoning the idea of finding the light switch, he shuffled forward with his arms stretched forward and down, like a blind man moving through a strange room. His left foot bumped into a footlocker and he pitched forward grazing his head on the wood crossbar of a cot.

"Looks like this isn't your day." Danly's voice floated out from the darkness.

Barnes rubbed his temple. "No shit."

"You just overshot. Go back a couple of feet and you can crash into your own cot."

"Yeah, thanks."

Barnes crawled back the way he'd come and bumped into his footlocker. Gingerly, he rose to a half-crouch and made his way to the side of the cot. He sat down with a sigh.

"Barnes."

"Yeah?"

"Don't be too hard on yourself; you're not the only one who's made that mistake."

"Then you should move your cot." Barnes had trouble getting the words out without slurring them.

Danly was silent.

"You hear me, Mike?"

"That's not what I was talking about."

"Then what . . ." Barnes paused. Jesus, he wondered, how does he know I fucked up? Nobody coulda told him. Door gunner don't know shit, and Mullen and Gunther went to the Seventy-first Evac. "I don't know what you mean."

"Yes, you do. Don't let one mistake fuck you up, Ray."

"Already has," Barnes murmured to himself. He tipped backward onto the cot. It felt like it was beginning to spin, and Barnes gulped, fighting a spasm of nausea.

PART THREE
WAR MINDS

As wounded men may limp through life, so our war minds may not regain the balance of their thoughts for decades.
  —FRANK MOORE COLBY, *The Colby Essays*

CHAPTER 13

MARCH 19, 1968
POLEI KLENG

Danly felt the light tickle of the fly's legs when it landed on his neck just above his Adam's apple. It crawled, in the erratic fashion peculiar to flies, up his neck, along his jaw, and then stopped on his chin. Danly remained motionless, his head tilted back, resting against the top of the armored seat. Small rivulets of sweat that began at his hairline zig-zagged their way through the stubble on his cheeks, flowing toward his already-damp collar. His breathing was slow, and he emitted a faint rasping sound each time the thick, humid air passed through his throat.

Above and to the front of him, stuck through the upper left corner of the windshield, was the outside air temperature gauge. It registered thirty-seven degrees centigrade, but to Danly, it seemed even hotter. It was 2:34 in the afternoon on the 275th day he had been in Vietnam. He did not know that, however, having long ago intentionally lost count of the days remaining. He did not wish to think about the end until it was very, very close at hand.

Eyes closed he sat, almost in a stupor, feeling the minute, featherlike prancing of the fly's legs as it moved toward his

mouth. The fly's progress reminded him of one of Spradling's screwy monologues: the proper technique for trapping
winged insects with the tongue.

Spradling had demonstrated the procedure one day at Dak
To. In order to execute the tongue-blot method, he had
instructed, it was necessary to induce the fly to enter the
mouth over the lower lip. Spradling had sat in the cockpit
of a gunship in the same position that Danly was in: head
tilted back and mouth open. It had not been long before one
of the little scavengers landed on the side of his face and
pranced around to his chin, heading for his mouth.

Relaxing his lower lip, Spradling had formed a cavity
between it and his teeth. When the fly crawled into the
space, he had thrust his jaw forward and tightened his lip,
trapping the insect against his teeth. Then with a theatrical
rolling of his eyes, he had slowly forced his tongue up and
over his bottom teeth into the cavity where the fly was
struggling to escape. After mashing it with his tongue, he
had spit the small, sodden mass into the chin bubble.

"It's slow, I admit, but *goddamn* it's fun," Spradling
had laughed, enjoying the revulsion of the more squeamish
onlookers.

The fly on Danly's face was now exploring the opening
to his mouth, and without thinking, Danly began relaxing
his lower lip and readying his tongue. Jesus! he exclaimed
silently. Is this what my existence has come to, half-
suffocating in a beat-up helicopter trying to kill flies in my
mouth? He sat up straight and coughed. The fly buzzed
quickly away, only to return immediately and land again
on his neck. He swatted at it halfheartedly, and yawning,
climbed from the cockpit out into the sun.

It was very quiet as he scanned the row of helicopters
parked on the ramp. All of the crews had sought shade
inside the aircraft, but outside, underneath the tailbooms,
small groups of infantrymen were sitting stolidly in rows,
like crows on a fence, availing themselves of the shade.

He walked slowly to the aircraft parked in front of his

own, looked inside, and saw only three people, two of whom were asleep.

"Where's Lieutenant Horvath?" he asked Gothard, who was reading a ragged paperback with a picture of a half-nude woman on the cover.

"He went to take a shit and the hogs ate him," answered Gothard without looking up. "Who cares?"

Danly couldn't decide to laugh or be angry. He understood Gothard's attitude, but he really couldn't let it pass.

"*I* do, Sergeant," he said sharply.

Gothard jerked upright, closing the book. "Sorry, sir. I think he went over by the Sneaky-Pete camp."

Danly walked to the other side of the gunship and looked across the ramp at the heavily fortified camp. Built almost entirely underground, it looked just like a low, wide dome of dirt with a few clusters of sandbags placed here and there. Eight rows of barbed wire ringed the camp in a series of concentric octagons, giving the dome the appearance of being in some sort of weird corral. Sitting on a metal ammo box next to the outermost ring of barbed wire was Horvath. He had an M-16 laid across his legs and there was a PRC-10 radio beside him. His head bobbed rhythmically as he carried on a private conversation with himself.

It gave Danly an eerie feeling. He walked back to his aircraft and removed the web belt that was slung over the pilot's seat. He unsnapped the canteen pouch and removed the green, plastic container. Swatting at the flies that buzzed his face while he drank, he spilled some of the brackish water. It mixed with the thin film of red dirt coating his skin and oozed warmly down the sides of his neck.

Discomfort, thought Danly, maybe that's it; maybe that's a big part of what Horvath's problem is. A constant barrage of aggravations and discomforts might be exceptionally disturbing to a person of Horvath's frail sensibilities. The cumulative stress of the heat and insects and shitty food and bouts of diarrhea and intermittent sleep and all the other irritating things might be what ultimately gets to him. Maybe he could handle the fear if not for the other stuff.

Horvath crouching on the ammo box was a pathetic and disturbing figure. His mere presence, considering his unsettled state, was dangerous. Fear tended to be contagious, and Horvath's was of the worst kind: uncontrolled and self-destructive. Danly's anger rose. *Goddamn Patterson!* If it were not for him, Horvath could be where he belonged—in some rear echelon job, *not* in combat. There were plenty of administrative staff jobs in secure areas. As a matter of fact, there were more rear echelon jobs than anything else. Why not transfer him?

Three days earlier Hawkins had agreed with Danly and had come to the conclusion that Horvath should be taken off flight status. However, his efforts to convince Patterson and the flight surgeon of the fact were futile. The flight surgeon was a kiss-ass who would never argue with Patterson, and Patterson dismissed the idea summarily, saying he wanted to hear nothing further about it. As far as he was concerned, Horvath was one of his best men.

With Hawkins having just left on R&R, Horvath was now in charge of the platoon. Danly had hoped Horvath would continue to assign himself to fly with the most experienced pilots, as Hawkins had been doing, but he had not; he had paired himself with Barnes. Danly had really shaken his head at that one. The blind leading the blind. What a crew: a basket case and a guy who had managed to get his ass shot down eight days earlier.

He didn't really hold it against Barnes—everybody made mistakes—but having him in the same cockpit with Horvath was a potential disaster.

Danly took another swig from his canteen. The flat, musky taste of the brackish water made him suck in his cheeks as if he'd just bitten into lemon. He forced himself to swallow some of the water, and then spit out the rest. Well, maybe nothing would happen in the AO today; maybe Horvath wouldn't get a chance to screw up. Sure, and maybe the sun would set in the east.

DAK HODRAI VALLEY,
WEST OF POLEI KLENG

Most of the automatic weapons fire tore through the engine compartment, shredding oil lines and damaging the turbine blades so badly that the engine literally chewed itself apart. The other rounds ripped through the cockpit. Lieutenant Alvarez, the pilot, was shot twice in the head and died before the aircraft hit the ground.

Gray was looking right at the small aircraft when it was hit. The high-pitched, panicky voice that screamed: "We're going down!" caused a jolt of adrenaline to surge through Gray's body. It was Bookman's voice; he had volunteered to fly with the scouts that morning. Gray felt sick as he watched the stricken LOH lurch awkwardly to the right. Twisting through a 180-degree turn, the crippled aircraft crossed back over the small stream it had been flying above and settled into a grove of small trees. It bounced hard, rotated forward, bounced hard again on its nose, and then rolled onto its side.

Bookman had been lucky. Although his right kneecap was shattered and his left arm was broken, he had been able to extricate himself from the mangled cockpit. Painfully, he had dragged himself clear of the wreckage before it had begun to burn.

Gray divided his attention between firing into the treeline across the river and watching the wreckage. Come on, get out of there, he pleaded silently, waiting for Alvarez to emerge from the LOH. But the plume of smoke coming from the aircraft flashed into a full-blown fire, and Gray knew the lieutenant wasn't coming out.

The other LOH working the area made a fast, on-the-deck pass over the downed ship and received more fire, this time from the treeline on the same side of the river as the wreckage. It was hit also and the pilot, worried about the damage, radioed that he had to return to Polei Kleng. Gray and Reinke maintained their racetrack orbit, providing protective fire for Bookman, who had crawled into some scrub foliage beneath the small trees.

Twice Gray saw men trying to advance from the treeline toward Bookman's hiding place, but fire from the gunships drove them back. Gray was very worried. All they could do was conserve ammunition and try to protect Bookman until help arrived. His concern heightened when the door gunner's voice blared excitedly on the intercom.

"There's more of them at three o'clock, sir! On the hill!"

Gray banked right and saw more NVA soldiers moving across a small hill about one hundred meters behind Bookman.

"Oh no!" Gray exclaimed, fighting his growing feeling of panic.

━━━━━━━━

Sitting on the floor behind the copilot's seat, Danly leaned against the cargo-door frame and watched Horvath with growing fascination. The lieutenant had gotten up from his perch on the ammo box and was walking around in small circles, much like a dog preparing to lie down. Still talking to himself, he was clenching and unclenching his fists, occasionally drumming his fingers on his thighs. Danly tried to convince himself that Horvath's antics were no more disturbing than those of anyone who might become agitated from time to time, but he couldn't make himself believe it.

Going crazy with fear, panicking, even pissing or crapping in one's pants—Danly had thought about all of them during his early training. Flight school meant a guaranteed trip to Vietnam, and that meant a guarantee of getting as scared as one would ever get. How would he react? Could he cope with the pressure? He had not been positive, but he figured he would be able to handle it. He believed there

were a lot worse things than dying, and he had known he
would rather act with courage and risk being killed than
stay alive by being a coward. Easy to say, he had found
out later, but much harder to do.

But at least he had given it much thought ahead of time.
He had known and accepted the fact that he would be afraid,
but he had been and still was determined to control his fear.
He had concentrated from the beginning on developing a
strength of will from which he could always draw courage.
So far it had worked.

Maybe Horvath had never considered his own fears;
maybe he had never developed an inner strength; or maybe,
and this was the disturbing thought to Danly, maybe Horvath
had planned and worked at it just as Danly had, but now
had finally reached the limit of his courage.

So how far away is your limit? Danly asked himself. The
question seemed to hang in the humid air, threatening to
haunt him like the demons that were badgering Horvath.
He tried to dismiss it, but the question remained. *What is
your limit, Mister Danly?* Suddenly, he grinned ruefully.
*This is exactly the problem with Horvath: he thinks about
it too much, letting his doubts gnaw away at his confidence.
Well, fuck that, my limit's a long way away.*

He looked away from Horvath toward the jungle-covered
hills rolling steeply away to the north. He tried to concentrate on the beauty of the valley, and the strong profile of
the mountains framed by the hard blue highlands sky. So
what's this now, asked a little voice in his head, a "strength
from nature" routine? Danly chuckled. *Whatever it takes.*

"Hey! Hey!"

Danly leapt out of the helicopter before he realized it was
Horvath who was yelling. The lieutenant was standing halfway between Danly's aircraft and the barbed wire, pointing
back toward the radio.

"What's going on?" Danly called as he trotted to where
Horvath was standing.

Horvath wore a hollow expression. ''A loach is down,''
he said.

''Where?'' asked Danly.

''Um, I...ah...ah, I'm not sure,'' Horvath stam-
mered. His facial muscles sagged, giving him the look of
a child about to cry.

Aw Christ, not now, thought Danly. ''Never mind, we'll
find out in the air.'' He turned and ran toward the gunships,
shouting at the other pilots.

''Got a loach down, get everybody in the air!'' He was
pleased to see his new copilot, Roper, already in the gunship
preparing to start it. When he noticed Barnes climbing into
Horvath's aircraft, Danly suddenly realized he could no
longer hear footsteps behind him. He spun around. Horvath
had stopped and was standing still as a statue, staring into
the distance.

''Lieutenant!'' he yelled angrily. ''Let's go!''

━━━━━━━

Barnes worked quickly through the starting procedure,
ignoring the checklist and relying solely on memory. Having
gone through the routine so many times, he sometimes felt
as if his arms had a life of their own. They weaved back
and forth automatically among the banks filled with gauges,
radios and circuit breakers, his fingers flitting like fat ser-
pents' tongues from switch to switch.

The whine of the turbine grew louder and he watched the
exhaust-gas temperature gauge closely. The engine was old
and it had a tendency to heat up too rapidly during the start.
Jockeying the throttle to keep the temperature below the red
line, he glanced briefly at Horvath, who was settling slowly
into the copilot's seat, mumbling to himself. Barnes returned
his attention to the gauges. The exhaust-gas temperature
hovered for a few seconds just above the red line and then
settled back into the green arc. Barnes sighed. He was
feeling progressively more uncomfortable. It was bad

enough that he had a lack of confidence in the engine and that he had a bad feeling about the area they were going to, but he now sensed impending trouble with Horvath.

Continuing to hurry through the remainder of the starting routine, he became aware that Gothard remained standing by the door after replacing the fire extinguisher in the rack next to the pilot's seat. Nodding toward Horvath, Gothard raised his eyebrows in a silent question. Barnes looked across the cockpit. Horvath was noticeably pale and was sitting motionless, seemingly transfixed by Danly's helicopter parked in front of them. Barnes shrugged irritably and motioned Gothard to his seat.

As he turned all the radios on, Barnes's irritation gave way to a strong feeling of apprehension. Something was about to happen that he did not know how to handle. All three radios crackled to life and the tone of Danly's voice indicated his impatience.

"Two-nine, radio check."

"Ah, rog . . . er," replied Barnes, his voice trailing off. His attention shifted to the shaking body in the copilot's seat.

"Okay, pull pitch in zero two."

Danly's crisp command went unheard. Aghast, Barnes stared in stunned fascination at Horvath. Tears streamed down the lieutenant's ashen face. His eyes were wide, and his fists were pressed tightly against his cheeks. Rocking forward and backward, his anguished moans were barely audible above the noise of the engine and the whirling rotor blades. Barnes sat frozen as Horvath seemed to shrink before his eyes, his shaking body drawing into itself, huddling against the unseen terrors that had finally consumed him.

━━━━━━━━━━━

Picking the gunship up to a low hover, Danly noticed his team's LOHs already taking off from the end of the ramp. *Must be nice to just pick up and go.* Quite a difference from nursing an overweight gunship off the runway.

"We clear left, Rollins?"

"You're okay, sir," answered the crew chief.

Danly hovered sideways from his place in the line of helicopters, then began moving the gunship forward toward the end of the ramp. "Two-nine, you up?"

There was no response.

"Two-nine?"

"Ah...I...we got a problem." Barnes's voice was subdued.

This is not the time for any bullshit, thought Danly. He could imagine Horvath getting bent out of shape because of some minor glitch like a low reading on the alternate generator. "If you're flyable, the hell with it. Let's go."

"The ship's okay; it's not that."

Danly knew right then. "Lieutenant Horvath?"

"That's affirmative," responded Barnes, the tone of his voice suggesting uncertainty as to what to do.

"All right, get him out of there and we'll get a replacement." Danly was surprised by the sudden pang of sadness he felt. This was a bad end for Horvath. It would have been better if he'd collapsed in battle—that way he'd have an excuse. This was no heroic breakdown in the course of a harrowing mission; this was just a whimpering collapse next to lonely Special Forces camp in the middle of nowhere.

"Blue lead, Two-six."

There was no answer. Jesus H. Christ, is nothing going to go right? Danly wondered. He considered calling one of the LOHs back, but they were already on the way to the AO, and their miniguns would probably be needed. The gunship reached the end of the ramp and Danly turned it onto the runway. Moving forward, the heavy ship began to settle, its skids lightly brushing the interlocking metal planks. Accelerating, it began to climb as it came abreast of Barnes's aircraft. As he flew past it, Danly saw Gothard helping Horvath from the cockpit. Horvath's movements were like those of an old, old man.

"Damn!" exclaimed Roper. "What's the matter with the lieutenant?"

"The lieutenant's done cracked up," said Rollins, not sounding the least bit unhappy. "Ain't that right, Mister Danly?"

Danly didn't answer immediately; he was irritated by the crew chief's tone of voice. Rollins seemed to take pleasure in Horvath's collapse.

"The lieutenant's had some health problems," Danly said finally. "He shouldn't've been flying." And, he added silently, it's a damn good thing for him—and Patterson—it didn't happen in the middle of a firefight.

"Blue lead, you up yet?"

"That's affirmative. What's with your other gun?"

"Got a sick pilot. How 'bout sending one of your guys over; we're going to need both ships."

"Stand by."

Continuing the climb, Danly banked the aircraft toward the west and told Roper to take the controls. He removed his map from between the seats and looked at the area marked as the AO.

"Two-six, Blue lead. Raider Six says he won't put anybody on the ground unless the whole platoon goes in, and we need all our birds for that."

Just fucking great, sighed Danly. He was going to start arguing with the slick leader when he saw the damaged LOH approaching from the west.

"Blue lead, Two-six. There's a loach inbound; how 'bout sending your copilot over to Two-nine now and then grabbing the loach driver for your bird when he lands?"

"Okay, Two-six, will do."

———————

Thick, black smoke billowed skyward and Gray knew the Air Force had just dropped napalm. Approaching from the east after a rapid refueling and rearming stop, he could

see an Air Force FAC circling lazily off to the south. A
pair of bomb-laden Phantoms took turns swooping from the
layer of cotton-puff clouds floating above the valley, dump-
ing their mixture of explosives and napalm into the NVA
positions encircling Bookman. The jets would disappear
momentarily behind the high ridge blocking Gray's view of
the valley, then suddenly pop skyward, climbing from sight
in a matter of seconds.

Searching for the other gunships, Gray finally spotted
them circling just on the other side of the ridge from the
diving Phantoms. The slicks were visible orbiting much
farther to the south, staying well clear of the mayhem. If
the troops weren't on the ground yet, it was a bad sign.

He wondered how Bookman was faring. He must have
known that his chances were pretty slim when he crawled
to the trees. The NVA were coming after him from at least
two sides, and there was little hope of an immediate rescue.

Perhaps the frantic firing from him and Reinke had given
Bookman some comfort; he couldn't be sure. But he did
know, although it may not have improved Bookman's
hopes, that the arrival of the two LOHs followed by Danly—
even without his wingman—had lifted his own spirits: he
and Reinke had just run out of ammunition.

While he had quickly briefed Danly on Bookman's pre-
dicament, his initial elation faded. The situation had still
been very grim—Danly couldn't possibly contain the situation with only one gunship, even if he did have two LOHs
to help. Where was the other gunship and when would they
get some help from the Air Force?

But as he had turned toward Polei Kleng with the FUEL-
LOW warning light glowing brightly on the console, he had
been forced to smile in spite of himself. The sight of the
little LOHs making gun runs alongside the much larger
gunship struck him as funny. It was like two little kids
leaping into a fray to help an older and bigger brother.

Now, with the valley floor being burned and blasted apart,
it was obvious that the NVA were paying heavily for their

prize of the downed LOH. The only question now was if Bookman would be found in one piece and breathing. There was certainly the chance that he'd be spread around the valley floor, charred bits of his remains mingled with those of the luckless NVA. A slightly off-target bomb would have done the trick.

Hill's gruesome pictures flashed through his head again, and he felt the now-familiar tightening in his stomach. *Goddammit, why think of that now?* He pushed it from his mind, but other images followed: a group of NVA soldiers was moving toward Bookman when rockets from Gray's gunship exploded in their midst, literally blowing one man apart and knocking the others aside like tenpins.

Gray jerked his head, shaking the scene from his consciousness. Was he going crazy? Why should he give a damn about the NVA soldiers? Bookman was worth the whole lot of them. Sweating profusely, he gnawed on his lower lip in frustration.

Finally the Phantoms finished their deadly air show and Danly's team popped back over the ridge. The east side of the valley, which had contained several groves of trees and had been blanketed with elephant grass and scrub vegetation, was now a smoldering, barren landscape pocked with bomb craters. Some of the trees still stood, but most were knocked down, their shattered remains strewn among the dirt and rocks. Gray's hopes for Bookman vanished; how could anything have survived that devastation?

One LOH, after a rapid pass over the area, slowed and finally came to a hover above the spot where Bookman had last been seen. The LOH pilot gave a running commentary as he searched for Bookman. A bomb landing near the grove of trees had exposed some bunkers. Apparently Bookman had crawled into an unoccupied bunker complex. The pilot said there were several bodies, "or what's left of them," about forty meters to the west, but none in the area of the bunkers.

Smoke and dust cast a pall over the valley and Gray

slumped in his seat. He watched with fading interest as the scout helicopter moved deftly over the mangled terrain.

"There he is! He's moving!" The scout pilot's exultant voice caused Gray to jerk forward, and he felt a slight pain as the shoulder harness locked and the canvas straps pressed tightly against his shoulders. He sank back in the seat, relieved but still edgy. The roller coaster of emotions was wearing him out. Closing his eyes and exhaling slowly, he wondered what kind of shape Bookman was in.

CAMP ENARI

Cradling an armload of unopened beer cans, Barnes shuffled unsteadily from the bar to the table. As he leaned forward to set them down, his chest jerked from the force of a powerful hiccup and the beers slipped from his grasp. With a series of dull clunks, they bounced on the tabletop and then rolled in different directions toward its edges. Danly and Gray moved quickly trying to catch the cans before they dropped to the floor, but Spradling, holding an open beer in each hand, just leaned back in his chair and laughed.

"The Army actually *lets* you fly its helicopters?"

Barnes stuck out his foot to intercept one can that was rolling along the floor back toward the bar. "Damn, I'm sorry."

"We know you're a sorry bastard, Barnes, but we thought you could at least carry some beer without fuckin' it up."

Picking up the can from the floor, Barnes emitted a loud burp. He set the can on the table and sat down heavily. "Hey, I'm sorry. The damn things just slipped."

"Forget it," said Gray, who reached out quickly and clamped his left hand down on Barnes's arm, "but *don't* open the can you just picked up. I don't need a shower."

"Oh, yeah. Sorry."

Spradling shook his head slowly. "Sorry? Is that all he ever says now, Mike?"

"Apparently so. I think Horvath really shook him up this afternoon."

"That and he never could drink worth a damn."

"Boy, I hated to see the lieutenant go like that," mumbled Barnes. His speech was slurred and he began swaying forward and backward as if in a trance. "I'm sorry, but I hated to see that."

"Steve," said Danly, pointing to the beers in front of Barnes, "get those things out of his reach before he tries to drink any more. He and I have got to take an aircraft down to Qui Nhon tomorrow for some maintenance on the gun system, and I'd like for him to at least be able to stay awake during the trip."

Barnes watched dully as Gray moved the beers away from him.

"Hell, he's young," said Gray, "he'll recover by morning."

"Speaking of recovering," said Spradling, "what's the word on Bookman?"

"He's got to be the luckiest son of a bitch alive, that's for sure," said Gray. "When the observer helped him out of the hole he'd been hiding in, he couldn't believe Bookman was still in one piece. In addition to his broken arm and leg, he was bleeding from more holes than the observer could count. He was also deaf. The Phantoms put their bombs damn near on top of him and the concussion blew out his eardrums. The word from the Seventy-first Evac is that he's going to make it, though."

"Why in the hell did he volunteer to fly with the scouts anyway?"

"Damned if I know," said Gray, "but that oughta make anybody else think twice about it."

"No shit. Well, Mike, how about the other gun platoon casualty for the day? Is the master of the grand twitch gone for good?"

"Yeah, Horvath's finished. Nervous breakdown—in spades."

"Here's to Lieutenant Horvath," intoned Spradling, raising his glass. "From a flak jacket to a straight jacket. *Xin loi*."

Gray drummed his fingers on the table. "It's really a damn shame," he said softly.

Danly opened his mouth as if he were going to comment, then pressed his lips together and shrugged. He stood up and reached over to grab Barnes by the arm. "Come on, Ray, we've got to fly in the morning. You've been in here too long already."

"Oh yeah. Sorry, Mike."

CHAPTER 14

MARCH 20, 1968
QUI NHON

Waving a handful of what from fifteen feet away appeared to be a deck of playing cards, the old man hobbled toward them. Danly glanced sideways, but continued walking leisurely toward the medical compound. Barnes, despite his continued uneasiness in the presence of Vietnamese, stopped and waited for the man to come closer.

"Hey, hold on, Mike. I want to look at what he's got there."

Danly stopped and turned around with a bemused smile on his face. "You haven't seen any of that stuff yet?"

"No, just wait a minute."

The man shuffled to a stop, holding the small deck of cards out in front of him. Barnes took several of them from the man's dirt-streaked hand and whistled softly. The black-and-white photographs, many of which were slightly out of focus, showed Oriental women participating in a variety of sex acts. Animals were involved in some of the pictures, and despite his initial revulsion, Barnes could not stop himself from eagerly examining the lurid displays. The old man suddenly reached out and closed a gnarled hand around the ends of the cards protruding from Barnes's cupped hand.

"You look. Now you buy," the old man said sternly, tugging at the cards.

"Hold it a minute," said Barnes, tightening his grip. "I gotta check all the merchandise."

"No more look!" the old man cried forcefully. He grabbed Barnes's wrist with his other hand. "Now you buy!"

Barnes looked down at the old man's hands. The fingers were stained a nicotinelike brownish yellow, and his fingernails were caked with dirt. The man's hands were rough and dry; it felt to Barnes like a sheet of coarse-grade sandpaper was clamped to his wrist. Barnes's gaze shifted to the man's face. Flecks of dirty-gray foam stuck to the corners of his mouth, and his small, dark eyes stared coldly from the shadow of his straw hat. Feeling a wave of revulsion, Barnes jerked his arm violently from the man's grasp.

His arms folded across his chest, Danly stood patiently watching the two men. "Barnes," he said evenly, "either buy 'em or give 'em back to the guy. I think his friends are getting pissed." He nodded toward a group of younger men who were observing the confrontation from a short distance away.

Still holding the cards, Barnes looked quickly in the direction that Danly had indicated. A half-dozen young men, their eyes shielded by sunglasses, sat on their motor scooters watching him. Afraid of them, but still angry, he spun around and swung his arm in the direction of the old man.

"*Don't* throw them," Danly ordered sharply. "Hand them back."

Barnes froze, and then feeling like a little boy who has just been chastised by his father, held the cards out for the old man to take. The man's bony, crowlike fingers grasped the cards and pulled them away. Then the man lowered his head and spat at Barnes's feet. The ball of saliva hit the ground in front of him, gathering a coat of dust as it rolled toward his boots. Barnes's anger increased as the dirt-covered ball of moisture, shaking like a brown gob of jelly, stuck to the toe of his boot. Glaring, he took a step toward the old man.

"That's it, Ray, let's go." Danly's voice was calm, but insistent.

Reluctantly, Barnes turned and followed Danly to the barbed-wire gate of the Army compound, one block away.

As they entered the officers' club, Barnes felt a bracing swath of cool air brush across his face. It carried with it a faint, musty smell and the odor of stale beer. He could see nothing; constricted from the searing brightness outside, his pupils were having trouble adjusting to the cool darkness of the club. He blinked his eyes rapidly, trying to hurry the adjustment process along.

Danly, using a pilot's technique to preserve night vision in the presence of bright lights, had kept one eye closed for several minutes as they approached the club and had no trouble seeing when they entered. He smiled at Barnes's momentary blindness.

"Don't worry about it," he said, steering Barnes toward the bar, "there's hardly anything in here worth seeing anyway. Mostly a bunch of rear echelon goof-offs pretending they're fighting the war."

"What do you mean?"

"Barnes, only one person in ten over here is directly involved in the fighting. Of those that aren't, some just basically sit on their asses. With the exception of the medical people and a few engineers, most of the people in here fit into that category."

"Aw, Mike, they're probably doing their part."

"Good of you to think so. Wait'll you see what they think of you." Danly motioned to the bartender for two beers and sat down on a stool.

• • •

The air-conditioning units protruding from the walls hummed loudly as they strained in their battle against the sweltering, moisture-laden air that seeped in from outside. Intermittent clanking sounds resounded periodically from the unit nearest the bandstand, as if its bearings were intent upon colliding with one another until they all were reduced to metallic rubble. The jukebox was losing the decibel war with the noisy air conditioner, and the music was at times barely audible.

Barnes cupped his hand around his ear and leaned toward the jukebox. He could barely hear the faint lyrics: *"We got to get out of this place, if it's the last thing we ever do."*

"How 'bout turning that thing up," he shouted to the bartender, a heavyset sergeant who was talking to a captain at the other end of the bar. The sergeant ignored him.

Barnes nudged Danly, who was sitting on the next stool. "That's one song that shouldn't be played softly." Danly, engrossed in writing a series of numbers on a piece of paper, did not respond.

"The words are right on, though," Barnes said, leaning closer to Danly. "Gettin' out of this damn country is something to look forward to. The day I wave bye-bye to Vietnam will be one happy day."

Danly cocked an eyebrow. "I can hear you, Barnes, so get your nose out of my ear. I'm not all *that* fond of you."

Barnes grinned and sat up straight. "Okay, but you gotta admit it's a good song."

"It's wonderful," Danly said sarcastically, still concentrating on his column of numbers, "but I'm not planning on going anywhere until my year is up. You leave early, it's either on a stretcher or in a body bag. I'll wait."

"Yeah, yeah," intoned Barnes. "The real reason is you just like this shit. Hey, Sergeant! We need some beer here."

The sergeant and the captain both stared at Barnes before the sergeant finally walked slowly to the cooler. The captain continued to stare, frowning.

"What are you doing, Mike?" asked Barnes, as he

pushed some military script toward the bartender.

"Keeping score."

"What?"

"Keeping score; we're 26,761 bodies ahead," said Danly gravely.

Barnes was puzzled. "How in the hell can you figure . . . ?" He stopped, realizing he'd been taken in. "Fuck you, Danly. Go ahead and play with your numbers, I'm going to see what's going on."

He swung around on the bar stool so that his back was resting against the bar. What he saw pleased him. Many more people had come into the club since he and Danly had arrived, and that meant there was bound to be some nurses around. Some people were wearing civilian clothes, but most were in uniform. At one table, four men were wearing Class A's. Barnes shook his head in wonder. Why the hell would anybody wear a dress uniform in Vietnam? Dumb. Then he noticed that almost everyone's fatigues were freshly laundered and sported razor-sharp creases. Starched jungle fatigues? That was even stupider than wearing dress uniforms. He looked down at his own fatigues. They were reasonably clean, but very wrinkled. Well, he thought wryly, you can tell who's been living right around here.

Continuing to scan the room, his gaze finally settled upon two women sitting at a table near the bandstand. Barnes could not make out their insignia to see what their rank was, but he figured they had to be nurses. One had medium-length, golden hair, and was a little overweight. The other, who was laughing merrily at something, was slender and had close-cropped dark hair. Barnes felt an odd pang and realized that he had not talked to, seen, or even been remotely near a Caucasian woman in months. In fact, he had not even thought about a woman recently; he'd been so tired and preoccupied the past couple of weeks, all he'd cared about was food and sleep.

The two women were carrying on an animated conversation, and he found it a pleasure just to watch their movements. After living in close quarters with nothing but males and being subjected to a never-ending panorama of nose-picking and ass-scratching, this was a slice of heaven. The way the blonde lifted her chin and gave a soft jerk of her head to swing her bangs away from her eyes, and the way the brunette would gracefully take her cigarette from the edge of the ashtray, gently purse her lips and then slowly tilt her head back as she brought it to her mouth made him ache for female companionship.

He hopped off the stool. "Think I'll go talk to some ladies, Mike."

Danly did not look up. "I'm sure they'll be thrilled."

Approaching the women, Barnes felt confident. He was better than average looking, but more importantly, he was a combat soldier. She could never mistake him for one of the garrison troopers he'd seen all over around Qui Nhon— guys who never got dirty, who slept in actual beds in air-conditioned quarters, who strutted around in starched fatigues—in short, guys who were . . . well, soft. His fatigues were neither fresh nor ironed, but they had sewn on them the one thing that really counted: aviator wings. The women would have to know that he was one of those people who hung his ass out, a man with courage enough to brave the worst of it. Hell, anyone ought to respect that. He chuckled. What did they call aviator's wings in flight school? Leg spreaders. Humming happily to himself, he strolled to their table.

"Hi, mind if I join you?" he asked, and without waiting for an answer, slid a chair out and sat down next to the brunette. "My name's Raymond," he smiled. "What's yours?"

She stared at him for several seconds. "*Lieutenant* Burnett," she said coolly.

Danly completed his calculations and felt good. With the money he was saving, even after sending his parents $200 every month, he would be able to buy a sports car when he got back to the States. A fine sports car. *If* you get back to the States, a small voice chided him. He had to smile. There it was again. Whenever he started making plans for after his tour, which was rarely, the small voice would suddenly come forth to remind him that a return to the good ol' U.S.A. was anything but a certainty. He didn't like and seldom bothered to think about the end of his tour—not because of fear or superstition, but because he didn't see much point in torturing himself.

It seemed as if every time someone started dwelling on the topic, that person would end up depressed. He remembered Kramer, who had had a terrible time of it during his last month in Vietnam. When he had thirty days remaining, he tried to get off of flight status. With twenty days to go, he had begun sleeping in a bunker, and with one week to go, had started wearing his flak jacket and steel pot all day long, making sure he was never more than fifty feet away from the nearest bunker. It had been funny, but also pathetic.

Not me, mused Danly. Until my tour's up, I'll just keep flying. Wanna bet? asked the voice. To the last day if I have to, answered Danly. The hell you will, said the voice. Danly sipped his beer and smiled. If the flight surgeon knew I was carrying on a conversation with a little voice in my head, I could get a section eight and go home right now. Now you're talking, said the voice.

"Excuse me, Mister—" the man paused as he leaned in toward the bar trying to read Danly's faded name tag "—Danly, is it?" It was the captain who had been talking with the sergeant at the end of the bar. His fatigues, heavy with starch, made a crinkling noise as he sat on the stool that Barnes had vacated.

"What can I do for you?" asked Danly without looking up.

"I'm Captain Reynolds," the man said pleasantly. "Where are you from?"

Danly turned to face the man in the sharply creased fatigues and knew without looking that the man's boots would be shined as glossy as patent leather. Another garrison warrior.

"Iowa."

"No, no," laughed Reynolds patronizingly, "I mean where are you from in-country?"

Danly's face was blank. "I'm not *from* 'in-country.' I'm from Iowa."

Reynolds' smile vanished momentarily and he looked coldly at Danly. Then, just as quickly, his smile returned. "Hey," he said, "I know what you mean. I wouldn't want to have to say I'm from this country either. I meant what part of the country are you working in? What's your unit?"

"Central highlands. Fourteenth Cav."

"You based at Pleiku?"

"Yes."

Reynolds seemed pained at the lack of a 'sir.' "Lot of action up there?"

"Unlike around here, yes." Danly permitted himself a thin smile.

Reynolds' studied friendliness vanished. "Mister Danly, I am the officer in charge of the club, and although we like to be hospitable, we also expect certain standards to be maintained. Such as proper decorum and military courtesy. You and your friend exhibit an aura of disdain for those amenities. That will not be tolerated for long. Your friend already seems well on his way to a good drunk, not that that would be unusual in here, but we don't tolerate unruly behavior. Keep your eye on him.

"I also like to be addressed as 'sir' by those of lesser rank. Is all this understood, Mister Danly?"

"Perfectly, sir."

"Good," said Reynolds, getting up from the stool. "Just

one more thing. I know you gentlemen just arrived from
the hinterlands, but next time you come to the club, let's
get a hold of a fresher set of fatigues.''

Danly stifled his impulse to burst out laughing. Jesus! he
thought, this guy acts like he's a club officer in the States.
He watched the captain walk away and then turned to check
on Barnes. There were now three men sitting at the table
with Barnes and the two women. The captain was right
about one thing, Barnes was on his way to a good drunk.

The three crew-cut heads were grinning and Barnes was
fairly certain a joke had just been made at his expense. His
mood had begun to sour even before the three lieutenants
from the engineer corps arrived at the table—both nurses
had remained aloof from the beginning—but their presence
had made the situation worse. They were obviously acquainted with the women and exhibited no friendliness toward him. He thought if he could just talk with the nurses
further without distractions, he could break through their
inexplicable, hostile attitude. But now, with an appreciative
audience, the blonde in particular seemed to delight in being
rude to him.

Were it not for the alcohol he'd consumed, Barnes would
have abandoned the nurses shortly after his initial attempt
to get acquainted. But the belligerence that often welled
within him when drinking made him stay. He was determined to gain some satisfaction from the encounter, although he had no idea what kind of satisfaction it might be.

The blonde now had the full attention of the engineers
as she loudly recounted a story about something that happened at the hospital. Burnett did not appear to be listening;
she sat quietly, ignoring Barnes and gazing vacantly across
the room.

He tugged gently at her sleeve. "Look," he said quietly,

"let's cut the crap. Ever since I sat down, you've been treating me like I had the plague or something. I just don't understand why."

She turned her head slowly, the corners of her mouth tilted upward into a thin, cold smile. "Well, you don't have to stay here, do you?"

"No, but I'd still like an explanation."

"Do I owe you one?" she asked.

"Yeah, I think so." Barnes put his hand on her arm to keep her from turning away. "Nobody likes to be insulted. All I wanted to do was to sit down and talk, have a couple of laughs. If we didn't hit it off, I was going to leave. What's so bad about that?"

She pulled her arm away and raised her eyebrows in disbelief. "Just wanted to talk, huh?"

"Yeah."

She laughed scornfully. "What you really wanted to do was get in my pants, score, put it to me. Or," she said with a cold smile, "do you 'winged warriors' have a different way of referring to it? Probably just 'fuck'—it's easier to spell."

Barnes was taken aback by the intensity of her brief harangue. He was a bit woozy from all the beer, but still her response seemed overwrought. Well, this party's over, he thought ruefully, so what the hell, nothing to lose now. He grinned broadly and was pleased at her surprise. "As a matter of fact, that did cross my mind. So what?"

Angrily she stubbed out her cigarette, almost knocking the ashtray to the floor. "I've seen enough of you asshole pilots to last me forever. You come in here and strut around like you're the only ones fighting the war. You see any American woman and think she should automatically melt, just because you're wearing wings and that's supposed to make you some kind of goddamn hero." She was squinting in anger, her dark eyes radiating contempt. "Big bad gun-pilots. You guys think the war is fun—kill some gooks, get drunk, grab a piece of ass. Well I see what isn't fun: pain and misery; men crying for their mothers, pleading with us not to let them die.

"I haven't seen one of you yet who doesn't enjoy what you do. Go away; go back to your 'fun.'" She grabbed the arms of her chair and jerked it around so her back was toward Barnes.

The others at the table had stopped talking when her voice had risen, and they now stared at Barnes, their hostility evident. Stunned by her vehemence, he started to get up to leave, but then changed his mind and sat back down. Something about her intensity was way out of line. Maybe she'd been jilted by some war-loving pilot and now she hated them all. Whatever it was, he couldn't let it rest.

"Lieutenant, you're wrong," he exclaimed, grabbing her arm.

She spun around and glared. "Let go of my arm, dammit!"

"Listen a minute." His tone was half-pleading, half-angry. "I'm not like that."

The largest of the engineers stood up and leaned across the table. "Let go of her," he growled. Barnes eased his grip and she pulled her arm free. Her anger seemed to have drained her energy; she pulled her arms close to her sides and slumped forward, placing her hands in her lap. Barnes could barely hear her.

"Just leave," she said, softly.

"Can't you listen for a minute?" he pleaded.

The tall lieutenant started to walk around the table, his fists clenched. "You heard her, Mister. Leave!"

He stopped abruptly when Danly suddenly materialized between him and Barnes.

"What's the problem?" Danly asked pleasantly.

"Well, well, another pilot," the lieutenant sneered. "No problem; you and your friend are about to leave."

The other two engineers moved around the table, and Danly pivoted slightly to the left, keeping all three men in front of him. "Oh, really?" he said with a smile.

The tall man was surprised; usually people were afraid of him. Most men backed down if he threatened them, but the smiling warrant officer in front of him didn't show the slightest trace of fear. The lieutenant took a tentative step forward and glared down at Danly. "Yeah, you're going to leave all right, and I'm going to help."

Danly continued to smile. "You're too kind. The only problem is: we're not ready to go."

"Forget it, Mike; it's my fight," said Barnes as he struggled to his feet. He knew he was in no shape to fight, especially with someone as big as the lieutenant, but he was too angry to care. "C'mon, fuckhead," he yelled at the man as he tried to push his way past Danly.

"AT EASE!" a voice boomed from the direction of the bar. Danly, Barnes and the engineers froze momentarily, then turned their heads in unison toward the stocky, gray-haired man approaching them.

"What seems to be the trouble here?" he asked pleasantly, coming to a halt next to Danly.

"Colonel," said the tall lieutenant, pointing at Barnes, "that man was harassing Lieutenant Burnett."

Barnes started to protest, but the colonel silenced him with a wave of his hand. "Is that true, ma'am?"

She looked at Barnes and then shrugged. "It was just a misunderstanding, sir. We're on our way out anyway." She stood up, and followed by the blonde, hurried away from the table.

The tall lieutenant wasn't satisfied. "I beg your pardon, sir, but—"

The colonel waved his hand again, this time silencing the engineer. His smile was congenial. "I don't know what transpired here, gentlemen, but it's all over now. I think you should shake hands and then sit down and join me for a drink."

The tall engineer grudgingly proffered his hand to Danly, and Danly shook it.

"Good, good," said the colonel. "Sit."

With some muted grumbling, the men did as they were told. Leaning forward, the colonel spoke directly to Danly and Barnes. "These men," he said, nodding at the engineers, "are well acquainted with me because—as you may have guessed—I'm their commanding officer. Customarily," he continued, shooting a disapproving glance at his men, "we are more hospitable—after all, we're all in the same army." He furrowed his brow and his smile disappeared. "We expect, of course, that guests act in a cordial manner also."

He paused, then smiled again. "So, that being said, let's have a drink."

Barnes quickly finished a beer and started on another as the colonel began a long monologue about the trials of serving in Vietnam. The story was entertaining, but still Barnes found his attention wandering, partly due to the excess beer and partly because his feelings of anger and embarrassment would not subside. He was sure Lieutenant Burnett had made him look like a complete fool. *The bitch.* Why pick on him? Christ, all she had to do was say: I'm not interested; please go away. What in the hell was wrong with her? He guzzled more beer and then noticed he had trouble focusing on the colonel's face. Suddenly he realized the colonel was talking directly to him.

". . . and Mister Barnes, I suspect you were the unwitting victim of the time of the month, or perhaps because the ladies are naturally a little skittish about certain tropical diseases." The colonel paused and chuckled. "You are in luck, though. My men know of an establishment where you would be treated much more favorably by the women therein. Since some of these gentlemen will undoubtedly be making a sojourn there this evening, I think I can prevail upon them to take you along. Lieutenant?"

The tall man shrugged. "Sure, sir. Why not?"

"Good," said the colonel, getting to his feet. He offered his hand to Barnes and Danly. "Enjoy your stay in Qui Nhon and—" he paused, nodding toward the ample posterior of a female captain standing next to a nearby table, "—enjoy the sights." He turned and walked briskly toward the door.

One of the shorter engineers shook his head and laughed. "The colonel's a little different. But," he added hurriedly, "he's a damn good CO. Anyway, we're about to hook it to the 'establishment' the colonel referred to. You interested?" he asked, looking first at Danly.

"No thanks, I've had my case of clap for the year."

"These girls are clean!"

"Yeah, so was the one who gave it to me before. I'll pass."

The man shrugged and turned to Barnes. "How about you?"

Barnes's attention had wandered again and he now sat transfixed, staring at the large woman's buttocks, which moved in and out of focus.

"Hey! Knock knock, Barnes. You going with us?"

The material of the woman's fatigue pants was stretched very tight. Barnes tore his gaze from the woman. "Damn right," he said forcefully, his speech beginning to slur.

━━━━━━

The low-ceilinged room was smoky and dimly lit; Barnes had difficulty seeing clearly. It was as if someone had draped a thin, gauze veil over his face. The silhouettes of things in the room were blurred, and like-colored objects seemed to merge with one another. In the dim, orange light, the faces of the women sitting on the couches appeared fuzzy and out of focus. A peculiar, pungent odor that Barnes couldn't identify permeated the room.

A few of the women had stared at the four Americans as they entered the room, but most had ignored them and continued to talk among themselves in their rapid, singsong cadence. Barnes was surprised; he had assumed that the prostitutes would have approached them immediately, each vying for the chance at G.I. money. But other than a few come-hither smiles, the women acted as though the men weren't even present.

Barnes stood somewhat self-consciously near the door, irritated that he could not focus more clearly. It was like being in a hazy dream.

Opposite the front entrance was a doorway with a heavy curtain of beads that obscured the hallway beyond. Slivers of yellowish light knifed through the tiny spaces between the gently swaying beads and made a vibrating pattern of yellow dots on the floor. The oscillating pattern made Barnes dizzy and he had to look away. The beads suddenly issued an avalanche of soft clicking noises, and Barnes turned his head to see a small woman in a green dress push aside the strands and enter the room. She seemed to glide across the floor, coming to a stop in front of the tall lieutenant. Leaning toward them, Barnes tried to listen to their conversation, but the woman was speaking too softly. Suddenly she burst into laughter, her merry lilt sounding very much out of place in the murky room. Smiling, she turned and disappeared back through the doorway.

"All right, Barnes." The lieutenant turned to him with a leer. "We got you fixed up. And don't worry about it," he added, reaching for his wallet. "This is on the Corps of Engineers." He slapped Barnes on the shoulder and grinned.

Barnes thought briefly of protesting, but then shrugged and grinned at the lieutenant. *What the hell? Why not?* He turned as the small woman returned with another woman, equally small, in tow. The second woman—she seemed to be more of a girl, actually—was different from the others in the room, but the reason eluded him for the moment. She looked up at him, her face impassive. "This way," she said, walking toward the beaded doorway.

The beads closed behind him and he wavered slightly as he started down the hallway after her. Shouldn't have had so much to drink, he thought, might not be able to get it up. Shit, he admonished himself quickly, never failed yet.

He focused on the dainty woman walking in front of him. She was kind of pretty and he felt his penis begin to harden.

Then the difference hit him—it was her hair. The other whores all had long hair; hers was cut short. Her bangs stopped just above her eyebrows; the hair on the side of her head was swept rearward, the ends curling forward underneath her ears, even with the back of her jaw. It was somehow very familiar.

He followed her in to a small room that was illuminated with a single, white light. There was a small cabinet, a bamboo stand with a tin washbasin, and a bed pushed against the wall, over which was hung a white, gauzelike mosquito net. She stopped at the side of the bed, where the netting had been pulled aside, and removed her *ao-dai*. The white light shining on her evenly proportioned body gave her skin the appearance of porcelain, smooth and hard. But the illusion of hardness faded quickly, the soft flesh of her thighs and buttocks undulating as she crawled onto the bed. She lay on her side, facing him. As he undressed, his eyes slowly swept across her body, from the small black triangle below her stomach to her tiny, pointed breasts, to the pretty round face framed with bangs. His heartbeat quickened.

He felt a tremendous urgency to have this woman. Hurriedly he removed his pants and shorts, disappointed to see that he was still not fully hard. He felt a stab of panic— what if he couldn't get a full erection? Quickly he grabbed his penis, stroking it as he moved toward the bed. He clenched his jaw. No, I am not going to miss this, he reassured himself.

Pulling her thighs apart, he knelt between her legs and tried to enter her. Bending, his penis slipped to the side. He cursed, but then began to relax as her small hand grasped it and began to move softly up and down from the base to the tip. Closing his eyes, he felt himself harden under her feathery touch. Moving his hands to cover her small breasts, he massaged them and began to tug at her nipples.

She winced and pushed his hands away. "No, no!"

His good feeling rapidly switched to anger. Another god-damn rejection? Grabbing her buttocks, he pulled her up-ward and plunged into her roughly. She emitted a faint grunt and lay still as he began to push in and out. *Come on, come on.* It was taking too long; he couldn't feel anything. Grimly determined, he kept up the rhythm, the small woman jig-gling roughly beneath him. Yes, there! He could finally sense an orgasm building and he moved faster, sweat drip-ping from his chin onto her tiny chest. It wouldn't be long, he was almost there.

Then the tingling feeling subsided.

Oh, God! I've got to come, he thought, gritting his teeth.

She began to wiggle uncomfortably. "Hurry," she said, as he pushed into her harder. Her hand groped for his tes-ticles and finding them, squeezed gently. "You come," she pleaded in a small voice, "you come."

"Dammit," he moaned. The feeling kept slipping away.

Both her hands were now on his chest trying to push him away. Air escaped from her throat in short grunts as he continued frantically pushing into her. "Stop," she gasped, "you stop."

Oh no, lady, he thought drunkenly, I ain't going to be told to fuck off again. He clapped his left hand across her mouth. His vision blurred by alcohol and sweat, he tried to focus on the body pinned beneath him. Though her features were fuzzy, the short, dark bangs and close-cropped hair that framed her face were not.

No more bullshit, Lieutenant Burnett! You want it and I'm going to give it to you.

Desperately he drove into her faster, the fingers of his left hand tightly squeezing her cheek, his right hand beneath her buttocks, trying to pull her closer around his softening penis.

Then, for a moment, he saw her clearly.

The fuzziness was gone and just above his cupped left hand, he saw the small, almond-shaped eyes squeezed tightly shut, tears trickling from the edges down the sides of her face.

He pushed himself away from her, revolted by what he'd been doing. She lay crying softly, her small chest heaving. She looked very young.

"Oh Jesus, no," he said in anguish, covering his face with his hands. "I'm . . . I'm sorry," he said, his hand moving hesitantly to touch her shoulder.

Opening her eyes, she recoiled and swung her arm, knocking his hand away. She curled into a sitting position, her back against the wall, and stared at him with hate-filled eyes.

He backed away and dressed as rapidly as he could. Taking all the money from his wallet, he stepped forward and placed the bills on the end of the bed.

"I'm sorry," he said, his voice shaking, "I didn't mean to hurt you." He searched her face for some response.

She sat immobile, staring at the opposite wall.

Barnes turned and rushed from the room. As he walked quickly down the hall toward the beaded doorway, the woman in green stepped from the shadows. Stopping abruptly, Barnes looked down into her smiling face.

"You have fun?" she asked sweetly.

He nodded dumbly and fled through the beaded doorway, across the hazy, orange-hued room and out the front door. Sour bile burned his throat and nose as he leaned against the building and vomited.

CHAPTER 15

APRIL 11, 1968
CAMP ENARI

Gray walked slowly along the shoulder of the road, his jungle boots kicking up small clouds of red dust, which hung for a time in the still air, then settled slowly to the ground. To his right, the Pentaprime-covered road glistened under the baking heat of the sun, stretching like a wide, flat ribbon of moist licorice toward the main gate. Oblivious to the speeding jeeps and the occasional deuce-and-a-half that lumbered by, he moved as if in a trance. Head bowed, he shuffled forward, the bag of supplies from the PX swinging loosely from his hand, bumping gently against his thigh.

It was getting worse. At first he thought it was just one of those things. After all, everyone had trouble sleeping now and then. But if he did not start sleeping normally soon, he was in trouble. It had been sporadic at first, but now it was happening almost every night. He would wake up sweating, or sometimes holding tightly to the sides of his cot, his body rigid. It was difficult to get back to sleep, and when he did, he would sleep fitfully, often to awaken again.

It had to be nightmares, but about what? He never re-membered once he awoke.

"How ya doing, sir?"

Startled, Gray jerked his head up, causing his cap to flip off. Several feet to his left, two bare-chested men were attempting to dig out part of a collapsed ditch. The one who had spoken leaned on his shovel and looked at Gray with a mixture of amusement and apprehensiveness. It was his experience that officers didn't usually take kindly to being embarrassed.

Sheepishly, Gray bent over and retrieved his cap. "I'm fine," he said to the two men. "If you guys can surprise the Charlies like you did me, we gotta be winning."

"I'm a cook, sir," said the man leaning on the shovel. "Only way we can kill anybody is with food." The other man grinned. "So if you can march them motherfuckers into the mess hall, sir, we can fix their asses good."

Gray laughed. "That," he said emphatically, "I can be-lieve."

His spirits buoyed momentarily, he began to walk faster and soon came upon the side road that led to the troop area. He turned right, walked a few paces and then stopped. Another joke about killing, and he'd laughed. Nothing wrong with that, really—or was there? Didn't each death joke chip away at the enemy's humanity, making them "its" rather than men, making their deaths easier to accept?

Or was he making too much of it? Had death become a running gag because a mental safety valve was needed? Were the jokes just a whistling-in-the-graveyard balm to soothe the fear that lurked beneath the surface? . . . *Not me, Jack. They're not going to get my ass. . . . How 'bout an-other chorus of the "Body Bag Song"? Okay: You're goin' home in a body bag, doo dah, doo dah. . . . How does the scoring go again? Well, you get four points for an armed gook, three if he's unarmed, two points for a woman and one for a kid. What if the woman's pregnant? Then ya get one and a half—har, har. . . . Another song? Sure: Oh do*

you remember sweet Nguyen from Pike; shot through the
ass as she ran 'cross the dike; zapped her old man while he
hid in the grass; reloaded the minis to blast some more
ass. . . .

Suddenly, Gray realized there were men staring at him
from the doorway of a nearby barracks. How long have I
been standing here like an idiot? he wondered. Any more
of this and they'll be coming after me with a butterfly net
like they did for Horvath. I don't want that; I want to keep
flying. I just don't want to kill anybody anymore.

He resumed walking down the road, depression settling
on him like a heavy, stifling blanket. I've got to start sleeping normally, he thought. A tired pilot is dangerous. Might
make a mistake and kill somebody.

The irony of his words hit him, and in spite of his depression, he had to laugh aloud. Kill somebody if you do your
job right—kill somebody if you do it wrong. In the end,
the joke's on you.

YA KRONG RIVER, WEST OF KONTUM

Innocent looking as the sampans were, something about
them still caused Captain Miller to be suspicious. He
wheeled his LOH back around to the right and made another
pass over the long, narrow boats. Six hundred feet above,
Barnes also banked sharply in an attempt to keep Miller's
LOH in sight. The C-model's rotor system made its familiar
thick popping noise as the broad, heavy blades slapped
against the air.

There were seven sampans in the small flotilla. Barnes
was too high to see their cargoes with any clarity, but the
boats appeared to contain an assortment of baskets and bags,
which he guessed to be full of rice. The men in the boats
ignored the clatter above them and continued poling, moving
the boats steadily upstream.

"Miller smells a rat," said Webb, beating his hand on his thigh in time with a song by the Rolling Stones. The ADF radio was tuned to the Armed Forces Radio Network, and in anticipation of a slow day, Webb had turned the volume up higher than normal.

"Yeah, sure does," said Barnes, yawning. "Better turn that thing down in case he comes across something."

"But it's the Stones, sir," pleaded the crew chief, his right boot tapping on the metal floor.

Webb laughed as he turned the music down. "War is hell, Kittle."

Barnes wore a sour expression as he watched Miller and Snead flit around the riverbank near the boats. The flight had been on its way to the AO, a sleepy-looking valley south of Polei Kleng, but Miller had stopped to check the sampans. Why take a chance on screwing up an easy day? Barnes wondered. The AO was undoubtedly as cold as could be. The only creatures sneaking around the jungle in that valley were monkeys.

Barnes had come to believe firmly in Danly's idea about acquiring an instinct for trouble, and he'd bet his life—which is just what he did every time he totally relaxed on a mission—that there were no NVA in that godforsaken valley. Just why they were assigned to search it was a major mystery to him, but he'd long since given up trying to figure out the reasons why certain orders were given. Why fight it? All they would have had to do for the rest of the afternoon was to poke around some more in the AO, and then get on back to Enari where the cold beer waited. Too bad Miller got curious.

Barnes felt like he needed a break and he motioned for Webb to take over the controls. Leaning back, Barnes closed his eyes. Since returning from Qui Nhon, he discovered to his chagrin that he had lost his enthusiasm for flying, his eagerness for combat, and worst of all, his sense of humor.

In addition to his disturbing lethargy, other concerns weighed heavily upon his mind. He was still bothered by his behavior with the prostitute, although he at least could understand why it had happened. But that was more than he could say for the run-in with Lieutenant Burnett. Her venomous attitude remained a puzzle. Just because he enjoyed and took pride in being a gunship pilot, it didn't mean he loved the war itself. Why couldn't she understand that?

He had always considered himself to be an honorable, ethical person, but the encounters with the two women now had him questioning his morality. And he didn't know how to deal with that. What he did know was that his self-confidence had been dealt a blow when he'd been shot down near Ben Het, and that his interactions with the women weren't helping that situation any. He fervently wished that he'd never gone near Qui Nhon.

Webb's tap on the shoulder roused him from his thoughts and he opened his eyes. He looked in the direction Webb was pointing. The boats were near a sharp bend in the river, where it branched to the northwest and to the east back toward Kontum. Thick groves of trees bordered the eastern fork on both sides. Abutting the groves was a patchwork of irrigated fields, each bordered by lines of trees and scrub vegetation. The LOHs continued to buzz the flotilla as it turned east at the fork in the river. The men in the sampans, who had previously ignored the helicopters, now were casting occasional, nervous glances skyward. They began to steer the boats close to the riverbank as Miller's LOH came to a low hover directly above the lead sampan.

Barnes began to feel edgy. If nothing happened, they would be on their way to Enari within the hour. But he had a growing feeling that he was going to have to wait longer for the beer than he'd originally planned.

Gray hoped no one but Danly would be in the tent. Everyone would know eventually, but the longer he could keep it from being common knowledge, the easier it would be

on him. At least Hill was gone, flying in an LOH on his
day off—some people just could never get enough action
to satisfy them. If Hill were to hear what he was going to
tell Danly, there would be trouble. He could picture Hill
accusing him of cowardice, which would naturally precipitate a fight. He was glad that that could be avoided. He
was not afraid of Hill; he just didn't want to go through the
hassle. Gray believed Danly would understand—he felt very
certain of that. In any event, his mind was made up and he
had to tell somebody.

He entered the tent and walked slowly toward his bunk.
Besides Danly, who lay on his cot reading a book, the only
people in the tent were Reinke and Winters. Sitting in the
far corner, they were concentrating on their card game. Gray
was relieved—maybe it could be done without everybody
knowing the entire story.

He sat down on his cot and tried to decide how to explain.

Danly looked up from his book. "What's the matter,
Steve? You sick?"

Gray shook his head. Well, here goes, he thought nervously. "Mike, I'm getting out of guns. I don't want to
kill anybody anymore," he said softly.

Danly lowered the book to his chest. He did not appear
surprised. "Getting out's fine," he said, keeping his voice
low, "but you better keep your reasons to yourself, otherwise you're going to put up with a lot of shit. You're sure
it's what you want to do, huh?"

Gray was relieved; Danly's opinion was important to him.
He had doubted that Danly would think badly of him, but
now he knew for sure that he had no cause to worry. "Yes,
I'm going to ask for a transfer tomorrow," he replied,
relaxing and letting his voice return to its normal volume.

Danly put his index finger to his lips, but it was too late.
Reinke had heard the last part of the sentence. "Transfer?
What's going on?"

Gray shrugged. "I just want out of guns, that's all."

"What the hell for?"

Gray hesitated. He should have made sure he talked to Danly in private. Danly was probably correct; the others wouldn't understand.

"Come on, Steve," pressed Winters. "What for?"

"You don't like us anymore?" Reinke asked, pretending his feelings were hurt.

"Get off his ass," said Danly. "It's personal."

Gray waved Danly's comment aside; he was suddenly weary of continually trying to conceal his feelings. "It doesn't matter, Mike. I'll tell 'em." He looked up at Winters, who had walked over and was standing next to Danly's cot. "I don't want to kill anybody anymore."

"What?" asked Winters, amazed. "Steve, you're in the wrong place for that attitude. In case you haven't noticed, there's a whole bunch of short guys in black pajamas willing to shoot your ass."

Reinke laughed. "You know what's going to happen if you ask for a transfer, don't you, Steve? Patterson's liable to put you in slicks. That ought to be enough right there to make you want to kill somebody. A slick driver?" He shook his head in disgust. "Goddamn, Steve. Use your head."

Gray managed a thin smile, but it quickly faded as Winters leaned forward with a patronizing grin. "It's because of Kontum, ain't it?"

Danly tossed his book aside and sat up. "Drop it," he said to Winters.

"Steve, forget those people, man. What the hell's the difference? It was just another dink kid who'd've grown up to be a VC."

Leaping to his feet, Danly grabbed Winters and pushed him toward the door. "I told you to fucking drop the subject!"

"Mike! Let it go," said Gray. He stared at the floor. "The Kontum thing's part of it," he said wearily, "but not all. Look, I'm tired of guns; I need a change. Let's leave it at that."

Danly glowered at Winters. "His reasons for wanting out

aren't for public consumption. You got any problem with that?''

"No," Winters replied, backing away. "No problem. I'm not going to say anything."

Danly shifted his gaze to Reinke. "Harry?"

"Doesn't matter to me, Mike. I forgot already."

Returning to his bunk, Danly sat down. "Steve, unless you want to get harassed to death, you better keep all this to yourself. Whatever you do, don't tell Patterson your real reason for wanting a transfer."

Gray nodded. "I suppose you're right." He no longer felt as good about letting the truth out as he had thought he would.

━━━━━━━━━━

Buffeted by the small gale blowing from the LOH's rotor blades, the men in the lead sampan crouched lower among the rice bags and baskets. Suddenly, near the stern, the swirling wind plucked the straw hat from the head of one of the men. He leapt to the side of the boat in a vain attempt to grab the hat before it flew into the water. Behind him, rising like a brown-sheeted ghost, the large piece of burlap he had been sitting on began to move toward him. Flung by the churning vortex, it hit the man's shoulders and clung to him momentarily, then whipped away, sailing off in the direction of the hat.

Now uncovered, neatly stacked between two large bags of rice, were a half-dozen AK-47s.

At that moment, however, the LOH was hovering directly over the weapons and neither Miller nor his observer saw them. As the LOH remained in a stationary hover over the sampan, another man in the boat gave a hand signal toward the trees lining the bank.

Barnes was jolted by Miller's shrill cry reverberating in his headphones.

Out of position, Barnes cursed as he jerked the cyclic,

swinging the nose of the gunship around and pushing it into a dive. Miller's LOH had darted to the left, dipped toward the bank and then, yawing erratically, had climbed over the treeline and headed for an open field. Snead, in the second LOH, had immediately fired a burst of minigun into the treeline and then had turned to the east, paralleling Miller's course.

Miller's anguished "I'm hit" echoed in Barnes's earphones as he punched off the first pair of rockets. He fired a second pair and turned away. Mackin's gunship was coming in behind him, grenades spitting from the stubby gun in front and curving earthward to explode among the boats. Continuing his turn, Barnes saw Miller's LOH drop to the ground about 150 meters south of the river. It bounced twice, yawed left, and came to rest upright, pointing north.

"Two-six, One-four. I need help. One-one's now getting fire from the south."

Turning toward the downed LOH, Barnes saw Snead's ship spit a stream of tracers at the nearest treeline and then break sharply away.

"One-four, we'll be there in zero one, coming in from the northwest with a right break."

"One-four, roger."

"You copy, Two-nine?"

"Affirmative."

Lining up for the attack, Barnes suddenly realized how energized he felt. For the moment, anyway, his lethargy had vanished. The excitement, the noise, the sudden peril—all were tonics for his soul.

He was coming to recognize that risk was a fine narcotic; it energized and calmed simultaneously. His power of concentration increased exponentially. Though every nerve ending clamored for attention simultaneously, no signal was lost; each impulse registered sharp and clear. Yet you could pick and chose among them, putting the body on "automatic pilot" and letting the mind focus on the most important thing.

In the dive toward the target, Barnes's hands and feet controlled the aircraft, but his mind was detached. Peering through the iridescent circle in the rocket sight, the things at the periphery of his vision faded like the edges of an overexposed photograph. Barnes felt as if he were looking down a long tunnel while one, then two, then three pair of fiery red dots sped away from the rocket tubes toward the trees that filled the distant opening. As the dots merged with the trees, they mushroomed into bright yellow flashes, jolting Barnes from his target fixation.

He blinked and the world returned: the smoking trees grew rapidly larger and the ground rushed at the windshield. He quickly turned the gunship away from the target and began to climb.

"Two-six, One-four, we're going to try and pick them up."

Banking hard, Barnes tried to spot Snead's LOH as it swooped in fast from the north. The gunship shuddered, a strong one-to-one vibration shaking through the aircraft with metronomic precision. Everything in front of him jiggled, and for a few brief moments, Barnes saw two LOHs flaring steeply near the ground. The two merged into one as the gunship's vibrations waned, and Barnes saw Miller and his observer rise from the cover of a shallow ditch and run toward the landing LOH.

They only made it a few feet before bullets from the treeline stopped them, the observer seeming to rise as if in the power of some unseen force before slumping back to the ground. Barnes made another tight turn, passing directly over the LOHs as the gunship's nose swung back toward the treeline. He craned his neck to keep Snead's helicopter in sight. A man leapt from its left door and sprinted toward Miller and his observer. But then the LOHs disappeared from Barnes's sight beneath the gunship, and he returned his attention to the target. He began a dive, once again framing the trees in the glow of the rocket sight.

CHAPTER 16

**APRIL 30, 1968
CAMP ENARI**

Stepping into the crowded room, Patterson let his gaze sweep across the assembled pilots, pausing momentarily as he looked into Danly's cold stare. He strode to the metal desk, which was located directly in front of the briefing map hanging on the wall, and placed on the desktop the tablet of paper he'd been carrying, taking care that it was positioned in the approximate center. He nudged the tablet with his forefinger, moving it so its edges were perfectly parallel with the sides of the desk.

The wrinkled jungle fatigues and the unkempt appearance of some of the pilots contrasted sharply with Patterson's crisply starched fatigues and his boot-camp haircut. Standing perfectly erect, he folded his arms across his chest and once again let his gaze sweep the room. Some of the pilots looked away or fidgeted nervously when his eyes met theirs, and he smiled inwardly. He believed in using intimidation to command.

"I have a list," he said sharply, his voice loud and hard, "of unsatisfactory conditions within this troop." He reached forward and tapped the yellow tablet emphatically with his index finger. "And there should not be so many things wrong that I should have to make a list." He frowned, still thumping the tablet with his finger. "I don't like making lists."

He began to pace back and forth in front of the large map. "Nor do I like wasting time discussing standards for behavior and appearance that all officers, even warrants, should be aware of." He stopped and leaned toward the assembled men, his jaw jutting forward like the prow of a ship. "*But,* it appears to be necessary. Now I'm not going to go through the list item by item, because," he paused for sarcastic emphasis, "I don't have that much time."

Sitting between Barnes and Danly near the back of the room, Spradling rubbed his forehead with his fingers and, through the spaces between them, peered at Patterson. "Oh goody," he muttered softly. "He's going to keep it short and simple, like his dick and his brain."

Biting his tongue, Barnes fought to keep from laughing. Danly, however, just continued to stare at Patterson with the same impassive expression he'd had when Patterson first entered the room.

"Your platoon leaders," Patterson continued, "will be going over the deficiencies with you, one by one, but there are some that warrant special emphasis."

"Warrant? Freudian slip?" whispered Spradling.

Patterson's lips parted in a thin, mirthless smile. "So I'll just take this opportunity to discuss those with you now. First of all, there is the matter of military courtesy. Now I know we all work closely together in the air and on the fight line, and that it is somewhat cumbersome and inconvenient to salute and address your superior officers as 'sir' all the time. That's fine and our policies regarding courtesies during those activities take that into account." He frowned again. "However, there is no excuse for not maintaining the proper courtesies at all other times. As a matter of fact, I was just told yesterday by a section leader that two warrant officers passed by him near the PX and without saluting, addressed him by a nickname."

"Is Horvath back?" mumbled Spradling, still hiding behind his hand. Barnes couldn't suppress his laugh and did his best to turn it into a cough. The resulting croak attracted Patterson's attention. His eyes searched the back of the room and finally locked with Danly's. He suspected that Danly's large moustache hid a smirk, but he could not be absolutely sure. He glared at Danly for several moments before resuming his pacing.

"From here on out," he thundered, "the proper courtesies will be employed! Now, the second issue has to do with proper appearance, or more accurately," he paused, his eyes narrowing, "the lack thereof. It would be impractical to insist upon starched and pressed fatigues, but it is not impractical to insist upon clean ones. I will not tolerate further the dirt-, oil- and grease-stained uniforms that some of you people favor—and are sporting even at this moment."

He walked behind the table and paused again. "Nor," he barked, slapping the table for emphasis, "will I tolerate the hirsute appearance that has become the fashion around here lately. You people are not in some goddamn commune; this is the United States Army! From now on your haircuts *will* be regulation. There are also a number of you with moustaches, and as I'm sure you are aware, this is permitted under current regulations. However . . ." Patterson paused again, standing at parade rest with his jaw jutting forward.

Has this guy been taking drama lessons, wondered Barnes, fighting his urge to laugh. Either that or he thinks he's a reincarnation of MacArthur. Please, lord, don't let me laugh. Make it one of the others, not me.

". . . I feel strongly, and I might add, so does the colonel, that all the Fu Manchu and handlebar moustaches detract from the image this unit wishes to present. Therefore it is my desire that all the men under this command have either neatly trimmed moustaches or bare upper lips by zero eight

hundred tomorrow morning. I know you gentlemen will
wish to cooperate.''

Barnes looked at Danly, whose moustache drooped well
below the corners of his mouth. He nudged Danly and raised
his eyebrows in question. Shaking his head slowly, Danly
continued to stare impassively at Patterson.

"All right," said Patterson, resuming his pacing, "that's
enough on that subject." He smiled. "It is now my pleasure
to present some good news. Captain Miller, who as most
of you know was shot down west of Kontum yesterday, is
reportedly doing well at the Seventy-first Evac and will be
transferred to a hospital in Japan in a couple of days. Although wounded in the shoulder and both legs, the doctors
say he should recover fully. Chief Warrant Officer Richard
Hill, who rescued Captain Miller, is also at the Seventy-
first, but will be rejoining us in a week or so. He has two
superficial leg wounds.

"For those of you unaware of the circumstances of the
action involving Captain Miller and Mister Hill, I'll give a
brief description. Captain Miller discovered an arms cache
being transported by a group of sampans. The cache, incidentally, was recovered by our infantry units and included
about sixty AK-47s and thousands of rounds of ammunition.
In addition, the bodies of more than twenty NVA were found
as a result of helicopter and artillery fire.

"In any event, after Captain Miller made the discovery,
the enemy opened fire, severely damaging his helicopter
and wounding his crew. Captain Miller was forced to land
in a nearby field and subsequently came under heavy fire.
A loach flown by Mister Snead with Mister Hill riding as
observer landed immediately near the downed aircraft. As
Captain Miller and . . . uh . . . um . . . I don't recall the observer's name, attempted to run to the other loach, they
came under withering fire. The observer was killed.

"Mister Hill, with complete disregard for his own safety,
jumped from the second loach, ran through the hail of fire,
lifted Captain Miller up to his shoulders and, despite his

own leg wounds, carried him to the rescue aircraft.''

Patterson was talking quickly, his eyes bright, his arms moving rapidly up and down as he described the incident. Barnes watched him with growing fascination. He really loves this stuff, thought Barnes.

Patterson smiled broadly. ''There was some humor in all of this. Atop Mister Hill's shoulders, Captain Miller noticed that the loach was sitting in an indentation and that his head was at the same level as the main rotor blades. Thinking he was being rescued from the NVA only to be chopped up by Mr. Snead's loach, he started screaming, 'Put me down! Put me down!'

''Mister Hill, running with his head down and thinking that Captain Miller was delirious, just kept heading for the loach. Waiting for them, Mister Snead alertly tilted the edge of the rotor disk upward to give them more clearance. But Captain Miller continued to yell and wiggle frantically, causing Mister Hill to lose his balance and fall. He then dragged Captain Miller the rest of the way. Mister Snead, who had also been wounded while waiting, helped pull Captain Miller aboard and then flew out of the area. They will all receive Purple Hearts. In addition, Captain Miller has been put in for a Bronze Star, Mister Snead for a DFC, and Mister Hill for a Silver Star.''

Patterson beamed as murmurs of approval were heard throughout the room. ''It's a good thing Mister Hill wasn't any taller or faster, or Captain Miller would now be bald,'' he said, smiling.

Danly's voice cut through the ensuing laughter. ''Sir?'' Patterson's smile faded. ''What is it, Mister Danly?''

''What about Sergeant O'Brien?''

''Who?'' asked Patterson, looking puzzled.

''The man who was killed,'' Danly responded dryly. ''Was he put in for a medal?''

Anger flashed in Patterson's eyes; he'd been caught off guard. ''Well, uh . . . certainly he'll be awarded the Purple Heart posthumously. We all regret his loss.'' His face hardened again, his jaw once more thrusting forward resolutely. "These men have exemplified the spirit of the cavalry and have brought great credit upon themselves and this unit. I'm fully confident that we all will act with similar courage and fortitude in the future. You gentlemen are released to your platoon leaders."

He picked up his yellow tablet and strode resolutely from the room.

━━━━━━━

"You gonna trim it up, Mike?" asked Gray, opening a can of beer.

"They don't make blades that sharp," said Spradling.

"Yeah, Mike," asked Barnes, "are you going to accede to—what did Patterson call it?—his 'desire'?"

"No," replied Danly, leaning back against the row of sandbags. "Christ, there's even Fourth Division staff officers running around looking like Yosemite Sam; he's not going to go to the mat over this one. It's just more harassment."

The four men sat on the ground outside the officers' club using a wall of sandbags as a backrest. The horizon to the east glowed yellow against the blackness of the moonless sky.

"Lot of flares over there south of Pleiku. Must be some kinda shit going on," said Barnes.

"Yeah, somebody run and tell our exalted leader," said Spradling. "He'll probably want to hike his ass over there and demonstrate his"—Spradling shifted to Patterson's short, clipped pattern of speech—"'courage and fortitude in the future.'"

The laughter faded into silence as they continued to watch the pulsing glow several miles in the distance. A stream of tracers, barely visible from that distance, erupted from the blackness above the flares. They watched in silence as the

Air Force gunship spit its deadly cargo. As many times as they had seen it, the work of the minigun-laden C-130 still evoked a sense of awe.

Gray lit a cigarette. "I think you ought to think about this moustache thing, Mike. You embarrass him on this and he's really gonna be pissed."

"That's right," agreed Spradling. "He'll be all over you like maggots on a dead dink's ass."

Danly shrugged. "He can't dislike me more than he already does. Fuck 'im."

"I don't know, Mike," Gray said slowly. "I don't think it's worth the trouble. In light of things, I'm trimming mine up."

"In light of what?" asked Spradling.

"What about you, Ray?" asked Danly, quickly, not wanting Gray to reveal his problem. "You gonna toe the line?"

Barnes fingered the sparse wisps of blond hair on his upper lip. "Yeah, I guess so."

Spradling laughed. "What the hell for, Raymond? Nobody can see it anyway. Only way Patterson would know you've got it is to kiss ya."

"Stick it, Wendell! You talk big; what are you going to do?"

Spradling twirled one of the scraggly tails of hair at the corner of his mouth. "I'll keep mine as is. I figure he's just out to hang Mike; he doesn't give a shit about me. He figures I'm a hopeless case anyway."

"I'll be damned," said Danly. "Patterson and I do agree on something."

━━━━━━━━━

"So what happened with Patterson regarding your transfer request?" asked Danly.

Gray watched the figures of Barnes and Spradling disappear into the darkness as they walked toward the latrine. "He got madder than hell and accused me of being a coward."

"You told him the reason right off?"

"No, I told him the other stuff first, that I wanted a change of pace, a new challenge. He wasn't biting, though, so I finally got tired of screwing around and told him the truth. First he looked at me like I was talking another language. Then he asked me if I was sick."

Danly spit. "The guy's a royal asshole."

"I told him no, of course, and that I wasn't trying to get out of flying. I said I'd fly as much as he wanted, but I would like to do it in slicks. That's when he got really pissed. Said if I was too scared to fly guns then I was too scared to fly anything. He said if I wanted to be permanently grounded, to just say so, otherwise to get the hell out of his office and start acting like a man."

"Jesus!" said Danly. "I wish I knew a way to fix his ass."

They sat silently for several minutes, their thoughts interrupted sporadically by the sounds of raucous laughter from the club.

"Mike," Gray said dejectedly, "I don't know what the hell I'm going to do. I'll keep flying, but I'm afraid there's going to come a situation when I won't shoot and somebody's going to get hurt because of it."

Danly sighed. "Look, Steve, you gotta stop playing head games with yourself. You haven't fucked up anything in the air yet, and you're not going to. All you've got to do is stick it out for a while. I think we can get Hawk to swing a transfer to another unit for you. *He* didn't give you trouble when you told him, did he?"

"No, no. I talked to him before I saw Patterson and he seemed to understand. He just said that he had to get Patterson's approval for a switch to slicks. I told him I'd let him know the outcome of the meeting with Patterson."

"Okay, then we'll both talk to him, but forget the transfer

to slicks. We'll see what he can do about getting you out of E Troop and into another unit.''

Gray remained somber. ''I don't see how he could get that by Patterson.''

''It's a different sort of deal. Hawk could play it up as a trade for some hotshot pilot he could say he heard about. It's damn sure worth a try.'' Danly stood up. ''C'mon, let's get a beer.''

Gray slowly got to his feet. ''No, I'm going to hit the sack.''

''All right; see you later.'' Danly watched Gray walk away. Gray's posture reminded him of a picture he'd seen of a man on the way to the gallows. He was not given to premonitions, but Gray's situation gave him a bad feeling. If Gray's confidence eroded, he could become like Horvath—fearful and uncertain, paralyzed by the frightened babblings of imagined ghosts.

CHAPTER 17

MAY 14, 1968
KONTUM

The deafening whine of the huge twin turbines grew steadily louder, giving ample warning of the impending dust storm. The row of weary men, sitting on the ground with their backs resting against the side of an ammunition bunker, appeared to be oblivious to the growing cloud of red dust behind them. Each was just summoning his energy, however, waiting until the last second to move, like a jackrabbit hunkering down next to a country road, primed to dash across just inches in front of a speeding car.

Poised above the slingload of howitzer rounds like a colossal dragonfly, the giant skycrane generated a mini-hurricane with its whirring, seventy-two-foot rotor disk. The thick, expanding ring of magenta-hued sand and dust was almost upon the men when all but three of them leapt to their feet and raced toward the parked helicopters.

"Aw, fuck it," said Danly. He remained seated. To his left, Spradling and Mackin pressed back against the bunker and pulled their caps down tightly. They hunched their shoulders and tried, like turtles pulling back into their shells, to draw their heads back into the protection of their upturned collars.

"Now you know how Lawrence of Arabia felt on a bad day," shouted Spradling above the noise, just as the dust engulfed them.

"You mean like a dumb fuck?" yelled Danly.

"You got it!"

Sitting next to the open cargo door, Kittle watched the group of officers running toward him. They were barely managing to stay ahead of the swirling dust.

"Why'd they wait so long?" whined the door gunner, a fastidious youth who, ever since he had arrived in Vietnam, had been constantly distressed by his losing battle to stay clean.

"Damned if I know." Kittle spit a brown glob of tobacco juice, which fell short of the doorway and splattered on the metal floor. Seeing the dark, sticky liquid splay across the gray metal flooring, the door gunner moaned and looked away. Kittle leaned out the door. "If you ain't here before that dust cloud, you're staying outside!" he yelled to the approaching figures of Barnes and Winters.

Sand and grit began to tickle Barnes's nostrils as he and Winters scrambled aboard. Swirling threads of dust curled around the edge of the door as Kittle slammed it shut.

"Pardon me, sirs," said Kittle with exaggerated deference, "but this kinda suggests that pilots ain't particularly bright. You could hear that crane coming ten minutes ago. You had time enough to walk over here."

Barnes grinned. "Sure, but there was no challenge in that."

"Challenge? Seems like a matter of common sense to me."

"Doesn't matter. You see, Kittle, common sense isn't a requirement to become a pilot."

"I got news for you, sir: that ain't news."

Barnes laughed, thinking that perhaps Kittle's remark was

more accurate than he'd thought. The noise of the skycrane began to fade. Barnes leaned forward to look out the window and got a strong whiff of his own odor. Three days in the highlands' heat without a shower is the rough equivalent of three unwashed weeks in the real world, he thought. I can hardly stand to be around myself.

On the underarm areas of his fatigue shirt, white lines of salt made jagged patterns, like crooked filaments of frost on a tinted window. He could feel grit on his skin, particularly under the waistband of his shorts and where his collar rubbed his neck. It was like wearing underwear made partially of sandpaper.

An old, dirty hex tent next to the runway at Dak To had been the sleeping quarters for the last two nights and that had contributed to the problem. Barnes had wondered the first night whether it would be dirtier sleeping on the old cots with the dust-laden blankets, or just rolling around on the ground. It was a toss-up, he'd decided.

Winters poked him in the side as the skycrane moved away to the north. "Hey, look at that," he said pointing at two women clad in light blue uniforms of the Red Cross standing near a bunker about sixty yards away. One was bent over at the waist, shaking her head and running her fingers through her hair in an attempt to get rid of the dust. The other woman was halfheartedly brushing her clothes with one hand.

"Not too bad, eh?" said Winters.

"I think you've been out in the bush too long; they look a little too heavy to me," said Barnes.

"Heavy?" Winters exclaimed. "I suppose you'd rather have one of those scrawny hootchmaids. Either one of those donut dollies has got to be better than the last thing you got laid with."

Barnes winced, remembering all too well his last encounter with a woman. "Yeah, maybe so."

"Maybe so, my ass. Unless you got Joey Heatherton stashed away in the tent, these are the best females you've seen in a long time.'' He slid the cargo door open and hopped out. ''The ladies look like they could use some assistance.''

Kittle sent a gob of tobacco juice flying out the door after him. ''Mister Winters ain't going to get anywhere with them. If they was putting out, they wouldn't have to be hangin' around the runway trying to hook a ride. Somebody'd be takin' care of 'em.''

Barnes lay back on the floor, sliding a helmet bag under his head for a pillow. ''Hope springs eternal, Kittle.''

━━━━━━━━

Lieutenant Runnels' piercing voice jolted Danly from his half slumber, and he opened his eyes. From his position at the side of the ammunition bunker, he could see the tall lieutenant striding down the runway by the helicopters, waving a map and yelling at the crews.

''Should we go see what he wants?'' asked Mackin.

''Nope,'' replied Danly, closing his eyes and wiggling his shoulders to get comfortable.

''Only if he invites us personally,'' said Spradling.

''Must be something big going on; he's got his map all spread out and everybody else is crowded around.'' Mackin looked at Danly. ''Wonder why he hasn't called us over there?''

''Because,'' said Spradling, ''he's saving the elite troops for the truly big shit. Besides, Mike's got his copilot down there checking it out.''

''He better not be,'' said Danly. ''Didn't we elect him to go find some beer to take to Dak To tonight?''

''We did indeed, but he's either damn quick or he's failed his mission,'' said Spradling, looking at the group surrounding Runnels. ''Because right at this very moment, Barnes is standing amidst the rest of those highly trained killers.''

Danly shook his head at the information. ''I'll have to speak to the boy. He has no concept of duty.''

They watched as the briefing broke up and most of the men dispersed to their aircraft. Barnes, however, began walking leisurely toward them. Winters quickly joined him. The two men spoke briefly, then Winters nodded and trotted quickly to where Danly was sitting.

"Mike," he said, breathing hard as he came to a stop in front of Danly, "Barnes will tell you about the briefing, but you've got to do me a favor. There's two Red Cross girls over there and I told 'em we'd give them a ride to Dak To. They agreed to meet me tonight if we can get them up there. How about it?"

Danly looked up, amused. "You gotta be kidding. I haven't got room in a gunship for them."

"Come on, Mike, you can do it. It ain't like they weigh five hundred pounds apiece. You won't even know they're there. Look, you're supposed to fly up there in a few minutes to stand by for another mission; I'm going to tell the girls you'll take 'em." Winters turned and hurried off in the direction of the women.

Spradling stood up and watched him go. "He's serious, Mike. There's two women sitting by a bunker over there."

"Wendell, we're not in the taxi business."

"Aw, what the hell?" said Spradling, eyeing the women. "It ought to be all right."

Barnes shuffled up to the ammunition bunker and sat down next to Danly. "The rest of 'em have to go on some mission with C Troop. We're supposed to wait until they take off, then go up to Dak To and stand by. Runnels says we're supposed to contact the Fourth Division TOC when we get there."

"Fine," said Danly, yawning. "Now tell us where the beer is."

"Aw come on, Mike. I didn't have time."

"Go easy on him, Mike," said Spradling. "Winters got us something better."

"First of all, don't be too sure they're better until you've seen them up close, and second of all, it wouldn't matter if they were because they're not going with us.''

"Why not?" asked Barnes.

"We've got a rule about passengers in gunships: there can't be any.''

"Mike, let's not be hasty," said Spradling as he watched the women approach.

━━━━━━━━━

DAK PEK

Old C ration cartons cartwheeled across the scrub grass, blown along by gusts of wind from the approaching storm. A crumpled cigarette package, caught in a tiny cyclone, spun wildly in a circle near Gray's feet. He leaned against the tailboom of the C&C aircraft and kicked absentmindedly at the ground. Despite his uneasiness about continuing to fly gunships, he now had some hope for an end to it. Hawkins had liked Danly's idea of a trade and had contacted a friend who was a platoon leader in the First Cav. A switch looked promising.

There was still pressure, though; Gray knew he couldn't afford the slightest screwup or the transfer could be jeopardized. His stomach growled, and for a moment he felt a burning sensation. He hoped he wasn't getting an ulcer.

The C Troop commander and three other officers were still standing near the front of the aircraft, intently examining a map. Gray shifted his gaze to the darkening northwestern sky. An isolated group of towering, cumulonimbus clouds, their bases merged into a seething dark mass, moved steadily toward Dak Pek. Wide, gray sheets of rain were starting to soak the nearby hills.

Gray shifted irritably. He had no desire to get wet. If the briefing could just get under way, they might get off before the rain arrived. He stared at the circle of officers. *Come on, let's get this show on the road.*

As if responding to Gray's silent plea, Major Ansel began

beckoning the pilots. "Let's go, gentlemen, gather 'round."

Gray stood at the edge of the group and listened as Ansel described the impending mission. Several massive bomb strikes had been made west of Dak Pek the previous night. The Fourth Division commander decided that a damage assessment was now in order, and it had to be accomplished quickly. All available aircraft were going to sweep the target areas simultaneously. Ansel held up his map to show how the whole area had been partitioned into sectors for the reconnaissance, and two large raindrops hit the plastic map cover at the same time, exploding into tinier beads that clung to the transparent surface. Ansel glanced at the sky and then back to the men gathered around him.

"I'll finish this as fast as I can," he said smiling, "but, what the hell, none of us will melt."

"Maybe not, sir," piped a short, redheaded pilot known as Muskrat, "but I kinda like to take showers with my clothes off."

Ansel laughed. "Okay, okay, I'll hurry."

How unlike Patterson, thought Gray as he listened to Ansel complete the briefing. If someone joked during one of Patterson's briefings, he'd be in big trouble. Patterson would take it as an affront to his authority, and he would not forget. Gray regretted not being in C Troop; he was sure Ansel would have honored his request for a switch to slicks.

Rain began to splatter against Gray's back as he hunched over, copying the outlines of the bomb-strike areas from Ansel's map to his own.

"Everybody got it copied? Okay, that's it then. We'll crank in zero five."

Gray turned and started to trot down the row of helicopters toward his own aircraft. Gauging the speed of an approaching wall of rain, he cursed. He would not reach the gunship in time. Quickly he rolled his map into a tube and stuck it inside his shirt. Bent over at the waist, he charged into the barrage of rain.

His feet made loud, slapping noises as they came down on the wet clay, and he suddenly felt foolish. He imagined he looked like an ungainly old man, futilely trying to avoid the elements while helplessly pursuing a departing bus. Finally reaching his helicopter, he scrambled aboard, tossing his soggy cap on top of the instrument panel. He grabbed his helmet bag from under the seat and attempted to dry his head.

"Here, try this," said Platz, the new copilot who had been waiting in the aircraft. "It's more absorbent." He tossed Gray a wrinkled green handkerchief.

"Thanks," nodded Gray.

"Hope I live long enough to be an aircraft commander," said Platz with a sarcastic grin. "Then I'll get to go to briefings in the rain too."

Gray finished mopping his face and stared at the water cascading down the windshield. Nothing was visible beyond the gray curtain of rain. He turned toward Platz and tossed the limp, soggy handkerchief back to him.

"With any luck," he said, thinking of the impending transfer, "you won't have to wait too long."

━━━━━━━━

"Mike," said Spradling, "I want you to meet Cheryl and Candy." Spradling beamed as he made the introduction.

Danly, still leaning against the bunker, did not want to meet them. *Candy? Oh, no. I'm surprised the other one's name isn't Misty or Tawny or some other jerkball, cutesy name.* He looked up and saw two rather plain-looking young women wearing hopeful, expectant expressions.

"Hello, ladies," he said coolly, his own expression not giving any hint of friendliness.

"Mike here is what we call the gun team leader. He's the man you've got to convince. He may look like a hardass, but he's reasonable, so just tell him your story."

Danly shook his head. "I'll save you some time. If you're asking for a ride, the answer—"

"Mike, Mike," Spradling interrupted, "just listen a minute. These girls are in a hell of a bind. Maybe we can help."

Danly shot Spradling an exasperated glance and sighed. "Okay," he said to the blond woman who was now standing directly in front of him. "What is it?"

She squatted, putting one hand on his knee, and looked at him earnestly. Her face was chubby, but her dark green eyes were as pretty as any he'd ever seen. He felt his resolve beginning to crack.

"We've been trying to get to Dak To for two days," she said, "but we can't seem to get a ride. We've got some gifts and some special messages from home for the men up there. It's really important."

"Yes," agreed the other woman, her oval face framed by long brown hair still disheveled from the skycrane's winds. "It really means a lot to them to get these things from home." Her faced brightened. "And Wendell here was such a dear; he said you could probably take us."

"Well, dear Wendell—" Danly paused to give Spradling a hard look "—is sometimes mistaken." He felt the pressure of the blonde's hand on his knee increase and he stared into the face of the woman crouching in front of him. She looked at him sadly, her eyes pleading. He had to look away.

"Please?" she asked softly.

Feeling his resistance fade, he decide to move. Grasping the small hand resting on his knee, he stood up, helping her to her feet in the process. Her lovely, questioning eyes kept staring at him.

"Look," he said uncomfortably, releasing her hand, "I'll let you know in a couple of minutes." He turned and walked toward the parked gunships.

Spradling smiled broadly at the women, winked and gave them the thumbs-up sign.

═══════════

WEST OF DAK PEK, NEAR LAOS

His eyes open wide, Platz gave a long, low whistle. The area below appeared to be completely covered with craters. At their edges, broken trees lay strewn about, splintered by the force of the explosions. It was the first time Platz had seen the destructive power of a B-52 strike, and the desolate, pockmarked ridge reminded him of pictures of the moon.

Gray had instructed his team to begin its reconnaissance at the southwest corner of its assigned sector, where, it now appeared, the heaviest damage had been done. Flying slowly up the side of the long ridge, they searched carefully for any sign that the NVA had been present when the bombs landed. Gray was sure no one on the ground in that area could have survived.

Reaching the northern border of the sector, they turned back south, paralleling the original course two hundred meters to the east. Gray, though he had seen the results of a B-52 strike before, still marveled at the destruction. Huge trees had been split apart as if they were made of straw, and then had been tossed by the explosions into jumbled piles, like so much discarded kindling.

Gradually, the helicopters moved away toward terrain that had not suffered quite as much damage, and the LOHs began to stop and circle more often. They made sporadic reports of bunkers that had been blown open and of small remnants of human bodies. Gray dutifully recorded each report and noted the location on the map. He checked his watch and frowned, they had only been in the area for twenty minutes.

Shifting uncomfortably, he tugged at the soggy clothes clinging to his body. His chest felt sticky hot, and it itched where the weight of the chicken-plate pressed his gritty, wet T-shirt against his skin. He tried ignoring the discomfort, but could not. The heat rash on his buttocks burned, and his feet, encased in clammy wool socks, began to itch. He wiggled his toes and sighed.

Got to concentrate on something else, he thought as he tugged again at the wet material bunched at his crotch. Looking at the torn-up landscape beneath him, he remembered a bomb damage assessment mission he'd flown two months earlier. It had been just a few miles southwest of Dak Pek, not far from where he was now. Before starting the reconnaissance, he had been told the mission had to be completed by 1300, because another bomb strike would start at 1315 just to the north. He hadn't felt comfortable about the times; they were much too close.

Just before twelve o'clock, the crew chief had asked him to look up to the southeast. Very high, in sharp contrast to the deep blue of the cloudless sky, numerous sets of parallel, white lines were tracking directly toward them. Naa, it couldn't be, he'd thought at first, the bombers weren't due for another hour. But there was no denying the contrails. Either the B-52s were going further north, or there had been some foul-up and the helicopters were about to get dumped on. He was not going to take any chances and they had left the area quickly.

When he had looked back, a very large section of the mountainside seemed to be boiling. The treetops shook as the shock waves spread, clearly outlining each wave as the bombs hit. He could still picture the awesome display, the force of the explosions rippling acres of trees as easily as a dropped rock would ripple the surface of a pond.

The mental image faded like a mirage as Gray realized Platz was talking to him.

"After all the shit that was dropped on their heads, you don't think anyone could be alive down there, do you?"

"Sure," Gray replied, "but not close to the point of impact, only along the edge of the strike zone. There's some pretty solid bunkers built all around in this general area, and they'll hold up if they aren't hit directly. Anybody in 'em would have a damn big headache, but at least they'd be alive.''

Platz grunted. "If I were still alive after one of those strikes, I'd be hauling ass out of this valley as fast as I could."

"The NVA won't. They're down there somewhere."

Smiling, the two young women listened intently to the instructions Danly was giving. "You've ridden in helicopters before, so you shouldn't be nervous. If, and I'm certainly not expecting any, we have any difficulties, just do exactly what the crew chief tells you to do. These birds may look pretty battered, but they're rock solid."

The women nodded, but their expressions betrayed their lack of confidence in the worn-looking gunships. Seeing their hesitant expressions, Danly suppressed a smile. "If you'd rather not go, I understand," he said, hoping they'd change their minds. He was already regretting his decision to give in and allow them to come along.

The women were silent, and Spradling, who had been leaning against the gun mount, stepped forward quickly. "Come on, ladies," he said with an enthusiastic grin, "this is gonna be fun." Gently he took the arm of the woman named Candy and led her toward his aircraft. "Look, you can cheat death just like the rest of us."

The blonde looked at Danly and smiled nervously. "Okay, let's go," she said gamely, holding out her hand for Danly to help her climb aboard.

The gunships climbed sluggishly, as if protesting the onerous burden of the added weight. As Barnes turned the aircraft toward Dak To, Danly lit a cigarette and reflected upon his decision to give the women a ride. There was little chance of something bad happening, but their presence was still an unnecessary risk. If Patterson knew he was violating the rule about passengers in gunships, he'd have a court-martial convened before the helicopters landed. But that wasn't the main thing that worried Danly. Nor was it the threat to the women's safety—hell, they were at serious risk just being in the country. No, his real concern was just how a woman's presence in the aircraft might affect his decision making in the event of trouble. If there was a mechanical problem, or worse yet, if they were shot at, would he react differently—and possibly less effectively— because she was there?

He glanced back over his shoulder. She was sitting with her knees pressed tightly together, her hands in her lap. Leaning to the left, she craned her neck in an attempt to see the ground. He suddenly wished he had not bothered to look at her. She was so out of place, so foreign to the little world that had become comfortable to him, that her presence was starting to unnerve him.

Turning his head back to the front, he leaned forward and stubbed his cigarette out in the small ashtray mounted underneath the instrument panel. He leaned back in the seat and stretched his legs. Well, he thought ruefully, a tired Huey gunship has become the focal point of my existence. Instead of a helicopter, it's more like a cramped apartment— work in it, eat in it, sleep in it, relax in it, everything but go to the bathroom in it. And sometimes it even smells like I've been doing that.

He sniffed. Gunships always reeked of oil and stale sweat. They were often dirty; they rattled and vibrated; they made strange noises, and though their workhorse durability had saved his ass several times, one of them still might be his coffin one day.

He had always spurned attachments to things, but in spite of himself, he had developed a strong fondness for gunships. He quite simply loved to fly them. It was a visceral feeling, linked to the sound and the smell and the feel of a C-model as it churned its way through the air.

But with a passenger—especially a woman—it just wasn't right.

A mess sergeant or a general's aide would have been out of place sitting in back. But placed between the door gunners cradling their M-60s, the form of a woman was particularly disconcerting. The C-model was a brutish gun platform with no room for extras. Especially no room for reminders of gentle touches and soft laughter.

Funny, mused Danly, it doesn't take all that long for the gentleness of a woman to become so foreign. Once again, despite his intention not to do so, he looked back over his shoulder. She still sat primly, although more relaxed, gazing at a group of small, puffy clouds floating lazily over the rice paddies to the south. Her lips were parted ever so slightly, the corners of her mouth turning upward at some private, pleasant thought.

For an average-looking woman, she sure looks beautiful, thought Danly.

His reverie was broken by the voice of Holman. "Bulldog Two-six, this is Striker Three."

"Go ahead, Three."

"Roger, got a convoy being hit about ten klicks from Dak To. You ready to copy coordinates?"

Shit! I should've known. "Two-six, affirmative."

"Zulu Bravo, one five zero, zero eight one. Contact Comet Three on up from Larkin two-point-six."

"Two-six, good copy. We're on the way."

Quickly locating the ambush site on the map, he gave Barnes a new heading.

"Hey Two-nine, Two-six. You copy Three's transmission?"

"That's affirmo," responded Spradling cheerily.

Danly shook his head in wonder. To Spradling, Holman's call had about the same impact as if he had told them to "take the girls to the club for a beer." Spradling was probably delighted to get a chance to show off his gunnery skills for the woman. Danly turned to look at the crew chief. "Lopez, tell the woman that we've got to do some shooting, but it's no big deal. Tell her there's no reason to worry.

Tell her just to hang on and we'll get her to Dak To safely. Also, take that box of smoke grenades off the extra armored plate and give her the plate to sit on.''

He watched as Lopez leaned toward the woman, yelling to be heard above the engine noise. She nodded as her eyes grew wider and her hands squeezed one another tightly. Lopez unfastened his seat belt, moved to his right and squatted just to the left of her. He pulled the armored plate out from under the grenade box and slid it under the woman's buttocks as she leaned forward. He tightened her seat belt and gave her a reassuring pat on the shoulder before returning to his position by the door.

Her left foot began tapping nervously on the floor.

Before fastening his shoulder harness, Lopez pulled apart the Velcro strips that held his chicken-plate in place. "I'll give her my vest too, sir."

"No!" snapped Danly, "keep it on."

"But sir—"

"She'll be fine; you're the one who's going to be hanging out the door. Keep it on and strap in." He turned his head quickly and stared out the windshield. He couldn't bear to look at her frightened expression any longer.

Danly watched Barnes out of the corner of his eye, looking for signs of nervousness as they approached the ambush site. There didn't appear to be any, and Danly wasn't really surprised. In the air, Barnes was all right—it was on the ground where he seemed to be slowly tying himself in knots, making life hard for himself by brooding about his mistakes.

Thin columns of smoke twisted skyward in the distance. "That's it," said Danly, pointing at the smoke.

Barnes nodded.

Danly swung the rocket sight down and then put his hands on the flight controls. "Compared to some of the shit we've been seeing lately, this ought to be like a stroll in the park."

"Yeah," Barnes answered, his voice flat.

The ambush had been fierce, but its intent was only harassment, not the destruction of the convoy. After firing several salvos of rockets and a barrage of automatic weapons fire, the attackers had retreated. The brunt of the attack had come from the north side of the road, and four of the convoy's five tanks were pursuing the fleeing NVA into the scrub vegetation at the base of the foothills. The remaining tank had chased a group of attackers a short distance to the south, and had stopped at the creek's edge. Low on ammunition and concerned about getting bogged down in the mud, the tank commander asked Danly to fire into a small orchard on the other side of the water.

Danly decided the NVA would flee in both directions along the creek's edge, where the heavier vegetation provided the best cover. But for the first 150 meters in both directions from the orchard, the cover was sparse. He felt sure the gunships could put enough fire into the orchard to drive them out where the tank could also get a clear shot at them.

"Comet Two, we'll be coming in from the west; we'll try and flush 'em out."

"Roger that. Get their asses outta there."

On his second pass, as he began the break, Danly saw half a dozen men dart from the eastern edge of the orchard toward a group of trees further east along the creek.

"Miguel, they're running east!"

The crew chief stepped out of the doorway onto the skid, and leaning over the gun mount, fired at the men as the aircraft turned. Suddenly he let out a whoop. "All right! The tank got 'em! It must be firing canisters, sir; the gooks just evaporated."

Danly banked back toward the orchard and saw Spradling's gunship turning hard to the right.

"Two-six, I'm getting fire from the west side of that orchard."

"Roger, we got the spot," said Danly. "Ray, walk some minigun up that treeline; they gotta be coming this way too."

Barnes nodded and squeezed the trigger. Tracers disappeared into the leaves about one-third of the way up the rows of trees.

As Danly leveled the rocket sight on the spot where Barnes's first tracers hit, he saw red flashes down between his feet through the chin bubble.

"Two-six receiving fire! They're right below us." He heard several sharp smacking sounds as he rolled the gunship almost on its side in a steep bank.

"We got a couple of rounds through the floor," yelled Lopez.

The horizon was almost perpendicular in the windshield and the gunship shook strongly. Danly rapidly scanned the instrument panel and the console warning lights, relaxing as he saw that everything was in the normal range. Easing the pressure on the controls, he watched Spradling's aircraft spew tracers at the treeline. Three pair of rockets, leaving thin, smoke trails, followed close behind. Two bodies tumbled from the brush onto the riverbank. Spradling may be a screwy bastard, thought Danly, but you could always count on him.

"God-fucking-dammit!" Barnes exclaimed through clenched teeth.

Danly rolled out of the turn. "No sweat, Raymond, we'll get 'em next pass. Everybody okay back there?"

"Yes, sir, no problem," answered Lopez.

Breathing a sigh of relief, Danly began a turn back toward the target. "How much you got left, Ray?"

"Couple hundred in the left; right gun's out."

"I got two pair of rockets; we'll make one more pass."

"Hold it, sir," Lopez's voice sounded worried. "The woman is hit!"

Quickly looking over his shoulder, Danly saw the stream of blood running down her left leg. Its sticky, red sheen stood in bright contrast to her pale skin. "Dammit," he cursed, looking up at her face. She lifted her eyebrows in

a silent question. Then, her lips trembling, she smiled
weakly.

He gave her a quick thumbs-up, a gesture he hoped would
assuage her shock and fear, and returned his attention to
the cockpit. Glancing sideways, he saw Barnes pounding
his thigh with his fist.

"Easy, Ray. It wasn't your fault. We'll get 'em."
Just fucking great, he continued to himself, Barnes's confidence and Cheryl's leg. Two wounds for the price of
one.

He dove toward the treeline to finish off the remaining
NVA.

━━━━━━━━━

The bombing had unearthed two large bunker complexes.
The camouflage and log supports covering the tops of the
bunkers had been blown away, and the sharp geometric
outlines of the rectangular holes seemed totally out of place
amid the chaotic pattern of scattered debris. Pieces of clothing, utensils and paper were scattered about, attesting to
Gray's certainty that the bunkers had been occupied.

Platz was puzzled. "Why aren't there any bodies?"

"The survivors drag them away. They'll even pick up
the pieces."

"Man, I could see it if it was just a couple of guys, but
there must've been a lot of bodies down there."

"Yeah," agreed Gray. "I think there probably were."
The images of Hill's photographs flashed through his mind,
and he felt a tightening in his stomach. The now-familiar
depression was settling upon him once more.

"Hey, Platz, why don't you fly for a bit?" he asked
wearily.

"You bet," said Platz, eagerly grabbing the controls.

New guys, thought Gray. They've always got lots of
energy and enthusiasm. Just wait a few weeks, Mister Platz,
then you'll be dragging ass like the rest of us.

Gray slumped back in his seat and stared blankly at the scarred landscape below.

Standing about fifteen feet away from the helicopter, Gray watched the crew chief as he tugged at the gas cap on the side of the aircraft. The sun shining through the spinning blades produced a strobe effect that made the crew chief's movements appear jerky. It also started to make Gray dizzy. He turned away and looked up at the high mountain ridges to the west. Although it was temporarily clear above Dak Pek, the clouds that had been gathering in the west were steadily edging closer. The highest ridges, and even those just a few klicks west, were now covered by a gray shadow. It was a gloomy vista, matching his mood.

He had removed his helmet and the whine of the turbine rang loudly in his ears. He splashed a little more tepid water from his canteen upon his forehead, took several deep breaths and then massaged his temples with his fingertips. The dizziness passed, but he still did not feel totally well.

He pivoted around to see if Gothard was still having trouble with the gas cap. The crew chief was still standing by the opening to the gas tank, but was now holding a heavy nozzle as JP4 surged through the line. Gray walked slowly back to the gunship and noticed Platz staring at him as he approached.

He climbed into his seat, fastened his seat belt and shoulder harness and pulled his helmet on. Platz was still staring. Gray grabbed the cord that dangled from the ceiling and plugged in his helmet.

"Are you all right?" Platz asked.

"I'm fine," said Gray. "Just a little hot."

"You sure?"

"Yes."

Platz's expression showed he didn't quite believe it, but he shrugged and looked away. Gray picked up the map and began to examine the new area they'd been assigned to check. It was further to the west, on higher ground, just on the periphery of the bomb strike. He began to feel more apprehensive. Anyplace in the shadow of the towering mountain had a palpable aura of menace, and the bomb strike had merely added to it. If the NVA were well dug in and had survived the bombing, they would be hell-bent on exacting revenge on the nearest target. And that was going to be the LOHs and gunships.

Platz, in a change from his usual cockiness, was also subdued. "Why in the hell are they sending us out there, when one of CTroop's own gun teams just left to go back to Dak To?"

"I don't know," said Gray.

"Major Ansel rather have *us* take the risk than his guys?"

"Watch it!" Gray responded angrily. "Ansel's got a damn good reputation; he's not the type to screw anyone."

Platz scowled and looked away.

Absorbed in the takeoff, Gray began to relax. He knew it seemed contradictory, but it was true: the more he concentrated on flying, the more relaxed he became. Flying, the activity that could cause the most tension, ironically, was also the activity that provided the greatest relief from tension.

The gunship creaked as it slid along the short runway, its skids tapping the black surface as the aircraft struggled to fly. Gray's control movements were almost imperceptible as he smoothly coaxed the gunship into the air. As it climbed just above the treetops at the south end of the runway, he gently banked the aircraft to the right. The darkening mountainside filled the windshield. A few drops of water splashed on the Plexiglas, breaking into small beads, which slid quickly off to the side.

Eyeing the deepening overcast, Platz scowled. "I wish it would either piss or get off the pot."

"You might as well relax," said Gray. "We're nearing monsoon season and we're going to be seeing a lot of days like this."

"Great," said Platz.

The LOHs flew directly to the northwest corner of the new area and then turned south. Gray followed, weaving to maintain the proper separation as the scouts zigzagged their way south just above the trees. Gray looked out to the horizon and marveled, as he had many times before, at how beautiful Vietnam could be. Columns of sunlight poked through breaks in the clouds further south, where a brief thunderstorm had soaked the valley below. The wet leaves were shiny, their deep, emerald green contrasting sharply with the softer, yellow-green grasses that spread across the few clearings on the valley floor. Shifting beams of light framed a rainbow that oscillated slowly in the rising mist.

"One-four receiving fire!"

Gray's attention snapped back to the two small aircraft in front of him, six hundred feet below. The LOH pilots banked wildly in a frantic effort to avoid the fusillade that burst from the jungle beneath them. Gray felt a surge of panic as the entire area below him seemed to erupt with muzzle flashes. Lowering the gunship's nose, he swung the rocket sight down into position.

The jolt was terrible. A searing pain spread across his forehead—it was as if someone had hit him with a giant club. More jolts rocked the aircraft, and a wail of panicky voices blared through his earphones. He tried to focus on the instruments, but his vision was blurred and he could not hold his head erect. He felt his body being pushed against the side of his seat and he knew the aircraft was rolling over. Clutching the controls he tried to stop the roll, but his hands and arms had lost their strength.

He could feel a sticky warmth flowing down his forehead into his eyes and along his nose and cheeks. Desperately he tried to blink away the sheet of dark red that was coating his eyes. *Oh God, I can't see. Jesus help me!*

Terror stricken, he realized the helicopter was tumbling slowly, and he knew he was going to die. *Oh no, no, no, no, please no!* Tears, mixed with the blood that coursed down his face.

Then he stopped fighting for hope. His body sagged and the terror melted away. Now it was over; no more pain, no more weariness, no more anguish. Still clinging to the controls, he tried to curl himself into a ball. The gunship seemed to be dropping in slow motion. His body swayed from side to side, tugging against the shoulder harness, as the helicopter corkscrewed toward the trees.

The fall seemed to take forever.

"Come on," he whispered, blood dripping from his lips, "hit the ground."

CHAPTER 18

MAY 15, 1968
CAMP ENARI

Taking a large pinch of shredded tobacco leaves, Spradling opened his mouth wide and stuffed the brown wad between his cheek and gums.

"Wendell, you keep chewing that shit, you're going to wreck your teeth."

"So?" said Spradling, sending a brown glob of saliva flying toward Winters' feet. "Then I won't have to waste time eating; I'll just drink."

Winters hopped sideways, avoiding the liquid missile, and glared at Spradling. "You hit these boots an' you're gonna eat that wad."

Spradling loosed another brown blob at Winters and grinned. "I doubt it, shortstuff."

Sitting on the top row of sandbags that encircled the tent, Barnes watched as Winters spun away from the second slimy missile. "He's right about your teeth, Wendell. If you keep it up, you're going to look like the hootchmaids."

"Might be an improvement," said Spradling. "Some of 'em are pretty cute."

"Yeah," Winters countered, "until they open their

mouths; then they look like they've been eating dirt all their lives."

"Maybe you should give them something else to chew on, Winters . . . like your dick. I've seen a picture of your girlfriend; you're not going to be needing it."

Barnes flashed a tired smile as Winters threw his hands up in despair.

The sound of rotor blades drew their attention and they looked up briefly as three new Cobra gunships passed overhead. Spradling chewed distractedly; Barnes slowly swung his legs forward and backward bumping his heels against the sandbags; and Winters stood with his hands in his pockets, rocking back and forth on his heels.

"What's Patterson going to do to Danly?" asked Barnes, breaking the silence.

Spradling shrugged. "Try to court-martial his ass."

"Damn," said Barnes. "That was bad luck with Patterson standing on the ramp as we came in."

"You got that right."

"I didn't hear the whole story," said Winters. "What exactly happened?"

Spradling spit again and then wiped away a string of brown saliva that hung from the corner of his mouth. "The C&C was parked on the far end of the ramp, down from POL, and Patterson was standing out there picking his nose or something when we came in. Danly goes right by, heading for the medevac pad and I pulled in to refuel. As I hovered over to POL, I saw Patterson standing there staring after Danly. He figures something is up and starts running down toward the medical tent. Obviously Danly's on his way to being up shit creek, so I call him and tell him that Major Fuckhead's on the way. Danly just says, 'Figures,' like he's not surprised at all and couldn't give a shit less.

"Until he gets there, Patterson can't see what's going on because he's got all those buildings and tents between him and the pad, so Danly has a chance to dump her and get out of there before Patterson arrives. But he doesn't; he helps her into the aid station.

"Patterson gets there just as Danly's leaving and makes him wait. It didn't take him long to find out what happened and that was it. Told Danly that at the end of the day his flying career was over." Spradling winced, as if he felt pain. "It was my goddamn fault. I talked him into giving the women a ride."

"What about the donut dolly?"

"Aw, she got her leg sliced by a flying piece of metal when the rounds came through the floor. Bled pretty good, but the cut wasn't too deep. A few stitches and she was fine."

"So Patterson didn't find out about the girl in your ship?"

"No. When I first saw him, I told the crew chief to get her out of sight, so he had her lie on the floor. I hovered just off the edge of the ramp to raise a bunch of dust, that way it looked natural when he and the door gunner quickly slid the doors closed. After refueling, we parked in the far corner and the door gunner snuck her out.

"But when Mike came back to refuel and I found out what happened, I figured I should turn my ass in and take some of the heat off him. Danly got pissed, told me that would be pretty fucking dumb, and if anything, would just make matters worse. So I didn't."

"He was right," said Barnes.

"Maybe."

"C'mon, Wendell. Wasn't your fault. Nobody talks Danly into doing something he doesn't want to do. He makes up his own mind."

Spradling hopped off the sandbags. "Still doesn't change what *I* did."

Barnes scuffed the dirt with his boot. "If it's anybody's fault, it's mine. If I'd fired right on the end of that treeline, then the woman would never—"

"Bullshit, Barnes. You don't know what would have happened. Besides, none of us knew the dinks were that far west."

"Hey, look on the bright side," said Winters. "Patterson got his man and he'll probably forget about the chickenshit stuff like haircuts and moustaches."

Spradling spun around and took a step toward Winters, who backed away.

"You ain't worth hurtin' my fist on," Spradling spat. He turned and stalked off.

Barnes glared at Winters.

"You know," Winters said, "it could be the best thing that ever happened to Danly."

Barnes cocked his head. "What in the hell are you talking about?"

"Risk. Danly hangs it out a lot, takes big chances, won't refuse a mission."

"So? He's a damn good pilot."

"Sure, but there's limits, and he goes past them. If you don't believe me, ask some other guys that have been around here a long time. Ask Webb about stupid night-convoy support missions in pea-soup fog. Ask Beeman—if you can find out what hospital he's in—about hanging it out for some crazy medevac pilot. Ask—"

"Sounds to me like he's just doing his job."

"Just his job my ass. He goes too far. He's been flying on borrowed time for months."

Barnes snorted derisively.

"You don't think so, huh? Tell me, how many hits have you taken?"

Barnes paused and tried to picture the holes in the aircraft he'd flown. "Seven; so what? Most gunnies get hit now and then."

"I've taken twelve," said Winters. "Know how many Danly's taken?"

"How could I? No."

"Well neither does he. All the rest of us keep track; we may not write it down, but we know. Not Mike, though, he doesn't care. If you ask him, he just shrugs. He really doesn't know."

"Do you?"

"Yeah. Thirty-four."

"How do you know?"

"The crew chiefs," answered Winters. "Some of 'em have been keeping track of every damn hole and who was flying at the time. Petty showed me this chart they got down in maintenance. Danly's leading the league—by a lot." Winters stared at Barnes intently. "Mike's *pushing* his luck."

"Everybody over here is."

"Not like him."

Barnes shook his head. "I'm surprised, Winters. I thought you liked him."

"I do."

"But it's still all right with you if he gets grounded by some chickenshit court-martial?"

"Beats the hell outta dying."

━━━━━━━━━

From the outside, the chapel was indistinguishable from the many other long, low, wooden-sided, tin-roofed buildings that provided housing for Fourth Division troops. Inside, instead of the usual rows of cots and footlockers, there were neatly spaced pews, and at one end of the building there stood a small altar. Although the sun had set more than an hour earlier, it was still very hot, and the body heat from the men crowding the room made the building progressively more uncomfortable.

Standing in the rear of the room, just inside the doorway, Danly leaned against the wall with his arms folded across his chest. He wiggled his nose. The chapel was beginning to smell like a locker room. The irregular damp blotches on the shirts of the men squeezed into the pews in front of him grew larger and darker.

His attention shifted to the pews, and he could not help but notice their excellent quality. But the rich, dark brown wood looked out of place amid the sea of green-clad, sweating bodies. Danly wondered where the pews had come from. They looked like they'd been recently lifted from a Stateside church. He was beyond the point of getting too upset at misplaced priorities, but he could easily think of many things that the troops had a greater need for than deluxe pews. He remembered when the troop had first arrived at Enari, and how they couldn't shower for days because they couldn't even get the rudimentary building materials to make a simple shower. Yet, as sure as he was staring at them right now, somebody had gotten the pews within twenty-four hours from the time some colonel decided he wanted them. There was probably a special arrangement to have a C-130 fly them in from the States. Hell, two C-130s—one to carry spares. You never know when you might need some extra pews.

The chapel was full; men lined both sides of the building and filled the center aisle. They stood silently, their attention directed toward the front of the room. Eight pairs of boots, each pair representing one of the men who had died at Dak Pek the day before, were set, evenly spaced, on the floor in front of the altar.

A minister—Danly couldn't determine what faith he represented—strode solemnly to the altar and faced the silent men. Bowing his head, he read from a piece of paper he held close to his chest. "Let us pray. Dear God, we are assembled here to commend unto You the souls of Your faithful servants: John T. DeMarco, Darnell Green, Steven F. Gray, Donald D. Platz, Aubrey A. Gothard . . ."

As each name was read, Danly tried to picture the face that went with it. He knew all of Gray's crew and had seen the LOH pilot and observer before, but he did not know the two infantrymen who were killed while trying to retrieve the bodies of the downed flight crews. There was something he never understood: risking lives to retrieve bodies. Particularly when a "missing in action" designation could not reasonably apply. When a helicopter fell out of the sky from a couple hundred feet, landed inverted and blew up and burned, like Gray's did, then the crew was dead. Period. They should not have to be listed as missing in action because no remains were recovered; the eyewitnesses could verify without a doubt that they were dead. Danly could think of no good reason why other lives should have been risked to recover the bodies.

A chorus of subdued amens interrupted Danly's thoughts. He shifted his attention back to the minister, who was silently gazing around the room. The man raised his right hand in the air, clutching a small Bible.

"The Bible teaches us that God has a plan. He has a plan for each and every one of us. Indeed, we acknowledge that truth in the Lord's Prayer: 'Thy kingdom come, Thy will be done.' *Thy* will be done!"

Lowering the Bible to his side, the minister paused and let his gaze pass along the row of boots. "But," he said, raising his head and looking toward the ceiling, "we can't always know what God's will is. We can't know all His plans, all His mysteries. So, we don't know why He chose to have eight of our fellow soldiers, our friends, join Him in Heaven yesterday.

"We can imagine the terrible grief their loved ones will feel as they receive the news, and we can imagine the hollow feelings in the hearts of their wives and children. Our own hearts cry out, 'Why, why?'"

Danly narrowed his eyes and a look of disgust replaced his normal impassive expression. What was this maudlin "why, why?" crap? Was this guy an idiot? People get killed in wars because of one of two reasons: a random fatal event or someone's stupidity. The idea that a deity was sitting around deciding which people were going to die that day was absurd.

"I know many of you feel great sorrow; these men were your good friends. But you must temper your grief with the knowledge of God's mercy and His love. And you must trust in His wisdom."

Danly clenched his jaw and groaned softly. *Not that shit. Don't try and tell us that it's really all right.*

"You see, even in the depths of your sorrow, you can rejoice. Yes! The battle is over for our friends. We can be happy for them; they have been drafted to a higher calling."

You sorry bastard. I'm supposed to rejoice over the death of one of the best friends I've ever had?

"They died in God's service. Good soldiers. Good men."

"How in the fuck would you know?"

Several men, shocked expressions on their faces, turned quickly to look at him, and Danly realized he'd just said out loud what he'd been thinking. As the minister turned a puzzled glance in his direction, Danly pushed between Spradling and Winters, who were blocking the doorway, and stepped out into the darkness.

He walked aimlessly, strolling past rows of dusty tents housing young men who had so far avoided being reduced to empty pairs of boots. Murmuring voices, raspy snores, and occasional bursts of laughter carried through the night air, disembodied sounds of the living that clashed with Danly's thoughts of the dead. Without conscious intent, he found himself nearing the flight line. Familiar silhouettes, framed by the glow of lights from the south perimeter, loomed in front of him. Rows of squat-bodied Hueys crouched in their revetments, only the blades and upper portions of their fuselages showing above the protective walls. Even in the darkness, and even from a distance, it was easy to identify the different types of aircraft. The wide, heavy blades of the C-models drooped in weary contrast to the longer, thinner blades of the D-models, which angled slightly skyward from their masts.

Danly walked to the front of the nearest gunship and stared at its stubby body. *You want an example of a good soldier, preacher? Here it is. A metallic, uncomplaining purveyor of death. It's dependable, tough, and it has no fear. This is the good soldier, not Gray. Gray was a bad soldier—a very, very good man, but a bad soldier. He let his feelings get the best of him.*

Pulling with his arms and giving a quick push with his legs, Danly hoisted himself onto the top of a revetment wall. Perched on the wall, looking at the dim lights twinkling in the Montagnard village south of the perimeter, he thought that maybe he should be crying. Gray had been a very good friend. Maybe he should cry, but he just didn't feel like it. As a matter of fact, he wasn't feeling much of anything anymore. Even his anger at the minister had been shallow and short-lived. Hell, the preacher was just like Patterson, another lifer wed to the military. Lifers dealt with everything as it pertained to the good of the unit. Gray's death was just a matter to be taken care of in a way that hurt morale the least. Better yet, see if it could be twisted around to raise morale. All the "good soldier gone to Heaven" stuff was just aimed at accomplishing the mission. Get the troops humming "Onward Christian Soldiers" and they'll be itching to get out the next day and kick some commie ass. Individuals cannot matter in relation to the overall mission.

Danly's sorrow was fading just as his anger had, because he knew that was the way it had to be. There really wasn't any point in yielding to his emotions. All they could do was get in the way.

People were going to keep on dying. Too bad.

You didn't belong over here, Steve. You took it too personal; you made yourself suffer. You couldn't accept that your job here—killing people—was just that, a job. That's what soldiers have to do.

I'm sorry, Steve; I hope you died in peace.

The lights in the Montagnard village were blurred. Danly blinked several times and they became clear once again. He looked at his watch; he'd been sitting on the wall a long time.

PART FOUR
A LONELY
IMPULSE

Nor law, nor duty made me fight,
Nor public men, nor cheering crowds.
A lonely impulse of delight
Drove to this tumult in the clouds . . .
>   —WILLIAM BUTLER YEATS,
>   *An Irish Airman Foresees*
>   *His Death*

CHAPTER 19

**MAY 21, 1968
CAMP ENARI**

He was sliding backward down the hill. With his feet in the air, laying on his back, he clawed at the ground. But he kept sliding, sliding away from the firebase perimeter into the dark, oppressive jungle. He tried to turn his body, but his muscles seemed paralyzed. His yells for help were soundless bursts of air, sucked like his writhing body into the suffocating, dank undergrowth.

Clutching the sides of his bunk, Danly jerked awake. He looked up between his feet at the two men who were holding the end of his cot about three feet off the floor.

"Morning," said the man on the right, grinning.

"He doesn't look well," said the other man cheerfully.

"Jesus," sighed Danly. "I thought it was a bad dream." He closed his eyes, then slowly opened them again. "It still is."

The man on the right shook his head in mock disgust. "How some of these people get to be pilots I'll never know. Give them a little unusual attitude training and they go to pieces. We'll have to pink-slip this one."

Danly rubbed his eyes. "Why don't you just put the

goddamn cot down and go play with your little baby windup helicopters.''

The man on the left looked at his partner. "Have you ever noticed the prejudice against loach pilots on the part of the cretins who fly guns?''

"Yes, sadly I have. But as you've pointed out, it comes from those of diminished capacity. Let us not hold a grudge against ignorance.''

The two men lowered the cot to the floor and stood staring at Danly.

"Okay, so I can go back to sleep, what the hell do you want?''

"Well, first of all," said the larger of the two men, "you're not going back to sleep; you're gonna go flying— as my observer.''

"In case you haven't heard, Frogert, I'm grounded.''

"Yeah, we heard some ugly rumors. That's why we're here. We wanted to get you on one last flight before you start rotting away in the Long Binh jail." Frogert picked a set of fatigues from the footlocker and tossed them on Danly's chest. "Yup, that's why you're riding with me today.''

Danly pushed the fatigues aside. "Frog, I really appreciate the offer, but I'm grounded, period. No sense in getting you or anybody else in trouble.''

"Yeah, right," Frogert replied dryly, "they might send me to Vietnam. Mike, I don't give a shit about Patterson. Look, he'll never find out anyway; he wouldn't get within a hundred yards of a loach. So, what do you want to do, vegetate in here or go for a ride?''

Slowly, Danly swung his feet to the floor and then shrugged. "Okay," he said with a small smile. "But I'll say it one more time: you can get your ass in big trouble.''

"Mike, you've obviously mistaken me for someone who gives a shit.''

———

DAK POKO VALLEY

Winding its way through the dense vegetation, the narrow path paralleled the creek that meandered along the valley floor. From above, only short segments of the trail were visible. Both Frogert and Danly had seen the path at the same time and they were now moving over it, heading slowly to the west.

"Bastards are here somewhere," Frogert said with a trace of edginess.

Danly cradled the carbine in his lap, its muzzle pointed at the trees below. "Agreed."

Like a water bug moving erratically across the surface of an algae-filled pond, the LOH darted back and forth just above the shimmering treetops, following the stream's meandering course. The two men stared intently through the leaves, their eyes straining to identify the varied shapes that occupied the shadows below. Was the thing that moved a plant caught by the wind from the rotor blades? Or was it a man with a gun seeking the safety of the shadows, hiding until he had a clear shot?

Crisscrossing the stream, they inched their way along just above the valley floor. Danly rubbed the back of his hand down his nose and along his mouth in an attempt to wipe away the sweat. The LOH passed slowly over an old, weathered footbridge that spanned the creek about twenty feet above the water. Frogert turned the LOH in a tight circle, so it passed over the bridge a second time. There was no sign of anyone below and Frogert began to hover away.

Leaning out the door of the aircraft while the bridge passed beneath it, Danly blinked as a rivulet of sweat trickled down his temple and entered his right eye. For a split second, he thought the movement at the edge of his vision was an illusion, a false shadow caused by his blinking. But the shadow moved onto the footbridge and he knew it was no illusion. Swinging the muzzle of his carbine toward the bridge, he stomped on the floor intercom switch. "Frog, on the bridge!"

Before he could squeeze the trigger, the aircraft spun to the right, the force of the turn pulling his head and shoulders back inside. Frogert pressed hard on the left pedal to stop the turn and fired the minigun at the bridge. Danly leaned out the door again to fire, but lowered his carbine when he saw the stream of tracers cut into the man, throwing him against the rope railing. The man's AK-47 fell from his grip as he literally folded in half and slid off the bridge. A swath of bright red stained the ropes where he'd been thrown against them.

The LOH hung above the trees swaying gently, while both pilots, breathing hard, stared at the bridge.

"Christ!" Frogert exclaimed softly. "I cut him in half."

"Better him than us," Danly replied, quickly resuming his scan of the area beneath them. "Frog, we better move."

Frogert continued staring for a moment, then tilted his head to the right and moved the aircraft away from the bridge. The other LOH, which had been flying a parallel course further south, was now moving directly toward them.

"Red One-four, One-six. What have ya got?"

"One Charlie K.I.A.," answered Frogert. "He might have some friends."

"One-six, roger. How 'bout we each work one side of the river?"

"How about you take both sides and I'll go home?"

"Sorry, One-four, that's against union rules."

Danly permitted himself a thin smile and continued to strain to see beneath the gaps in the trees. His armpits were wet, and the acrid odor of tension-induced sweat filled his nostrils. His tongue scraped against the dry insides of his mouth. Fighting the urge to pause and open his canteen, he gripped the carbine firmly and kept his attention focused on the ground.

No movement could be seen beneath the trees. The jungle spread placidly beneath them, sunlight dancing on the swaying leaves. Two large birds circled lazily nearby, watching their mechanical counterparts with vague interest.

═══════════

CAMP ENARI

The air inside the tent was stagnant. Even though the canvas sides had been rolled up, the inner layer of mosquito netting hung motionless in the still air. Heat waves shimmered from the top row of sandbags surrounding the tent. Barnes, his body slick with perspiration, lay on his cot staring blankly at the tent ceiling. On his stomach was perched a half-empty can of beer.

Keep in control. That's what Danly had said so long ago. Always keep in control. Good idea, but just how in the hell do you do it?

Barnes dragged his palm across his brow to push away the sweat. His forehead felt hot and slimy, like a greasy plate left in the sun. Control took effort, and he wasn't sure he could maintain enough energy to keep trying. He'd screwed up bad enough when his energy level was high; what was he going to do as it kept declining?

He was worn down, and he still had almost half a year to go.

Bringing the can of beer to his mouth, he tilted it quickly. The warm fluid gurgled from the triangular opening and fell short of his lips, splashing on his chin and neck. He tossed the can on the floor and absentmindedly scratched the ugly rash on his groin.

Well, tired people make mistakes, Ray old boy; better try and get some rest. He closed his eyes. He imagined he could feel the hot, humid air lying across his face like a gauze veil. His breath made a raspy sound as it escaped through his mouth, and he felt as if he were beginning to suffocate.

Aw, fuck this. He rolled over and pulled another beer

from a small cooler on the floor. *Might as well get bombed, I'm good at that.* He took another drink of beer, laid back, and closed his eyes. His shorts and T-shirt were plastered to his skin, and he felt as if he were covered with a thin coat of mucus. *A pool of slime, that's what you become in Nam. If you don't get shot, you melt.* He laughed mirthlessly, and then poured beer into his mouth until it overflowed. Streams of foam ran down his cheeks onto his pillow.

"Barnes, you trying to get your ass in a sling too?"

Opening one eye, Barnes turned his head toward the doorway. Winters was standing just inside. "Fuck you. You got nothing else to do but bother me?"

Winters ignored the question and sat down on the nearest cot. "You're just like Danly—flouting the rules. You know Patterson said no drinking in the daytime, period."

Barnes grunted. "The major's out menacing the airways and the only way he'll know is if some asshole tells him."

"Don't get pissed at me. You've been drinking a lot lately, and I'd just hate to see you get in trouble."

"I'm eternally grateful. Good-bye."

Winters stood up, but instead of leaving, began to pace back and forth in front of Barnes's cot. "Ray, I had a hell of a realistic dream last night."

Rolling onto his side and propping his head up with his hand, Barnes peered at Winters with half-open eyes. "And you're going to tell me about it, no matter what."

"Look, I've had them come true before, and this one was—"

"Bullshit," mumbled Barnes, rolling onto his stomach.

"—as real as any. I was at some kind of ceremony after the war. There were a lot of veterans there and they were honoring those who had served in Nam. Someone was reading a list of names from each unit. They were the names of those who had been killed."

Winters stopped pacing and stood at the end of Barnes's cot. "I heard names from this unit."

Barnes grunted. "Big deal."

Winters leaned forward. "Like Danly's, for instance."

"Winters, you're a ghoul, and I'm not fucking interested in your dreams. Take a hike."

"Okay, okay," said Winters, retreating toward the door, "I guess you don't want to know if your name was read."

Barnes belched.

"Go ahead and scoff, but dreams can predict the future and the only way to protect yourself is to know what might happen."

Barnes rolled over and pushed himself to a sitting position. "And the only way for *you* to protect *yourself,* creep, is to get the fuck out of here."

━━━━━━━━━

"Shit, there they are!" said Danly, motioning to a knoll just underneath the LOH on the left. Frogert leaned across the cockpit and caught a glimpse of the fresh-cut logs forming the top of a bunker. He turned the helicopter to the right and increased its speed, moving away from the knoll in a shallow arc.

"How many bunkers did you see?"

"Three. They must have 'em running all the way around the knoll."

"Damn, we were right on top of 'em; they coulda shot our ass."

"Jungle's pretty thick there, probably figured we couldn't see 'em."

"We fly back over them, they're going to get the idea pretty quick."

"Yeah, but we ought to try and get an accurate estimate of what's down there."

Frogert pursed his lips, puffed his cheeks and blew out a long stream of air. "I know."

"Frog?"

"Yeah?"

"Do me a favor, keep this thing moving."

"Don't worry, we ain't getting slower than sixty knots. All Striker aircraft, Red One-four. We got some new diggings on that knoll to our south. We're going to take another look." He pushed the cyclic forward and the LOH accelerated quickly, dipping to within inches of the treetops. The foliage rushed by, occasionally flicking the skids as the LOH closed with the knoll from a different direction.

"Red One-four, this is Striker Six. What is the situation?"

Frogert cursed. "Look's like Major Shithead's back on station." Hugging the crease of a shallow draw, the LOH moved up the side of the knoll. "Stand by, Six," Frogert said tersely.

There was a sudden break in the green blur, and during the short seconds the aircraft passed over the opening in the trees, Danly saw two more bunkers with rifle barrels protruding from the narrow openings in their sides. As the blur of foliage resumed, Danly motioned to Frogert to turn. "There's people in 'em, let's get out of here!"

Frogert banked sharply to the right and the LOH rapidly curved away from the knoll.

"Red One-four, Striker Six."

"Go ahead, Six."

"What have you got down there?"

"Six, the whole area around the knoll appears to be filled with bunkers. They're definitely occupied."

"Did you take any fire."

"Negative, Six."

"Roger, One-four. Then I want you to make another pass and get a more complete count."

Frogert looked at Danly, his eyebrows raised. "Is he crazy? Let the gunnies work it over first. Until then, I'm not going back over there."

"That's good," said Danly. "If you change your mind, let me out first."

"Red One-four, do you copy?"

"Jeez," said Frogert, "somehow I feel we're about to have radio trouble." Grinning, he clicked the transmit button on the cyclic several times, producing static, then reached to the console and turned his main transmit switch to the intercom-only position. "Hell of a time for the radios to crap out, huh Mike?"

"It's a damn shame."

"Red One-four, Red-One-four, this is Striker Six, acknowledge!"

Frogert held the LOH in a tight circle to the north of the knoll. "What a dumb shit. Why doesn't he just let the gunnies, or better yet the Air Force, lay some fire in there?"

Before Danly could respond, Patterson's voice was back on the radio. "Striker aircraft, Six is coming down to take a look. White team, get in position to support."

Anger surged in Danly like a dose of adrenaline. To use a D-model like an LOH was stupid anytime, but to do it over an occupied bunker complex was criminally negligent. If Patterson would get only himself killed that was one thing, but there were three other people in the aircraft. Looking to the east, Danly saw Patterson's aircraft descending toward the knoll in a slow, shallow approach.

"Jesus H. Christ! He's going to come to a hover right over the bunkers." Danly reached over and turned the transmit switch so he could talk on the UHF radio.

"What are you doing?" exclaimed Frogert. "If he hears your voice, you're really screwed."

"I'm going to try and dissuade the dumb bastard. Striker Six, this is One-four," said Danly, taking momentary pleasure at the shock his voice must be to Patterson. "We say again, there are numerous bunkers with automatic weapons."

There was a long pause before Patterson's terse reply. "Roger, One-four. You are to return immediately to base."

The D-model continued its descent.

"Sorry, Frog, didn't want to get you in trouble, but I had to try."

"That's all right; forget it."

"He's going to need help," said Danly.

Frogert nodded and pushed the cyclic forward, aiming the LOH directly at the bunkers.

"RECEIVING FIRE! RECEIVING FIRE!" Patterson's panicked screams rang in their earphones as they saw the D-model yaw violently to the right and sink toward the east side of the knoll. Frogert opened fire with the LOH's minigun at the same time the gunships began to attack. The D-model stopped descending after a few agonizing seconds and, with its skids brushing the trees, moved away from the knoll. Slowly it began to climb.

Two sharp cracks startled Frogert and he pulled the LOH into a steep bank away from the bunkers. "Shit! We've been hit."

Danly looked quickly at the gauges. "Everything's still working."

A weak voice from the stricken D-model drew their attention from the gauges. It was Patterson's copilot. "We're badly hit. I'm going to try and make Dak Pek."

"Not a bad idea," Frogert said to Danly as he turned to follow the D-model. "Roger, Striker, One-four will stay with you." He smiled thinly across the cockpit. "Patterson has always made the radio calls himself; he must be hit pretty bad. Might call it a just reward."

"No one deserves it more," Danly said, "but I hate to see his crew have to pay for it too."

CHAPTER 20

JUNE 4, 1968
CAMP ENARI

The plate of spaghetti hovered in his mind's eye like a tempting mirage. It floated there, a big, steaming pile of thin noodles, dripping with thick tomato sauce. Right next to the red and white mound was a crisp, green salad high-lighted with wedges of fresh tomatoes and doused with creamy garlic dressing. A long, thin basket suddenly hove into view, filled with thick, crusty slices of garlic bread. Danly held his eyes tightly closed, tying to maintain the mouth-watering vision.

It was no use. The rank odor surrounding him filtered through his daydream, and the images faded. It had been a long time since he'd eaten good pasta, but it wouldn't be much longer until he could do so again. Just three more weeks to go. He reluctantly opened his eyes.

In front of him was the rusty sheet of screen that covered a long, thin rectangular opening in the latrine wall. He looked out across the dusty expanse between the latrine and the perimeter road. A few scraggly-looking weeds clung tenaciously to the hard, red clay. Exactly like a lot of people around here, he mused, just hanging on. Hold it together

for a year and with any luck at all, you're out, on the way
back to the real world. Back to hot showers and clean clothes
and smiling women and frosty mugs of beer and heaping
plates of spaghetti.

Leaning to his left, he began to reach for a roll of toilet
paper lying on the other side of an adjacent hole. The powerful odor wafting up out of the opening made him recoil.
It seemed to him like a mixture of decaying cabbage and
rotten eggs. Funny what circumstances can do, he thought.
Sitting in the middle of this god-awful stench, the main
thing I think of is food.

The latrine door swung open and Spradling rushed in.
After quickly unzipping his pants and pulling down his
shorts, he hopped on the nearest seat. "Fucking emergency," he said breathlessly. "Christ! I've never gotten
used to those goddamn malaria pills."

Danly laughed. "It's your sensitive nature, Wendell."

"My ass!"

"I always had the feeling that's where it was located."

A series of loud noises echoed from the area beneath
Spradling as the pent-up gas and fluid escaped from his
bowels.

Putting an index finger in each ear, Danly shook his head
and shuddered. "Up until now, I'd been enjoying a leisurely
crap. You've kind of killed that, Wendell."

"My heart fucking bleeds. In three weeks you can take
all the leisurely craps you want, in sanitary splendor on
toilets that flush. You can sit there like royalty in a sweet-
smelling bathroom till your ass gets welded to the seat.
Drop dead, Danly. I got no sympathy for short-timers."

"What are you moaning about? You won't be far behind.
What do have, about six weeks?"

"I have exactly forty-six days. Which, at say fifteen
chances of getting killed a day—" Spradling paused, count-
ing on his fingers "—gives me another six hundred eighty
chances of getting zapped before I'm due to get out of here."

"That's six-ninety, actually, but you can't fly on the last

day, Wendell—you'll have to out-process.''

"Well that sure lifts my spirits; that knocks it down to only six-seventy-five. Piece of cake.''

"Yup, nothing to it.''

"Like I said before: my ass!''

Danly grinned. "I think we covered that already. Toss me that paper there, will ya?''

Spradling's expression turned serious as he handed Danly the roll of toilet paper. "You ever get a final word on Patterson?''

"I reckon he's on his way to Japan, then home. He got shot up pretty good, including one round in the jaw, but he's supposed to recover all right.''

"That sorry bastard. The crew chief gets killed and he gets sent home.''

"Justice doesn't abound over here.''

"Well, at least he can't fuck up your life anymore.''

"Yeah. You know I thought I would be happy when that day came, but the way it happened, I'm not. I was looking forward to a resolution of things. Just him and me.''

"Hey, cheer up, Mike. You're off the hook. I heard that Patterson didn't get the paperwork on you up to squadron, so Hawkins just threw it away.''

"Yeah, that's the good part. I'm saved from jail and back on flight status.''

"The good part is there's no court-martial, but I'm not so sure about the flight deal. Why don't you just take it easy, Mike? When you get down to two weeks, you won't have to fly unless we're really hurtin' for people.''

Danly stood up and zipped his pants. "I'd rather keep flying. I think I'd go nuts just sitting around, even if it was for only a few days.''

Spradling looked at him earnestly. "I'd rather go home loony than in a body bag.''

"I'm not planning on either contingency.'' Danly pulled open the latrine door and looked at his watch. "Better not

take too long, Wendell; Hawk wants the guns that are going
to Polei Kleng to be off by eight-thirty.''

━━━━━━━━━━━

POLEI KLENG

Squatting on the front of the skid, Barnes stuck a white
plastic spoon into the shallow tin of peanut butter. He
frowned as the thin handle bent almost to the breaking point.
The sticky brown paste was a far cry from the creamy
concoction he'd always loved; it was firm and crumbly like
a block of hard cheese. He dug out a small chunk and put
it on top of one of the round, brittle crackers that came with
the peanut butter.

''That,'' said the crew chief, who was also sitting on the
gunship's skid, ''looks like a rat turd on an albino Ritz
cracker.''

Barnes grimaced. ''Thanks, that's all I needed. Jesus!
Rollins, my stomach feels bad enough already.'' He contemplated the cracker briefly, then flipped it to the side and
watched it roll under the chin bubble. Picking up the empty
can that had contained wieners and beans, he tossed it into
the half-empty C ration case along with the uneaten peanut
butter and crackers. He took two long drinks of warm water
from his canteen, and then leaned forward, supporting his
head with his hands. He felt queasy and his forehead
throbbed.

Rollins tried to suppress his smile. ''One too many beers
last night, eh sir?''

Raising his head slowly, Barnes glared. ''Maybe you
ought to do something useful, like preflighting the aircraft.''

Rollins started to protest, but seeing the angry look on
Barnes's face, shrugged and walked away.

Rubbing the back of his neck, Barnes groaned and moved
his head gingerly from side to side. It was then that he

noticed Danly leaning against the gun mount, watching him with a noncommittal expression.

Barnes grinned sheepishly. ''I guess I shouldn't have had those last couple of beers.''

''True.''

Barnes shifted uncomfortably under Danly's gaze. Danly made fewer mistakes and had a greater force of will than anyone Barnes had ever known. What troubled Barnes most was how inadequate he was in comparison with Danly. He doubted whether he was as smart or as courageous, and he knew he didn't have the personal discipline. The current monumental hangover amply attested to that.

He wished that Danly would at least say something. Call him an asshole or a jerk, or just tell him he was stupid. Anything but the stare and the silence. Anything but the silent message that said: ''You're slipping. You've got to try and act like a man.''

Struggling to his feet, he fought off a faint wave of nausea. He had to get out from under Danly's microscope. He picked up his canteen from the floor of the gunship and walked toward the zigzag row of barbed wire that formed the outermost line of defense for the Special Forces camp.

There were eight rows of barbed wire forming the wide protective barrier surrounding the underground hovels the camp's residents called home. Barnes had been inside once and had found it very claustrophobic. In fact, he thought the entire existence of the Special Forces troops was claustrophobic. If they weren't in their subterranean quarters, they were out worming their way through the jungle, moving slowly and cautiously through the dank tunnels of undergrowth.

Barnes reflected upon the seeming futility of the war in the mountains and felt even more depressed. It was a strange partnership in the highlands—the moles and the eagles. What an odd existence the whole thing was. Men who lived in holes searched for men who hid in the jungle, and then called on the men who soared above to rain bullets and bombs upon the men who were hiding. Men from all the groups died and what was accomplished? No ground was taken; no villages were secured; nothing was resolved.

The jungle could swallow an awful lot of men and machines. It would be there forever; the vines and ferns would grow over the soldiers' bones and the skeletons of wrecked aircraft, absorbing them as it had done for centuries with the rotting remains of trees and animals. In time, there would be no traces of the war at all.

Like the aircraft skeletons ensnared by jungle vines, the war's purpose was often caught in the undergrowth of the mind, twisted from men's consciousness by the grasping tentacles of tension and fatigue. For weary soldiers, numbed by the seeming futility of their efforts, the fighting became a soulless exercise: a hollow, violent ritual sustained only by its own fury.

The distinctive whapping noise of a C-model pulled Barnes from his depressing reverie and he looked up, searching the sky for the approaching gunship. He finally saw it, skimming the trees about two hundred meters to the south. Considering the number of helicopters parked all the way around the edge of the parking ramp, he wondered idly where it would fit once it arrived. In the center of the ramp, three C-130 transports had taken almost all of the space, and another C-130 was in the process of making a wide, circling approach. All in all it looked like mass confusion. Some brass back in an underground bunker had decided on an impromptu, big-deal operation, but as usual, the units that had to carry it out didn't quite know what the hell was going on.

Scores of infantrymen were milling around near the C-130s and several officers were scurrying around consulting with one another. Most of the pilots stayed close to their aircraft, but some of the gunpilots had wandered down the slope between the ramp and the outer perimeter of the camp, and were lounging on the ground next to the barbed wire.

As he strolled toward them, something nagged at him. He had the growing feeling that something was wrong, but he did not know what it was.

"Here comes the human sponge," said Mackin.

"You manage to walk it off?" asked Webb with a smirk.

"Yeah," answered Barnes, only half-aware of what had been said to him. Distracted, he chewed on his lower lip. What was it that his unconscious was trying to tell him?

"You ask me," said Mackin, "he looks worse."

"Shit!" exclaimed Barnes, wheeling around and looking to the west.

"Well," said Webb, "the man is taking this criticism kinda hard."

"No, it's the transport," said Barnes, staring into the distance.

The other pilots looked at one another with puzzled expressions. Mackin shook his head sadly. "Move over, Horvath; you're about to get some company."

Barnes ignored them. At first he couldn't see it, but then he picked up the silhouette moving across the sides of the hills. The camouflage paint on the C-130's top made it almost invisible against the jungle background as it banked on its circling approach. He was right; the transport was about to turn on final to land to the east. Quickly he turned back to where he'd seen the helicopter. It was approaching to the west.

"I hope to hell they see the C-130," he said pointing at the gunship.

"Aw, they will," said Mackin, but as he searched for the C-130 himself, his expression registered doubt.

The gunship came to a hover at one end of the runway just as the transport rolled level about one hundred feet from touchdown. Neither crew seemed aware of the other.

"Oh no, big trouble," said Barnes.

The C-130 touched down on the steel planking and a thundering roar split the air as its pilot reversed the pitch of the propellers and added power. The C-130 pilots hadn't seen the gunship and the big plane was committed to land. It was obvious to Barnes that the gunship pilots hadn't seen the C-130 either, until after it touched down, and they were now in serious trouble. The gunship was too heavy for a short, quick takeoff. The pilot had no choice but to move it sideways off the runway.

"Be careful in the dust," said Mackin, who had gotten to his feet and was watching anxiously.

Moving sideways at a low hover, the gunship was immediately engulfed in swirling red dust as it left the runway. Barnes watched in horrified fascination as the helicopter began to rise straight up, its pilot making a desperate attempt to fly free of the blinding dust.

"No, no! Set it down!" yelled Barnes.

His futile plea was lost in the noise from the aircraft engines, and Barnes suddenly realized he was running toward the gunship. Feeling foolish, he stopped. There was nothing he could do.

The gunship was fighting for altitude and still moving sideways when its weight overcame its power and it began to sink. Barnes guessed it was about thirty feet high—almost free of the dust—when it settled. His heart pounding, Barnes began running again.

The gunship hit the ground hard and the impact caused the main rotor blade to flex violently into the tailboom. The aircraft bounced and then rolled on its left side as the force of the disintegrating rotor system ripped apart the fuselage, rupturing the fuel cell. Barnes was still sixty yards away when he saw the small fingers of flame begin to grow, climbing their way up the sides of the broken fuselage.

Three men, one from the cockpit area and two from the cargo area, emerged from the wreckage and stumbled free of the burgeoning fire. As he got closer, Barnes could see that someone was still trapped in the cockpit. Who was it? The man was lying on his side, struggling frantically to free his left arm, which was pinned between the armored seat and the crushed door. The flames were spreading rapidly and Barnes strained for more speed as he realized he might not reach the aircraft before it was completely engulfed by the fire. His legs felt heavy and his chest heaved.

As he drew near the helicopter the intense heat caused him to throw up his arms to shield his face, and he reluctantly came to a halt. He squinted, peering between his arms into the inferno.

Spradling's face was framed by flickering, yellow tongues of fire. His eyes were wide, his mouth wrenched open in a soundless scream as his free hand swatted feebly at the raging blaze within the cockpit.

Barnes's arms dropped to his sides. The horrible image of Spradling's agony shocked him, rendering him numb. Closing his eyes, he stood paralyzed as the skin on his face reddened and his eyebrows began to shrivel from the intense heat.

He dimly realized he was being tugged backward, but he felt no sense of relief. Two sets of arms had hold of him now, dragging him away from the burning wreckage. There were yells and small sharp explosions from the ammunition being cooked by the blaze. He forced his eyes open and saw three men with fire extinguishers spraying the fire. Despite the exploding ammunition, they grimly and bravely edged forward. Their efforts seemed to Barnes to be as futile as trying to douse a burning barn with a garden hose. The columns of carbon dioxide cut ineffectually into the wall of red, disappearing with no discernible effect.

Tears flooded Barnes's eyes and involuntary sobs shook his body.

The medic dabbed at the reddened skin with cool water. "It's just like a sunburn, sir, you'll get over it pretty quick," the young man said cheerfully.

Barnes nodded dully, but did not speak. His face and hands felt warm, like they were glowing, and his eyes were watering, but he knew he was not burned badly. He would be all right. Physically anyway. His hands trembled as he rummaged in his shirt pocket for a cigarette.

"I wouldn't smoke right away, sir."

Barnes ignored him and lit the cigarette.

"Can I do anything else for you?"

Barnes blew out a stream of smoke and stared at the ground. The medic shrugged and walked away.

Why Spradling? Why like that? Barnes had prepared himself for the loss of a friend during combat. He had made a great effort to imagine the shock and grief he'd feel. But he was not prepared for the horror he had just witnessed. Dying in combat was one thing, but Spradling's death was entirely wasted. It was for nothing. Absolutely nothing.

Barnes felt numb, having neither the energy nor the desire to move. He heard Hawkins' voice; it was like a floating echo, the disembodied monotone of an unseen person in a foggy dream. It drifted in and out of his consciousness, the words beating a soft tattoo on his unresponsive mind. Finally, recognizing his name, he attempted to break free from his semistupor.

"Mister Barnes is over there. There'll be a D-model here shortly to take the survivors back to base camp, and Barnes will be going back also."

Yes I will. Might even stay there for good. The cigarette smoke curling up around his forehead felt very hot, and he suddenly realized he'd been continuously jerking his head to the side trying to avoid it. He stubbed out the cigarette on the ground and closed his eyes. *God, what an awful way to die!*

He tried to make his mind blank. A void would be the best thing now. No more thinking about Spradling. No more thinking, period.

━━━━━━━━━━

Danly leaned against the tailboom of his gunship and watched Barnes sitting motionless on the end of the parking ramp. He tried to imagine how Barnes felt—Barnes and

Spradling had grown to become good friends—but his own reservoir of feelings seemed to have run dry. How many of his friends was it now had died? Too many. And there would be more. Spradling would not be the last.

Kay had been the first, and her suicide had devastated him. He'd literally fled into the Army, anxious to put as much distance as possible between himself and the constant reminders of her death. It had not been a well-considered move. He'd fled right to death's own playground.

But he'd learned. With the death of each friend, he learned how to ward off the grief better and how to suppress the stirrings of unwanted emotion. The sky had become his refuge now; it provided the separation he needed. In the air, his carefully nurtured defenses weren't required. It was as if gravity pulled away the crushing sadness of the carnage below, freeing him to fly and fight with calmness, freeing him to experience the exhilaration of beauty and risk in the sky.

He looked at his watch. It was just about time to depart for the next mission. Reaching into his shirt pocket, he extracted a bent cigarette. Gingerly he straightened it, then tapped the end on his thumbnail and put it between his lips. As he held a burning match near the end of his cigarette, he looked through the flame, which was superimposed over the figure of Barnes sitting cross-legged on the ground. For a fleeting moment through the tongue of flame, Barnes looked like a Buddhist monk who had set himself ablaze.

Danly frowned. Barnes shouldn't be sitting there consumed with grief. It damn sure didn't do Spradling any good, and it damn sure wasn't doing Barnes any good either. Going back to base camp to stew in his grief wasn't the answer. Danly knew what was.

Standing directly in front of him, Danly looked down at Barnes.

"Change of plans, Ray. Let's go; you're now flying with me."

Barnes stared at the ground. "No, I'm going back."

"Yeah, later. We've got a mission right now."

Barnes rubbed the hot, tender skin on his forehead. "Hawkins said I'm going back. I'm not flying anymore."

"I just changed his mind. Come on." Danly's tone was gentle, but insistent. "Get up."

Barnes raised his arm and flicked his hand, trying to shoo Danly's persistent voice away. Danly grabbed his forearm and pulled him to his feet.

"It's not over for you yet."

Still gripping Barnes's arm, Danly steered him toward the gunship.

CHAPTER 21

The needles in the gauges vibrated gently as the gunship squatted just off the runway. An early morning cloudburst had saturated the ground, and wisps of steam ascended from the asphalt where the sun baked away the last skimpy pockets of water hiding in the crevices. Although the increase in humidity made the ninety-eight-degree temperature seem even hotter, Barnes was still thankful for the rain that caused it—at least the dust would be suppressed for an hour or two.

Beads of sweat formed on his upper lip and he swept them away with the tip of his tongue, savoring the salty taste. He was thirsty, but at least it wasn't the awful thirst that accompanied a hangover. He never again wanted to experience the nausea and energy-sapping dehydration that always followed his bouts of heavy drinking.

He had not been hung over in ten days—the ten days since Spradling had died, the ten days since Danly had jerked him from his cocoon of shock.

He thought back to the night of Spradling's death, when he had sat hunched over a table in the officers' club staring into a glass of beer. The mood had been very somber. There had been no banter, no laughter and no music—just groups of men conversing in the quiet tones generally reserved for hospital corridors and funeral homes.

Mackin had performed the short ceremony that always followed the death of an E Troop pilot. He cut off the name tag and wings from a fatigue shirt extracted from Spradling's locker and nailed them—the wings positioned just above the name tag—to the wooden plaque that he'd removed from above the bar. The large plaque was shaped like a shield and had the motto ABOVE THE BEST emblazoned across the top. On it had been four rows of name tags and wings, each row containing four names. The faded swatches of cloth from Spradling's shirt, added right below Gray's name tag, started the fifth row.

Barnes was sure Spradling would have hated what happened after the plaque was hung back in its place: the assembled pilots had drunk a silent toast; there had been some muted expressions of sorrow; and then the entire group had lapsed into a tomblike silence. A raucous wake would have been the fitting thing, but no one had the spirit for it.

Finally—Barnes didn't know who had started the singing—the muffled lyrics of a familiar song were heard. There were just a few voices at first, but gradually the number swelled. But the voices weren't loud and spirited like they had always been on other occasions; they had remained soft and low, lacking the defiant edge that before had always mocked the words of the song.

Barnes had listened with a growing sadness. Pathos had been foreign to Spradling's temperament. The dirgelike quality of the singing just wasn't appropriate.

You're going home in a body bag, doo dah, doo dah.
You're going home in a body bag, oh, doo dah day.
Your wings stay with the best,
*   Your mama gets the rest;*

You'll fly home in a body bag,
  oh, doo dah day.

Barnes had added his voice to the chorus, but it had been painful. Afterward, he'd walked out of the club leaving his half-finished beer on the table. The numb drunkenness that he usually sought for comfort had lost its appeal.

He'd resolved that night to try Danly's way of coping: keep in control. Develop an iron will. Don't give in to pressure. Avoid the highs and lows. Prepare for the worst; do the best you can.

If he was going to die, then so be it.

He licked away the sweat from his upper lip again and focused on the gunship parked in front of him. Its squat body shook rhythmically as its spinning rotor blade made a gauzy, sweeping shadow on the ground. A blanket of heat waves from its exhaust made its rotor mast shimmy in the harsh sunlight.

Here we are again, he thought. Hurry up and wait.

The order to crank had come twenty minutes earlier, but the mission was now on hold. The plan was to provide gun cover for some Fourth Division slicks while they extracted bodies from a firebase that had been overrun two days earlier. A continuous low overcast and steady rain, which had finally moved away to the south, had prohibited any prior attempts to remove the corpses. The battalion commander was exceedingly anxious for them to be retrieved before they became too badly decomposed.

Now, for some unexplained reason, the slicks weren't ready to go. That was all right with Barnes. At the moment, he and Danly had the only two aircraft available to provide gun support for the mission, and that didn't seem like enough. Mackin was en route from Kontum with two more gunships, and the longer the slicks stayed on the ground, the better the chances were of doubling the amount of firepower available when the mission began.

The battalion commander had told them at the briefing

that the area around the firebase was no longer hot. Barnes had been barely able to keep from laughing. What a fucking joke! Did the colonel think they just came from the replacement depot? There was no place within thirty miles of Dak Pek that wasn't hot.

The number of radio transmissions from the division TOC to the lead slick was increasing, and the colonel's voice was becoming louder and angrier. Barnes reached over and turned down the volume on the FM radio. He rubbed his eyes and yawned. Another day at the Dak Pek circus.

———

Puffing on a cigarette, Danly hunched forward and peered closely at the map. The vibrations of the idling helicopter made it difficult to focus on the closely spaced relief lines that outlined the hills. But hard to focus or not, it was still apparent that the peak on which the bodies were located was in a lousy spot. Situated on one of the steep, craggy knobs that protruded from the jumble of ridgelines four miles east of the Laotian border, it was surrounded by an uneven array of rugged peaks, several of which towered above it.

Retrieving the bodies was going to be a difficult and dangerous task. The helicopters would be vulnerable to enemy fire from both below and above. The slicks would be forced to make steep approaches no matter which direction they descended from, and the gunships would be spending far too much time in the "dead man's zone," an area from fifty to five hundred feet above the ground. It looked like they would have to fly in a low, tight orbit, and the terrain varied so sharply that it would be impossible to stay out of the zone for long.

Tossing the map on the top of the instrument panel, he sat back and frowned. *The shithead who picked the location for that firebase ought to have to climb up there and carry out the corpses by himself, one at a time.*

As was customary for the lead aircraft when lining up

for departure, Danly had parked perpendicular to the other gunship waiting behind him. Directly to his front, about two miles distant, was the mountain that had always appeared so sinister. Its huge mass practically filled the entire windshield. Danly thought about its sinister reputation. It seemed as if almost every time an aircraft came near it, something bad happened. Giving credence to that supposition were the numerous twisted skeletons of various types of aircraft that littered the nearby slopes. If evil omens exist, he thought, that goddamn mountain is one.

"White Two-six, Striker Three. Stagecoach is now en route to the Foxtrot Bravo. He'll be on our push. The ground element will be Smokey Six."

"Two-six, copy. We're on the go. Two-eight, pitch in zero two. Mackin will have to join us there." Danly rolled the throttle to the full open position and brought the gunship to a low hover. Glancing one last time at the mountain, he hovered forward, made a right-pedal turn and began to slide the helicopter lightly along the ground, coaxing it gently into the air.

Some of the bodies were visible from where the gunships were making their tight orbit. Arms and legs jutted awkwardly from the dozen or so green bundles scattered down the steep slope on the east side of the firebase. A few more bodies were visible near the bunker entrances, and Danly was sure there were more inside.

LOHs had flitted among the nearby peaks and ravines, but had not drawn any fire. Danly was sure the NVA were still nearby, it was just a question of when they would come out of hiding and fight.

The lead slick landed in a cleared area on the top of the peak, and several troops scrambled out, each carrying a supply of body bags. Two of the men disappeared into the nearest bunker, and the other four moved down the slope. Danly saw the men on the slope stop to tie handkerchiefs over the lower half of their faces. Gingerly, like they were handling something easily breakable, they began to place the corpses into the bags.

The orbit for Danly's gun team was taking the aircraft very close to the sides of two much taller peaks, and Danly was tempted to climb to a safer altitude. Flying above the highest peaks would decrease his vulnerability, but it would also put him far above the potential target areas, so he decided against it. If the men on the ground were attacked, he needed to be lower to provide the instant, accurate covering fire they would need.

As he watched the progress of the men on the slope, he grew progressively more uncomfortable; it was apparent that the retrieval was going to take much longer than he'd first thought. He watched uneasily as a D-model came to a hover and began to move sideways down the slope. Slipping and sliding, the men hoisted the bags one at a time into the hovering aircraft. It swayed back and forth, its main rotor blades coming perilously close to the ground on the upslope side.

A second slick landed on the summit, and more men jumped out and moved down the slope. To Danly, it seemed as if a sense of relaxation had begun to settle upon the men on the firebase. They were moving much less quickly—almost casually—as they fanned out among the bodies. Danly definitely did not like the way things were going.

He saw the tracers and heard the yells from the ground commander almost simultaneously.

"Bulldog! My Smokey One element is receiving fire."

The fusillade of automatic weapons fire erupted from several locations, but the most intense fire came from the middle of the mountainside directly across from the men working on the slope. The D-model hovering above them jerked quickly upward, causing one of the large, black plastic bags to tumble from the cargo bay. The body bag plopped in the mud and began to slide down the slope like an unwieldy toboggan. As Danly turned toward the area where the heaviest fire was coming from, he saw the men of the retrieval detail trying to burrow into the mud. Although they had no cover and were almost certain to be hit by the withering fire if they stayed where they were, they were obviously afraid to move. The lone man who had tried to scramble up the slope had been immediately cut down by the hail of bullets.

Danly fired three pair of rockets, and they burst against the opposite slope. Streams of tracers from the miniguns worked back and forth across the target, and as he broke away, he saw that Barnes was already laying fire beneath him. He breathed a momentary sigh of relief when he saw that the ground troops had begun to move up the slope toward the protection of the bunkers near the summit, but his attention quickly shifted back to the target. Although the enemy fire had decreased, there were still bullets thudding into the muddy slope of the firebase. One more pass, he thought—that will give them enough time to get to the bunkers.

As he rolled level, Danly saw several flashes from a ledge about two hundred feet above him, straight up the mountainside from the target. Simultaneously, he heard two sharp, slapping noises and knew his helicopter was hit.

He began to bank away and then froze, thinking of the men frantically scrambling for safety.

Reversing course, he again dove toward the site of the heaviest fire. Under the onslaught of more rockets and minigun fire, the muzzle flashes from the target winked out. Pulling the gunship into a steep turn, Danly caught a glimpse of more tracers spewing from a rocky ledge above him.

A wave of bullets swept the side and belly of his helicopter. The windshield disintegrated, the needles in the engine gauges fell to zero, and Danly winced as a fragment of metal tore into his cheek. His pulse racing, he slammed the collective down to enter autorotation, and the gunship descended rapidly toward the trees. Guiding it toward the flattest area he could see, he forced his shaking hands to become steady. *Relax; don't rush. Just relax. Bring it in level*. The treetops rushed upward at the chin bubble. Danly eased back on the cyclic and pulled pitch to cushion the impact with the trees.

Sinking into the leaves, the gunship jerked violently to the left and ripped off branches as it plunged toward the ground.

━━━━━━━━━━

When Barnes saw the tracers from above angle toward Danly's aircraft, he gasped as if he'd been punched in the stomach. He pulled back on the cyclic, trying to swing the nose of his aircraft upward to aim his rocket sight at the ledge. But it was too late, Danly's aircraft was already sinking toward the ravine below the firebase.

Barnes's first impulse was to follow Danly's aircraft to provide covering fire for the downed crew. But he checked himself. The tracers from the ledge were now redirected at the men retreating up the slope. *Oh, Jesus, what do I do?* His hands began to shake. Was he to protect Danly and his crew or the men on the slope?

Keep in control. Do it right. He forced himself to take a deep breath. Danly's crew could already be dead.

He aimed at the ledge and fired.

"Hey, Two-eight, this is Two-four. We're zero five out." It was Mackin's voice.

"Two-four, we're getting heavy fire from east of the firebase. Need you ASAP!"

"Roger, Two-four. Hang on."

For the next few minutes, everything Barnes did was from instinct, while his mind's eye fixed on the image of the gunship disappearing into the trees below. His body went through the ritual motions as tracers and smoke danced and swirled above the jungle. The familiar cacophony of firing weapons and nervous voices rang in his ears while the horizon bounced and tilted in the windshield.

Barnes felt himself fighting to maintain his composure;

his recently acquired confidence in willpower and self-discipline was crumbling. The Fates had made a horrible mistake. People like Danly weren't supposed to get shot down.

He tried to nourish the small hope that flashed through his mind when Danly's gunship disappeared into the trees. He repeated the optimistic words over and over until they became a reassuring mantra: *It went in almost level. He's got a chance!*

The fire from the ledge stopped, and Barnes quickly turned toward the ravine where Danly's aircraft had sunk into the trees. The jungle had swallowed the gunship and Barnes's heart sank when he realized he didn't know exactly where it went in.

"The miniguns are out!" Webb yelled across the cockpit. "Wait for Mackin."

Barnes ignored him and dove toward the ravine. There were no more rockets, either, but the door gunner still had a little ammunition. Barnes could imagine what Danly would be saying as he looked up: "Don't be stupid. You can't help now; just get out of here."

Fuck you, Mike. We'll get you out.

Suddenly, there was a burning sensation in his left hand, followed quickly by a hard, sharp pain in his right leg. He gasped. It felt like his kneecap had exploded. Reaching forward, he clutched his leg. Blood spurted between his fingers and splattered on the cockpit floor. The new barrage of fire was spewing forth from the jungle at the base of the ravine.

Clenching his jaw against the pain, he fought a wave of nausea. He stared at the red, sticky mess beneath his flight glove, and noticed for the first time that the thumb was missing from his left hand.

He felt a tug on the cyclic.

"Let go, Ray! I've got it," Webb shouted.

Barnes glanced up and realized that his right hand was still squeezing the cyclic, still aiming the gunship at the area where he thought Danly's helicopter had disappeared.

"Dammit, Ray, LET GO!"

Letting his hand fall away from the cyclic, Barnes slumped to the side. The pain was awful.

Webb jerked the cyclic to the side, pulling the gunship into a steep turn.

"Hang on, Ray. We'll get back to Dak Pek."

"But . . . Danly," grunted Barnes through clenched teeth.

"Jesus, Ray! We're hit ourselves; there's nothin' we can do."

Barnes looked up and saw Mackin's gun team churning by, headed for the ravine. The familiar odor of hydraulic fluid began to creep into his nostrils and he knew that Webb was right; they had to leave.

The FM radio crackled to life and Barnes heard the voice of the ground commander.

"Smokey One, this is Smokey Six. What's your status?"

"This is One. We lost one K.I.A. on the slope, the rest are safe in the bunkers."

Slumped against the side of his seat, Barnes tried to feel some joy—he'd saved the guys on the slope—but all he felt was a cold emptiness.

He looked down at his hand, which was still locked, crablike, on his knee. The flow of blood had changed from a stream to a trickle, and the pain was easing slightly. It dawned on him that he was clutching his blood-soaked ticket home.

EPILOGUE

NOVEMBER 13, 1982
WASHINGTON, D.C.

As had been the case all week, fatigue jackets were very much in evidence in the bar. Barnes sat quietly in a booth near the door, absentmindedly tapping a half-empty package of cigarettes on the table and watching beads of condensation slide down the outside of his beer glass.

It was almost over. In the morning he would go back to the monument and say a final good-bye. He didn't know yet what he would do about looking for Danly's name— that was the last piece of unfinished business—but tomorrow would be the end of it, one way or another.

It was about time. Long past time, actually.

Staring at the tiny bubbles of carbonization that streamed upward from the sides of the glass, Barnes pondered the hold that Danly's uncertain fate had upon him. Even now, after fourteen years, it still seemed horribly unfair that Danly had been shot down. Barnes closed his eyes; he could still picture the stricken gunship disappearing into the thick jungle, sinking like a large, odd-shaped rock in a murky green sea.

Barnes remembered the relief he'd felt in the Seventy-

301

first Evac hospital upon hearing the news that only two bodies were recovered from the wreckage of Danly's aircraft, and neither one was Danly's. He'd been sad for the dead men, but happy that Danly could still be alive. Missing in action was okay—it didn't mean dead. Not then, anyway.

But it would now.

Why Danly? It wasn't supposed to work that way—the very best should have been immune. And Danly was among the best. He'd been smart, dedicated and extremely courageous.

He had also done Barnes the biggest favor of Barnes's life: he had forced him to fly the day of Spradling's death.

Barnes fingered the faded combat patch on the right shoulder of his fatigue jacket. It was a badge of honor. How would his life have been if he'd have quit that day like he'd planned? How would he have coped with the fact that he'd given up on himself and his friends?

If it hadn't been for Danly, he would have spent the rest of his life trying to hide from the shame of quitting.

He'd spent enough time hiding from war memories as it was.

He could have kept in touch with guys from the old unit to find out if Danly had walked out of the jungle sometime later. He could have tried to find Danly's relatives and learn of his fate from them. Or he could have at least paid attention to the news when the POWs were finally released to see if Danly was among them. But he'd done none of those things.

He had never been quite sure he'd made the right choice that day. The men on the slope might have made it to safety without his help. Maybe it had been Danly and his crew who had needed his help the most. The question had begun to haunt him, and so to stop thinking about it, he started ignoring everything concerning the war—and ignoring one feeling in particular: it was he who'd deserved to have been shot down, not Danly.

He drank the last of the beer, slid to the edge of the booth and pushed himself slowly to his feet. He massaged his leg; cold weather made the knee stiffer than usual.

═══════════════

NOVEMBER 14, 1982
WASHINGTON, D.C.

It was cloudy and cold as Barnes made his way from the cab down to the path in front of the monument. The overnight rain had beaten down the many bundles of flowers that had been placed along the base of the wall the day before. They lay bedraggled and forlorn next to the many cards, photographs and notes, which had been reduced to soggy clumps of paper.

He limped slowly across the wet grass to a Park Service volunteer who stood near the east end of the memorial. She was a small, blond woman, whose mouth and nose were covered by a bulky, blue scarf that was wrapped around her face and neck. She held a thick book against her chest, as if it were a infant whom she was shielding from the chilly wind. The book contained the names of all those people killed or missing in action, and—since the names on the monument were not arranged in alphabetical order—the panel and line number where each name was inscribed.

He began to feel a cold dread. Maybe he should let it be.

"Can I help you?" she asked.

"I . . . I'm wondering if the name of a friend is on the wall."

"What is it?" she asked, opening the book. "I'll check for you."

"Warrant Officer Michael R. Danl— . . ."

"What was the last name again, please?"

He hesitated for a moment, then shook his head. "I'm sorry," he said. "Never mind."

He walked back and stood before the center of the monument, staring at the rows of gray names etched in the black granite walls. The cold wind stung his face and he squinted as his eyes began to water.

Mike, I need to let the war be over, and for that, I need to know your fate. But somehow I just can't ask. I don't want to know if you're dead.

He turned and hurried to the waiting taxi without looking back.

The blond woman held the book open and watched a nearby man who was standing in front of the wall. His body was rigid and he squinted at his reflection in the shiny black marble. She was sure she knew what would happen when he touched the wall—physical contact with the monument provided an amazing catharsis.

Like so many persons before him, the man reached out and touched a name. As he slowly brushed his fingers across the indented letters, the woman could see the tension in his body drain away, as if it were drawn through his hand into the stone.

She looked down at the book and thought of the man with the limp, the man who had hurried away. He'll be back, she told herself. He'll be back.

Her eyes rested on a name: CWO Michael R. Danly.

APPENDIX A: TYPES OF HELICOPTERS

The helicopters mentioned most frequently in this book are the C-model, the D-model and the LOH. The first two were manufactured by Bell Helicopter Company and were part of the UH-1 (or "Huey") series, which constituted the bulk of the helicopter fleet in Vietnam. The LOH (Light Observation Helicopter) was manufactured by Hughes Aircraft.

The C-model was a gunship. It carried four crew members: two pilots and two door gunners, one of whom was usually the crew chief. The pilots sat side by side, separated by a radio console. Behind them was a passenger/cargo compartment accessed by two large sliding doors on either side of the aircraft. During combat—and most other times—the doors were slid back along the fuselage and secured in the open position. The door gunners sat on either side of the aircraft at the rear of the passenger/cargo compartment and fired from the open doorways with M-60 machine guns.

Beyond door guns, the armament of C-models commonly came in two configurations. Both configurations included a pair of rocket pods, one pod mounted on each side of the aircraft. The pods contained seven rockets each. The first configuration had a minigun (a high-speed Gatling-type gun) mounted above each rocket pod; the second featured a nose-mounted grenade launcher instead of the two miniguns. Usually the pilot in the right seat would fly the aircraft during gun runs and would fire the rockets. The other pilot would have control of the miniguns or grenade launcher.

The C-model was replaced in the late 1960s by the Huey Cobra, a sleeker, faster, and more powerful aircraft.

The D-model, like the C-model, had a crew of four and was quite similar to the C-model in appearance, but had a slightly longer fuselage and a different-size rotor system. It was commonly referred to as a "slick." It was used to ferry troops and carried no weapons systems except the door guns.

The LOH, commonly called a "loach," was much smaller than a Huey and had a fuselage shaped like an egg. It was flown with the doors removed. Used as a scout aircraft, it carried a crew of two: one pilot and one observer. The LOH had one minigun mounted on the right side of the aircraft that was fired by the pilot. The observer was usually armed with a small, rifle-type grenade launcher and/or a carbine, which he would fire through the doorway on the left side of the cockpit. There was a small area behind the pilots' seats that could be used to carry a passenger or two in an emergency.

APPENDIX B: HELICOPTER FLIGHT CONTROLS

There were two complete sets of controls in all Hueys and LOHs, one set for each pilot.

Cyclic: Extends vertically from the floor and stands between the pilot's legs. The cyclic tilts the rotor disk (the plane formed by the spinning blades of the main rotor), enabling the pilot to accelerate, decelerate, or turn the aircraft during flight. A two-position radio/intercom transmit switch is located on the cyclic grip. (On gunships and LOHs, a button to fire the weapons is also located on the grip.)

Collective: Extends from the floor on the left of the pilot's seat at about a thirty-degree angle, pointing toward the front. It controls the pitch of the rotor blades. When pulled up, the helicopter ascends; when pushed down, the helicopter descends.

Throttle: Located on the end of the collective, it resembles the "twist grip" throttle on a motorcycle. On turbine-engine helicopters, such as Hueys and LOHs, once the throttle is in the full-open position, the power is controlled by an automatic governor. The power is controlled manually with the throttle only during the starting and shutdown procedures, or in the event of a governor failure.

Pedals: Located on the floor out in front of the pilots' seats, they are used to control yaw during flight, and to keep the front of the helicopter pointed in the desired direction during hovering maneuvers.

GLOSSARY

ADF: *Automatic direction finder;* a navigation radio that tunes to AM radio beacons.
AK-47: A Soviet-made automatic rifle.
AO: *Area of operations.*
Ao-dai: A type of Vietnamese dress.
APC: *Armored personnel carrier.*
ARVN: *Army of the Republic of Vietnam.*
ASAP: *As soon as possible.*
Body Bag: A thick plastic bag for holding a corpse.
Caribou: A twin-engine Army transport plane.
Chinook: A twin-rotor Army transport helicopter.
CO: *Commanding officer.*
Conex: A large, square, corrugated-metal storage container.
CWO: *Chief warrant officer.*
C-123: A twin-engine Air Force transport plane.
C-130: A four-engine Air Force transport plane.
DFC: *Distinguished Flying Cross.*
Di-di: A Vietnamese expression meaning "leave."
Deuce-and-a-half: A two-and-a-half-ton truck.
Dustoff: A medical evacuation helicopter.
FAC: *Forward air controller.*
Firebase: A small, temporary artillery base.

Free-fire zone: An area in which anyone may be fired upon without provocation.

Hootch: A small dwelling.

Klick: Kilometer.

Lima Zulu: See LZ.

Loach: See LOH.

LOH: *Light Observation Helicopter;* also called a "loach."

LZ: *Landing zone;* also called "Lima Zulu."

Medevac: A medical evacuation helicopter.

Minigun: A high-speed, Gatling-type machine gun with six barrels.

NVA: *North Vietnamese Army;* a group of North Vietnamese soldiers, or the North Vietnamese Army as a whole.

POL: *Petroleum-Oil-Lubricants;* the refueling point for helicopters.

PRC-10: A small portable two-way radio.

Push: A radio frequency.

Slick: A troop-carrying helicopter.

SOI: *Signal Operating Instructions;* a small, loose-leaf notebook containing frequencies and codes.

S3: The operations officer.

Tracer: A bullet that glows bright red in flight.

TOC: *Tactical Operations Center.*

WO1: *Warrant officer, grade 1.*

Xin loi: A Vietnamese expression meaning "I'm sorry."

XO: *Executive officer;* the officer second in command.